The young man was starting to breathe over-fast. What if he got nervous and pulled the trigger on his weapon?

"I wonder," said Jake, turning sideways to his right as if to address both father and son at the same time, "if I might sit at one of your tables?" He put his left arm out slowly, pointing to the side, all the while watching the lad. "If I am to wait, then I cannot stand all night."

"Well—" started the father. The rest of his sentence was cut off by the loud crash of the blunderbuss discharging.

Into the ceiling. Jake had thrown himself into the boy, taking care to push the gun upwards first. The thick brass of the gun barrel flamed hot as ten balls exploded from its mouth; fortunately they found their home in the thick ceiling beams.

The boy . . . Jake stood back after his push into her proved the matter beyond doubt . . .

"You're a girl," he said.

Other books featuring
Jake Gibbs, Patriot Spy

THE SILVER BULLET
THE IRON CHAIN

THE GOLDEN FLASK

★★★★★★★★★★★★★★★

JIM DeFELICE

St. Martin's Paperbacks

THE GOLDEN FLASK

ISBN: 0-312-95762-9

Printed in the United States of America

St. Martin's Paperbacks edition/April 1996

10 9 8 7 6 5 4 3 2 1

THE GOLDEN FLASK

Introduction

By now, many readers will be familiar with the history of these stories, which are loosely translated from some old manuscripts found in the root cellar of an eighteenth-century farm. Whether the originals were intended as history or fiction is difficult to tell. The places described are verifiably real, as are most of the people and situations. Anyone interested in some of the surrounding history will find some notes addressing it at the end of the book.

The original author's sympathies were clearly on the side of the Revolutionists, and so we must forgive his occasional lapses into partisanship. My contribution has been to update the language here and there, and fight against his habit of puffing out the simplest descriptions and going on for pages when a single paragraph will do.

In one of the strangest and most bewildering events of the war, the British army that had been harrying New Jersey during the early summer of 1777 suddenly gave up its efforts to force General Washington into a decisive battle. Under the command of Sir William Howe, some 20,000 redcoats, Hessians, and various hangers-on marched onto ships and disappeared into the mists of the Atlantic.

They were obviously preparing for a new invasion, but General Washington wasn't sure where. On the one hand, Philadelphia seemed a logical choice—difficult to defend, it was the capital of the Revolutionary congress and had ostensibly been Howe's target during his Jersey campaigns. Yet there were rumors of an attack up the Hudson toward Albany, and intelligence pegged Boston as the next British prize.

The loss of any of these cities would be devastating,

but Washington could not guard all three. Just at the moment he was about to choose where to march his army, a letter fell into his possession from General Howe giving his place of attack as "B—."

The writing was in Howe's hand, and even a schoolboy would realize "B—" was Boston. But was the letter a ruse?

The commander-in-chief faced the most perplexing dilemma of the war. March to Boston, and Albany and Philadelphia were free for the plucking. Hesitate for more than a few short days, and the British would dance their way through New England.

There was only one way to discover Howe's true intentions:

Send the most illustrious member of the Secret Service into New York to find out what Howe was up to. And therein lies our present tale.

—Jim DeFelice
Chester, N.Y.

One

*H*e was unarmed, his ribs throbbed from several recent injuries, and he was about to come under severe attack.

A lesser man might have quaked in his low, silver-buckled shoes. But Lieutenant Colonel Jake Stewart Gibbs took the charge manfully, extending his uniformed arm with grace as Mother Schuyler took his hand and led him through the minuet.

Jake even smiled. It was the price one paid for dancing with her daughter Betsy.

"You are as fine a dancer as a soldier," said Catherine Schuyler as the music ended.

He bowed gracefully, his hand carefully placed on his side to keep the bandages on his ribs from bursting. He'd only risen from the convalescent bed this morning—against the wishes of his nurse, who happened to be Betsy herself.

"I can see where your daughter learned her charms," Jake told his hostess as he took her arm and steered her from the dance floor. "I wonder if you two conspired against me."

The ball was being held in the Schuylers' Albany mansion, known as the Pastures. Despite the poor news from the north, most of the city's social elite had gathered.

"My husband's orders were quite specific," said

Catherine Schuyler. "You are to stay in Albany this evening and meet him tomorrow only if your wounds have healed sufficiently. You look quite handsome in that uniform," she added. "And your hair has completely covered the awful slash you arrived with."

"I have had more severe cuts from errant barbers," replied Jake.

This was just the sort of lie dashing young spies are always telling young women, but it had a considerably different effect on the middle-aged matron. Mrs. Schuyler frowned and her soft, sweet voice transformed to a scold. "Don't tell me your tales," she said, waving her finger up at his face. "It is only a miracle you survived. The first night they laid you in the bed, I thought you were dead."

"Oh, I've been much closer to death. There was the time in Quebec when the governor caught me in his office, for instance. And two months ago on the *HMS Richmond* the noose was already on my neck. Your friend Claus van Clynne saved me from that predicament."

"You were close to death indeed," interjected Colonel Thomas Flanagan, appearing at Jake's right. General Schuyler had pressed Flanagan into serving as his substitute at the ball while he attended to more difficult matters further north.

"Van Clynne is no friend of ours," sniffed Mrs. Schuyler. "He goes about styling himself a squire when he has no land at all."

"He is a bungler and a thief," charged Flanagan.

"Come, Colonel, I understand you have done business with Claus yourself."

"Business, yes—I should like to meet him here tonight. We have a matter to discuss."

"Claus van Clynne was not invited," said Mrs. Schuyler. "Nor would he be welcome."

"He speaks highly of you," said Jake.

"That is a bolder lie than the one about your wound," she replied.

"I am surprised to see you in uniform," said Flanagan. "I did not think the Secret Service was given to wearing them."

"I think it is quite becoming," said Betsy Schuyler, fluttering her skirts as she reached them. She had temporarily managed to extricate herself from a line of suitors to check on her patient. "Much better than the clothes he arrived in." Betsy hooked her arm in Jake's. "Our own tailor made it. I think the blue of his jacket matches his eyes. His breeches are pleasing as well. Very snug."

"And here I thought you were spoken for," Flanagan hinted to Jake.

"I have heard of no wedding vows," answered Betsy sharply. "Nor an engagement given."

"Sarah has been in Boston to attend a sick aunt," Jake explained. "I have not seen her since I returned, though I sent word to her father."

The muscles in Betsy's arm tensed, telling Jake she wished he would reconsider the points he had made in their conversation that afternoon. In truth, he found Betsy a nearly perfect woman, beautiful and intelligent, plucky and brave. She had only one short-coming: General Phillip Schuyler, commander of the northern department of the Continental Army, was her father. And despite Schuyler's recent kindness, Jake did not have a particularly high opinion of him.

He kept that opinion steadfastly to himself, however. Sarah's claim was older and deeper, as he had explained to Betsy—though it was obvious she had not accepted his words as final.

"Perhaps one of you gentlemen will get me some punch," hinted Betsy's mother Catherine.

"I have some business to attend to," said Flanagan. "But I'm sure Colonel Gibbs will oblige."

Mrs. Schuyler was waylaid by an old acquaintance as the trio headed across the room, leaving Jake and Betsy to find the table themselves.

"You are the only one here who does not seem on

edge," said Betsy. Her lilac perfume tickled his nose as the hoops of her brocaded skirt swirled against his side. He had to admit there were much less pleasant ways to spend an evening.

"Don't believe everything you see. I would much prefer to be doing something useful."

"Do you think Burgoyne will attack Albany?"

"He will try to reach it," said Jake.

"Does my father have the troops to stop him?"

The note in her voice surprised him. Jake took hold of Betsy's elbow as he looked down into her eyes. The girl was devoted to her father, but even she couldn't hide her doubts.

Despite his own feelings toward the general, Jake's first impulse was to try and reassure her.

"Don't tell me not to worry," she said before he could speak. "Don't be like the others. Be honest."

The spy nodded, his lips tightening before he spoke. "We won't give up."

It was the most he could say. The recent fall of Ticonderoga—without a fight—was a sobering reminder of how precarious the Revolution was. Jake knew there were plans for waylaying Burgoyne's advance—he had been wounded initiating some of them—but he could not be confident they would be enough.

"Well, this party is supposed to boost everyone's spirit," said Betsy resolutely. "Let us try this punch."

The concoction included a small amount of rum and a much larger portion of sugar—ordinarily too sweet for Jake, but some sacrifices were expected during war.

Betsy turned back to the room, smiling at a knot of admirers who were pitching together their courage to ask for a dance. While there was some sentiment that her older sister Angelica was prettier, Jake would have to cast his vote in Betsy's favor. Indeed, there was only one woman he could think of who was more fetching and she was many miles away.

But if that was so, who was wearing the red velvet

dress and making a beeline directly for him, young men swooning in her wake?

"Jake, how long have you been in Albany without coming to see me?"

"Sarah?"

Jake took a step forward and found himself nearly consumed by Sarah Thomas. He hugged her to him, running his fingers through her auburn hair and savoring the crush of her round, rich breasts. For a brief moment he forgot everything—the war as well as Betsy Schuyler behind him.

"Your father said you were in Boston," he told Sarah.

"I hurried back when I heard your life was in danger," said Sarah, taking a step away and surveying him—with one eye cast menacingly at Betsy. "Apparently I arrived not a moment too soon. What happened to you?"

"Among other things, a Mohawk made the mistake of trying to carry off a piece of my scalp without taking care to make sure I was dead first." He held her hands a moment longer, then loosened his grip to gesture to his side, where Betsy was standing in a pose that would have intimidated Minerva. "Sarah, I believe you know Betsy Schuyler. Her family nursed me back to health."

"Indeed."

Rarely has a simple word contained such understated venom. In a clash of arms, Jake Gibbs had few betters, but he felt temporarily overmatched as the air around the two women sparked with the electricity of a sudden summer storm.

"Sarah Thomas," said Betsy Schuyler. "I hadn't realized you were invited."

"I wasn't," said Sarah. "A friend of mine escorted me. A most distinguished gentleman, as it happens."

Any question as to the gentleman's identity was forestalled by a loud harangue just now rising near the orchestra.

"I should think that another violin would be needed

for proper dancing. In my day, accompaniment was accompaniment, and we did not cut corners with it."

As he had done on so many occasions, Claus van Clynne made a most timely entrance. Pushing his way through the crowd, he temporarily displaced Sarah and Betsy, whose hostilities were interrupted by the small whirlpool created by the squire's arrival.

The portly Dutchman, freshly combed and dressed in a fine russet suit, might have been termed a dashing figure, assuming one made proper allowances for the antique quality of his clothes, his large stomach, and his somewhat scraggly, if over-full, red beard. His shoes bore large golden buckles, and he had not one but two watch chains. His buttons were silver, and his sleeves very properly ruffled. His hat was by far the finest in the hall, circling his head like the clouds over Olympus, and nearly as gray. The beavers that had volunteered their coats for it had been truly noble beasts.

"I had not expected you out of bed for at least another week," said van Clynne, giving Jake a pat on the side so sturdy the spy gasped with pain. "But of course, I had not counted on Dutch cures."

"You seem to have made your own recovery," said Jake.

"A trifle," said the Dutchman, whose most serious wound during the adventure consisted of the loss of an entire bushel of wampum. "A misunderstanding. The Maquas and I have always been on the friendliest of terms. Indeed, we have done much business together, and will do so in the future."

"Not the near future," said Jake. "They've all gone over to Burgoyne."

Van Clynne dismissed this as he might dismiss word of poor weather. "A temporary indiscretion. Now that you are fully recovered, perhaps you can accompany me to Peekskill. I have some business there and aim to leave in the morning."

"I can't," said Jake. "Schuyler will need me."

The Dutchman sniffed and pulled at his beard, but

noting Betsy nearby, did not voice his opinion of the Albany aristocrat turned commander. Instead, he took a glance at the tables, searching for something to drink. Besides the punch, the Schuylers were serving the best Madeira they had, but as of yet, no ale had been liberated from the kitchen. While van Clynne went to perform that mission, Jake returned his attention to Sarah and Betsy.

The British and American armies were exchanging less threatening glares. Under the guise of complimenting each other, the two women traded pointed insults. Sarah noted that Betsy's new dress was most becoming, considering that it had been let out twice in recent months. Betsy opined that the rouge on Sarah's cheek was very much in fashion, no matter what the word from Europe might suggest. Sarah allowed as how no one in the room would notice that Betsy mixed a little clothes dye with her hair soap; Betsy complimented Sarah on the handkerchief discreetly stuffed in the front of her dress.

By now a knot of women had assembled, and the atmosphere was heavier than a late winter's fog. While somewhat flattered to be the object of such attention, Jake was not about to let the two young women come to blows. He owed Betsy his gratitude for her service as nurse, and Sarah much more. Surely a smile to one, a kiss to the other and peace would break out.

Or at least a truce that would facilitate tactful withdrawal. But as he stepped forward to propose a cease-fire, Jake was grabbed from behind by a most unfeminine hand.

"You, sir, are a scoundrel and a villain. You will accompany me outside, where we will arrange to redress our difficulties on the field of honor."

Two

Wherein, Jake is summoned to meet with the commander-in-chief, and the Bard is misquoted.

*J*ake, unsure what he had done and somewhat annoyed at being interrupted, spun around to face his challenger.

He was met by a young man of twenty with a disheveled mop of hair, mud-soiled if nicely tailored clothes, and a broad, impish smile on his face.

"Alexander Hamilton, what the hell are you doing in Albany?"

"Come to rescue you from a tight situation, I see," said Hamilton, whose buff and blue uniform proclaimed him a member of General George Washington's staff. He swept his tricornered hat toward Betsy and Sarah. "Ladies."

"Colonel Alexander Hamilton," said Jake, introducing them. He was as glad of the company as the interruption. "Be careful of him, ladies; he is most ambitious. Just a few weeks ago he was a captain."

"Charmed," said Betsy as he took her hand to kiss it. She fluttered her eyes at him, making sure Jake saw.

"I hope you will excuse me if I remove Colonel Gibbs from your presence. But first let me say, Miss Thomas, that dress is particularly fetching. And you, Miss Schuyler, I hope my delay in making your acquaintance to this point won't be held against me, for surely it has been my great loss."

The reader will be spared the swain's additional bouquets, though the women were not. Sarah immediately became suspicious, but Betsy's eyes filled with a sort of light a poet might devote a lifetime to describing.

"Outside," Hamilton whispered to Jake as he turned from them. "We must not be overheard."

Jake, with a sinking feeling that he was about to become embroiled in the political fallout from the Ticonderoga fiasco, reluctantly bowed his apologies and followed Hamilton through the room. They passed through the ornately worked portal, leaving the faux woodlands on the walls behind.

Jake had been to the Pastures before the war, and knew its interior passages fairly well. He took Hamilton to the east door, passing down the steps onto the broad brick walkway. They walked onto the lawn, away from the house and the nearby bushes.

The moon was at its fullest. The two men might have had a proper game of skittles, or perhaps the duel Hamilton had promised, had the situation been different. Both remained silent until they reached a point where eavesdropping was impossible.

"General Washington must see you immediately," said Hamilton. "It is a matter of the greatest urgency."

Though softly spoken, the words could not have elicited a sharper reaction in Jake had they been shouted in his ear.

"I've ridden all day and half the night without stopping, except for fresh horses," continued Hamilton. "The general has removed you from Schuyler's command. You're to report to him immediately. No excuses."

"I have none."

"Schuyler is in disrepute for abandoning Ticonderoga without a fight," Hamilton added. "His Excellency had one of his famous fits when he heard the news. Several chairs were damaged."

"As I have heard it, Schuyler's not entirely to blame. St. Clair neglected to reinforce Sugar Loaf Hill, as he did not think the British could send artillery there."

"A costly mistake, for which Schuyler will be justly blamed," said Hamilton. "A commander must take responsibility."

"I haven't heard he's ducking it," said Jake. He was honor-bound to defend his commander, even if his assignment had been temporary.

"Arnold is being sent north, along with more reinforcements. The matter will be taken in hand. You and I have more pressing problems."

"More pressing?"

"Come, we have a long ride before us."

"Wait." Jake caught Hamilton by the arm as he started away. He was only three years older than Hamilton, but had seen enough danger since the war started to make them seem like decades. "Let me change from this uniform first. And I have to say good-bye to Sarah."

"No time. Besides, the suit looks quite dashing."

"The breeches are too damn tight."

"You can find other clothes after we reach the general. We're to meet him below Newburgh by noon, and even if we start now I'm not at all sure we'll make it."

"Let me just catch Sarah's eye. And a Dutch friend of mine is here who has proven himself useful in difficult situations; the general may want to make further use of him."

"Colonel—sir." Hamilton's grip on Jake's arm was as powerful as any British grenadier's, but there was a note of respect and even supplication in his voice.

And something else.

Ordinarily, Hamilton was happy to rely on the commander-in-chief's authority and address even major generals as if they were privates. But speaking now to Jake, genuine admiration mixed with fearful worry; his words nearly trembled in his mouth.

"I would like nothing better than to stay on a few hours myself. But the entire British army has disappeared from the Jerseys, packed themselves into ships, and rode out to sea. If we don't discover their inten-

tions within the next few days, we risk a disaster that
will make Ticonderoga look like milk spilt at a maids'
picnic. No one must be informed of our business, not
even the closest friend. You would know that much
better than I."

Duty having clamped her heavy arm on Jake's shoulder, he nodded and followed Hamilton to the horses
without comment.

The Dutchman whose value Jake had mentioned
would have welcomed an interruption. He happened at
that moment to be deeply engaged in discussion with
Colonel Flanagan. Not in itself unusual, except that he
was spending considerably more time listening than
speaking.

Ordinarily, van Clynne would use any meeting with a
close confidant of the commanding general of the
Northern Department to press his claims for the return
of his ancestral lands, stolen from the family by English
interlopers. But it happened that a month earlier the
squire had been engaged by the colonel to sell a variety
of items, including a very fine carriage.

"What a coincidence. I was planning to work on that
transaction tomorrow," said van Clynne.

"That would be very good—I could use the thirty
crowns, believe me."

Van Clynne ignored the note of sarcasm in the colonel's voice. In actual fact, the wagon had fetched forty
crowns at Half Moon some weeks before, just before
the Dutchman ventured north to assist Jake in his dealings with the Mohawk. But such a large interval had
transpired in the meantime that his memory of the details of the business had faded.

Or so he would claim if pressed. For the moment, he
frowned, allowing as how there was a great shortage of
money and an oversupply of wagons, which made
achieving a favorable price difficult. Perhaps, he
hinted, his usual broker's fee could be boosted as an
incentive to a deal.

"I doubt that," said Flanagan. "We have a contract. Your word is your bond, you said."

"As it remains, stronger than any rope. Indeed, stronger than the chain across the Hudson—which I saved, by the by, and which I am due to, er, inspect directly."

Flanagan caught van Clynne's cuff as he attempted to retreat. "I saw a carriage that looked very similar to mine in town just the other day. Another coincidence?"

"As I said, there is quite an oversupply." Van Clynne looked eagerly for a diversion. He saw one in the person of a servant who entered the room carrying a tray of Port. "Here we are, Colonel—something to drink?"

"No."

"Of course, you are a beer man. As am I, in fact. Indeed, I had set out in search of some ale when you bumped into me. Here . . ." He called over to the servant. "Two cups of your finest ale. Wait—better make it porter; my friend and I have just been discussing some stout business."

"Excuse me, sir, but I am serving the wine."

"Just so," said van Clynne, "but it is a venial offense and I won't hold it against you. Hurry now; the colonel is a military man and has many important things to attend to."

As the waiter retreated, van Clynne took a step to follow.

"Hold it, Claus." Flanagan extended an arm and hooked his finger in a buttonhole on the Dutchman's vest.

"I promise to give the carriage my top priority."

"There is another matter I'd like to discuss. General Schuyler told me you have recently been among the Mohawk. I would like to know their strength and plans."

"Yes, the Maquas." Van Clynne frowned, running his eye up and down Flanagan's dark blue uniform. Undoubtedly, Flanagan was merely making a pretext, planning a return to the obnoxious topic of his wagon as soon as possible. "My friend Mr. Gibbs would do better to fill you in. He was gathering intelligence, while I served primarily as facilitator and interpreter. The interviews were not all together pleasant, as I'm sure he will tell you with his usual flair."

"Jake left a short while ago," said Flanagan. "And you're here now."

"Where did he go?" demanded Sarah Thomas, who had been silently observing their conversation.

"I'm sorry, Miss Thomas, but I saw him leave the room a short while ago," said Flanagan.

Tears welled in Sarah's eyes as anger flushed her cheeks. "He's gone to see Betsy I'll bet. She claimed to have a headache and went upstairs."

Flanagan had a daughter about Sarah's age and well understood her consternation. "I saw him go outside with another officer," he explained. "Not with Betsy."

"Colonel Hamilton?"

The words were scarcely out of Sarah's mouth when van Clynne began to bluster. "Hamilton?" he demanded. "Alexander Hamilton? Are we speaking of the young officer who handles much of His Excellency General Washington's correspondence? A man at Washington's beck and call every hour of the day?"

Before Flanagan or Sarah could answer, van Clynne was asking which door they had taken and throwing himself hastily in that direction. The Dutchman ran into the hallway, seeking out his friend with loud entreaties and a sprinkling of even louder curses.

A personal meeting with General Washington had always been a prominent feature of van Clynne's strategy to win back the rights to his property—and here was his chance to arrange one. Surely Jake would tell Hamilton that the Dutchman's plea was a righteous one. Surely the young aide would escort him directly to the general.

But they were nowhere to be found. The landless squire expended a considerable portion of complaints and not a little wheezing before he discovered a stable-hand who had seen them and their mounts head south from the estate. With a great shout, van Clynne realized Dame Opportunity was about to slip off his doorstep.

Not if he could help it. Nor did van Clynne let the fact that the man had only a hazy notion of where the two were going delay him. He trusted to his wits and Fate to reunite them, ere Jake met the general.

Assuming he set off right away.

"A horse, a horse!" he demanded. "My land for a horse."

What Shakespeare might have thought of this plagiarism will not be recorded here. A horse was produced nearly as quickly as the gold from one of the Dutchman's four purses. He thundered into the night, pushing the beast with more fire than Paul Revere displayed the night of his famous tour of the Boston suburbs.

Three

Wherein, Jake and Colonel Hamilton make the acquaintance of several shady fellows.

*T*he cool night air and the rush of excitement at being summoned by General Washington invigorated Jake, and he urged his horse southward with the enthusiasm of a boy released from school the day stripers start their river run. Hamilton was right beside him; the two men took advantage of the strong moon and clear night sky to thunder at full speed through the Hudson Valley hills. They reached the small settlement of Coxsackie, some twenty miles below Albany, in barely the time it would take to spell the name. The horses Hamilton had chosen were slender but sturdy beasts, identically colored—roan, with a single white daub at the left eye. Their muscled legs seemed capable of outrunning the wind.

As fast as the horses strode, Jake's mind went quicker. He began to fear what might lie ahead. It was not fear for himself. Until presented with a specific danger, Jake Gibbs was not the type to dwell on contingencies. But he realized that the Revolution had reached a tremulous point. Already, there were rumblings of discontent in the army, and the chronic shortage of funds was becoming acute. While delegations had been sent abroad to seek foreign support, European powers such as France would not back a cause that appeared headed for defeat. Another major setback—the loss of Boston or Philadelphia, or even Albany—could easily end all hope of assistance.

The area Jake and Hamilton rode through had been among the first visited by white men after the continent's fortunate discovery. The Dutch, including members of the van Clynne family, had made this land their own, exploring, farming, and trading for furs. It was still sparsely settled, however, for various reasons beginning with the geography. Hills and mountains rose up in jagged lines from the river; between them, all manner of ponds, creeks, and streams flowed in crazy-quilt patterns, now shimmering in the moonlight.

A few miles south of Coxsackie, a stream crossed the roadway to mark a perfect *X* on the darkened landscape, and it was here that the two Continental officers stopped to refresh their horses and stretch their own arms and legs.

The spot was idyllic, but the choice was unfortunate, for no sooner had the men slipped off the backs of their mounts than they were warned to stand away, with their hands held out at their sides.

"You will do what I say, or I will kill you," said the voice sharply. "Identify yourselves."

Jake, his barely healed wounds smarting from the bumping they'd been treated to on the ride, stretched his arms stiffly and studied the shadows. A man with a gun was standing to their right.

"Excuse us, sir," said Hamilton brightly. "We are on our way to New Paltz."

"No one travels at night on this road," said the man. Tall, he cast a wedgelike shadow forward from the woods. His accent was odd, though his words were perfect English. The intonation reminded Jake of the Iroquois, among whom he had just spent several harrowing weeks.

"We are good patriots," answered Hamilton. His service as an artillery officer had not taught him the caution that was second nature to Jake. This was secure patriot country, after all, and his assumption that the men must be part of the local militia was logical. "I am Lieutenant Colonel Alexander Hamilton, and this is my friend, Colonel Gibbs."

"A pair of colonels," said another voice, this one to their left. There was no mistake about his accent—it was direct from one of London's cruder neighborhoods.

Jake quickly surveyed the nearby woods, looking for a safe line of retreat. His only weapon was his Segallas pocket pistol secreted at his belt. And Hamilton's larger officer's pistol was snug in the holster on the side of his saddle on his horse.

"If you've come to rob us," said Jake, "it will do you no good; we've got no money."

"We're not interested in your money," said the man with the Indian accent, who seemed to be the other's leader. He took a step from the shadows.

"Come now, friends, who is your commander?" said Hamilton, taking a step forward.

Jake groaned. "Alexander," he said as he put his hand to his vest, "I believe my stomach is acting up."

"As well it should," said the leader. "Bring up the light."

A third and then a fourth man emerged from the shadows near the bushes, the last holding a candle lantern. Its flame was hardly enough for anyone to read by, but it gave Jake enough light to see there were no other reinforcements.

"Gentlemen," he said, still feigning illness as he stepped forward, "I must speak to you alone."

"That's an old trick," said the first man who had accosted them, standing to their right. The dim light illuminated white skin, but his forehead and cheek were tattooed with the unmistakable markings of an Iroquois warrior. His head was completely shaven, except for a scalp lock; tied with a large golden feather and brass ring, it hung down the side of his head to his shoulder. His clothes were a curious mixture of European and Indian dress. He wore a black, tailored jacket but no shirt. A long red ceremonial slash cut a diagonal across his chest. His breeches were leather. In the darkness it was impossible to tell what if anything he wore on his feet.

Jake had come across painted whites before. Some called them changelings, men who had been adopted or stolen as youngsters to live among the Indians and converted to their ways. Others called them renegades, race traitors, and worse.

It was difficult to generalize about where such men's loyalties lay. But these had already given themselves away. Jake guessed the white Indian and his escorts must be messengers working between the British northern and southern frontiers; they were too far and too misplaced to be scouts.

"This is not a trick," said Jake. He had used his feigned stomach ailment to put the Segallas into his hand, and now contemplated how best to use its store of bullets. "The name I have used until now is false, a fiction to make travel among these rebels safer. I am Major Doctor Keen, assigned to General Bacon's intelligence service. I am on my way to our lines with valuable information."

Keen's name was unfamiliar to them, but the mention of Black Clay was enough to give the quartet pause. Bacon ran the British intelligence service headquartered in New York City under General Howe. They were ostensibly if indirectly under his command.

He was also a man who must not be crossed in the least way. The Englishmen took a step backward, nearly as a group.

The tattooed man was not impressed. He spat on the ground.

"Egans, let us examine him," suggested the Londoner. "He should bear a token if he is a messenger."

"I did not say I was a messenger," answered Jake, working his way slowly toward the man with the candle lantern. He tried to use the same haughty tone Keen would have used. The spy felt safe in usurping Keen's identity as well as his voice, as he had watched the doctor sink to the bottom of the Mohawk River a week before.

"What are you then?" demanded Egans. Jake's guess about the man's origins was correct—he was an adopted member of the Oneida nation, among whom he had proven his worth and earned the name of a warrior some years before.

"I would not talk to one who pretends to be an Iroquois," said Jake, as savagely as if his mother had been accused of being a whore. The white Indian at first did not react, but his anger quickly grew as Jake began to rattle off a series of curses in pidgin Huron. While these ill-pronounced words represented all he knew of the tongue, still they were of sufficient slander to accomplish Jake's purpose. No matter that the stress and accent were wrong; the hate for the Huron nation's eternal enemies, eaters of people and robbers of skins, was perfectly clear.

"I have spent many weeks among the Huron," Jake told the Englishmen as they strained to hold back the infuriated Egans. He embellished his preposterous tale with a boldness that made it sound plausible. "Working on an alliance. You will help take me to Howe."

"What about him?" said the candle-holder, gesturing toward Hamilton.

"Oh, he's just a convenient rebel," said Jake, walking to him. "We shall take him along as ransom. I doubt he's really a colonel, though," he added. "I should be surprised if he's even a captain."

Hamilton might have objected at this demotion, but he was too busy flying to the ground. This sudden action was dictated by Jake's shout as he upturned the lantern into its bearer's face. In the next instant, he fired the Segallas at the next closest Englishman.

Jake's finger inadvertently nudged both of the gun's small triggers, and thus two poisoned bullets instead of one struck the man in the chest. Cursing, Jake dove at the last Briton, whose pistol discharged as they tumbled backwards.

Egans took a step backward, calmly drawing back the lock on his musket. He caught the bare outline of Hamilton springing to his feet and fired in the young officer's direction, ducking as a projectile flew at him. The missile was a medium-sized rock, which missed Egans's head by a half-foot. Fortunately, his bullet missed Hamilton by the same margin.

Jake and the Englishman fell together into the stream, the Segallas dropping by the wayside. The patriot had just spotted a jagged rock to thrash his man's head against when he felt his leg warm considerably. This sensation was followed by a strong, sharp poke, which the patriot spy recognized only too well—his enemy was endeavoring to stitch his name on Jake's leg, if not his abdomen, with a small but still considerably sharp knife.

The Englishman's head was thrust three times on the stone, each time harder than before, so that with the third blow his brains burst in a gruesome mess from the skull. Jake jumped to his feet as the man's ghost ran from him.

The patriot had just enough time to duck as the candle-bearer charged straight at him. The maneuver sent the man flying face-first into the stream. It also brought Jake within reach of the dead man's discarded knife, which he appropriated before wading after his prey.

While his first approach had ended in a comic flip, the Englishman aimed quickly to redeem himself. He had equipped himself with a hatchet, and took two quick swipes at Jake to halt his advance. Knee-deep in water, the two men faced each other in the moonlight oblivious to all else around them.

Hamilton, meanwhile, had managed to take a few strides for his horse, where his pistol sat waiting. Egans got there first, shoving him aside and grabbing at the saddle holster for the gun. Though of average height,

Hamilton could extend himself when enraged, and he was rarely so hot as he was now. He flew headlong at the man, knocking the gun from his hand just as the lock was pulled back. The woods exploded with the misfired shot, but neither Hamilton nor the adopted Oneida was injured. Egans slipped and the pair rolled in the mud beneath the animals' hooves, the horses pulling and yanking at their tied reins.

Fury aside, Egans was more than a match for Hamilton. But Hamilton was persistent. They continued to grapple together, until the white Oneida spotted the fallen pistol a short distance away. Then began a desperate game of leapfrog, each man trying to reach the weapon first.

Meanwhile, Jake and his opponent thrashed back and forth on the creekbed. Twice the American took a feint with his knife, falling back under the weight of a vicious flail from the Englishman's ax. On his third try, Jake's luck seemed to run out—he slipped on the muck and fell backwards in a tumble. In the next instant, the Englishman fell upon him, hand curled back with the heavy hatchet.

The weapon fell aside harmlessly. Jake had employed a simple ruse to take his enemy off his guard, plunging his knife full into his stomach as he charged. He held the hilt firmly as the man first pushed then pulled, triumphant charge turned to desperate retreat.

On his knees in the water, Jake levered the blade through the man's organs, holding him tight with his left hand. No lover's grasp was as sturdy as this death grip; by the time he let the man collapse backwards into the moonlit water, his soul had long since escaped earthly bounds.

And now Jake turned his attention to the shore where Hamilton was deep into his own hard struggle. Egans's superior skill and strength were showing; he managed to grab the pistol from the dirt and brought it back in a crash across Hamilton's head.

Jake scooped up his Segallas and spun its barrels to

fire, but both bullets whizzed wide of his mark. Oblivious, the white Oneida pulled Hamilton's empty pistol back for a second blow as a hammer when Jake crashed into his back. Knocked to the ground, Egans managed to tumble around and spring to his feet, and Jake found himself staring down the barrel of a gun.

It took a moment for him to realize the weapon had already been fired. By that time, Jake was diving to his right, out of aim. The Indian smiled brightly and leapt to the nearby horse.

Jake took a step to give chase, but Hamilton caught him by the shirttail.

"Our mission is too important to risk following him," he said between winded puffs for air. "We've already lost too much time."

"That's quite a little pistol you have there," said Hamilton when he had caught his breath. "It fires four shots?"

"Two, then you have to twist the barrel around to fire two more," said Jake, inspecting the dead men's bodies for papers or other signs of their mission. Besides a small collection of British and other coins, which he left in their pockets, they had nothing incriminating. "The bullets are small but at close range they're effective. These were poisoned by an old acquaintance."

The irony encased in the last word escaped Hamilton. The poison had been supplied by one of Jake's most severe enemies—the now deceased Keen.

"Effective. The men seemed to be farmers."

"That's just their dress. They are British soldiers, except for the one they called Egans."

"Why would a white dress as an Indian?"

"Possibly adopted as a boy. Or simply a renegade. It doesn't make much difference, at the moment."

Under different circumstances, Jake would ride to the nearest militia unit and alert them of Egans's presence. But there was no time to alert anyone, or even bury the dead men. He restored his pocket pistol to its hiding place and dragged the bodies to the side of the road. Then he bowed his head.

"Don't tell me you're praying for them," said Hamilton, incredulously. "They're the enemy."

For every hard inch of callus applied to Jake's body by these years of struggle, another part of his inner self had softened. Enemy or not, he could not help but feel remorse at the death of a fellow human being.

Someday, this growing well of sorrow might prevent him from fighting, despite the great justness of his cause. For now, he merely finished his silent memorial and walked to where Hamilton was sitting on his horse. As Egans had made off with the animal Jake had been riding, their remaining horse would have to be pressed into double duty. Fortunately, they were to change mounts only a few miles down the road, and then press on to New Paltz, where another fresh pair awaited.

Jake grabbed hold of Hamilton and hauled himself up behind him. "If you have any influence with this horse," said the spy, squeezing onto the saddle, "ask him to avoid the bumps. My ribs feel as if they've just been broken again."

"I'm afraid we've only just met," said Hamilton, spurring the stallion.

Four

*Wherein, a carriage and traveler stop along the road,
with unpleasant consequences.*

$\mathcal{H}$elios had not long strung his bow in the eastern
sky—nor had the sun been up very long—when a
mahogany-paneled carriage happened to pass on the
road near where Jake had placed the bodies. As the
patriot spy had surmised, the dead men quickly caught
the attention of these passers-by, and an order was
given from within for the driver to halt.

The large, gilded wheels skidded to a stop in the dirt
as the horses were curled back sharply at the bit;
though he had held his position as driver and guide
only a short while, the Indian whose hands were
wrapped around their reins knew his master was best
obeyed promptly.

Even so, the door had swung open before the carriage stopped. As if caring little for his fine, bright blue
jacket and buckskin breeches, the vehicle's occupant
dashed into the swirling dust. His energy belied his age,
which was now past fifty. Though he had lately spent
considerable time recuperating from a variety of
wounds, he sprung forward with great energy to inspect
the dead men. Brandishing his walking stick, he waved
it over them as if it were a bishop's scepter, imparting
some blessing to the already vanquished souls.

But the man had not stopped to administer Christian
niceties. He was instead a connoisseur of death, con-
genitally interested in examining the nuances of each

individual tragedy, hoping to increase his already considerable stock of knowledge on the subject. For the man who now pushed the bodies back and forth like so many laboratory specimens was no less than Major Dr. Harland Keen.

The very same man Jake had seen fall over the Cohoes Falls to the bottom of the Mohawk River less than a fortnight before.

The reader is entitled to some explanation for the shock of that last line, and we shall here deliver it as succinctly as possible, to avoid losing the thread of our present tale.

As a young man, Harland Keen had left his native London to tour the world, gathering the esoteric knowledge that would supplement the skills he learned at Edinburgh and render him among the most brilliant practitioners of the medical arts in Europe. He had not yet become the evil-hearted assassin who would eventually forget his fraternity's oath against causing harm, though already his character shaded toward Life's darker vales.

It was during a stay in Venice that he came upon an old woman, reputed of Borgia stock, who had gained great fame as a reader of the Egyptian cards. On a cloud-besotted day on an obscure piazza overlooking the Grand Canal, the woman plucked the Magician from the deck and nodded approvingly. But then she found Temperance inverted, and crossed severely by the Moon. Keen himself shuddered when the next card of her divinatory layout proved to be Death, mounted aboard a white charger with the red rose as his banner.

Even a reader unfamiliar with the portents must sense the message the cards foretold. As the reading proceeded in a progressively darker vein, Keen felt his anger grow. He had never been superstitious, yet something in the woman's manner convinced him not only to believe what she said, but to take it as a curse rather than an objective interpretation of Fortune's wheel. He pounded the table and upset the cards, demanding to know what, if any, good news she had for him.

"You shall not die a water death," proclaimed the woman. "You cannot be killed by water."

Suddenly, he was seized by a fit. "Let us see if the same is true of you," he shouted, picking the woman up and throwing her into the canal.

Immediately, he repented, threw off his boots and coat, and dove into the dark water to save her. But despite the long hour he searched in the putrid stream, he could not retrieve her body.

The full explanation for the dark roiling of his soul is perhaps more complicated, involving other choices and decisions as well as personal reverses. But it is nonetheless true that his path took a severe turn that afternoon. The woman died without relatives. Keen found himself not only free but in possession of her considerable texts and potions, and in a few hours gained knowledge his instructors at Edinburgh could not have dreamed in a lifetime.

His career progressed, and at length he returned to London and became doctor to the highest elements of society, including the king himself. Despite his fame, his experiments brought him disrepute. He was accused of heinous crimes before King George III exiled him to America, in exchange for his life. By then, he had joined the king's secret department, sworn to carry out assassinations and other assignments in utter secrecy.

Once a member of the department, there is no resignation short of death. Keen continued to carry out assignments under the direction of General Bacon, who besides being the intelligence chief was the king's personal representative at the head of the clandestine order of assassins.

A few months after his arrival in New York, Keen was given the red-jeweled dagger signifying a mission— and told to kill Jake Gibbs and his friend Claus van

Clynne. The doctor was bested by the pair below the great iron chain that spans the river at Peekskill, but he did not despair. Instead, he traced the two men north, and as they worked on a mission among the Mohawk he struck again.

Keen believed van Clynne perished in a burning building, where he had left him tied and gagged. In fact, the Dutchman had escaped through a basement passage used by an earlier occupant as a beer cellar.

Jake, meanwhile, proved harder to find, let alone kill. Keen joined forces with the local Mohawks, and was able to trick the American spy into a meeting just above the Cohoes Falls. The two men fell upon each other and engaged in a death struggle. Keen, aided by drugs that increased his stamina and natural strength, throttled Jake, then had him bound and gagged, placed into a canoe and sent tumbling over the falls.

But the doctor himself became tangled in the tackle trailing from the boat, and plunged over in the torrent. The canoe, loaded with heavy supplies, sank at the foot of the falls—as Jake had seen.

Jake saw this because he had not been fooled by Keen, but rather played the trick back to ensnare the doctor. With the aid of a confederate . . . ah, but we do not wish to give the plot away to those who have not read the adventure. Suffice it to say Jake watched Keen fall, and observed the commotion on the riverbank below as the doctor's Indian allies debated what to do. By the time Jake left to complete his mission, Keen had been underwater ten minutes at least; no one, he thought, could have survived the tumult without drowning.

But he had not counted on the Borgia curse or prediction—whichever it might be—nor did he know that Keen had found a pocket of air within the overturned canoe. The British assassin reached the shore intact. His Indian cohorts were dumbstruck to see him. As fooled as Keen by Jake's plot, they assured him the

white man had died, and after a lengthy search produced a blond scalp to back up their claim.

The hair now rested on the bench of Keen's carriage.
He was fully confident that it belonged to his nemesis.
But how to explain that one of the dead men bore the
unmistakable signs of having been killed by a poison
few men besides Keen himself could concoct?

A poison that had been on the bullets when Gibbs
stole his Segallas pistol back in their fateful fight before the falls?

There might be many theories. Perhaps one of the
Indians had managed to find the gun on the body and
then used it here.

But why? The man's rough outer clothes were not
exceptional, but he had on a silk undershirt. That and
his pocketful of coins suggested he was an English
agent, but not a robbery victim.

Very few people in this province would not ransack a
body before death. Keen knew full well Gibbs was one.
He felt his blood rising against the rebel's sham virtue.

But he was dead, wasn't he?

The doctor saw the death wounds of each man before returning to the carriage, where his Mohawk assistant waited. The man had lived among whites for many
years, and had acted as an interpreter during Keen's
recent travels.

"Clouded Face," said Keen, addressing him as he
stood by the side of the carriage, "come down a moment."

"Doctor, sir?"

"Simply say 'doctor.' I am not a knight, nor do I
aspire to be. Knighthood, in fact, is out of the question.
Come down here."

There was nothing specifically venomous in Keen's
voice, yet the assistant trembled as he put down the
reins. He slipped to the ground, then held his hands in
a tangled, sweating knot before him, where they would

be conveniently situated should he have to beg for mercy.

"Clouded Face, you assured me Jake Gibbs was dead, did you not?"

"Yes, sir, yes, Doctor, yes I did."

"And you did that because of the scalp?"

"I saw him go over the falls myself," said the assistant. "And heard the death wail. I kicked the body with the others on the shore below. You have the hair."

"The ribbon is the same. The color, of course. But tell me . . ." Keen tapped the man's uncovered head with his cane. "Tell me if a scalp could be taken without a man being killed. Or if the wrong scalp could be taken and dressed with another man's ribbon?"

"Impossible."

"Let us try the first, then, and see," said Keen, producing a knife. "Your knot is convenient."

The Indian made the mistake of starting to run. Until that moment, Keen had not completely decided to kill him—he was still largely a stranger to this country, and if Gibbs were truly alive, a guide would prove useful. But he could no more allow an assistant to run from him than he could let this Gibbs continue to live. He pointed his stick and pressed a hidden button near the end of the shaft. The ornate gold head flew off with a tremendous burst of velocity, striking Clouded Face in the back of the head. The man fell forward immediately, his brain pan shattered.

"I think that I have my answer," said Keen. "I don't suppose it will be of much use to scalp you then, but I will do so anyway, for the practice."

Five

Wherein, more of Mr. Egans's particular history is explored, with unsatisfactory results.

While Jake and Alexander Hamilton continued south, Claus van Clynne headed in the same general direction. But even though he took every shortcut he knew and urged his horse forward with epic entreaties and a few unvarnished threats, his progress was not half as sharp. Indeed, as the sun dawned, it found him just seven or eight miles south of the spot where Jake had left the dead Englishmen, on a dusty but sturdy road whose dips and turns ran somewhat in harmony with the nearby river.

His lack of speed was partly caused by the fact that he had to stop every so often and search for signs of his friends and their direction; their trail was difficult to trace. But a more substantial portion of his problem was due to his horse's slow gait, which was in direct contrast to its advertised attributes. This was especially annoying as van Clynne had paid dearly for the animal. Under ordinary conditions, the Dutchman would not have allowed himself to be so ill-used, nor would he have concluded a deal without several minutes', if not hours', worth of haranguing. He did not wish this taken as a sign of weakness, as he explained to the beast in great detail as they rode. Only the prospect of seeing General Washington and presenting his case made him accept the outrage as the price of doing business.

Van Clynne's tongue was no less prolific because he

was traveling alone; indeed, he found it easier to give full range to his feelings, as he was not constantly being interrupted by a companion. After he finished complaining of the high price of transportation, his topic naturally moved to the injustice of Jake's flight southward without him. Occasional jabs at the patroons who unlike him had managed to keep the vast land holdings he was riding through led to the subject of injustice in general, whereupon the British bore the brunt of the complaint.

He soon turned to the Esopus Wars, the great conflicts of the seventeenth century during which the Dutch had tamed the native inhabitants near Kingston, only to find themselves tamed in turn by the English invaders. Without following the entire path of van Clynne's logic, let us say that it left him in a sympathetic, nay, charitable frame of mind when he came upon a dusty, Indianish fellow traveler sitting astride a horse on the river road not far from Murderer's Creek.

The traveler was Egans, who had restored both his strength and his anger during the several hours that had passed since encountering Jake and Colonel Hamilton. He had also recovered sufficient composure to cloak his business in the guise of a semi-innocent wanderer.

"Good morrow to you," said van Clynne. "Which way are you going?"

"To the river," replied the man.

"Not far to go, then." Van Clynne stroked his beard a moment and attempted to puzzle out the man's ancestry. Though his skin was white, his wardrobe was just the sort of mixture an Iroquois might consider his Sunday best. Obviously this was a European adopted by natives at some point in his past.

Such men had an unsurpassed ability to slide between the two worlds and were invaluable in business. They were generally easy to enlist, and rarely understood the nuances of European exchange rates. Van Clynne hated to miss an opportunity that might lead to future profits. But his beard scratching brought him back to his true priority: finding Jake and winning an appointment with Washington.

"I wonder if you have seen a man about six foot tall and heading south on horseback," he asked the stranger. "An early riser two towns ago thought he caught sight of him hurrying this way. He has blond hair, a fine Continental uniform, and a habit for getting involved in difficult situations, from which I inevitably rescue him."

"I have seen no one," claimed Egans.

"He would have been in the company of another man, a Colonel Hamilton. My friend's name is Gibbs—a remarkable individual. I have no doubt posterity will learn a great deal about him, though the edges of his story will have to be rounded for easier consumption. Modesty prevents me from describing my role in his adventures, but it has been considerable. The times I have plucked him from Hades's vestibule are too many to count."

"You look familiar," suggested the white Indian. "What is your name?"

"Claus van Clynne, at your service," said the Dutchman. "You, too, seem familiar," he said. Now that he'd had a chance to think about it, he placed the man's signs and jewelry definitely among the Oneida. There were not many white men who would wear the simple stone and symbolic tree, and fewer still who would have been accorded the honor of the eagle feather tied to his scalp lock. He searched the cubbyholes of his brain and retrieved the name: "You are Egans, are you not?"

Despite a secret hatred of the Dutch—van Clynne's ancestry was easily deduced from his clothes, to say nothing of his name and accent—Egans's stoic mask dropped for a moment. "How do you know me?"

"You are quite famous," said the Dutchman. He slipped off his horse and approached, holding out his hand. "You were a white child kidnapped by the Mohawk and then adopted by the Oneida during troubles thirty years ago. Your white family came from land not far from mine, and your adopted uncle and I have made one or two suitable arrangements regarding furs and corn in the past, before the war. I believe you were baptized Christof—"

"My Seneca name is *Gawasowaneh*."

"Yes, yes, Big Snowsnake," said van Clynne, waving his hand as if he knew a thousand men with the Indian name. The Oneida were a touchy lot, and he did not want to provoke even an adopted son. Van Clynne was temporarily weaponless, his customary tomahawks left behind in Albany and his unloaded pistol resting comfortably in his saddlebag. "You have earned it for your role in the ceremonies."

"I have earned it for my role as a warrior," said the Oneida. Indeed, his ceremonial names could not be uttered except at the council fire.

"Just so, sir, just so. Would you prefer I use *Gawasowaneh* in addressing you? I myself am known by many Indian names." Van Clynne did not add that most of these might be translated loosely as "Big Tummy and Longer Tongue."

"Call me what you will."

"Thank you, sir, thank you. I know your entire life story; I congratulate you on your endurance. What brings you here?"

Egans did not answer his question, but van Clynne was undaunted.

"One of your native uncles and I had quite an arrangement three summers ago," continued the Dutchman, the memory of the profitable deal warming his heart. "I delivered certain blankets to the great chief Cornplanter, in exchange for wood carted down the mountain path. An unusual arrangement, but favorable to both sides. With your connections to the Iroquois Federation—strong friends of mine, I might add. I have recently spent much time among the Mohawk, turning them from the English path into more profitable areas. Perhaps we have mutual acquaintances?"

"As it happens, I am to meet my uncle at the river," suggested Egans. "Ride with me."

Van Clynne wondered what a seventy-year-old Indian whose home was far to the northwest would be doing near the river. A belated if sharp sense of danger hastened him to postpone further talk of a business arrangement indefinitely.

"I have urgent business further south," he noted, bowing and then reaching to pull himself back onto his horse. "Perhaps in a few days we can meet in some local inn."

"I think you will come with me now," said Egans, pushing aside his coat to reveal a secreted pistol.

"I should think it cold without a shirt beneath your coat. There is a fine tailor not too far from here. Perhaps if we took that road, I might be able to shave a few pence from the price."

"I think not," said Egans. "We are almost at the river now."

"Does your uncle know that you have allied yourself with the English?" asked van Clynne, steadying his horse as it climbed down the obscure, rock-strewn path. They were far from the main roads, approaching a wooded bluff overlooking the Hudson. The water was so close the Dutchman could catch glimpses of the gently rocking waves through the trees. "I would think he would have something to say about it."

"I have not seen my uncle in many years, fat man."

"I would think, sir, that personal insults will not forward our relationship in the least. But let me mention that your uncle still grieves your family's loss."

"No other man has lost two fathers," said Egans suddenly, turning on van Clynne. "And now I suggest that you keep silent, or I will fill your mouth with lead."

"As you wish, sir," said van Clynne. "Though I

would think you much wiser to align yourself with the patriotic cause, as it is one that argues for freedom and should be most compatible with the native lifestyle. These English—"

"Enough! It was a Dutchman who killed my second father. Do not tempt me to take revenge."

With great effort and a strong glance at the pistol lodged against his nose, van Clynne stopped his tongue. Egans's red father had in fact been killed by a German—the story was well known in the inns near the family's old homestead—but his friend was not in a mood to be corrected.

Egans was a wily fellow, and he made sure to stay several yards behind van Clynne. He had also taken the precaution of removing the squire's pistol from his saddlebag, as well as confiscating his four purses. The pistol was of little account, as it hadn't been loaded, but the purses had a certain sentimental value—the Dutchman nearly cried over the bills they contained. True, he had taken the precaution of leaving nearly all his coins with Sarah Thomas's father for safe keeping before attending the ball, and had a good supply of New York pounds and a few British notes besides hidden in his heel. But this he considered emergency money, and of dubious authenticity besides.

What van Clynne really wished for was a tomahawk. He was well known as one of the best ax chuckers in the province; were one in his hand right now, Egans would be wearing his hair much differently.

"Stop," said the white Oneida as van Clynne's horse reached a high point in the trail. The trees immediately to the east had been cleared, giving them a good view of the Hudson below. The river was a bright expanse of blue, gleaming with the sparkle of the midday sun. Only a few boats were about.

With Egans's attention turned toward the water, Escape was flapping her wings and heading for greener pastures. But the Dutchman needed a weapon to gain tactical advantage, and only one thing presented itself—his large and well-treasured silvery-gray beaver hat. Desperately, van Clynne flung it, startling Egans as he turned, and causing him to misfire his gun. In the same motion, van Clynne kicked his horse sharply. The animal leapt forward, but stumbled after only three steps, sending the Dutchman in a heap into the hillside brush. The considerable slope of the terrain added momentum to van Clynne's tumble, and the Dutchman was soon rolling down the hill with the force of an avalanche, throwing all manner of debris and dust in his wake. He was just barely able to steer himself by shoving his arms in front of him, managing to avoid several large rocks but crashing over a number of smaller ones.

Egans started through the brambles at the top of the bluff, then realized he would have to find an easier passage. He jumped atop his horse and rode down the path, toward an abandoned step-back trail leading to the river bank.

With a great groan, van Clynne bounced against a stone wall that stood a few yards from the edge of the water. He could hear the struggles of Egans's horse just to the south and knew he would not get very far on the ground in that direction before the Indian arrived. The way north was blocked by a large patch of overgrown blackberry sticker bushes; escape in that direction was likewise improbable.

Indeed, the only path open was the river a few yards away. Not only did its waters beckon with a disarming calmness, but a canoe had been placed on the bank to make his exit child's play.

Except that van Clynne was deathly afraid of water. Given the choice, he would have walked barefoot through a field of burning corn before being berthed in the captain's quarters of a fine sailing ship.

The sound of Egans's horse crashing through the woods vanquished his fear. Or rather, it gave the

Dutchman courage enough to close his eyes as he dove into the canoe, his weight helping to move it out onto the water as the current caught hold and pushed it toward midstream.

Six

Wherein, a certain flask is opened, and a perplexing problem pours out.

Jake and his guide passed through the fertile farmland of southern Ulster and northern Orange counties without encountering any other difficulties. For the most part, the people here were strong patriots who had already suffered much for the war. A good number had been deployed as militia in the Highlands a few months before. The long rail fences and haphazard stone walls that marked the boundaries of their lands teemed with tall grass and summer flowers; truly Nature had blessed the area with an abundant flow of life.

Had we the leisure, we might dally in one of these meadows or walk among the furrowed corn. The stone houses of the Huguenots that made up New Paltz might be of special interest, not merely for the architecture but the stories these stones might tell of harrowing winters and violent struggles in the old wilderness. But Jake and Colonel Hamilton did not linger here, taking without comment their fresh horses from the waiting militiaman, a tall fellow named Schenck, who had stood a lonely vigil by his yard's gate all night. They thundered onward, sucking hard bread crusts between their teeth, the fresh animals soon wheezing with the difficult pace.

There was much the two men might have said to each other. Hamilton was especially interested in Miss Schuyler, whom he'd already heard rumors of from an-

other of Washington's aides, Tench Tilgham, but their
haste precluded idle chatter. Immediately south of the
village, Hamilton left the main road, heading over a
series of obscure paths that would have made van
Clynne proud. The Shawangunk mountains stood at
their right shoulders, watching their progress through
the foothills. Newburgh and New Windsor sat off to
the left, closer to the river. Red-tailed hawks, surveying
the fields for a midmorning snack, circled warily overhead, anxious lest the hurrying travelers suddenly covet
their feathers.

It was just about noon when the two men neared the
vicinity where the rendezvous with the commander-in-
chief had been arranged. The tangled area is known as
the Clove. With the Highland mountains guarding the
approach from the river, the land dives down into a
lush valley, overgrown with all manner of Nature's
bounty.

Jake and Colonel Hamilton pushed down a path narrowed on both sides by massive bolts of daisies, laurel,
and other wildflowers, their sweet scents filling their
lungs. Hamilton suddenly veered to the right, crossing
into what seemed at first a field made entirely of black-
berries. But the bushes gave way to a meadow inter-
sected by a firm path; Jake let his horse follow
Hamilton's lead as they dipped down a gradual incline.

Ahead, the two riders spotted a tall, regal man on
horseback, gray hair flying beneath his hat as he paced
with his mount on the hilltop. Some trick of the light
washed out all else before them, and for a moment it
seemed as if horse and rider were walking on air.

Jake spurred his horse at the sight; many months
had passed since he had seen General Washington.
Crossing a stream that lay between them, a shout went
up. The general's guard appeared from both sides and
intercepted the men. Recognizing Hamilton, they
joined in escort, and the commander-in-chief found
himself besieged by an eager body of young men whose
emotions stirred even his fabled constitution.

There are those who have made General Washington into a latter-day Caesar, only wiser and bolder. Another contingent, smaller but nearly as vociferous, crayons him a tyrant and fool. Those closest to him can speak equally of his steady faith and ready temper. Let us agree that he is neither demigod nor demon, but if the compass should shade toward one extreme over the other, let it be the former. No other single man has embodied our noble struggle so completely. No other man has pulled us together so completely, nor inspired so many tattered soldiers, ranks broken by bayonet charge, to turn round and face the enemy one last time, and thereby win victory and honor.

The first sight of the long blue coat with its wide collar turned out gave Jake a flush of inspiration and strength. Any doubts over the outcome of the war were vanquished at the sight of this surrogate father on the hilltop, watching them approach.

Washington's majestic blue uniform was fitted out with buff lapels and topped by gold epaulets, its swallowtails buttoned for riding. The light tan vest and breeches snugged a powerful body, draped by a diagonal light-blue ribbon. This ribbon, along with the unadorned cockade on his black, three-cornered hat, showed his rank, much as the yellow cockade had confirmed Hamilton's.

With no hat to doff in salute, Jake held out both arms in exaltation as he drew up close. "General, sir," he exclaimed, "I have come as quickly as I could."

Washington's light tone belied his words as he chided his young officer. "You look as if you've come straight from the dance floor. Is that a tailored uniform? On a member of the Secret Service? When I sent you to Schuyler I thought he'd put you to serious work."

"I've had my moments, sir."

"I rescued him from Betsy Schuyler's clutches, your excellency," said Hamilton, drawing near. "It was a difficult fight, and I shall stand for a medal."

"It's I who rescued him," countered Jake. "Your secretary was ready to give himself up as a prisoner."

Washington smiled, but already gravity was returning to his face. "Hamilton, there is some business for your immediate attention," he said, dismounting. "Harrison has a critical dispatch. Young Jake, walk with me a bit."

The long grass brushed against the tight breeches of Jake's fancy dress pants as they walked. A clump of daylilies sat at the edge of the hilltop meadow, their red-and-yellow faces basking in the sun. Sprigs of daphne mixed in behind them, their berries just shading from blue to black.

It would not have taken much imagination to think themselves on a picnic. Until the general began speaking.

"You met Howe a few months ago," said Washington. "Or so I have heard."

"Aboard his brother's ship in New York Harbor. They thought I was a spy—for their side."

Washington laughed heartily. Certain of the younger men always tickled his sense of humor, and Gibbs had been among them from the first day they met. "I wonder how they got that idea."

"You know the British. Always adding two and two and finding five."

"What was your opinion of Sir William?"

"The general is the letter of the reports about him, perhaps worse. He's vain and indecisive. Given to drink and whoring."

"Yes, and I'm sure the British say the same of me."

"In his case it is true."

Washington was silent a moment, as if considering the field around him. But his thoughts were much further away.

"The general has helped us many times without knowing it," he said. "Still, he is more formidable than you give him credit for, and he can be perplexing."

Washington reached into the inside pocket of his coat and pulled out an ornate golden flask. If King

George had appeared on the hilltop before them, Jake would not have been more surprised.

"General?"

"Take the flask and open it, Jake. Go on; it's not one of your poisons, I assure you. Nor is it rum."

Beautifully worked, the flask was made of metal, shaped like a flat shovel used in a stable, though naturally much smaller. The stout neck had a delicate flute, stoppered with a common cork, in great contrast to the glimmering metal it fit into. There were no identifying marks, no signs of ownership or even the initials of the man who had made it. About the size of Jake's hand, the bottle appeared to have been hammered from pure gold, and must have been worth a considerable sum.

Jake opened it slowly. Instead of liquid, it contained a tightly rolled parchment.

In an ornate hand, the writing on the paper greeted General Burgoyne, congratulated him on his successes, and then declared that things were proceeding as planned.

"If," the writer said, *"according to my expectations, we may succeed rapidly in the possession of B—, the enemy having no force of consequence there, I shall, without loss of time, proceed to cooperate with you in the defeat of the rebel army opposed to you. Clinton is sufficiently strong to amuse Washington and Putnam. I am now making a demonstration southward, which I think will have the full effect of carrying our plan to execution. I have sent this message by duplicate couriers, to ensure its prompt arrival."*

The message was signed by General Howe.

"*B* is Boston, obviously," said Jake. "But can it be?"

"Perhaps," said Washington. "We bloodied Howe's nose in the Jerseys but he was still quite strong. At first I believed he was aiming for Philadelphia, but it became clear his true strategy was to draw us into a fight on poor grounds. When that didn't work, he took his men back to Perth and Staten Island. Now he's loaded them aboard ship and disappeared." There was an impish twinkle at the corner of Washington's eye as he added, "Not to return to England, I'm afraid."

"Where was the message found?"

"The message came into our possession yesterday morning. A man stumbled into a patrol of General McDougall's soldiers in the Highlands. Clumsy, for a Tory spy."

Jake nodded. Not two months before, he had trailed a British messenger south from Canada to New York City. The last thing the man would have done was stumble into an American patrol and get captured.

But the paper in his hand certainly seemed genuine. And the container it had come in was not something to be given up lightly.

"Have you asked the Culpers for their opinion?" Jake asked. Culper was the code name for the leaders of the patriot spy ring in New York City. Their information on British intentions had proved extremely reliable in the past, and Jake had made use of both Culpers—Junior and Senior—in several of his operations. As contingencies continue to demand discretion, we will use only the name Culper in referring to the man at the head of the patriot spy ring, wherever we shall meet him in our tale.

"Another problem," said the commander-in-chief. "We haven't had a message out of New York City for more than a week."

"Nothing?"

"I fear our men have been captured or worse. This is the longest I've gone without a message. I've even sent two men in for word. They haven't returned."

The general turned his attention briefly to the daphne at his feet. The beautiful plant and its berries contained a deadly poison, easily extracted.

"You want me to go to the city and find out if this captured message is genuine."

Washington nodded. "We have sentinels on the coast looking for Howe's ships. Our best information is that they wait just over the horizon. But I can't afford to sit still until Sir William decides he's had enough of his mistress Mrs. Loring and goes on."

"If I were to guess," said Jake, "it would be Philadelphia. Boston is not a logical attack."

"Agreed. But if I were attacking Philadelphia with his army, I would simply march across southern Jersey. He could try the Hudson, to join up with Burgoyne after this news of Ticonderoga. After all our efforts—after all your efforts particularly—it would be a great blow. Meanwhile, the South is wide open to him, and it would cause us considerable difficulty if he were to attack there. But Boston?"

"It is Howe we're speaking of," said Jake lightly. "Anything is possible."

Washington laughed. "It would be an imaginative stroke, though we can't rule it out on those grounds alone. The despair if we lost the city after regaining it would be tremendous, and we couldn't hope he would neglect the defenses a second time."

The general had a certain mood that came over him when he contemplated a strategic situation. His head tilted down slightly, and his eyes seemed to focus on something inside his mind. Meanwhile, his arms deposited themselves behind his back.

Jake, walking at his side, studied the supposed message from Howe. There seemed no doubt that he had written it—but in truth or as a deception?

"If I am to protect Boston, we must march by the middle of next week," said Washington finally. "It is the last possible moment, and I would be depending on the local troops to hold Howe, if he lands, until I could arrive and counterattack. It is a desperate strategy, but it is the best I can do until his destination is found. At least from here I can go in whatever way is necessary."

Jake nodded. The consequences of losing any major city would be great, but losing Boston a second time might crush the Revolution completely and would certainly end all hope of foreign aid. Jake knew the commander-in-chief would never say that, however; he would never bring himself to even hint that the war might ultimately be lost.

The spy slipped the letter back inside the flask and handed it to his commander.

"I'll leave for New York immediately," said Jake. He had no idea, as yet, how he might find out what Howe was up to, but clearly there was no time to lose worrying up a plan.

"If our friends in the city are still alive," said the general, "they may already know the answer."

Jake nodded, realizing that the general was implying that he feared the worst. "It will be an easy trip then, in and out."

"If not, your imagination will be put to good use in creating a solution."

He felt Washington's strength in his large arm as he patted him on his back. The Virginian came off stiffly in certain formal settings, but easily relaxed among the small coterie of men who knew him well. He could be a warm and doting uncle, as Jake well knew. And once he took a shine to you, mountains could erode to ant-hills before his faith wavered.

"Four days is all I have, Jake, and even that is cutting the hare's whisker close. If I don't hear from you and the British fleet is still unsighted, I must march for Boston." Washington began striding back towards his aides. "Get some new clothes. Hamilton will give you letters of credit. You'll have need of a fresh horse as well."

Jake thought of mentioning his friend van Clynne and his petitions, but realized this was not the time for it. He was already trotting ahead, looking for his horse. "I will be back as quickly as possible, sir. And we will have a few rounds of throwing shot."

"I won't stand you or the rest of my family an advantage this time," the general called out. He always referred to his staff members as family, and indeed he treated them as such. "I have heard you learned much from the natives during your recent visit with them."

Seven

Wherein, Jake meets a weaver but not his daughter.

While Hamilton led him south of Suffern's Tavern to a small village to see to a disguise, Jake worked his brain around a plan to enter New York.

The spy had last trod the city streets a month and a half before. His coming and going had created such a stir in the Westchester environs that he felt it would not be wise to enter from that direction again. Likewise, taking the river south, which would be the quickest route, was too dangerous. Jake had almost been hanged on the deck of the *HMS Richmond,* which Washington's men said was patrolling off Dobbs Ferry; its master bore him a serious grudge and would not be easily fooled by any disguise. And the men on at least one other ship—the galley *HMS Dependence*—would like to see him displayed high on their yardarm, or perhaps launched in pieces from the massive cannon they carried at their bow. Prudence dictated that his best course was by land south through New Jersey; there were any of fifty places where he might sneak into the river, take or rent a boat, and steal across to the city.

A few papers forged in Benjamin Franklin's son's name would come in handy if he ran into problems. Though a stout patriot himself, Franklin's son William was royal governor of New Jersey. He had been turned out the previous year and arrested, but his signature still impressed British authorities and Tories. It was also readily available to the Americans, and Washington's staff often amused themselves by duplicating it.

As they came to the village, Hamilton bade his friend farewell.

"I assume we will see you in a few days," said the aide. "And we'll be singing your praises again."

"Have some strong ale ready," suggested Jake.

"With pleasure."

Jake's first stop was an inn, where he had a quick breakfast—for such it was, even though the clock was past midday—of apple pie and fresh pheasant. The fowl was well prepared and left him in good spirits as he walked down the street to a weaver named Brian Daley, reported by Hamilton to be an especially hot friend of the Cause. The scouting proved accurate, though a bit more information might have prevented the misunderstanding that followed Jake's mentioning the colonel by name.

"Colonel Hamilton sent you, did he?" asked the man, setting aside the bolt he was working and rising from his loom.

Jake nodded in the affirmative, turned to take note of a fine piece of cloth, and suddenly found himself threatened by a sharp and rather nasty poker, its business end dusted with hot ashes.

"Stay away from my daughter, do you hear?" said the man. "All you macaronis in your fancy suits—if you attempt to sweet-talk her the way that West Indies bastard did, I'll have you skinned alive."

Jake managed to nudge the pointer from his face and delicately assured the man that his interest was in clothes, not daughters.

"It will help our cause a great deal," the spy added. "And you will be paid properly by General Washington's men, as these letters show."

The warrant allowing funds to be drawn—initialed by General Washington himself—helped clear up matters, and the weaver took him into the back room, where material was piled in haphazard fashion.

"I don't have time for a suit to be made," said Jake.

"I wasn't proposing to delay you," said the man, pushing aside several blankets to get to a store of knee breeches prepared for other clients. He looked back at Jake. "You're a tall one, though. It won't be easy to find something suitable. Although . . . Kristen, fetch me the trousers I set aside for Master Sullivan."

"Trousers? You're going to make me into a sailor? I am bound for New York, and must fit in there."

The weaver was unmoved by this confidence, much less the complaint. "You weren't aiming for any high society balls, were you?" he asked gruffly.

Indeed, he might be, thought Jake. The British in New York were famous partyers, and it was quite easy to pick up important command gossip at their celebrations. But he had no time to argue. The pants soon made their entrance in the hands of the weaver's daughter Kristen, who entered from the stairs. Hamilton's interest in her was well justified; the girl's smooth, unblemished face was as round as a ripe tulip, and even in plain working clothes and apron, she added light to the room upon entering. Jake endeavored to keep his mind on his business. Excusing himself, he went behind a small screen and changed. The white trousers were a little tight in the thigh, but serviceable.

"How do they look?" Jake asked, stepping from behind the screen.

Kristen had barely time to blush before her father ordered her out of the room.

"Back to work with you," he yelled at her, chasing her up the stairs. "And you, sir—"

"I'll keep my pants on, I assure you. Have you a waistcoat and jacket?"

"I have a hunting shirt, though it has seen better days," said the weaver. "It should be about your size."

"That would be fine," said Jake.

The shirt proved somewhat large at the stomach, but

Jake donned it gladly. His clothes were more than a bit mismatched, even for these desperate times, but virtue often comes from necessity, and it did so here. The costume would make it easy for Jake to pass himself off as a poor militia deserter; the woods and swamps of north Jersey were full of them, and none would be wearing the latest fashions.

As the weaver adjusted Jake's coat, he suddenly fell back in pain.

"The damn gout has my shoulder." The man's face was white and drawn.

Jake eased the man around and pulled up his shirt, looking at his back. His nimble fingers, so used to grappling with enemy soldiers, found a knot below the weaver's shoulder blade. With gentle but steady pressure he poked it down, and the man's color returned.

"Are you a doctor, sir?" asked Daley, with obvious relief.

"Of sorts," said Jake. "Is there an apothecary in town?"

"A liar and a thief, as are the entire breed."

Jake smiled. "I want you to obtain a cure from him called the Gibbs Family Remedy. It contains an extract from the Caribbean sea whip. A teaspoon when this flares up, and you will feel a new man."

The weaver looked at him suspiciously.

"If he tries to charge you more than a dollar for the bottle, tell him you know he paid but ten pence."

Jake's father had discovered the properties of the fish from an aboriginal doctor and sold it at close to cost, determined that it would be his lasting contribution to the science of cures.

The weaver was so pleased that he produced a pair of boots and a large beaver hat with a hawk's feather, adding them to the bill at half-price. Jake's next stop was at the stable owned by a certain Michael Eagleheart, a farmer and smithy who had helped find horses for several of Washington's officers. Eagleheart, a bluff fellow with a quick hand and ready laugh, allowed as how Jake had come just in time; the day before he had taken possession of a mount ridden only by an old woman to church on Sundays.

To say that Jake was dubious of the tale is to say a donkey has four legs. Nonetheless, the claim was backed up in the flesh, as a three-year-old filly in fine mettle was soon found standing atop fresh shoes and shouldering a gentle disposition. Her price, at fifty pounds, was half the going rate, and Jake had her saddled, boarded, and galloping for the road south within a few minutes, the farmer having thrown a small sword in to seal the bargain.

Eight

Wherein, Squire van Clynne has several experiences on the river, some unpleasant, and others more so.

While Jake rushes through the rough land of southern Orange County into the hills and barrens of northern Jersey, we will rejoin his friend and late companion, Claus van Clynne, who has been amusing himself by trying to escape the villainous white Indian, Egans.

Kneeling as his canoe flowed from the riverbank, van Clynne picked up a paddle and attempted to accelerate his progress downstream. The Dutchman had lost his weapons and purses, but not his considerable store of passes and pin money, and thus was able to comfort himself with the knowledge that, if he could merely overcome this tiresome interlude, he might yet complete his voyage to General Washington successfully—assuming, of course, he could discover where the general was.

These optimistic thoughts were not the only goad to his progress. Egans followed behind him on the shore, sending bullets so close that his hatless hair fluttered with the passing breeze.

The Oneida was one of those men who learns greatly from mistakes. When he reloaded and fired again, he was able to correct for his earlier aiming inadequacies, and was rewarded with a direct hit on van Clynne's canoe. The musket ball smashed against the hull with such ferocity that the Dutchman lost his balance and nearly fell over. The bullet sailed through the side into the floor of the canoe and thence into the depths, where it descended with an ominous hiss.

The squire was too busy holding the craft upright at first to realize the import of the noise. But he soon discovered a geyser rising in front of him and noticed at the same time a severe list developing in his vessel, the small hole magnifying steadily.

The Hudson is perhaps the mightiest of our native rivers. Before the war, it was a veritable highway of commerce, as choked with traffic as the streets of New York City or Philadelphia. Even now, no stretch of it is ever completely empty, and as van Clynne began to scream for rescue, there were three or four vessels close enough to hear his call.

Could they reach him in time, though? As his canoe swamped, the Dutchman paddled madly for the nearest craft, a single-masted gondola steered by a large tiller at the rear. Its two sails were filled with the wind, and as it tacked to head toward the floundering canoe, the squire began to feel the icy lap of the waves on his thighs. He pushed his oar violently through the water, his concentration remarkable, his progress less so. As admirable a vessel as the birch canoe may be, it was not designed to operate with a punctured hull.

Van Clynne could not swim, and as the water reached for his chest he feared that he had breathed his final breath of dry air. With heavy heart and a last burst of energy, he gave his oar one last brutal push, determined to meet his maker as a brave Dutchman, fighting adversity to the last.

It will be to his credit to note that his usual habit of complaint was not suspended in the moment he interpreted as his last. Indeed, by now his cursing had reached epic proportions, so that, beginning with Egans and ending with the Englishman who had discovered the North River, not a single living being could be truthfully said to have escaped his verbal wrath. His words were not stilled until the water splashed full in his face. He dove forward fitfully, writhing in what he hoped approximated the manner of a fish.

During the Dutchman's struggle, the gondola had managed to slip against the wind, and a sudden trick of the current sent it streaking toward the floundering canoe. A sailor in the bow leaned over and caught van Clynne's coat just before the Dutchman disappeared below the waves. The weight was so great that the poor man fell in with him.

The rest of the small crew quickly hove to. Within a minute, both men had been hauled from the depths and pulled aboard. Van Clynne had temporarily lost consciousness; he was brought around by some vigorous pumping of his chest and a dose of stiff rum.

"That is the most infernal excuse for liquor I have ever tasted," coughed the Dutchman, sitting upright on the deck. He reached up and grabbed hold of a rope ladder that led to the mast above. "Please, don't attempt to poison me further. If you are trying to kill me, send me back into the river. If you want to restore my health, fetch me a good keg of ale."

"We've no ale aboard," said the man in charge of the boat, a thick-chested fellow whose words were punctuated with whistles, owing to the large gaps in his front teeth.

"Porter then, or in a pinch, lager," demanded van Clynne. "Something with body to it. Brewed by a Dutch housewife if possible, or at least a German." He looked around the deck. The gondola was typical of the smaller vessels one finds in various river ports. The deck was well scrubbed and the hull freshly painted yellow, which implied somewhat more flash than the ship actually possessed. But the broad white sheets could hold the wind handily, and the vessel was surprisingly fast and even maneuverable. So much so that it occurred to the Dutchman that this small misadventure might end in his advantage, if only he could persuade the captain to take the craft south.

The direction it was currently heading, however, was west, toward the shore he had so recently vacated.

"I believe, sirs, that I have arrived just in the nick of time," declared the Dutchman, rising to his feet. "I have a business proposition that will do us all very handsomely, indeed. Do I have the honor of addressing the captain?"

The man answered gruffly that he was in charge.

"If I might make a suggestion," said van Clynne graciously, "this shore ahead ought to be avoided for the time being. It is frequented by a dastardly Indian, or I should say a white man painted as an Indian. A renegade, a changeling, a chicken in turkey feathers. He is obviously in the pay of British thieves and villains, and endeavored to murder me here. In fact, the poor condition of my vessel related directly to his actions. He—"

Van Clynne stopped short when he saw Egans climb over the side, a nasty grin on his face and the Dutchman's crumpled beaver hat in his hand.

"You lost your hat," sneered the Oneida. "And I have come to return it."

The Dutchman, finally sensing the wind's direction, reached to the mast and grabbed one of the staves. Three sailors fell upon him as he reared back to throw it. He managed to launch it nonetheless, and despite the interference scored a direct hit on Egans's skull, laying him out.

Van Clynne flicked off one of his assailants as he grabbed for another cudgel. By now the captain had picked up his sword, a fact van Clynne only realized when he felt the sharp blade flick past his face. He fell against the heavy wood of the mast, his weight sending another of the sailors to the deck.

"You will surrender this vessel to me, sir," declared van Clynne, "or I will be forced to vanquish your entire crew."

"Brave words, traitor," said the captain, showing off

the gaps in his teeth. "You will not repeat them once I cut out your tongue."

Van Clynne just managed to avoid the slash. He slid well below a second, but the third came remarkably close to his chest.

This was partly by design, however. He had placed himself near the mast, and the swordsman yelped with the vibration as his sharp, heavily weighted sword crashed into the wood. A quick roundhouse blow took care of the captain's chin, and he was next seen sleeping like a baby on the deck, basking in the warm glow of the midday sun.

But van Clynne still had half a dozen men to contend with. Two of these grabbed his legs and were unlikely to let go, despite his best efforts to bruise their arms and fingers. A sailor climbed against the sheet and sprang down at him. The Dutchman felt his knees give way and got his arms up just in time to prevent more than a glancing blow to the nose as he crashed face-first against the deck and an anchor chain. The same chain was quickly wound around his legs, but the redoubtable van Clynne did not admit defeat until Egans's voice, still slightly dazed, ordered the others to leave off hitting his prisoner.

"Anyone who fights this hard will fetch a stiff price below, I warrant," said Egans, pointing his musket at van Clynne. "Surrender, sir, or I'll test the theory that you're worth as much dead as alive."

"Alive would increase the price, I daresay," grunted van Clynne, striking his colors.

Nine

Wherein, the Jerseys are briefly praised, and Jake measures the mouth of a blunderbuss.

The hot sun of the afternoon did not impede Jake's progress. While much of the land he passed through was still comparatively wild and wooded, it should be noted that the owners were for the most part firm patriots. The strife of the past few years had not shaken their faith in the grand cause of Freedom.

So committed was Jake to reaching New York quickly that he let supper time slip without stopping; his only delays were a few brief pauses at streams to let his horse catch her breath. Eagleheart had made a good bargain; it was almost as if the old woman who had raised the filly had this mission in mind all along.

Still, even the most motivated horse and rider must eventually pause to restore themselves. And if it were well past nine by the time Jake decided he must finally rest, it meant only that his hunger was more acute. Though the lieutenant colonel is blessed with a constitution barely in need of sleep, his appetite is second not even to Claus van Clynne's.

On a road but a few miles removed from patriotic Hackensack, a sign soon caught his eye as he traveled: a boar curled before a fireplace. Heartened by the fact that the tavern windows were still lit with candles, Jake dismounted and took the three short porch steps to the front door in a single jump.

At first he was surprised to find it barred from the

inside, but on reflection he realized the hour and the times in general made this completely natural. Still, he thought his prospects of finding another inn more hospitable at this hour unlikely and decided to press for entrance.

"Hallo there," he called, knocking. "Have you food for a hungry traveler who can pay with hard money?"

The latter hint was not necessarily to be taken lightly, yet it failed to bring anyone to the door. Jake looked into the window but could not see much inside. His alert nose soon detected a simmering kettle of beans and he fell back on the door with good-natured—to say nothing of hungry—vigor.

Finally, Jake heard footsteps crossing the foyer. But instead of opening the door, their author pushed against it and yelled at him to stop.

"We've no room tonight," claimed the voice.

"I only want food," said Jake.

"We have none."

"I can smell it."

"Go away."

On another night, Jake might have satisfied himself with a curse—surely the keeper was harming himself more than his prospective customer. But Jake was anxious to eat quickly and move on. So he pounded again, announcing that he would pay twice the normal fee.

The keeper answered back that the visitor had been observed and marked as a Tory, and under no circumstances would he be admitted.

Rather than answering that he was a patriot, and possibly giving himself away to any spy inside, the spy shouted that he was a Quaker, completely neutral.

And willing to pay three times the normal charge, if his horse was fed as well as he.

The offer—or Jake's continued knocking—finally moved the tavern owner. He opened the door and revealed himself to be a thin man with a high-pitched voice, an unshaven face, and breath that betrayed several pints' worth of cider.

"Stop pounding my wall, Tory," said the keeper. "You'll get no food here."

Jake accepted the challenge, pushing the door entirely open and taking two strides inside. Just as he was about to repeat his story that he was a Quaker—and add another shilling to the price he was willing to pay—a lad stepped out from behind a curtain at the side.

The boy had not come into the room empty-handed. He pointed a large and most efficient-looking blunderbuss in Jake's face.

"Put your hands up, traitor," said the young man. The peach fuzz had not yet bloomed on the fifteen-year-old's cheek, but he had a sharp look in his eyes nonetheless.

The sheer number of projectiles in the thick barrel of his gun made it very difficult for the weapon to miss—a fact Jake was acutely aware of as he held out his hands in surrender.

"I'm afraid there's been some misunderstanding," he ventured. "I'm just a poor traveler, come for a bit of food. I saw by your sign that you were an inn."

"And I see by your dress that you are a deserter," said the innkeeper, putting his hands on his hips with some satisfaction. "We watched you ride down the road. You are heading south toward the river and the British strongholds. You are under arrest."

The boy with the gun stood motionless. No doubt this was his first time holding someone at gunpoint; Jake hoped his finger didn't develop a sudden itch.

"The fact that I wear a hunting shirt does not make me a member of the militia," said Jake calmly. "Nor does my destination mean I am a deserter."

"The militia and all of the army have gone north," replied the keeper, rubbing his hand on the front of the smock he wore over his clothes. "The alarm has gone out that there are redcoats abroad, and we have been told to be on the lookout for deserters."

"But I'm not one."

The keeper gingerly reached beneath Jake's shirt, removing the gun and knife from his belt. He also took a small, water-tight pouch that contained some papers, Franklin's pass among them.

The keeper thumbed through the documents so quickly that it was obvious he had not paused to read them. Nonetheless, he proclaimed that he had proof Jake was a deserter.

"The committee of safety is meeting a short distance away in the morning," said the man. "You can beg their mercy, though I doubt it will do you much good."

"I wonder," said Jake, turning sideways to his right as if to address both father and son at the same time, "if I might sit at one of your tables?" He put his left arm out slowly, pointing to the side, all the while watching the lad. "If I am to wait for the committee, then I cannot stand all night."

"Well—" started the father. The rest of his sentence was cut off by the loud crash of the blunderbuss discharging.

Into the ceiling. Jake had thrown himself into the boy, taking care to push the gun upwards first. The thick brass of the barrel flamed hot as ten balls exploded from its mouth; fortunately, they found their home in the thick ceiling beams, adding a decorative circular pattern to what had been simple if stout pine timbers.

And the boy . . .

"You're a girl," said Jake, rising. His push into her had proven the matter beyond doubt.

"I'm as strong as any boy my age," she replied, bolting up after him. "And I'll get you, Tory bastard."

She tried to make up for mishandling the gun by wrestling the intruder to the ground. Jake picked her up in his arms, twirled her around the room as she flailed, and, as gently as possible, tossed her at her father. The pair collapsed backward into the fireplace, sending a spray of dust and embers into the room. Jake picked up the blunderbuss from the floor where it fell, then stomped on the cinders to keep them from starting a fire on the chestnut floorboards.

"What will you do with us now, Sir Tory?" demanded the keeper indignantly after retrieving himself from the fire.

"I'm not a Tory," said Jake. As the man had proved himself a stout if less than fully effective champion of the Cause, the spy decided to trust him. He reached into his sock and pulled out the paper with Washington's signature. "Few deserters carry a warrant from the commander-in-chief," he said.

The keeper grabbed his daughter as she was about to fly into Jake. "Read these for me," he said, adding in an apologetic voice, "the light here is too dim for me."

Which of course wasn't true, though Jake thought it more polite not to mention that fact, especially as it had possibly saved his life a moment ago, the keeper deciding to bluff rather than actually discovering the evidence against him.

The girl could read very well, and she was soon nodding at her father, telling him in an awed voice that the man they had tried to arrest could charge "whatsoever honest amount he deems appropriate" and was "to be regarded with respect" as dictated by His Excellency, General Washington.

"A hundred apologies, sir. A thousand, indeed. Paul Brown, at your service. Ask for anything. This is a patriot house. Stout patriots, as the neighbors will attest. Let me get you something to eat and drink. You must be tired after our—our discussion as it were."

"It has been a long day," allowed Jake, replacing the pass in its hiding place.

The keeper showed him to a seat at a table near the fireplace and presented him with a wooden bowl of baked beans and a full pewter tankard of very hard cider.

"Those beans are our best," said Brown, who was now hospitable to a fault, fussing over each bite Jake took. "Alison learned the recipe from her mother, God rest her soul. Daughter takes after her, lucky for me."

"Your wife dressed as a boy?"

"I am close to the river here, sir, and not far from the British for all that," said Brown. "With a fifteen-year-old girl. As you appear to be a man acquainted with military matters, I need not tell you of certain indecencies the British have taken of late in this province. What I said before is true; there are strong rumors of redcoat raids this evening."

But her father's opinion and Alison's reasons for wearing breeches were perhaps not in total harmony. For the girl clearly chafed as he spoke.

"I'm not afraid of any British soldier," she declared. Her pants were a size or so too big, as was her shirt, but Jake judged that she would soon burst out in ways that shorn hair and rough clothes could not disguise. "I am as brave as any boy, and twice as strong."

Jake smiled at her.

"I am, sir. And I am as great a lover of freedom as anyone in the country, of any gender. I wish to serve the Cause and enlist. Other women have done so, and helped out quite handsomely."

"Hush now, Alison. Let the man eat."

"Please, sir, if you know General Washington, take me to him. I would like to be a soldier."

"Alison!"

Jake looked up from his food, bemused. "A strong patriot, eh?"

"As strong as anyone."

"You make good beans."

"Do not try to sweeten me with your tongue, sir. I know that is what spies are always doing."

"What makes you think I am a spy?"

"With a note from General Washington and a direction toward New York, what else would you be?"

Jake winked at her father. "I wouldn't think of joining the army if I were you," he said. "Sleeping on the ground night after night puts a sharp kink in your back. And the food is not as good as this."

"You mock me, sir." Alison stood before him at the table, hands on her hips.

"I do have need of a guide," said Jake, addressing her father. "I would like to find the most inconspicuous way to a ferry near Perth Amboy. I realize I'm quite a distance off."

"You are indeed, sir," whistled the keeper. "You'll never make Perth tonight, and would spend a good portion of tomorrow, if not the next day. It's in British hands, besides."

"I need to be in Manhattan by daybreak."

Brown shook his head. "There are ways to the island, but tonight—"

"I can take him, father. He should cut straight to Torman's, descend the Palisades, and find a boat there."

"Hush, dear, we don't want to interfere in the man's business."

"Actually, sir, I'd be happy for your help," said Jake. "And another share of this food."

Alison took the plate and refilled it.

"You are asking much," said Brown. "My home would be undefended. Even some of my neighbors covet it."

"If you can spare a few hours to guide me," Jake told him, "you would do our Cause a great deal of good."

"Let me go instead, father. You have to mind the inn. I know the way as well as you, and shortcuts besides."

A complicated melange of looks crossed the poor innkeeper's face. While his instincts told him the man before him was in great need, he had no real proof that he should trust him beyond the letter from Washington. Truly, such a document could be easily forged; neither Brown nor his daughter had the vaguest notion what Washington's hand was like.

But the tavern keeper was a strong patriot, determined to see the Cause prevail. Sacrifice was demanded of all, and chances had to be taken or the British would never be beaten. He could guide Jake to the river and be back by daybreak—a small risk, surely.

"I will take you," Brown finally decided. "As soon as you are ready."

"I am ready now," said Jake, taking a last bite and then draining the cider. "Let us get something for my horse and be off."

"Father, please take me, you must." Alison wrapped herself around her father like a snake around a tree.

"It is too dangerous," said Brown, but it was clear from his voice that he was wavering.

"Listen to your father," suggested Jake.

"I have the gun," Alison told her father. "I am the best shot in the neighborhood, you know it."

"Better for you to stay."

Alison took a shy glance at Jake, then put her arm gently on her father's arm. "But, papa, please. If it's not too dangerous for you, it won't be for me. We are a pair; you have said so yourself many times."

The keeper sighed. In truth, he had never refused his daughter the slightest favor since his wife had died. This was nothing more than a quick midnight ride, and perhaps it would quench her thirst for adventure.

"All right. Come along."

Jake scowled, but decided against objecting. He wanted to leave as quickly as possible, and did not want to risk his guide changing his mind.

And really, how much trouble could a young woman be, even one who insisted on wearing breeches?

Ten

Wherein, the river is not quite reached.

*T*he innkeeper and his daughter were most efficient guides, taking Jake across a succession of open meadows and close woods in the moonlight as easily as if they were riding down city streets. The keeper, who inside had appeared anything but athletic, proved to be a considerable horseman, and his skills had obviously been passed on to his daughter.

The willingness of ordinary folk to do extraordinary things in the name of Freedom continually amazed Jake. Many times he had been helped, even saved, by some farmer or housewife, who under other circumstances might have lived the most undisturbed life since Methuselah.

While he was more than happy to take advantage of their assistance, the spy also felt some obligation to repay their kindness. In this case, it seemed to him he could do that by informing Alison of the hard dangers of soldiering, in case she should run away and try to join the army. But every remark he made as they rode was answered by some optimistic comment. She loved the mud; she could exist for weeks on gruel; the damp earth invigorated her when she slept. She was three times as tricky as any boy, and able to hold her own should it come to that.

Jake could hear her father sighing beneath his

breath; evidently these arguments had been made before.

Finally, she capped her retorts by declaring that if she couldn't join the line and march, then certainly she would become a spy such as her new friend, who was obviously not subject to the deprivations he was boasting so strongly of.

"I wonder, have you ever met Abigail Adams?" Jake asked, huffing a moment as he muscled his horse over a hedge.

Alison cleared the obstruction without the slightest exertion, and answered that she had not.

"You would like her. She is a Boston lady with ideas as bold as yours and wit twice as sharp."

"Then we shall have a pleasant time shooting redcoats together," retorted the girl.

The trio passed over a large creek and found a wide road. They traveled along it briefly, then crossed back into a cultivated cornfield and found an old path through a fallow field. The moon, missing only the slightest sliver, illuminated their way so completely they left the torches the innkeeper had prepared unlit.

The keeper had stuck an old, rusty sword in his saddle scabbard. Alison had been allowed to wield the blunderbuss. She rode with it across her saddle, half-cocked. Her father had made her take the precaution of securing the lock mechanism with a twig that prevented accidental firing; he claimed that it was faulty and given to slipping. Twig or no twig, Jake made sure to stay out of the line of fire.

Jake's ribs had long since given up complaining about the jostling they were taking, settling for a long and constant groan nagging at the back of his chest. The horse Eagleheart had sold him was a strong beast, powerfully winded, but far from the smoothest platform to ride on. Jake soon began to believe the horse understood English: while she would fight the hard pulls of his arms and legs, she moved quickly to the right and left when directed to do so by voice only. And when he said "whoa," the horse stopped short before he could pull the reins.

"Aye, trouble ahead," said the keeper, who had spotted the figures by the bridgehead the same moment Jake had. "Don't think they'd be on our side."

"You'd best go back," said Jake. "Thank you for your help. I can find the river from here; it won't be far."

"We can't leave him, father," said Alison.

As Jake was starting to assure her he would be fine, one of the sentries shouted at them. His stiff English accent made it all too clear whose side he was on.

"Let's go," said Jake, turning his horse to lead the retreat northwards. But the beast had taken no more than two steps when shots rang out. From the corner of his eye, Jake saw Alison's mount fall.

"Keep going!" he shouted to her father. He sailed around, pulling his pistol and sword out as he jumped down. He fired as he ran to the girl.

The men on the bridge were part of a detachment of His Majesty's marines, who had come ashore and moved a mile inland to prove the general principle that they could go anywhere they wanted. The figures on horseback were the first rebels—the first people—they'd spotted all evening, and the British advanced from the bridge with the enthusiasm of a gambler who has waited for the cocks to appear all night.

Jake's shot caused them to pause briefly and reload for a fresh volley. Fortunately, it was not concentrated nor well aimed, and Jake was able to duck it by flinging himself into the dirt.

The girl had taken cover behind her fallen horse. As Jake crawled toward her, he saw several other figures heading for the bridge, their shadows thrown forward by a signal fire.

The vanguard meanwhile made sure their bayonets were fixed and commenced a charge. They covered the ground quickly enough to make the god Hermes jealous. When the keeper saw them advancing on his daughter, all instinct of prudence and caution flew from his head. He took his sword and began flailing it like the Grim Reaper as he charged past Jake and Alison. He caught one of the marines straight across the neck, slicing the man's head clean off. The head flew through the field like a pumpkin kicked from the vine, while its late body staggered forward a few grotesque steps before collapsing.

As the keeper regrouped, he felt a sharp prick in his side. Thinking it no more than a splinter, he steadied his horse in front of Jake and Alison and told them to run while he held off the advancing knot of marines.

The Britons' shouts of attack were drowned out by the sound of the blunderbuss, which exploded with the deep crackle of a light cannon. Alison had handled her gun as well as any hard veteran of the Connecticut line, waiting until the last possible moment and bowling over the tight clump of lobstercoats charging against her father. Four or five figures collapsed in a great tumble of hot death, their thirst for blood quenched forever by their own.

Only one redcoat from the vanguard escaped unscathed. He had already turned his attention toward the girl, and now charged bayonet-first, aiming to avenge his fellows. Jake managed to knock him off balance by diving at him with the sword, striking his bayonet with a sharp crash.

The Briton rolled to the ground but quickly recovered, wielding his Brown Bess in time to ward off a second blow so expertly that the short sword flew from Jake's hand.

A quick slash and the silvery blade of the bayonet nicked through the patriot's hunting shirt, catching his ribs and tickling the recently healed wounds. Jake fell to the ground with the pain, and the marine kicked him in the side before heaving the gun back for a fresh thrust.

The marine shouted as he prepared to make his murderous stab. His high note of glee broke into a

shocked riff of surprise and pain. Alison had exchanged the discharged blunderbuss for a knife she
kept secreted at her waist and sprung on the man like a
badger defending her young.

The wound she inflicted was no more than superfi-
cial, but its timing was critical. Jake flew to his feet and
grabbed the man by the neck, pulling him with such
force that the redcoat lost his will to fight as well as his
weapon. As Jake pulled his arm around the man's
neck, Alison picked up the marine's bayonet-tipped
musket and skewered him. He fell to earth with a dying
gasp.

War is never a pretty sight, especially at close range.
Both Jake and the girl were splashed full with blood.
But Alison stomached it as easily as Jake, and had he
the leisure, he might have commented on her bravery.

He did not. A new volley sounded over their heads
as the reinforcements from beyond the bridge charged
into the field to renew the assault. Jake led Alison
toward the spot where he had left his mare; the horse
stood calmly by, gently nickering that her owner had
best get a move on.

Alison's father, in the meantime, had been dashing
on horseback to and fro, his sword flashing as he made
sure the fallen redcoats would rise no more. Fresh out
of opponents, he followed to where Jake was pushing
Alison aboard the horse.

By the time he arrived, he was gripping his own
mount's neck. He waved them forward, telling them to
hurry and escape before the reinforcements caught up.

"Father!" Alison shouted. "What's happened?"

"I'm all right, all right," mumbled Brown. In fact, he
was anything but. He fell over from his horse, landing
in a heap as his bloody sword dropped nearby.

Eleven

Wherein, Melancholy shows her tearful face, and Jake confronts a development that will have diverse consequences for our tale.

"*F*ather! Father!"

Alison jumped from the horse and ran to the stricken figure. Jake followed, scooping up his dented sword on the way.

Brown rolled out on his back, stretching up to look square at the moon. The golden orb hung above like a benign party lantern. An owl, startled by the carnage before him, crossed before it, his path a compass toward blessed Avalon.

"Papa, papa."

"It's fine, my dear. I see your mother."

"No!"

The redcoats were charging across the field toward them, shouting. Oblivious, Alison kneeled down, and held her father's head in her arms.

"Papa, papa," she told him in a shaking voice. "I need you, papa."

"Don't worry, child. You have our friend here." Brown reached up his hand to Jake, who took it gently. Already the grip was cold and weak. "Take care of her."

"I will, sir," said Jake, his eyes locking on the dying man's.

"I'm coming, Mary."

"Father!"

A haphazard volley of shot fired on the run missed

Jake and Alison, but caught Jake's mare. The spy yanked Alison to her feet and pulled her with him toward a row of trees at the edge of the field. The girl stumbled and fell; Jake ducked back, took her under his arm, and began running again, holding her like a log plucked for the fire.

Only a macabre coincidence kept him from being speared through the back by the swiftest of their pursuers. Just as the redcoat reached out to stab him, the soldier tripped over the discarded head of his comrade, the same man Brown had earlier decapitated. The marine fell forward, and discovering what he had fallen over, began retching violently.

The two patriots reached the tree line barely ahead of a second lobstercoat. Jake tossed Alison roughly into a bush, then ducked as the marine charged; he was able to upend the man and grab a large tree limb as another soldier reached the woods. A swift slash disabled this attacker, and Jake turned his attention back to the first, still sprawled on the ground. A blow from his boot dispatched him from the active duty rolls; Jake helped himself to the man's bayoneted weapon and went to the bush where he had thrown Alison.

She wasn't there. He pushed through, stickers grabbing at his clothes and face. Jake had just yanked a particularly nasty branch from his cheek when his injured ribs were creased by a thin but still hurtful tree limb.

"Jesus!"

"I'm sorry," Alison exclaimed. "I didn't know it was you."

"Come on, before the others find us." Jake pushed her forward. The woods were just thin enough for them to run through, and the top cover filtered the moon's light, sheltering them with a veil of darkness. After they had gone a hundred feet or so, Jake pulled Alison to a stop, whispered that they should be quiet, and thus changed their tactic from rapid retreat to organized withdrawal.

The marines had lit torches and were scouring the field and the edge of the woods. The fight, however, had been knocked from them. Jake and Alison moved stealthily to the east, and within a half-hour could no longer hear the English shouts, nor see their lights.

Another half-hour of walking brought them to a road. Jake motioned with his hand that they should stop and rest; they were both so tired they flopped down right into the dust.

"I am sorry about your father," Jake told her. "I am truly sorry."

The girl did not say anything, but began softly weeping to herself. Jake knelt and held her in his arms. Back at the tavern, her body had felt considerably harder, more muscular, and though there was no mistaking her sex, he did not doubt her boasts about being stronger than many boys. Now, she felt as weak and soft as a tender kitten, stranded after its mother has been snatched away.

"I must go," said Jake. "I'm sorry for you, but my mission is critical. It will be light in a few hours, and I must find a way across the river. Hide here until dawn. The soldiers have given up their pursuit and will soon return to their boats. I'll continue south and find my way across with the light."

"We are barely a mile from the Hudson," said Alison, springing to her feet. "Come on."

"Wait. You can't come with me."

"You need me to show you the way. You can't go south here. And you will never get down the cliffs by yourself."

"Wait!"

Jake's protest was useless. The girl was already running full speed down the road in the direction of the river. Cursing beneath his breath, he ran to catch up. He soon found himself sliding off the road down a ravine Alison seemed to know as well as the furrows of her garden. His feet finally found a solid path, and once more he had to run to catch up with her.

Those who have sailed up the Hudson from the bay will well remember the massive rock ledge that seems to leap from the Hudson's waves straight up toward heaven. This part of Jersey appears to stand upon a solid platform, raised like the bank of the Nile by Moses against some foreign horde. Indeed, these natural defenses helped secure the patriots during the dark days of the British rush to take Manhattan.

But the fortress rocks are not as impenetrable as they seem from the water, and there are many points where they fade back from the river. Countless crevices and paths wind their way down, ancient ways first explored by the Indians who made their homes here. Alison led Jake down one now, slipping and dodging through the mazelike natural wall as if she were a raindrop descending to earth.

Here Jake's height and bulky shoulders proved something of a disadvantage. Normally sure-footed, with the balance of a squirrel, he found himself continually sliding one way or the other. It did not help that the route, though direct, was long as well as treacherous; he grew more and more tired as he went. At length, the lieutenant colonel began to wonder when he would reach the bottom, and even doubted the wisdom of his choice to try Manhattan from the Jersey shore.

"Here we are," said Alison finally, poking her way past some saplings that had forced themselves up in the crocks of the river stones. "God, look at the ships upon the river. They must belong to the redcoats we fought."

They did indeed. Three schooners, escorted by a fifth-rate, stood off the shore, while a dozen whaleboats scurried back and forth, taking men from the Jersey side to the ships. Fires burned on the ground above, and lanterns and torches glimmered in the boats, covering the proceedings with a golden glow.

"I don't suppose they've done me the courtesy of leaving a boat nearby," said Jake. Though his voice was sardonic, he nonetheless glanced up and down the shore.

"We can take that log and float across on it," suggested Alison, sprinting across the narrow ledge of shore.

"*We* can't do anything, miss," said Jake. "You have to go back to your inn."

"Why? What luck will I have there?"

"I'm sure you could run a good business, if you put your mind to it. You are a good cook."

"The inn will be taken from me in a day, and you know it," said the girl. "Even if I were a boy, it would be so."

"Some neighbor will help you, I'm sure," said Jake. "Here, this log will do nicely. Come now. You promised father you'd look after me."

Before he could grab her, Alison threw her weight against a large, broken tree trunk sitting at the waves' edge. Jake was surprised to see that she was strong enough to get it into the water by herself.

But if he had once been bemused by her determination, he had a considerably different opinion now. He could not traipse through the city of New York with a child at his elbow. She would be an unimaginable liability.

Or would she? Jake was known, but surely this girl was not. A brave young woman might serve the Cause in countless ways; many were doing so already.

The question was moot. Alison was already several yards from shore. Cursing, Jake slipped off his boots and took a few ginger steps on the rocks before diving into the river.

Twelve

Wherein, van Clynne's progress is briefly examined, as is Jake's prowess as a swimmer.

*C*laus van Clynne at that moment was contemplating somewhat similar waves, if a vastly different situation. His captors, having recovered from their wounds, found it difficult to contain their animosity toward him, especially as he was chained and could not retaliate. The poor Dutchman therefore suffered sundry blows before Egans, worried about the bounty he would receive for returning a rebel spy for interrogation, ordered he be left alone.

"I don't know why you think I'm a spy," complained the squire.

"Your forged papers are proof," said Egans.

"They are not forged, sir. I am purely a man of business."

"A fancy name for it. Personally, I don't care; you'll bring me twenty crowns whether you're a cousin of the king or George Washington himself."

"Twenty, is that all?" asked van Clynne. "I've got more than that in my purse."

"You did indeed," answered Egans, "in each purse. I have never seen such a collection of notes in my life."

The Dutchman's grumbles about thieves not being trusted were ignored. The open boat continued southward, her two small sails, set atop each other, puffed full with the wind. The moon gave her more than enough light to sail by. There were no American river patrols to stop her, and the only complication lay several miles downstream, where the chain at Peekskill stopped all river traffic.

Van Clynne's head rested against the hard oaken rails of the vessel's side. He was consoled by the fact that his hat had been returned; not only was it a longtime companion, but no self-respecting Dutchman considered himself properly dressed without one.

Perhaps the return of his headgear was a positive omen. He knew from recent experience that the river barrier was impenetrable, and that these British miscreants would therefore have to make landfall in patriot territory. As van Clynne realized he had good hopes of meeting friends once ashore—there was not a man or woman of Dutch descent in the valley whom he did not know—his outlook on the adventure began to brighten. Surely this difficulty would prove but another arrow in the quiver of accomplishments he would present when he asked General Washington for consideration in the matter of his land. The general, and afterwards, the Congress, would consider the great trials van Clynne had overcome and see justice served. And who could doubt that the Dutchman, as resourceful a man as ever to have trod these shores, would find some stratagem to ease his escape once embarked on dry land, where the air was clearer and the beer free for the taking?

So van Clynne began to feel optimistic, and as always when he was optimistic, he began to talk, and as always when he began to talk, he began to complain. It was good-natured criticism, meant for the edification of the listeners.

"This is an adequate vessel, for its purpose," said the squire. "But there are certain recommendations I would make for its improvement. If it were constructed in the Dutch manner, it would be two or three times faster. We would be in New York already."

"And why would you want to get there quickly?" demanded one of the sailors.

"Oh, I am in no hurry. I will get there when I arrive," said van Clynne philosophically. "But I should much prefer a Dutch sloop."

"Bah."

"The Dutch have been sailing this river for considerable time," essayed van Clynne. "We have learned to make the vessel flat-bottomed—"

"As is this one."

"—with a shallow draft that can tiptoe across the sandbars. The sides are much lower, much broader. This vessel is barely big enough for both you and I, while on a Dutch sloop, half the province could stretch out. And your sail arrangement: inefficient in the extreme."

"What's the trouble here?" demanded the captain. "What is this shouting about? Are you aiming at waking the entire shoreline?"

"The prisoner's giving us advice to make the ship better."

"Oh he is, is he? Well perhaps the improvements would begin with using him as an anchor."

"Tut, tut, sir; I won't be moved by idle threats."

"Idle, is it?"

But it was, so long as the crew kept Egans aboard. And as these men—British sailors under special order—had been detailed to transport Egans southward, they were forced to leave his prisoner in peace.

Which was more than van Clynne did for them, continuing his loud harangue on such diverse topics as the quality of Dutch hemp and the fine art of skimming stones across the water. His talk was not precisely idle. The Dutchman hoped some citizen ashore might hear it, recognize its timbre, and knowing his great antagonism toward the sea, row out to investigate. His heart perked as they neared Poughkeepsie, as the city's residents were especially alert, but the good citizens of the town seemed all abed. Fishkill Landing was the same. No matter how loud he spoke—and he was soon nearly hoarse with his shouting—he could not raise a response.

Finally, van Clynne saw that they were tending toward the eastern shore. He marshaled his tired body, still heavily chained, and decided he would save his strength for some new effort, as yet uninvented.

"So you've finally shut your mouth, have you?" asked Egans.

"My mouth opens and shuts as it pleases me," said van Clynne. "And as for you, sir, there are several facts regarding your past of which you are quite mistaken. It would please me greatly to straighten you out on them. First off, regarding your ancestry—"

"I think it will please you very much to be quiet now," said Egans, revealing his pistol. The dim light made his tattooed face, as well as his grin, all the more sinister.

Van Clynne saw no alternative but to nod in agreement.

Jake spat a mouthful of water from his throat as he grabbed onto the tree trunk. The strong tides of the river were pushing it rapidly downstream, toward the British and their ships. Alison struggled, but her exhausted body was no match for the strong current. She felt her grip slipping; suddenly, she fell headfirst into the waves.

The patriot spy grabbed the back of her shirt and hauled her up over the floating log.

"All right," he said. "I suppose I'm stuck with you. Let's not visit any sea rays along the way."

Alison was too winded to celebrate. Jake kicked hard, pushing the log before him as he aimed toward the dark shadow of Manhattan island.

The Hudson is no simple stream. Like a great lady, she moves back and forth as much according to whim as the edicts of the moon. Between her various eddies and flows, she is constantly changing direction, and often goes three different ways at once. Tonight she

was feeling particularly capricious; Jake had no sooner
found a suitable spot to aim at on the eastern shore
than the Hudson took it into her head to send him
back west.

In seconds, Jake found himself floating a mere
dozen yards from the British fifth-rater, a frigate-sized
warship retired from the line but still a considerable
power in these waters. The deck was awash with light,
and reflections leapt across the waves, the shadows
dancing in a wild, silent procession. He had no choice
but to drift; furious kicking might raise all manner of
unwanted attention.

Fortunately, the British eyes were drawn to the
Jersey shore, where word had just come of a major
land battle near a rebel bridge. Rumor had inflated the
encounter that had claimed Paul Brown's life; had the
wind been different, Jake might have heard whispers of
two battalions of rebels encountered, with George
Washington himself at their head. Such are the strange
fortunes of war; the same skirmish that made an or-
phan of Alison now allowed them to pass unnoticed by
a considerably larger and more dangerous British
force.

The Hudson now pushed the two patriots toward the
Manhattan shore. Jake felt the current take him as if
he were a feather on the wind; the log lifted nearly out
of the water, and in a trice they were speeding toward
land, within sight of the former Fort Washington just to
the north.

The rushing current and riptide threatened a fresh
disaster for Jake and Alison. The way before them was
filled with large and treacherously sharp rocks, plunging their nasty beaks into the night air like the mouths
of the Furies themselves.

"Watch out!" Jake yelled as the log rode forward.
Alison slipped to the side, barely saving her arm from
the craggy jaws of a boulder. The maneuver took the
last of her energy, and in the next second, she fell off
the tree trunk.

Jake dove face-first over the log after her. The moonlight was by no means bright enough to illuminate the depths, and he flailed blindly with his hands and feet, trying to feel for the poor girl. His right shin struck so hard against a rock that he involuntarily cursed; this led him to take a huge gulp of water into his lungs, and he fought to the surface coughing.

Her father's dying plea sounded through the sharp rap of the water against the rocks, and as he cleared his chest of water, Jake cursed himself for stopping at the inn, cursed himself still harder for suggesting that the pair guide him to the river.

For a brief moment the torrent around him seemed to cease and the din fall away. Jake heard a faint burble to his right, more animal than human. He dove toward it, catching Alison as she slipped downward for the third time.

He grabbed her under the arm and pulled her to the surface, tossing her limp body into the air with all his strength. Eliciting a hopeful cough for his efforts, he tightened his grip and spun back to face the rocks—and just barely managed to get his free hand before his face as the tide slammed him into a large, moss-covered crag.

The entire world might be coming to an end around him, but Jake could see nothing but black granite, feel nothing but the young girl clamped in his arm. His fingers pounded against the rock as if to hold it off, while the current took his feet and shot them to his right, upsetting his balance. But this proved fortuitous, for they landed against a sandbar, and in the next moment Jake was able to lever himself and Alison into a protected pool of water and get to his knees.

The shoreline proper was still some yards off, but the way now was easy. With his last bit of strength, he hauled Alison over his shoulders and crawled onto dry land, collapsing just as the first rosy fingers of dawn poked through the east.

Thirteen

Wherein, a weaver's measure is retaken.

*H*aving released his anger in disposing of his guide and driver, Major Dr. Keen mounted his coach and took stock of the situation. Once launched on a mission, a member of the secret department must carry it to completion. In this case, Gibbs's escape was doubly vexing, as the doctor had already sent a dispatch to his master, General Bacon, indicating the spy's demise. Should Bacon learn of the error, he would be well within his rights to punish Keen for his premature optimism.

There was only one punishment meted out to members of the secret department, no matter the offense: death, as untimely and unpleasant as possible.

Keen had not yet received an acknowledgment from Bacon, and so there might be a short opening for him to ransom the situation, assuming he could do so without Bacon finding out. In any event, there seemed no other option. He whipped his horses southward toward the largest settlements, reasoning that it would be the most likely direction for Jake to travel, as he must by rights have come from the north. Still, the British assassin knew from experience that finding the spy would not be an easy task.

At least, Keen thought to himself, he would no longer have to deal with Gibbs's vexing sidekick, the obnoxiously rotund and endlessly talkative van Clynne.

In violation of all natural law, the Dutchman had frustrated him consistently until his fiery death in the north country camp. It was not so much being bested that he hated as the scoterkin's inane chatter and grating air of superiority, which pretended the Dutch—of all people—were God's chosen race.

Keen's coach, though elaborately styled, was not well adapted to country highways. Despite his various alterations to the axle support mechanisms, it bumped along uncomfortably as soon as the horses attempted more than a walk. Still, it was excellently suited for what might be called its secondary purpose—providing Keen with a roving laboratory and storehouse of chemical and scientific wares. The back portion of the vehicle was shaped like an immense trunk; once open, it revealed a workbench any alchemist would envy. Keen had not been able to replenish his supplies since leaving New York some weeks before; he nonetheless had sufficient stores to accomplish his purpose.

One of these formulas, concocted from the venom of a snake found only on the western coast of Africa and enhanced with powder from an oak tree fungus, was sufficient to elicit information late that afternoon from a shopkeeper in New Paltz. The man told Keen two patriot officers had been met nearby with fresh horses before dawn. This news—the first tangible information of his prey he had had all day—was soon expanded by the man who had prepared the horses, whose tongue resisted the drug but not the pistol pushed against his cheek. Keen thus discovered not only Jake's direction, but the fact that he had been summoned by Washington himself—or at least he had been riding with Lieutenant Colonel Alexander Hamilton, a member of the rebel leader's staff. Simpler, less showy methods of inquiry easily provided the Continental Army's general location and the best route thence.

The English assassin had no more regard for Washington than he did for a common cur, though he realized he must take precautions approaching the camps.

Thus, when he reached the small village where Jake had eaten and clothed himself, he stopped more to discover the lay of the land than in actual hope of apprehending the patriot spy.

Keen's fancy coach, to say nothing of the fine buckskin breeches and embroidered coat he wore, marked him as a man of wealth. In certain Whig circles, this would immediately arouse suspicions, and so when he climbed down near the public house, the doctor began promulgating a cover story to any who would listen: He was a private citizen appointed to a committee of inspection by Governor Clinton, and was looking for a friend said to be traveling with a Colonel Hamilton.

"And who might that be, sir?" asked the tavern owner when they were introduced.

"A man with blond hair, an inch or two over six foot," said Keen. He placed his weight on his walking stick, picking the pocketwatch from his vest as if concerned about the fact that it was already well past seven P.M.

"Fella like that was in around dinner, midday or so," said the keeper. "Said Colonel Hamilton directed him here. Ate like a horse."

"That would be him," answered the doctor. "We were to meet in town, but I was delayed. I wonder where he's gone to?"

The keeper shrugged. "Seemed in a hurry. Asked after the weaver, if I recall."

Keen thanked the man, left a shilling on the table, and walked down the weedy, dust-strewn street to the weaver's shop.

Candles were lit in the small building, which was factory, home, and sales floor all in one. The doctor rapped his stick on the side of the old Dutch-style split door before opening it himself and stepping into the large front room. He was greeted by the steady whisking sound of a loom.

The large, wood-framed machine took up nearly a third of the room. Its levers and pedals were being worked with great concentration by Kristen Daley, the daughter whom the weaver had strenuously tried to protect earlier in the day.

The girl was so absorbed in her work that she did not notice her visitor at first. Keen likewise was transfixed, for here was a perfect American beauty, bundled in mobcap and baggy smock, but no less beautiful for these plain coverings. In London, the doctor had been quite a partaker of feminine charms, and if the world might be said to be filled with connoisseurs of female beauty, he could rightly be accorded a place of honor among them.

The doctor doffed his hat—rare was the Colonial who earned this honor—then tapped his stick on the floor, tilting his head at an angle calculated to give off a good perspective on his jaw.

The girl looked up with a start.

"Excuse me," said the doctor. "I am looking for a friend." He stepped forward and bowed. "Allow me to introduce myself: Dr. Harland Keen. I am on a mission for Governor Clinton."

"Oh," said the girl. She started to get up from the loom, but caught her dress on the bench; the frame, pedals, and cloth mechanisms formed a kind of cage for the operator, making it difficult to exit quickly. Keen flew across the room, catching her in his arms. He lifted her up as if she were a princess, twirling her away from the machine and then setting her down, bowing with all the flourish he had once used on the floor of the king's palace.

Under other circumstances, Keen would have been sorely tempted to pursue his interest in her. Indeed, he had to fight severely against his nature, reminding himself that Gibbs's existence was a threat to his own life. "I hope you are all right, my dear," he told her, stepping back. "I am searching for a friend of mine, a Colonel Gibbs. He is tall, well-built, with blond hair. I believe he came here searching for a suit."

"A stranger bought clothes from my father this afternoon," said the girl. "He was tall and more handsome than any man I have ever seen."

"Some women find Mr. Gibbs pleasing," allowed Keen, suppressing a reaction to her flutter. "Though I could not say but his nose seems over-large for his face, as well as his health. We were supposed to meet in this town, or I thought we were."

Keen walked to a table near the side, where some fine polonaise gowns were displayed. It took little imagination to picture the girl in one.

"He said he was going to New York," she told him.

Keen barely heard. It had been too long since he partook of beauty, and the temptation to satisfy himself on this morsel was overwhelming. Whether the girl understood the look in his eye as he turned or not, she took a step backwards. Keen advanced arms forward, his body literally shaking in anticipation.

"Another step toward my daughter and I will blow your head off."

Keen stopped dead, then looked up with a contrite smile at Kristen's father in the doorway.

"This is an interesting way of greeting customers."

"What business have you in my shop?" demanded the weaver, unimpressed. "State it quickly."

"I am looking for a friend," said Keen. Walking stick in hand, he took a tentative step toward the man. His gun appeared to be one of the colonists' infamous Pennsylvania rifles, though at this distance, its legendary accuracy was hardly essential.

"You have no friend here," said the weaver. "Out with you."

"Now, now, my good man. We are all friends in one way or another," said Keen.

The weaver's answer was cut short by a sharp jab of the doctor's cane in his stomach. The gun fired harmlessly into the ceiling; Keen smacked the side of the man's skull and sent him to a deep but unrestful sleep against the cabinet.

"And now, my darling," said the doctor, turning

back. "Perhaps you would like to come with me to New York? Have you seen the sights there?"

"She will not see them today," said a sharp female voice.

Surprised, Keen turned to his right. Standing in the doorway to the back of the house was a woman holding a musket.

"I don't know who you are," declared the girl's mother, "but if you do not walk backward from this building this instant, you will sing with the angels in heaven."

"As you wish, madam."

Keen was a man of science, but he considered that there are certain times in life when Fate herself may be playing a hand, and it is best not to interfere. He could always return here at some future date, once his job was complete.

He paused at the door, and reached inside his vest for his purse.

Mrs. Daley brought the musket up and steadied her aim.

"Permit me, madam, to pay for your troubles," he said mildly. "And a little extra."

He threw thirty crowns on the floor, a princely sum in this, and indeed most, households.

"I hope that you will spend a portion of it on that beautiful gown," he told Kristen, pointing it out. "It would look most beautiful on you."

He did not pause to hear the reply.

Fourteen

Wherein, Alison promotes Jake to fatherhood, without the usual preliminaries.

Jake's exertions, along with the tide and current, had delivered them to a point not only across the river but far south of the shore where he and Alison had departed. If the reader were to stand on the ridge at the girdle of the island—in the same batteries that slowed the Hessian advance the previous fall—he would find the two patriots to the south, though still beyond Cadwallader's mansion in the rocky portion of the city's outer precincts.

Anyone who has only visited the seaport and close streets at the tip of the island before the war will do well here to adjust his vision from brick buildings to farmland, or more properly, swamps and rough shoreline, which is where Alison and Jake found themselves as dawn ran its fingers through their damp hair.

Alison was the first to wake, roused from slumber by some warm licks on her face. These came from a large but friendly mastiff, who stood over her with a quizzical look. When she opened her eyes, the dog took a half-step back and gave a triumphant bark, as if he had breathed life into an inanimate object.

Alison recoiled from the brown-toned dog, with its well-meaning but spittle-ridden tongue. The tragedy of the previous night returned to her in a flood of horrible memories, and tears flowed freely, sorrow and fright combining in a way the fifteen-year-old had never felt before. Kneeling against the rough sand, she buried her head in her hands as the dog looked on in confusion.

"Do not cry, young man," said a gentle voice. "Here now, you're all right."

Alison—whose hair was cut short and who was still wearing the breeches, shirt, vest and coat of a boy— was helped to her feet by a woman in a spotless white dress and bare feet.

"Am I in heaven?" she asked.

The woman laughed. "I doubt Manhattan island has ever been considered that, or it wouldn't have been sold so cheaply. Were you shipwrecked?"

"Our boat sank. My father—"

Alison looked back at the rocks where Jake was lying, his arms crowded over his head. The dog was standing over him with a quizzical air, perhaps not knowing quite where to apply his tongue.

"Back, King, stand away." The woman patted the dog's neck lightly. "He means well, but he is such a slobberer. Come with me to the house, young man. We'll send some servants back to help your father while we get you some dry clothes. What is your name?"

Alison, well aware now that they had washed up in enemy territory, hesitated for only the slightest moment before answering "Al."

"Mine is Lady Patricia. Come along." The woman took her by the hand. "King, stay here until I send one of the soldiers down."

At the sharp tone, the dog's ears became erect. He gave a quick bark and bared his teeth, then began strutting back to Jake. No member of the Black Watch mounted a prouder patrol.

If the woman had appeared to be an angel when Alison opened her eyes, the building she led her to could have been heaven's own mansion. The gabled roof gleamed bright red with the light from the rising sun behind it, and the brick front was glazed with a glowing warmth that welcomed her as she stepped on the oyster-covered path leading to the door.

Lady Patricia led her gently by the hand, opened the mansion door and then called to a servant to assist. A young black man only a few years older than Alison appeared; he was dressed in a silk suit finer than any clothes her father or any of their customers had ever owned. He bowed as he received his instructions. Addressing Alison as "sir," he soon led her down the hallway and up two flights of a back staircase to a small guest room.

"If you take off your clothes, sir, I will have them dried."

"I can't do that," blustered Alison.

"Sir?"

"I—I'm afraid of catching a cold."

"That would be the point of your taking the wet clothes off your back, sir."

"I won't change until I have something to change into."

The servant frowned, but as he had been planning on fetching new clothes anyway, merely bowed and left.

Alison closed the door and examined the room. It was sparsely though elegantly furnished. The bed and curtain cloths were thick and sleek beneath her fingers, ten times as luxurious as any her father had ever used at the inn. The wardrobe and small chest of drawers glowed a reddish brown, their surfaces so strongly polished that Alison could see her reflection in the wood as clearly as if it were glass.

The harsh river currents had scrubbed her body clean of the blood that had bathed it last night. With her short hair and thin face, she did indeed look like a boy—an exceedingly fair one, and a few years younger than she actually was, but a boy nonetheless.

Her clothes were very damp; finally feeling the chill through them, she made sure the door was barred and window curtains closed, then whipped off her coat and shirt. She peeled back the breeches and walked naked through the room, her toes tickling the fine wool of the carpet, feeling as if she had been reborn.

Her father's death was as yet a bad dream, unreal to her. Jake, on the other hand, was very real, and her feelings toward him sharp in a way she had not felt before.

It was as if some new part of her had grown inside; if she were able to reach inside her chest she might find a new heart or lung there.

It took a few seconds for Alison to hear the knock on the door, and a few more to realize it was for her.

"Sir? May I come in, sir?"

"Wait," Alison said, running to the door. She wedged her bare foot against the floor, then leaned her head over to the edge of the doorway as she creaked it open. "What do you want?"

"I have your clothes, sir, if you'll permit me."

"Give them here."

"Sir?"

To open the door even another inch would be to give herself away. Alison eased her hand into the hallway— and pushed her weight harder toward her foot.

"Please give me my clothes," she told the servant. "I'll dress myself."

The servant sighed heavily, but nonetheless complied.

"Tell the lady I'll be down shortly."

"The lady is a dame," said the servant heavily, "being the wife of an earl. Her full name is Lady Patricia Eileen Buckmaster. You may call her Lady Patricia, if she so directs you."

"She already did," replied Alison. "Tell her I'll be right down."

"As you wish."

Alison whisked the clothes into the room, then fell against the door, closing it. She stayed against the oiled wood panel until she had finished pulling on a shirt and then the breeches.

The servant had not brought a coat, which presented

her with a bit of a problem. As Jake had discovered,
her chest was not so completely unnourished as to escape close scrutiny. She saw no choice but to wear her
damp waistcoat over the linen shirt, buttoning it despite the moisture.

Barefoot, she emerged from the room to find the
servant waiting impatiently.

"Here," she said, handing him a wadded pile of wet
clothes. "Can you dry these?"

"You are expected in the north parlor."

Alison had no idea what a north parlor was, much
less where to find it, and so followed quietly as the
servant led her back downstairs to a large paneled
room twice as large as her father's inn. The thick car-
pets covering the floors were the first thing the shoeless
girl noticed. Then a pair of massive chandeliers caught
her eyes and led them to a white marble fireplace that
took up nearly three-quarters of the wall. Despite the
fact that it was summer, a fire had been started, and as
Alison approached she felt the heat blow across her
face, chasing the last vestiges of the river's chill. Her
vest seemed to dry immediately.

"Isn't your waistcoat still damp?"

Startled, Alison spun quickly and took a step back,
avoiding Lady Patricia's touch. The woman moved so
silently and quickly, she might well be an angel or a
ghost.

"It's not wet at all," she told her.

Lady Patricia frowned briefly, dimples forming in her
round cheeks. But they soon slid into an indulgent
smile. "You are just learning the rules of decency, I
see. Very well. I am glad to see Thomas's old clothes
fit. They haven't been worn since he was thirteen or
fourteen, when he first came to visit his uncle."

"Is that long?"

"Too long, now," said the woman. "Take this chair
and sit by the fireplace, child. With luck, the servant
will find you some shoes."

Alison nodded and sat.

"Tell me how you came to be on my brother's beach while we wait for your shoes," said Lady Patricia. "Then we will go inside and eat."

"There's not much to tell, ma'am. My father and I were fishing."

"Fishing?"

Alison nodded her head up and down. She could tell that the woman did not believe her, but had no other lie to offer.

"And what happened to your boat?"

"The waves took it," said Alison. "We had to swim to shore, from at least midway. My father—saved me."

"Fishing? At night?"

"It was only late afternoon when we sank."

"Your father seems quite young to have a boy your age," said Lady Patricia.

"He seems old to me. But he has said my mother and he were young sweethearts."

"I see. And where is she?"

"She died. I was to have a younger brother."

Lady Patricia, who despite her high birth knew the trials of childbirth all too well, nodded sadly. "Let me have George get you some breakfast. My husband and brother are in the city," added the woman as she rose, "or we would have been able to greet you properly. With the rebellion, of course, times are strained. And my brother's ways here are somewhat different than our own—refreshingly so, I think."

Alison nodded. She belatedly realized she should have gotten up when the woman did—it would have been considered the gentlemanly thing to do.

Fatigued by his exertions and relative lack of sleep, Jake found it difficult to shake off Morpheus's shackles. He pushed his arms against the hard rocks beneath his chest several times before actually rising. When he succeeded he found himself squinting not into the sun but at a member of Her Majesty's Light Dragoons, an impressive if slightly haughty unit whose members spent considerable time each day primping the smart blue facings on their red uniforms—and a lot more time practicing with their swords and carbines.

Only the fact that Jake's legs were still weighed down by the invisible forces of exhaustion kept him from bolting.

"Lady Patricia directed that I wait on you," said the man. He was nominally at ease but still gripped his carbine tightly. "Your son has already been taken inside."

"My son?"

"He's quite safe inside Mr. Clayton Bauer's house. Were there others in your boat?"

"In my boat—no. Just myself and my son," said Jake. Fatherhood had come upon him unexpectedly, but he saw no option but to accept the condition gracefully and without comment. "Is he all right?"

"He has been seen to, sir. Please come with me."

Jake nodded and followed. He'd picked a fine bit of shore to wash up on. He wasn't sure who the lady would be, but Clayton Bauer was responsible for a good number of Tory spy rings around the freshly declared nation. He was an important member of the city commission, known as the police, besides.

Nor was he reputed to be particularly hospitable toward "rebels," no matter how cheerful the guard promised breakfast would be.

Fifteen

Wherein, Jake learns features of his past heretofore unknown to him.

"*F*ather!"

Caught off guard entering the hallway beyond the front door, Jake staggered backwards as Alison abruptly leapt into his arms.

"My name is Al and our last name is Stone," she whispered quickly. "We were fishing."

"Your son told me of your shipwreck," said Lady Patricia, coming out of the room behind Alison.

"My son told you, did he?" Jake put her down. "He's a remarkable young man."

"I'm just glad you're alive," Alison said. "I did not think we would make it."

"It must have been quite a storm," said Lady Patricia, her arms folded. "Yet I did not hear any thunder last night."

"Surprising currents," said Jake, who read her smirk all too well. "Not a storm. What else did Al tell you about our misfortune?"

"He has told me quite a lot. How the rebels burned you out of your home and left you penniless, so you had to make a living fishing. How you saved his life on the water last night, and plucked him from danger a dozen times. You sound like quite a hero."

"I'm sure every father is a hero in his son's eyes," said Jake. "Though I would allow as how he may tend to exaggerate at times."

"I am Lady Patricia," she said, smiling in a way that suggested she was entering into a mild conspiracy with him.

"Pleased to meet you, m'lady." Jake returned the smile. "Your husband is most famous. I had not heard he had wed, but then it has been long since I was in the city. Is he awake?"

"Clayton Bauer is my brother," she answered. "He is awake but not at home. My husband and he are seeing to business in town."

"Excuse me for my mistake." Jake's air, at once gracious and mildly flirtatious, could not have been more finely tuned if he were at King George's court.

"I have only recently arrived from England," continued Lady Patricia, "where I can assure you my husband William is almost completely unknown, despite the fact that he is the third earl of Buckmaster and a peer."

There was just the slightest hint of annoyance in her voice.

"I'm sure you exaggerate," said Jake. Lady Patricia's skin was nearly translucent, lighter than the downy white of her long, low-waisted white gown. The stomacher pulled tight at her waist rose like a funnel of silk tissues to the large scoops of her bosom. Undoubtedly considered simple, everyday wear in her circle at home, it would have passed for a ball gown in America. Though she might be close to forty, she had the body of a woman barely older than Alison, and carried herself with the simple grace of a woman born not merely to station but beauty as well. Her face was light and cheerful; Rubens, perhaps, would have used her as a model when contemplating beauty.

"You are charming as well as mysterious," Lady Patricia told him. "George, show Mister . . ."

"Stone," said Jake.

Lady Patricia nodded, though it was clear she did not believe most if any of what Alison had told her. "Show Mister Stone upstairs. I believe my brother would not begrudge him a fresh set of clothes. And thank you for the shoes. Your son has fit perfectly into my poor dead son's old clothes," Lady Patricia added to Jake.

With her last sentence, the studied polish of light chatter chipped away, and the woman showed her true face. It was no less beautiful for not being daubed with rouge, and considerably warmer.

Alison's expression clouded. She had not realized she was wearing a dead boy's clothes.

A thousand calculations fluttered through Jake's brain. Clayton Bauer was a close associate of Andrew Elliot, the hideous Scotsman who had returned from exile in the Jersey mountains to become the city's superintendent general, the highest-ranking civilian authority on the island. He could, on his own authority, have Jake put to death for as much as sneezing out of place—and with about as much thought.

On the other hand, Bauer's duties as spymaster would put him in a position to answer the perplexing question Jake had been sent here to answer. An hour of rifling his study might save the Revolution.

And a third hand, or at least consideration, presented itself: The beautiful woman standing before him fully realized he was not who he, or rather Alison, claimed. If they could not fool her, how could they hope to fool her brother? Already the redcoat guard behind him seemed edgy and suspicious.

"We must be on our way," said Jake.

"Do stay," said Lady Patricia, taking his arm. "My husband and brother will be in the city for several hours, and I would much appreciate the conversation of two people familiar with the rebellion. My only son was a young officer in Lord Cornwallis's army in the Jerseys this past winter when he disappeared. It would give me some solace to know more of this land."

"We have our own business in the city," said Jake. "But it would be ungracious of me to turn aside your kindness."

"I'll show you to the room where you can change,

father," said Alison, springing forward and taking Jake by the hand. "I know the way."

"I will see to breakfast," said Lady Patricia. "When you are done, we will be in the dining room."

"Yes, m'lady," said Jake, as Alison pulled him up the staircase.

His decision to stay involved more than the admittedly long-shot chance that he might search Bauer's office. Lady Patricia had charmed him. Her voice, while it contained the presumptive tone common to all British nobility, was softened in a most human way. How many earls' wives would condescend to seeing to breakfast themselves?

But life's more pleasing quandaries often must stand in line behind more pressing questions.

"Why did you tell them you were a boy?" Jake hissed at Alison after they closed the door behind them.

"She assumed I was. I thought it too dangerous to enlighten her."

"Her brother organizes Tory spy rings," said Jake. "And she has already seen through your fishing tale." He went to the window to peek through the curtains. Besides the man who had taken him from the beach, he had noticed two guards in the foyer and another pair on the front lawn. Now he saw two more posted at the rear of the property. Not overwhelming numbers, to be sure, but trouble enough.

"It's spooky to be wearing a dead boy's clothes," said Alison. "I feel as if I'm a ghost."

"That would be most convenient," said Jake. "You could slip through the walls and escape. Or search Clayton's office for me."

"Is that what we're going to do? I'm ready." Alison started for the door.

"No!" Jake grabbed her. "It's far too dangerous. There are redcoats all around, and God knows how many servants. We are not playing a game," he added. "We will have to tread very lightly here. You wanted adventure—well, here is some, and we must not lose our heads over it, you understand? If we are discovered, we will both be hanged."

"Yes, father."

Jake snorted. "We have some time before her brother returns. Let me discover what she knows. If I disappear for a while, continue talking with her."

"She is easy to talk to, though a bit suspicious."

"We will have to give away your story. It's too obvious that it's fake."

"Why?"

"Because I'm not your father."

"How would she know?"

A knock on the door killed Jake's sardonic reply. He found the servant standing outside the room with a set of clothes in his hand. Jake took them and dismissed the man.

"How did you fool him?" Jake asked when he had gone.

"I am more clever than you think."

"Yes, well, see that being clever doesn't get us in trouble."

"Should I close my eyes while you dress?"

"Can I trust you to keep them closed?" He didn't bother to wait for an answer. "Out the door with you."

"What if the servant comes back?"

"You'll just have to show again how clever you are. Wait for me, and add nothing to our tale. When I confess everything downstairs, play along completely. Until then, say as little as possible. You understand?"

Alison nodded solemnly—a bit too solemnly for him to trust, but there was no alternative. Jake pushed her out the door and quickly changed. The clothes the servant gave him were plain cotton breeches and shirt, serviceable and well made. A new pair of stockings and boots were also supplied; these were small and pinched his feet, but overall the re-dressed spy saw little reason to complain.

His Segallas was still in his belt, but as he had not

had time to place it in the water-sealed lining of his money belt, it was seriously fouled. He had no other weapon, save his tongue and wit.

The pass from Washington was a liability. Ordinarily he would have burnt it, but no fire presented itself.

Eat it?

As hungry as he was, Jake could not quite bear the thought. He had seen a fire flickering downstairs; he decided to go immediately and warm himself, disposing of the pass in the bargain.

Alison was not outside the door when Jake opened it—not that he was very surprised. Cursing mildly to himself, he descended the stairs patiently, the wadded pass in his hand. Jake turned into the large room where the fireplace was and discovered the servant just extinguishing it.

"M'lady is in the dining room, sir, with your son," said the servant. The accent on the word "son" made it clear he, too, did not believe Alison's story.

"I was just going to warm myself at the fire," said Jake. "I still feel damp."

"The dining room is quite warm, being bathed by the sun through the glass."

Jake allowed himself to be led to the room, slipping the pass inside his shirt as he walked. Alison was being waited on by Lady Patricia herself near the bank of rear windows. A full breakfast sat in silver trays and servers at the center of the small, round table used only on informal occasions. A much larger table, not quite fully extended with its leaves, dominated the rest of the room.

"I would love some more tea, thank ye, m'lady."

"I see you found your way here, Al."

"Hello, father. Lady Patricia has made us such a wonderful breakfast."

"The cook made the breakfast," announced Lady Patricia. "But it's my pleasure to serve you. My brother is a bachelor, and during these rough days there is no proper hostess besides myself. He has only the cook and his man George, besides the constant company of guards. Most of them are gone to the city with him."

"That's not necessary," said Jake as she pulled out his chair. "I think it improper to be waited on by a woman of your station."

"Oh, I shall not pour your tea for free. My son was at Princeton; I would like to know what you know of that battle."

Jake's blue eyes reflected the calmness of a summer day, but inside, he stormed. The spy had been employed to gather intelligence and had played a role in the battle; he wondered for a moment if this beautiful British woman might somehow know that.

But something in her face belied such artifice.

"Sit down, sir," she said. "Please. You are famished, and I would like the company."

She touched his sleeve gently.

"We are not entirely who we seem," he warned her, still standing. "Though I cannot give you every detail."

"I did not think you were Al's father. Stay and have breakfast. Do you want some tea?"

"Coffee, if you please. Something in me is allergic to tea, and I get a choking reaction."

"You should have that examined."

"I have, and apparently the cure is too dear." Jake touched his throat apologetically, then changed the subject as she nodded for the servant to fetch a pot. "The boy is a neighbor who sometimes proves useful. Unfortunately, the story he told of his house being burned is true. His real father perished in the flames."

"And you saved him?"

"I plucked Al from the fire, but could not rescue his father."

He glanced at Alison. She had a grimace on her face, and he could see her pinching her fingers together, as if to keep from saying anything.

As for Lady Patricia, it was clear that his hints had satisfied her, at least temporarily. She knew her brother was involved in spying against the Americans for the British, and would naturally jump to the conclusion that Jake was as well.

And something more. He brushed his hand over hers gently as he sat in the chair, and saw the light, brief flick of her eyelids.

"I know almost nothing of Princeton," he said, pulling himself to the table.

It was a moment before she gave him an embarrassed smile and sat herself. "Come now, surely you know something of the rebels who slew my son."

"Why do you think he was killed?"

"I—" Her lip quivered for a brief second before she regained her control. "Even Lord Cornwallis held little hope. The rebels have not asked for an exchange."

"That does not mean anything," said Jake. "They are not so organized that they would be able to respond quickly to inquiries, let alone take the initiative."

"That is something," she said, but it was clear she would no longer allow herself to believe her son might have survived. "Are they brave, at least? However misguided?"

"I would allow as the rebels are brave," said Jake carefully. "Their leader, General Washington, is certainly a noble man."

"You are the first person here with the courage to say so." She took the fine porcelain tea cup before her and held it to her lips, sipping as delicately as a fawn licks water from a stream. The servant, meanwhile, returned and served him. The cook had come from Pennsylvania, and her skill with scrapple was unsurpassed. Despite a token effort at restraining himself, Jake greedily gobbled two slices of the crisp fried pork mush without pausing for a breath. Sage and marjoram added to the flavor, and he had to control himself to keep from reaching for the last piece left on the ornate silver platter before him.

"Pardon my asking," said Jake when he was full, "but it is rare that we are visited by a noblewoman."

"My husband is indeed a peer, but you must remember, his position is inherited. We are not one of the haughty families your papers write of."

"Still . . ."

Lady Patricia smiled. "We are of some influence, and we live comfortably," she allowed. "But you notice no train of servants, nor rich jewels at my throat."

"You sound almost like a Whig," said Jake.

"You are of the King's Party?"

"I would not think to find many rebels on these shores any more. Would you, Al?"

"Not at all, father."

"Still sticking to your cover story?" Lady Patricia asked her pointedly. Alison pretended not to hear her, just as she had pretended not to hear Jake admit he was not her father. "There are many spies who show up at my brother's house," Lady Patricia added, turning to Jake. "Though I daresay few swim here."

"What makes you think I'm a spy? Just because I am not the boy's father, does not mean I am more than a wheelwright, which is my occupation."

"Come now, must I claim woman's intuition?"

"A woman as beautiful as you may claim anything she wants."

"There seems a bit of sauce in your reply, if I take your meaning one way."

"It may be taken any way you desire."

Lady Patricia picked up her napkin and dabbed gently at her mouth. She seemed to brush away her light manner with the cloth; it must be a well-practiced method of restraint, Jake thought.

"Lord Cornwallis said General Washington's army was nearly destroyed with the march," she said, "and it was only luck and desperation that made it succeed."

"It must be so, certainly," he answered. "But they are persistent. They fight for their homes and families."

"As you do."

"True enough."

Lady Patricia's hand shot out and took his so suddenly he was caught off guard.

"Do you think he is alive?"

"It is possible."

"How could I find out?"

And so, without even preparing for it, Jake found the way open to march to his goal. Was there a pang or twinge inside his heart at using this beautiful woman against her will, even for the good of the Cause?

"I would think that if you went directly to Sir William Howe immediately, the supreme commander might send personally after his status. But it would have to be done immediately."

"He is not in the city," said Lady Patricia. "Nor is his staff."

"I would go myself," said Alison. "You should go directly to General Washington and ask after your son."

This is what came of rescuing young girls from drowning, Jake thought. He loosed a glare at her that would wither an oak tree; if thoughts had any limbs, she would have been strangled in a trice.

"If he is the man they say he is," Alison said without taking notice, "he will seek out the truth immediately."

"Al, please."

"No, perhaps he is right. I would go, if I thought it would give me definite news, one way or the other."

"General Howe would have a much better chance," insisted Jake.

"A much better chance at what?" said a voice from the doorway.

Jake did not have to turn to realize he had overstayed his welcome. Lady Patricia's husband and brother were standing at the edge of the room—with a half-dozen well-armed and very red-coated soldiers right behind them.

Sixteen

Wherein, Jake and Alison exchange pleasantries with a most notorious Tory.

*I*t would please the reader, no doubt, to hear the Tory and his English brother-in-law described as carbuncled monsters, with hair tangled into snake tails and eyes the shape of melons squashed by winter's chills.

Such was not the case. The men who stood barring the entrance to the room were both handsome and well built, not quite as tall as Jake, though still of more than average height. They were naturally well dressed in the latest London fashions; it was impossible to tell from their suits which man had recently come from England and which had spent nearly his whole adult life in America. Indeed, even their features were somewhat similar, with high eyebrows, smallish noses and chins that might have been cut from wood blocks.

The scowl on Clayton Bauer's face was quite distinctive, however. It led him through the room with the ferociousness of a boar rousted from a lair.

"What nonsense are you talking, Patricia? Going across the lines to the rebels?"

"I've just been trying to talk her out of it, sir," said Jake, standing.

"And who the devil are you? Announce yourself, man."

Jake wondered if Bauer might recognize him. They had been introduced once before, but fortunately he had been disguised at the time. Still, Jake's recent ad-

ventures might have spread his true description
around, and it would not have to travel far to reach
Bauer.

"Jake Stone is my name."

"Search him. And the boy."

"That won't be necessary," said Jake, Washington's
pass burning a hole in his side. He reached into his belt
and pulled out the Segallas, handing it to Bauer for his
inspection. "This is the only weapon I carried when I
escaped from Jersey. Unfortunately, it is fouled. Excuse me, Lady Patricia." Jake turned and undid his
shirt to open the money belt's pouch and remove the
forged letter from Franklin. "I am assigned to General
Bacon. The boy is the son of another agent. He died,
unfortunately, on the opposite shore, and I did not
think it just to leave the lad to the mercies of the
rebels. They nearly killed us in any event as we made
our escape."

Bauer, who fairly winced at the mention of Bacon,
grabbed the letter and read it skeptically. "This is from
William Franklin, and says nothing."

"What do you wish it to say?" Jake shot back.
"Should it invite General Washington to hang me?"

"*Mister* Washington," answered Bauer. The insult
was a common one.

Jake ignored it, taking the letter back. "I thank you
for your hospitality; General Bacon will no doubt be
pleased."

Jake had not chosen the name idly. Bauer and Bacon
were more rivals than allies and scarce exchanged
pleasantries, much less information or agents. It might
even occur to Bauer that Jake had been sent here by
Bacon to spy on him.

On the other hand, an agent of Bacon's would know
he could find at least shelter here. Bacon would be
expected to provide the same to one of Bauer's men,
and had done so recently.

The Tory made a motion, and the redcoat who had
clamped a hand on Alison's shoulder—a very danger-

ous hand, given its proximity to her chest—immediately withdrew to the side of the room.

"You look familiar," Bauer said to Jake.

"I have a cousin who lives in this city," he answered. Jake gave a sign with his head to Alison that she should follow him out the door, but when he turned to go, he found the way blocked by Bauer's arm.

"Stay and finish your tea."

"Coffee," said Lady Patricia. "He is allergic to tea."

"You sound more and more like a rebel, sir."

"I know from personal experience that most rebels drink tea, given the choice," said Jake. He was indeed correct.

Lord William Buckmaster had lost interest in Jake. Going to his wife, he stroked her arm gently. "What is this about your going to Washington, dear?" he asked. Jake discerned in his manner a timid, almost wincing approach to life that confirmed the hints his wife had made. His peerage had been inherited indeed.

"If it will get us news about Thomas, I would go to the devil himself."

"An apt metaphor," spat Bauer.

Jake thought it wise to let the fresh insult to Washington pass. He gripped Alison's arm tightly, in case she had a different opinion, and once again started toward the door.

"We haven't been able to get information any other way," said Lady Patricia, tears welling in her eyes. "You were turned away again this morning, I can tell. Why else would you have returned so soon?"

"We were not turned away," said Bauer. "There was simply no one to receive us, as I predicted. Sir William's staff has all gone with him to the ships. The adjunct general and the city administration were very sympathetic."

"But of no use."

"Patricia, don't fret now." Bauer took her arm as gently as her husband had. His voice, too, had softened; clearly he doted on his younger sister. "We will call on William's cousin tonight and take him with us to the theater. There's an old Farquhar comedy; it will be a diversion. And if the engineering office can help us in any way, its entire resources will be thrown open to us."

"But he is just a child."

"They may have contacts that will be useful to us. Believe me; they have done work for me before. In any event, you deserve to take your mind off your son tonight. The theater here is quite good, despite what you've heard in London."

Lady Patricia ignored him, turning instead to Jake. "You are with General Bacon's staff. Cannot you help us?"

"I am not with his staff, merely in his service," said Jake. "I am afraid that I would not even recognize the general if I fell over him. You probably know better than I where he is."

Bauer scowled, returning to the business at hand. "And where have you escaped from? Why did you swim across the river to my house?"

"I did not swim across the river. Our boat was fired on. Only luck brought us here. Lady Patricia found us on the beach."

"Like drowned rats," she said.

"I thought Sir Henry used only Englishmen. Your accent seems native."

Jake shrugged. "There I cannot enlighten you. I have already said too much."

"If you worked for me, I would have you flogged for giving yourself away so easily. A rebel could win news of your entire mission in an hour."

"Come, Clayton, you are being much too harsh with the man," said Lord Buckmaster. "He is your guest."

"You are not used to the habits of our shores or this war, brother," said Bauer. "Please allow me to do my business, as I would allow you to do yours."

His lordship took the rebuke mildly.

"Come, Al, it is time for us to leave," said Jake, pulling her hand.

"Yes, father."

"You needn't call me father any more."

"He, at least, knows the business," remarked Bauer.

Jake grimaced. "We will have someone return your clothes tomorrow. I thank you most kindly for them."

He bowed to Lord and Lady Buckmaster before aiming for the door. The redcoat guards gave Bauer a glance, and for a moment Jake feared he was going to order them to carry out the forgotten search, if only to show that Bacon's agents were not above his own.

But he said nothing. Jake was able to guide Alison swiftly from the room to the front door without further interruption.

"Was that close?"

"Very."

Jake and Alison had by now walked a half-mile from the mansion, entering upon Bloomingdale Road. The city was still a long way south.

"I could not tell from your face that we were ever in danger," said Alison. "You must be a very good liar."

"I assume that was meant as a compliment." Jake stopped and retrieved Washington's pass from his belt. Making sure no one was nearby, he ripped it to shreds and then kicked a few pieces into holes he dug with the heel of his borrowed shoe. He fluttered a few others in small bits on the opposite side of the road, and scattered the rest near a tree trunk.

"Washington's letter!" exclaimed Alison.

"Had they found it, we would be guests of honor at a gibbet party," said Jake. "Come on now, do you feel up to running? I'd like to put some more distance between us and our late hosts."

"I can run as fast as you, I reckon," said Alison, dashing ahead.

They ran a good distance together, Jake trying to show her by his example that she must pace herself like a horse, aiming for a long stride and gradual progress. She was strong, there was no question about it, and energetic no matter her sex. They managed nearly a mile before losing their wind, and she did not tire until Jake did.

"Tell me about General Washington," said Alison as they sat to rest on the side of the road. "What is he like?"

"As tall as me, but much older."

"That isn't much of a description."

"He has white hair and a square face."

"But what is he like? How does he talk? How does he lead his men?"

"That is hard to say. He is like a father to us. One moment he seems kindly and gentle, the next hard and aloof. He is always pushing himself forward and cheering us."

"But I have heard—"

Jake jerked his elbow into her side to quiet her as he spotted the black helmets of British grenadiers just rounding the bend ahead. The patriots resumed walking at once, Alison grabbing her side with some discomfort.

The British soldiers took no notice of them.

"Why did you hit me?" she asked when they were once more alone.

"They would have seen if I had grabbed your mouth. You talk too loud."

"Ha! Listen to yourself."

"Come now, we are not in the clear. Remember where we are."

They proceeded mostly in silence the rest of the way to New York, passing through various patches of British encampments, many empty. Though he knew there would be considerable men at King's Bridge, and more on Long Island, Jake wondered if an attempt to regain the city might not be profitable. Its proximity to the water meant it could easily be reinforced by the British;

still, there was great value in striking a blow to the enemy's morale.

These and similar thoughts occupied the patriot spy as he headed toward Rivington's coffeehouse at the very heart of what was now the Loyalist capital. As for Alison, it was obvious that she had never been in the city. She stared with wide-eyed awe at the large and grand buildings as they appeared, most especially the English church, whose walls stood with careful grace above the adjoining mall, despite the congregation's politics. The gardens, too, had been tended despite the war, and the melange of colors and smells both pleasing and noxious nearly made the girl faint.

"Here," said Jake when they finally reached the coffeehouse door. "No matter what happens, you are to keep your mouth quiet."

"But—"

"No matter what happens. The British will hang me, and you as well, if we are caught. You are to wait here exactly a minute, then come in. If it appears that I am in trouble, stay far away from me. There is a man named Bebeef with an apothecary shop in the First Ward. If I am captured, you are to seek him out and say I am your friend. He is a druggist and a philosopher and a great friend of mine; he will shelter you. Stay out of Canvas Town, no matter what anyone tells you. And under no circumstances—none—are you to follow me to jail. Do you understand?"

The girl nodded soberly.

Jake took a full breath. He never knew whether he would be recognized or not here, and what the consequences might be.

"Take care of yourself," he said solemnly, patting Alison's shoulder as if it might be the last time he saw her. Then he pasted a smile on his face and plunged inside.

Seventeen

Wherein, Jake is accused of being a deadbeat, then asked about his German.

$\mathcal{R}$ivington, as any reader of our country's journals will know, is the notorious editor of the lying rag proclaiming King George III's vicious slanders against his former subjects. He is the same printer who published the infamous notes from the Westchester farmer at the beginning of hostilities, and a man who has done much to proclaim the word of tyranny throughout the continent. While it will be admitted that Rivington has also printed the occasional reply from the patriot party—including one penned by Alexander Hamilton—there are few in America and none in England who doubt his loyalty to the king.

Yet how to explain that, in opening the coffeehouse, he has entered into a partnership with Culper? How to explain that it is one of the best gathering places for the patriot spy network, and that even as Jake entered, three different pairs of patriot eyes noted his presence?

Some questions are better left unanswered, at least for now. Suffice to say that Jake quickly found himself approached not by a mere waiter, but by Culper himself. The spymaster wore a reddened mask of gouty displeasure, and sailed at Jake as a crusader descending on the Saracens.

"You, sir," he announced in a voice that scattered the pigeons nestling on the roof outside, "out of this establishment this instant! We will serve none of your kind here!"

"I always pay my bill promptly," sniffed Jake in return, not sure entirely what way the game was to be played.

"Not so readily as you claim. Out—and take the servants' entrance. I wouldn't want people of repute to see you."

"I resent the insult."

"Do you deny that you owe me past ten pounds?"

Jake glanced past Culper and saw Mark Daltoons standing near the side of the back hall. Daltoons, a young officer assigned to assist the city spies, was undoubtedly waiting to conduct him to a safer place.

"Perhaps we could make an arrangement," Jake offered, glancing around the room. "I am to come into money soon."

His glance had the effect of warning off a few of the more easily embarrassed patrons. "I must take the boy with me," said Jake in a whisper. "The lad in the tan vest without a hat just now coming through the door."

"I will retrieve him," promised Culper beneath his breath. "If you have coins, you may meet me in the kitchen," he said loud enough for the room to hear. "If not, do not darken my hallway any longer."

Jake was already heading for Daltoons. Tall and thin, with stained apron and unsmiling countenance, the fake waiter gave the most discreet of nods before disappearing into the back. Jake followed moodily; inside the hallway, he discovered an open panel and slipped through, landing uneasily on a twisting staircase.

Closing the door behind him meant enshrouding himself in a thick, dank darkness. He descended slowly, and counted five steps when he was suddenly grabbed from behind.

Just as he was ducking to flip his assailant over his back, he realized it was Daltoons.

"We have installed a new passage," said the young man. "Come quickly."

When they had last worked together, Daltoons had confessed to Jake that he had lied about his age when enlisting in his Massachusetts company two years before. At the time, he was barely fifteen, though he said he was nineteen. The fiction was carried off so perfectly that the others in his group elected him their officer. In their defense, it must be said that Daltoons generally carried himself as a man in his late twenties or early thirties, possessed of a bravery that knew no age limit. Barely seventeen when General Howe's army advanced on New York the previous fall, he had volunteered to remain in the city and help establish the spy network.

Jake had to duck to proceed through the passage, which burrowed beneath the building in the manner of a Roman catacomb. It narrowed so severely that at one point he and Daltoons turned and walked sideways.

"Quite a snug little nest we've made under the British, no?" Daltoons said as he reached a large chamber. "Wait now, and we will have a little light."

A lamp filled with whale oil lay near the entrance. Daltoons took it up, and with some trouble succeeded in getting it lit. The walls and ceiling of this dug-out room had been boarded over with wide pine boards, but it could not in any sense be called comfortable; many a dungeon seemed more handsome.

"The British have turned their screw wheels tighter of late," said Daltoons as Jake took a seat on an empty barrel. "The Tory bastard Elliot has been given broad powers, and anyone so much as criticizing the king is subject to arrest."

"An exaggeration, surely."

"Not at all," said Daltoons. "The British put a good price on your head after your last sojourn. Fortunately, they seem to have come up with a very faulty description."

The young man reached to a nearby chest and picked through some papers. He handed Jake a sheaf of circulars offering 100 pounds for the apprehension of "one of His Majesty's most pernicious subjects, Jake Gibson. Standing five-foot-three, with dark black hair and a scar above his nose, he has a French accent gained from his years of service in the maritime, where he lost partial use of his leg."

Jake's laugh shook the ceiling boards. "This is me?"

"I know a dozen men who would swear it."

The men's laughter stopped abruptly as they heard a noise above. The lieutenant took his pistol from his belt and steadied it at the narrow doorway, lowering it only when Culper pushed through with a grunt.

"You took a great chance meeting me here," said Culper gruffly.

"I asked for you at the governor's palace, but you weren't at home," returned Jake.

"There's a price on your head. It's fortunate we have friends willing to describe you so minutely, or half the company upstairs would have fallen on you."

Jake was just about to tell Culper why he had come when Alison burst through the opening with the joy of a newborn colt.

"Father!" she cried.

"It's all right, Alison, we're among friends," said Jake, holding her at bay.

She gave him a strange look.

"Father? Why are you calling me Alison? Do you think I've suddenly changed into a girl?"

"If you want, I'll let our friend Daltoons examine you." Jake ignored her scowl and turned to Culper. "Her father helped me find an easy passage to the city, but was killed by marines. We only just survived by swimming the river."

"You swam?" asked Daltoons incredulously.

"Not by design," said Jake.

As was her habit, Alison had adopted her own view of the situation. "I've come to New York to join the Sons of Liberty," she told Culper. "And to help General Washington."

Culper frowned. "You can't help him here. Where is your mother?"

"I have none. And no relatives either. I am a fresh recruit, without strings."

Culper was already shaking his head by the time Jake suggested a place might be found for Alison at the coffeehouse.

"She cooks very well," said Jake.

"I don't want a job as a cook or servant," said Alison. "I want to join the army—or be a spy like you."

"Alison, I think perhaps you should go and get something to eat. And get changed," said Jake.

"I want to stay here."

"No," he said firmly. "Lieutenant Daltoons will help you."

"Gladly," said Daltoons. Not only could he now see through the disguise, he was beginning to see more than a bit beyond it.

"Take her to Miss Tennison's," said Culper.

Daltoons started to object, but his commander would hear none of it.

"Tennison's. You could probably use a good supper yourself. Meet us at the infirmary when you are done."

Daltoons appeared nearly as reluctant as Alison now that the destination was given, but nodded and led her out through an entrance that led up the stairs of an adjoining house.

"Can we trust her?" Culper asked Jake.

"Without doubt, though she's the most rambunctious girl I've ever met. But give her her due: she just helped me lie my way off Clayton Bauer's estate."

"Bauer? He captured you?"

"No. I had the bad luck to wash up on his shore. Alison passed herself off as a boy there, and talked Bauer's sister-in-law into helping us."

At last Culper was impressed. "How old is she?"

"I believe fifteen, perhaps a year more."

"I don't know that we can keep her here. Things are

far too dangerous now. The entire city is turned against us."

"General Washington was afraid you might be dead."

"Not yet. But many of our people have been forced into hiding—or jail."

"The general needs to know Howe's plans," said Jake. "He has intercepted a message that claims he's attacking Boston."

"Very possible," said Culper. "His whole staff has disappeared from Manhattan. They're not on Staten Island either. Apparently everyone Howe values has been placed aboard ship and is sitting just over the horizon, whether waiting for the winds to change or some portent from heaven, it is impossible to say. Boston may be his target."

"Why would he go north? Why risk another defeat there?"

"If it were Philadelphia, why not just continue across the Jerseys?" answered Culper. "We have heard every city on the continent as a destination. I have sent a number of our men to try and discover Howe's plans, with nothing to show for it. My best hope was Robert Anthony, who infiltrated General Clinton's headquarters. Clinton has been left behind, though whether Howe is trusting him with his plans seems to vary from week to week."

"Where is Anthony?"

"Sitting in one of the city jails, waiting to be taken to the prison ships or hanged, whatever they decide."

"We must rescue him and see what he has found."

"I'm glad you feel that way," said Culper, a bit of his more usual spirit reviving in the twinkle of his eyes. "We have an operation planned this very afternoon. Tell me, how is your German these days?"

Eighteen

Wherein, Claus van Clynne is bundled in British rope and, more fearsome, red tape.

While Jake was enjoying his brief breakfast at Clayton Bauer's mansion, Claus van Clynne was in need of much stronger relief. Having been transported downriver to a small landing north of Peekskill, he was bundled and taken south in the back of a hay cart. The cart skirted the American patrols and defenses in the Highlands, which centered around the immense river chain and its neighboring forts on the river. South of King's Ferry, the small group of disguised British sailors and the renegade Egans took a road that led to the shore. Had he not been gagged, the squire might have remarked that he knew this particular lane well, as he had ridden down it during his adventures as the adopted general of a Connecticut brigade but a month and a half before. He might also have protested, with great severity, when Egans took up his hat and placed it on his own head, deciding to treat it as a trophy of war.

But then there was much van Clynne might have said at any stage of his journey. He could have waxed eloquent about the indignities of being lifted like a bag of year-old potatoes from the back of the cart and dumped unceremoniously into a longboat. He might have essayed at length about the untidy and haphazard rowing that took him to the river sloop waiting in the shadows offshore. He undoubtedly would have complained of the fickleness of the starlight as he stared at the sky for three hours while the sloop raced furiously south. Nor should anyone suspect that he would have stifled his complaints at the bidding of the marines who stood guard, nor Egans himself, who brooded at the front of the vessel.

More Indian than white, the Oneida was suspicious of his British paymasters, and his many dealings with them had made him less, rather than more, inclined to trust them. But he nonetheless had made himself their agent, and an effective one at that. His motivations were a mixture of revenge against the people who had killed his adopted father, a misguided notion that adventure against the whites was the equivalent of glory in battle, and a determination to use the wealth he received to increase his own position and standing among his adopted people. Indeed, the man who was called Snowsnake longed above all else for acceptance and honor, not merely from his immediate family but from Iroquois in general. The lines of power in his clan and nation ran through the maternal side, and Egans with some reason felt he had never been properly appreciated by his adopted aunts. Returning with the trophies British silver could provide was one way of raising their esteem.

His adopted father's death had left a great hole within his breast, which he felt could only be closed by over-awed respect. He would trade half the fingers on his hands for the position a man such as Johnson—also white—commanded among the confederacy.

For his part, Claus van Clynne believed Egans more misguided than evil. In the Dutchman's opinion, his alignment with the British was due solely to the misidentification of his adopted father's killer. The Dutchman placed a great trust in blood instincts, as well as his own abilities of persuasion, and felt that if the gag around his mouth were removed, he would soon have Egans leading the charge against the English. A word here, a hint there, and Egans would be among the hottest Revolutionists.

Alas, his theory was never put to the test, for the gag was not removed, not when the sloop pulled into Loyalist Spuyten Duyvil to discharge some other passengers, nor when it slipped along the shore to find the wharfs further south in Manhattan at early morn. The rag was still firmly around his mouth as van Clynne, with considerable straining from the crew, was loaded into a wheelbarrow and dragged ashore, where he was hoisted into a wagon.

If they chafed at taking directions from a man they might regard as a traitor to their race, the crew nonetheless followed Egans's orders and took some care as the trussed prisoner was lifted from the back and carried—again with a surfeit of groans—up the steps to the British administration building across from the jail.

Even in wartime, there are forms to be completed and papers signed. Egans waited stoically while the British went through their procedures for interning the prisoner. Van Clynne's money and his passes had been transferred to a satchel Egans kept at his side. He judged it unnecessary to produce them for the clerk, especially as they might be of use in his future endeavors.

It was a good thing, too, for otherwise the process would have taken three times as long, between the cataloging and accounting.

"An examination will have to be arranged," said the clerk at the desk, pointing at van Clynne after the forms were filled. "According to the calendar, it will not be before next week. After that, he will provide nice ballast at Wallabout Bay."

Egans did not join in the laughter. The mud flats of Wallabout Bay were the home of a series of derelict hulks used as prison ships. In his mind, there was no glory in keeping prisoners in such torturous conditions. Better to kill a man outright, so that his spirit might be used by the victorious warrior.

Needless to say, van Clynne had his own ideas. In fact, he tried to share them with the clerk.

"I cannot hear you through your gag," the man told him.

Van Clynne's gesticulations that it be removed were insufficient to convince him. The clerk was, however, required by the regulations to ascertain from the prisoner his name and role in the rebellion. Custom also dictated a few other inquiries, such as the nature of his religion. At length, therefore, the clerk nodded at the sergeant-at-arms, who removed the spittle-drenched gag.

"I was just about to wonder what had happened to the custom of law in this country," thundered van Clynne the moment his lips were freed. "To be tied like a common hog—"

"We were confused by your grunts," said the clerk dryly. "What is your name?"

"I am a personal friend of Sir William Howe. I demand to be taken to him at once!"

"The general will be with you shortly," said the clerk. "He is currently on his way to tea with Mr. Washington. What is your name?"

"It was not two months ago when I dined with Sir William aboard his brother's ship and debated the merits of Madeira versus ale," answered the Dutchman. (He happened to be speaking the truth, though the clerk should be forgiven for not thinking it possible.) "Take me to him immediately."

"This gentleman will show you there," said the Englishman, nodding at the sergeant-at-arms. "For the record, do you refuse to give me your name?"

"I refuse to answer any of your questions," said van Clynne indignantly. "I refuse to be a party to this injustice, and stand on my rights."

"You would do better to stand on your feet," said the clerk, making a notation in his book. "Take him away."

"My hat, I demand my hat!"

"You do not require a hat in jail," answered the clerk.

"I stand upon my rights," blustered van Clynne. "A man cannot be deprived of his hat under British law."

The clerk's brow knotted. He realized the Dutchman might indeed be correct, and in any case, there were considerable forms to fill out regarding its loss. The crisis was averted by Egans, who stepped forward and jammed the beaver on van Clynne's head. "Here it is," he said. "Wear it in good health."

"I demand restitution," said van Clynne. "I was without its services for several hours and am entitled to just compensation."

But the possibilities of delay, if not argument, had been exhausted. Van Clynne was taken, with great consternation, across the street to the jail.

With his prisoner gone, Egans asked the clerk where his reward was.

"Which reward would that be?"

"I am promised twenty crowns for each rebel spy I bring to the city," said Egans.

"I know nothing of that," said the clerk. He turned to his other work. "That is not my department."

"I will not leave without my money."

The clerk did not bother answering. Instead, he gave a minuscule motion with his hand, and the two guards who had been standing by the side door promptly came to take hold of Egans. The Oneida shook his arms out so fiercely they hesitated.

"I will have my money."

"Consult General Bacon's staff," said the clerk.

"Give me a receipt for my prisoner."

"That I will gladly do," said the clerk. "Once you complete the proper forms."

Nineteen

Wherein, Jake hears a familiar sound.

$\mathcal{J}$ust at the close of the afternoon dinner time, a procession of wagons piled high with bricks made their way down from Broadway toward one of the recently opened British jails, an auxiliary edifice converted from a warehouse and now generally used for holding suspected rebels and spies. The lead wagon, it developed, had a faulty axle pin, which gave way just as the vehicle passed the entrance to the jail. The load of bricks suddenly tumbled out, upsetting the horses behind, who in turn upset their own wagons. Within a short minute, the entire roadway was piled nearly waist-high with fresh clay bricks. Thick dust filled the air.

The resulting confusion caused considerable consternation inside the jail. The warden, his face two shades redder than most of the bricks, emerged and began shouting curses at the wagon drivers. His rants impressed the teamsters so much that they ran for their lives, abandoning the cargo. The warden, his curses crescendoing, had no option but to direct a party of his men to assist in the cleanup.

It was at this point that two inspectors general from the Prussian Council on Foreign Actions, Brunswick Division, arrived for an unannounced inspection. Personal representatives of the Duke of Brunswick himself, the graybeards were accoutered as royal officers.

Silver aiguillettes and tassels waved from their blue silk coats like pennants from a ship, and their bright sashes were wider than several local alleyways. The long swords at their sides practically dragged against the ground. These worthies were required by His Highness to ascertain that all prisoners of the allied nation were detained "according to practices in keeping with a civilized Christian nation." Otherwise, the terms of service as overseen by British commissioner and plenipotentiary Colonel William Faucitt would desist immediately, and all Brunswick troops would be immediately ordered back to Europe, at British expense.

"All zee troops," repeated the taller inspector, whose bushy eyebrows seemed like dyed caterpillars. "Ve vould not vant dis to happen, no?"

The inspectors were accompanied by copious paperwork and a small knot of regimental privates dressed in blue coats with red lining and turnbacks—to say nothing of very becoming yellow buttons. The Germans' English was sufficient only to annoy the jail superintendent, who understood from the papers that the men were minor dukes, just well-connected enough to cause him considerable trouble if they emerged from their inspection in ill-humor.

And that wouldn't be hard. Already they were complaining loudly to each other in a profoundly incomprehensible German. And taking notes.

"Is dis zee vay ve treat prisoners?" demanded the duke with the caterpillar eyebrows. "Vit dis dust everywhere in zee street?"

The superintendent apologized, ordered every available man outside to help with the bricks, and then ushered the Germans to his office inside the steel gate. He had just reached down to retrieve a bottle of Port wine to smooth their communication problems when he felt a cold sensation on his neck.

More specifically, it was a pistol barrel, sharply levered against the soft edge of flesh above the shoulders. It would be the last thing he felt for several hours.

"Ought to just kill him," said the duke with the thick eyebrows, who in reality was Jake Gibbs.

"They'll hear the gunshot outside," said the other duke—Culper himself. "Besides, he'll be in enough trouble once we're done. Killing him would be a mercy."

The two men quickly trussed the superintendent and abandoned their long scabbards, which contained only sword handles rather than the actual weapons. Littering the passage with broken German and pure gibberish—neither Culper nor Jake knew any German beyond a few odd curses and requests for food—they led their men through the prison proper, walking quickly down the central gathering area to the steps leading to the cell blocks. The guard at the steps snapped to attention and then practically snapped in half, as Jake returned his salute with a sharp kick to the stomach. The man was knocked over the head by one of the privates; another of the Brunswickers hurriedly exchanged coats and took his place.

Jake crept down the steps, pistol in hand, followed closely by Culper. The stairs took an L-bend and then proceeded to the landing via four short steps. A heavy metal door, the only one in the hastily converted prison, stood at the bottom.

Behind it was another guard, who patrolled the long corridor between the door and the dungeon cells. Jake returned the gun to his belt, fixed his jacket, and resumed the posture of a German inspector.

"Ve are zee prince's men," he told the man through the small, barred opening in the door.

"Talk English."

"I am. Ve are zee prince's representatives, to inspect zee prison."

"So?"

"So open zee door."

"I open this door only for my captain," responded the guard. "Or the superintendent."

"You will open it now," said Jake, exchanging the lousy accent for the more efficient pistol, "or I will shoot you."

But the redcoat was not to be taken so easily. He ducked to the side, out of Jake's range.

Jake waved one of the Brunswickers forward. The man's canteen contained a small explosive charge; it was placed at the door and lit.

"Last chance to give up," called Jake.

The redcoat stayed at his post. Jake gave him another second to change his mind, then threw himself around the curve of the stairs.

Even so, the force of the blast pushed him back against the limestone wall so sharply that water oozed from the rock onto his body. His fake eyebrows were blown off and his wig lost somewhere in the hallway.

Jake jumped up and ran through the hole. Parts of the dead guard lay to one side, below a large splatter of red and brown. The cell keys were lying in a twisted hunk at the far end of the hallway. Fortunately, the raiders had brought their own keys—a set of long axes were now assembled from parts carried in the privates' knapsacks.

Jake and Culper left three men to guard the approach while they raced down the long hallway to open the cells. Before they had gone halfway, however, Jake stopped short. A familiar sound, not precisely pleasing and yet comforting in an odd way, filled his ears.

"There was a time when a prison was engineered to proper specifications, with impenetrable walls and solid foundations. Even the rats were proud to be kept there. Now, these are flimsy things. Wooden doors and walls, indeed! Why if this were a Dutch prison—"

"Claus!" shouted Jake. "Claus van Clynne. Where the hell are you?"

"Here," replied the Dutchman indignantly. "Where do you think I am?"

Jake raced forward down the dimly lit passage.

The cell where his friend was kept was the first on his right.

"Stand back!" he yelled, swinging the ax. It took three swings before the wood began to give way. But with the fourth the door splintered sufficiently for a good kick to complete the job.

"What are you doing in New York?" Jake asked as the Dutchman shoved the door aside.

"I realized that you would need me to rescue you when the situation became difficult," answered the Dutchman. "Look at this hinge—another hour and it would have fallen off on its own. You cannot depend on iron any more."

"How did you manage to keep your hat?"

"A superior knowledge of British law always proves useful in these situations," van Clynne declared.

The Dutchman followed as Jake trotted to the next cell and once more swung his ax. He opened two more cells before Culper began yelling at the far end of the hallway that the British were coming.

"Everyone thinks he's Paul Revere these days," commented van Clynne beneath his breath.

The warning was soon underlined by the sound of muskets firing in the stairway. A volley of pistols answered. As they fell back, two of the privates took off their coats and the third emptied his canteen on them. The canteen contained pitch, and when the jackets were lit they began filling the stairway with a dark, heavy smoke. It stopped the pursuit, but the fog also began creeping into the basement, adding to the natural dimness.

"Here," Culper shouted to the liberated prisoners. "The cistern chamber is in the wall here. Hold your breath, dive into the water, and you'll reach a broader passage within three feet. Follow it quickly and wait for me." He took the back of his ax head and began knocking at the stones. "Jake, I don't know if your friend will fit through it."

"If you are referring to me, sir, let me assure you that Claus van Clynne always uses the front door when leaving a building. I have no need of crude expedients."

A bullet ricocheted down the corridor as the Dutchman finished speaking, sending him to the ground.

"Be my guest," Culper told van Clynne. He pushed one of the prisoners through the hole. A loud plop announced that the small, unlit passage beyond was filled with water, as promised. Culper immediately began shooing men through, much like cattle through a gate, then dove in himself.

"Come on, Claus, time to go," said Jake.

"Your men may proceed me," said van Clynne, waving the last fake privates ahead.

They were thankful on two accounts—firstly, the redcoats were beating through the smoke and flames and starting to advance down the cellblock, and secondly, to a man they thought van Clynne's large frame would act as a stopper in a bottle.

Jake removed a small cartridge from his belt and tossed it down the hall. The resulting explosion produced far more noise than harm, but it sent the British into a temporary retreat.

"Are you sure there isn't another way out?" van Clynne asked. "One without water?"

"In you go." Jake pushed the Dutchman through.

Van Clynne grabbed his hat and fell forward, receiving a mouthful of the dankest, most putrid liquid seen on earth since its invention. He flailed his arms, managed to crawl forward, and promptly stalled.

"I'm stuck," he blubbered.

"Like hell," said Jake, pushing from behind. The brick-lined passage rumbled with the disturbance, and suddenly the Dutchman was forcing his way forward like a mole on the scent of a garden patch.

The cistern had been part of an old scheme to supply the area with water. The supply of such plans has always been several times greater than the actual flow produced, but in this case it was most fortuitous. It led, not to the great lake of water north of the shipyards, or even to an underground canal, but rather to a former rain collection point—directly across the street in the British adjunct's present office.

Culper's arrival in the foyer there, though announced with a loud banging and bursting of the floorboards, went largely unnoticed. This was due to the fact that the building had been set on fire some minutes before by the same teamsters whom the jail superintendent had so severely abused. Culper, his escapees, and the fake Germans joined in the mad scramble to save the British documents from the flames, carrying armfuls with them as they ran down the front steps.

Jake and van Clynne followed some distance behind. By now the guards understood what was going on in the prison and filled the streets with shouts and alarms. As van Clynne emerged from the building, one of the guards began screaming words to the effect—we shall leave off the slanders about van Clynne's race and waist-size—that the ringleader was getting away.

A squad of soldiers rallied to his call as Jake and the Dutchman hopped through the brick-laden street and ran toward the end of the block. Jake pushed him to the right at the intersection.

"The others were going to the left," grumbled van Clynne as Jake yanked him along.

"Trust me. We have only to turn this next corner."

"And what do you have there? A pile of mortar to go with these infernal bricks?"

Actually, the surprise waiting for the soldiers was several times stickier than mortar and much sweeter. For a cart laden with barrels of dense molasses had been stationed there. Jake pulled a rope as he passed, and this in turn released a mechanism which sent a vast pool of the liquid flooding into the street.

As Jake and van Clynne ran down a nearby alleyway,

the soldiers found themselves slowed by a sticky swamp
that ran to their thighs.

"At least it won't be turned into rum," muttered the
Dutchman as he ran. "How anyone can drink such rot
when good ale beckons is beyond me."

Twenty

Wherein, Alison fights her own war, and a new plan is engineered.

*W*hile Jake and Culper were engaged in their afternoon's entertainment, Daltoons and Alison enjoyed slight diversions of their own.

Miss Tennison's house lay several long blocks from the coffeehouse, nearly on the outskirts of the city. Alison trudged along dejectedly, complaining at every step that she had much more important things to do. There was glory to be won, she said, hinting that, if left to her own devices, she would go straight to the British headquarters and blow it up.

"If you did so, you would kill one or two of our best operatives," said Daltoons, his tone slightly indulgent. "And then the British would retaliate by rounding up many of our men. The life of a spy is quite complicated; you cannot go off half-cocked like a French pistol."

"You're pretty young to be giving out advice," she shot back.

"Older than you," said Daltoons. "And I've fought in several battles besides."

"That's why they have you as an errand boy?"

"Ask your friend Jake about the Herstraw business," said Daltoons, his cheeks beginning to shade. "See who helped him on that mission."

"I have already saved his life two or three times," insisted Alison.

Their path took them right past a redcoat strong-
hold, the tavern owned by the notorious back-stabbing
Tory, William Hermann. Several of the patrons were
standing at the doorway as Daltoons and Alison
passed.

"Hey, ya cowards, ya," said a corporal. He reached
his arm out toward Daltoons, who shrugged him aside
and kept moving. "Yer the damned dogs we're gettin'
killed for."

"Go to hell," said Alison as the drunk reached out
toward her.

His hand brushed across her chest before she could
duck away. She responded with a bold and bright slap
across his cheek.

The redcoat fell back in amazement. "Hey now," he
called out, "there's something unnatural about this
lad."

His attempt to explore further ended in a high-
pitched screech as Alison kneed him in the groin. The
yelp had the effect of rallying his fellows, drunken as
they were, and Alison found herself facing five or six
large grenadiers recently returned from King's Bridge,
where they had had their noses bruised by a small but
efficient American raiding party.

"We'll teach ya some manners, brat," said one.
"Come in here with us."

Alison curled her fists as one of the men reached out
to grab her. In the next instant, she was yanked backwards by Daltoons.

"We meant no harm," he said. "The rebels have recently killed our father, and my sister is mad at the
world. She is only dressed this way so we could avoid
their guard in Westchester as we came toward the city.
Please excuse us."

The redcoats might not have accepted his apology,
save for the fact that the young lieutenant accented it
with a fully cocked pistol. He pulled back his coat and
revealed that he had not one but two more on reserve.

Drawing a weapon on British soldiers on a city street

was punishable in any number of ways, but the soldiers could not seem to cite the proper regulation prohibiting the offense. Daltoons hooked Alison by the arm, nudged her a few steps backwards, and then yanked her along as he bolted up the street.

When he realized the only things pursuing them were a few half-hearted oaths, he stopped.

"You could have gotten us killed or worse," he told Alison before releasing her.

"I won't be insulted by any British pig."

Daltoons was seized by a sudden fury and slapped her.

She slapped him back. And yet, immediately after the impulse, regret flooded into her eyes.

The lieutenant didn't notice it.

"You have a lot to learn," he said, storming towards Miss Tennison's. Alison followed, silent and somewhat chastened, if not wholly repentant.

The reader is no doubt familiar with the exploits of Mrs. Robert Murray, whose strategic introduction of tea and crumpets to the British leaders as their troops advanced up Manhattan island in the fall of 1776 allowed George Washington to escape their clutches. Though not as famous, surely Miss Tennison has served the Cause nearly as well. The refreshments this simple dressmaker serves are not intended for British officers, however, but for their women, and it is through their gossip that many an English plan has found its way back to General Washington. Her cookies, sweet as they may seem, are worse poison than bitter arsenic as far as the British war effort is concerned.

Nonetheless, some of Miss Tennison's habits might be said to be over-fastidious. It is not merely the insistence that her finely prepared clothes be worn a certain way, or that the cookies she serves be taken from the dish in a specific order. The old spinster also demands that her guests begin their visit by speaking to her cat, who must be addressed as Master Prickle. His health should be asked after, then his plans for the day. Anyone who does not follow this elaborate protocol is likely to be ushered from the house without pause.

Daltoons, already in a sour mood, bowed when Miss Tennison let him in. He then introduced, or attempted to introduce, Alison as a friend in need of a new dress.

"No, no, my dear young Mark, you have not greeted Master Prickle yet," insisted the spinster, pointing to the cat.

"A little light on cream, is she?" whispered Alison as Daltoons completed the mandatory ceremony. The cat did not bother waking from his nap to acknowledge the inquiries.

"Excuse me, dear," asked Miss Tennison. "Did you want cream?"

"If you please," answered Alison, rolling her eyes for Daltoons.

The old woman nodded approvingly. "Master Prickle was mentioning the same thing to me, a moment before you arrived."

"We have need of a dress for Alison," said Daltoons. "She needs a new disguise."

"I have a dress that would flatter you," said Miss Tennison. "My fitting room is right in the next room, behind the curtain."

Alison took her arm and walked with her a few steps toward the door. "Master Prickle advised me to proceed in breeches and a shirt, as if I were a boy. He says it is a safer disguise in a city full of soldiers."

"Yes, yes," nodded Miss Tennison thoughtfully. "I am sure he is right. Yes. He is quite clever."

"He is indeed," said Daltoons sarcastically behind her.

"You're not following us, are you?" Alison asked.

"Why not? If you want to dress as a boy, then I don't see why I can't."

She pulled the curtain across in his face.

* * *

After their escape, Jake and van Clynne made their way to an infirmary near Delancy's Square where Culper had planned a rendezvous. The bottom portion of the hospital was filled with actual cases, including a few British soldiers who could not be properly accommodated at the camp facilities, and in all likelihood would never recover. The top was completely taken over by the Sons of Liberty, who feted their rescued fellows with a hearty porridge and a few tasty pints. Van Clynne took one step from the stairs and immediately fell in with this group, anxious to quench his deep thirst.

Jake, meanwhile, sought out Culper, who was closeted with Robert Anthony, his rescued spy. Culper's office was an old storeroom, lined by long, shallow shelves. On one side various pans and jars sat waiting for use; on the other were blankets and bed linens. Culper had taken a piece of rough pine to use as a desk, and propped it against the shelf with the help of an old, narrow barrel that seemed to have been used to make cheese at one time. Perhaps that accounted for the smell of the room, whose paint blistered and hung in large flakes from the woodwork.

"Robert, this is our friend, Mr. Gibbs," said Culper as Jake entered. "He is seeking Howe's destination."

"You look nothing like your description," said Robert Anthony, shaking the agent's hand.

"I have been trying a new diet of late," said Jake. "What do you know of Howe's plans?"

"I was suspected before I could search General Clinton's office," said the spy dejectedly. "And there was no talk about Howe at all—except to call him an ass."

"No word of his destination?"

"None, though perhaps they were merely being careful. The guard had been tripled. I believe I was suspected from the moment I joined his staff."

"Yes," said Culper. "I fear we have a traitor somewhere among us."

"No hint at all?" asked Jake.

"I heard nearly every city mentioned, but only in passing. Which if any is Howe's target, I could not say. I heard of a letter being drawn to the citizens of Boston," he added, "but whether it is significant or not, who is to say?"

Jake nodded. Howe's knot remained untied. Had the British general concocted an elaborate charade for them, or was he truly attacking Boston?

Washington had told Jake to use his imagination, to create a solution. It was the sort of thing the general was always expecting, but in this case, Jake's Muse seemed to have taken herself off to another part of the continent.

Neither Anthony nor any of the other prisoners could be trusted. The same man who had informed on Anthony—and perhaps it had been Anthony himself—might now be among them.

Such doubt is the currency of a spy, who in constantly fooling others must always fear being fooled himself. Jake stood politely for a few minutes as Culper continued to ask Anthony questions about Clinton and his arrest, then excused himself to get something to eat.

As he might have predicted, he found Claus van Clynne holding court in the great room with several key members of the spy ring, commenting at length upon the quality of the small beer they had liberated from a Tory brewer.

"The hops are inferior, that is the problem," explained the squire in an authoritatively scientific voice. "They are ordinary hops. A true beer hop is a work of art, created over long generations by careful husbandry. It is a specific sort of creature, prepared by a knowledgeable craftsman."

"A Dutchman, no doubt," suggested Jake, who was well used to these arguments. The others were held in too rapt an attention to comment—and besides, they were busily investigating the quality of the liquid for themselves.

"It is not necessary to be Dutch to nurture a proper hop," allowed van Clynne. "But it helps."

"Dare I ask you how you came to be in New York?"

"I have already told you; I sensed you would require my assistance. Alas, in providing cover for your journey, I ran into a rather misguided fellow, whom I had to pretend to be beaten by in order to speed my arrival in New York."

"Pretend, eh?"

"You, sir, should be well acquainted with the ways of us secret agents, especially those of the Dutch stripe. We are continually pretending to be beaten, so that we may rise again. It is but one of our many tricks. And while we are on the subject, I wonder if you could assist me in preparing a writ for my misplaced notes. The sum is trifling, indeed, as far as Congress will be concerned, but there is a certain, shall we say nostalgic value for me, especially as I am still bereft of my land."

"Exactly how much money did you lose?"

"It is difficult to calculate a final sum," said the Dutchman. "But using British currency as a reference, I believe it would approximate fifty-seven pounds, two shillings, sixpence."

"You're taking the loss rather calmly."

"I am a calm man, reasonable to the core. I realize my losses will be made good."

"How much of the money was counterfeit?"

Donatello could not have painted a better picture of indignation. "I trade in only genuine currency. Four of my purses were stolen. Fortunately, my metal had been secreted away prior to the confiscation, or I would be beyond revival."

"You lost only paper money?"

"One takes certain precautions in difficult times," fussed van Clynne. "And money is money, let us not forget."

"Come, Claus, you seem to have an unquenchable supply of notes. What about the ones in your shoe? Or the lining of your vest?"

"Do you think me an alchemist, sir, who can conjure money from thin air?"

"No," said Jake. He left off the argument for two reasons: one, experience had shown it was useless to argue with the Dutchman when his mind was set, and two, Culper had dismissed Anthony and was signalling him from across the room. "Excuse me," he said.

Van Clynne rose so quickly behind him that he nearly upset the table.

"Claus, go on investigating your beer."

"We are an inseparable team," said the Dutchman, pulling his beard. "A machine that works as a set of wheels turning together. If it were not for me, how would you have escaped from the jail?"

"I suspect I would have run after the others."

"Balderdash, sir, pure balderdash."

Van Clynne continued to bluster so much that Jake tacitly conceded. Culper, however, had taken a dislike of the squire and demanded to know who precisely he thought he was and what he was doing.

A mistake, surely.

"Sir, I will have you know that my family's disdain for the British exceeds that of any other clan on the entire continent. Compared to Claus van Clynne, Patrick Henry is a poodle of flattery, a veritable fawn toward George and his German forebears."

"I'll not have a member of Congress insulted," thundered Culper.

At length, Jake was able to calm the situation by making van Clynne promise to keep his mouth shut in return for being allowed to stay. Neither the Dutchman nor Culper entirely agreed with the arrangement, but as Jake impressed them that time was of the essence, they eventually placed their mutual enmity on the shelf with the blankets.

Or perhaps with the pots, as it rattled in Culper's mouth as he told Jake the prospects for finding Howe's direction were limited. All of the members of the spy ring who had been liberated from prison must undergo a severe vetting before they could be trusted again.

"The evidence does point toward Boston," conceded Culper. "Such as it is."

"We need much more for the general. If he marches north, Philadelphia will be without protection. And if Howe were to show up off the Carolinas, the entire South would be lost to him."

"I have had the various city suppliers interviewed," said Culper. "But we have not gained anything."

"My friend Mr. Clayton Bauer would know," said Jake. "I should have gotten the information from him this morning."

"Bauer might know," said Culper, "if he has set up a network for Howe there. But he always has his guard with him. You did well to escape alive."

"His sister might help us," said Jake.

"How?"

"If I may offer a suggestion," started van Clynne.

"You may not," snapped Jake before turning to Culper. "She lost her son at Princeton. I doubt she would agree to tell us willingly, but she would do much to get information about him. We might be able to cobble together a deception."

"Too risky. Would Bauer be loose-lipped enough to tell his sister the greatest secret of the British army? If he even knows it? And then how would you use her to get to him? It's too complicated, Jake. There must be another way."

In any event, the mansion was as well guarded as any British headquarters; even if Jake would welcome a chance at gently persuading Lady Patricia to change her allegiance, there would be a host of men nearby to argue for loyalty. He ought to be able to puzzle out a plan to convince her—yet none would materialize in his brain, and it was much too dangerous to just knock on the door and count on his wits to carry him to an answer.

"There has to be someone in the city, not under constant guard, who would know where Howe is going," Culper said. "Someone who has been overlooked."

"If I—"

"Not now, Claus," said Jake.

With severe effort, the Dutchman clamped his mouth shut. He had given his solemn word not to speak, but this was almost more torture than he could bear.

At least the furrows on his companion's brow showed that he was working on a solution. With any luck, he would reach the conclusion van Clynne had already drawn without too much more delay. After all, it was only logical, and should be plain to all, even those not blessed with a Dutch intellect.

"I would think the engineering staff would know," suggested Jake to Culper.

"Surely. But they have gone with Howe."

"Not the entire staff. I heard them speaking of a member who is a relative at Bauer's."

Culper gave a snort of contempt. "If you are referring to the dissolute Lord Peter Alain, he wouldn't know Philadelphia from the local swamp. He was only shipped here to keep him from the London gutter."

"He's not an engineer himself?"

"He's barely in his teens. He has some skill at drawing, it is said, but no sense to back it. His father placed him here so he would be near his older brother, who was on Howe's staff. The brother was another man entirely, but he died of smallpox some months ago. Or so they say." Culper smiled. "We spent a bit of time trying to convert him. He would have been our best prize."

"Nonetheless, there may be papers that will give Howe away. Certainly he's had maps done."

"I don't know, Jake. Breaking into the engineer's office won't be easy."

"Much easier than a prison, I daresay. You have a map of the building?"

"I think we do."

"Personally, I think the whole plan is unnecessary,"

said van Clynne, no longer able to keep his peace. "I would take another approach entirely."

Before Jake could stop him, Culper asked, with some heat, what that might be.

"Well, sir. Now that you request my opinion, I will air it. General Howe is a man given to fine clothes, is he not?"

"What the hell is your point?"

"He has a tailor in the north ward, I believe, and undoubtedly consulted him before leaving. He would have the man prepare the latest fashions."

"Burning hell."

Van Clynne ignored Culper's comment and addressed Jake directly. "All we need do is ask the tailor what style of suits he made up. And as the tailor happens to be a fellow countryman with whom I have done some business—"

"I thought all Dutchmen hated the British."

"Alas, the man proves the rule by his exception. I believe he was dropped on the head as a small child, which may play a mitigating role."

"Thank you, but I believe we will proceed according to Jake's outline," said Culper. "Why don't you have some more beer? You look like you could use it."

"My associate always does things in the most strenuous way possible," tutted van Clynne, oblivious to the sarcastic tone. "It is effective in the long run, but much sweat is involved. Granted, you are dealing with a lord here, so he will be easy to fool. But still, an hour's stroll to the tailor's and I will have the solution."

"Go then," said Culper.

"I may, sir. I may."

"Claus—"

"First, however, I will accept your suggestion and see to my beer," declared van Clynne, opening the door.

"You'll pay for what you drink!" thundered Culper as he left. "Honestly, Jake, how do you stand him?"

"He has done me much service in the past," said

Jake. "His methods are unorthodox, but he has a knack of succeeding."

"I would think his success only the wildest coincidence."

Jake shrugged. He had learned long ago that there simply was no logical way to account for the Dutchman's ability to wrest victory from the most unlikely circumstances.

While the two men discussed other possibilities for discovering Howe's destination, van Clynne returned to the table to continue his study of hops. Alas, the men who had been eating here had dispersed, and taken most of the beer with them; the squire had to content himself with a half-filled tankard of the now slightly stale liquid.

No container is ever half-filled to a man such as van Clynne. He began to comment at length about the shallow nature of this pewter vessel, exposing the shortcuts modern craftsmen were taking with their work. His concentration was finally broken by the arrival of Alison, dressed in a fine suit of boy's clothes. She ran up the stairs and asked loudly where her father was.

"Who would your father be?" said van Clynne.

"The most noble soldier and spy in the entire Continental Army," she said, her voice puffing up with a pomposity that would put any parliament speaker to shame. "Working under the personal command of General Washington himself. He is worth five legions of troops, and his skills can save an entire army. He is resourceful and brave, and the British drop in fear at the mention of his name."

"You describe me perfectly," said van Clynne. "But I cannot claim to have sired you. Why are you dressed as a boy, when you are clearly a girl? Why is your hair fixed that way?"

"How do you know I am a girl?"

"The Dutch can tell such things."

"Alison, I'd almost forgotten about you," said Jake,

emerging from the office. "Culper is going to try and find you a job at the coffeehouse. In the meantime you can spend the night here. Why are you still wearing breeches? I thought Daltoons was going to find you a dress."

The lieutenant, just emerging at the stairs, shrugged and mumbled words to the effect that she had a mind of her own. Like any well-trained officer of the continental corps, he had long ago learned to choose his battles wisely.

"I don't want to work in a coffeehouse," said Alison. "Not while there is a war to be won."

"Listen to me, young lady." Jake caught her arm and held it tightly. "The first thing you must know about the army is that when a superior gives you an order, you follow it."

"I have heard this speech," remarked van Clynne into his cup. "A mission has but one chief."

"A mission has but one chief," continued Jake. "And I am it. You are a follower, and a follower follows orders."

"But, father—"

"I am not a father."

"Is that a blanket denial?" asked van Clynne. "Or a specific point?"

"You stay out of this."

"Gladly," said the squire as he rose. "I make it a habit never to interfere in a family quarrel."

"This is not a family quarrel."

"As you wish."

"This is deadly serious business, Alison," Jake warned. "I cannot play governess any longer."

"Governess! Is that what you think of me, a child?"

"You're young. And—"

"And a woman, is that it?"

"You're still a girl."

"I am fifteen, and as brave as any man. I want to fight for our freedom."

"No boy your age would be allowed to join the army."

"Piffle. I know many who have."

"Enough," said Jake. "Working for Culper is the same as working for General Washington. If you want to be treated like a soldier, act like one and follow orders."

"But, father—"

"And if you call me father one more time, I'll have you whipped before the entire company."

"They should like that, I expect," said the girl, folding her arms before her.

His C
less than
tee with
"I hop
suggeste
"And
guese ai
The u
venereal
tor need
nodded,
the serv
"My
gland,"
"How
Lord B
treated
before h
Bauer
Keen's c
well as t
individua
great de
had bee
event, th
nition ag
Thoug
fact trea
true nat
Bauer h
"I was
meet a f
"A fri
Assure
the impl
Keen pr
using his
noted. "
island. H

"I ar
man's
ately."
The
moving
hand fa
rolled
for this
him up
ing a y
"I w
captain
do you
"Th-
who re
shoe as
His
had be
times,
scendin
woken
somewh
walking
"You
carriage
tor. "Y
"Wh
"I an
staff. A
with th
knob I
have ar
would
in your
Similar
esty's s
four P.M
way: B

Twenty-one

Wherein, Dr. Keen makes his way back into our story.

*A*fter leaving the weaver, Major Dr. Harland Keen headed to the river near Tappan in as foul a mood as any man since Hudson found it necessary to concede his craft drew too much draft to pursue the passage to India up these waters. It was by now well past midnight. Any boat Keen spied would be his for the taking, but he feared some random guard or sentry near the docked ferries might cause complications. So he continued south to an area with less settlement, spotting a large, old flatboat as he drove his wagon over a pine-planked bridge spanning a creek that emptied into the river.

While Dr. Keen was a man on the other side of fifty and had spent much of his life in London besides, he was still in reasonable shape. His physique was aided by certain substances of his own concoction which he imbibed from time to time. He took one of these now—a small pill whose major ingredient was distilled from a member of the nightshade family, *Datura stramonium*—before climbing down from his carriage to inspect the craft.

This was nothing more than a serviceable vessel, of the type commonly used by farmers to carry wagons across the river. Several years had passed since its paint began chipping off, but otherwise the boat appeared sound and relatively solid; ropes were conveniently tied

"Where?"

Keen smiled. "He is quite a traveler, my friend."

"His name?"

"It is perhaps best not to say."

"When did he arrive?"

"I believe within the last day, though it is possible I am returning before him. He is the sort much given to delay. I am sure you know the type."

"Indeed. There was a man here this morning who washed up on shore. His name was Jake Stone or some other such thing, and he said nothing of you or of being a doctor."

"I would hope he would not."

"I think him a poor spy. He quickly gave himself away and even mentioned Bacon."

Keen smiled, not bothering to inform Bauer how completely he had been fooled. "I have had some association with General Sir Henry myself," said the doctor. "I would not think one of his men would give himself away."

"Bacon's intelligence people are not as smart as you believe. We are not enemies, General Bacon and I. Nor are our people. You are here, for example."

"Come now, surely you don't believe I am in his employ. I am assigned to the admiralty as a surgeon and doctor."

"Who rarely is aboard ship and is free to come and go as he pleases?"

Keen shrugged. "I wonder where my friend got to."

"Perhaps my sister Patricia could tell you more. She spent some time with him, seeing to his breakfast."

Keen stroked his chin thoughtfully, as if considering whether speaking to her was worth the effort. A few minutes later, he was listening as Lady Patricia recounted the entire meeting. Her continued reference to the man as being "unexceptional" told the doctor she felt otherwise.

"He was pleasant enough, but he seemed mainly interested in getting to the city. I encouraged him."

Keen nodded. Lady Patricia had changed from her morning white to a high-waisted gown whose yellow was the bright shade of spring's first daffodils. Though near forty, her face had a radiant, youthful smile, and her charm and grace could easily beguile a much younger man.

To say nothing of Keen himself. Her husband was a weakling, easily managed out of the way.

But duty called. Gibbs would not wait for him.

Perhaps Gibbs would return for Bauer, however. Had he been sent to assassinate him, then warned off by the guards? Clearly he was after the Tory—Keen's best path might well be to shadow the man.

"His eyes perked up when I mentioned the theater," said Lady Patricia. "I thought he was going to say something about it, but my brother insisted on dominating the conversation."

"The theater. You have been?"

"We are going this evening," said Lady Patricia. "After some supper and a few errands. We should leave soon, if we are going to eat."

"The theater in New York is surprisingly good," hinted Keen.

"So I have been telling my sister," said Bauer, his tone a harsh hint to Keen.

Which went unheeded.

"I go at every opportunity," said the doctor.

"Perhaps you would join us this evening," said Lady Patricia. Her tone was stiff. She did not truly want Keen to accompany them, but extended the invitation for form's sake. In England, it would be completely understood that she had meant the invitation for politeness only.

"I am in the mood for entertainment," said Keen. "Thank you, I accept your invitation."

"Lord Peter Alain is coming with us," said Bauer, hoping that would put Keen off.

On the contrary. The doctor saw quickly that the young fool might actually be useful. Keen had recently supplied him with certain medicines on account, and he would no doubt gladly make inquiries after Gibbs to discharge the debt. These would not attract the same attention as Keen's. Meanwhile, the doctor would stay close to Bauer in case an attempt was made at the theater.

To say nothing of being near Bauer's sister, reluctant though she might be. Keen rose, extending his arm. "M'lady, I am at your beck and call this evening."

"Come then, let me get my husband," said Lady Patricia, ruining the moment.

Twenty-two

Wherein, Claus van Clynne spies an old acquaintance.

The tailor whose shop Claus van Clynne sought was located not far from the tanning yards. It was a good distance from the Sons of Liberty hideout, and the Dutch squire would have readily accepted a ride, had one been proffered. It was not, nor was van Clynne a man who would readily condescend to hire a hack. He therefore contented himself with walking.

Despite his airs and general habits, the Dutchman could mount a considerable pace when motivated, and there was no motivation higher in his mind than the rightful return of his property. Having received a full briefing of the mission from Jake, van Clynne realized that this golden flask was for him a golden opportunity; Washington would react with joyful gratitude when the Dutchman rode into camp tomorrow with the news he was about to discover. There was little doubt but that the commander-in-chief would dispatch a company of men to immediately enforce van Clynne's claims on the purloined estate.

The squire's suit had been severely punished during his recent travails, and so he had a ready job with which to occupy the man and divert his attention. In addition, some months before van Clynne had arranged to supply the tailor with a good load of buttons at a considerable profit; he planned to broach the sub-

ject now in case a similar opportunity might present
itself.

It should be noted that, while his hate of all things
English remained strong and healthy, van Clynne's love
of profit was equally vigorous. If he would not sacrifice
the former for the latter, he would certainly endeavor
to shave or stretch the bounds of both to avoid conflict.

The Dutchman's course ambled across the foot of
Golden Hill in view of the harbor, though his personal
gaze consisted steadfastly of dry land. He had well
filled his month's quotient for wetness these past few
days. Though perhaps not as active as before the war,
the port still did a lusty business, and the usual mer-
chant vessels were greatly supplemented by military
ships and freelancers operating under what polite society referred to as letters of marque, and more simple
folk called pirates. The body of water between Manhattan and Long Island was dotted with masts; if it was
not quite the forest some commentators have compared it to, it was still a bit more than open meadow.

The red bricks of the tailor shop soon crowded into
the Dutchman's landlocked view, jutting toward the
street in a peculiarly lopsided fashion. Quinton van
Tassel had been speaking of repairing these for the
many years van Clynne had known him. One thing or
another had prevented him from letting the contract,
but he never failed to mention his resolve to fix the
bricks when he spoke with a customer, and today was
no exception. Never mind that the two men had not
seen each other for several months; the wall and the
failing foundation beneath it were the first topic
broached.

"The work must be done," opined Quinton without
explanation as van Clynne entered the shop, "but fifty
guilders is the lowest estimate, and too dear at half
that."

"I quite agree," said van Clynne. "The worst part is,
there is not a good Dutch mason left in the precinct to
do the work."

"Aye, nor do they make bricks properly any more," said Quinton. "The clay is defective."

"As is the water, a key ingredient. To say nothing of the trowels."

"Aye, the trowels. A sorry state." The tailor took a step back and surveyed van Clynne's suit. "A fine outfit, but in need of a patch and tuck," he declared. "And some pressing."

"No time for pressing," said van Clynne. "As for the repairs: how much?"

"Three guilders' worth."

"Outrageous! I could have an entire suit for half."

"Indeed. The cloth alone would come to six."

"I bought the suit for less than three guilders."

"Your father might have. It dates from then."

"For two guilders I'd expect a fine French weave, and see it pressed."

"You find me in a generous mood," said the tailor, extending his arm.

"I would need the work done on account," mentioned van Clynne after handing over the coat. "As I have recently been separated from my resources."

The tailor's face changed several shades as he promptly flung the coat back to van Clynne.

"I do not believe I heard you properly. Did the word 'account' pass your lips?"

"Indeed," lamented van Clynne. "But considering the affair of the buttons . . ."

"An arrangement to which I was forced only by severe want."

"As I am now."

The two men jabbed at each other for a good five minutes. In the end, Quinton agreed to accept four guilders for the work in two months' time, or five in three, along with a goodly supply of cloth at a reduced rate, when this could be arranged by mutual consent. He took up some thread and needle and promptly began the close stitch to repair the tear which ran along one pocket. In truth, his skills justified his fee, as he could put upwards of twenty-five stitches per inch. His stitches always looked more decoration than patch.

Van Clynne's efforts to elicit information about General Howe, offered as small bits of conversation as the man worked, were not nearly as efficient. In fact, they ended abruptly when the squire asked if the tailor had seen the general of late.

"Do not mention that damned bastard," exclaimed Quinton, dabbing the air with his needle. "He owes me twenty pounds since Christmas! Do you know the material I purchased for him? He looked at it and waved his hand, saying he did not like it now that he saw it. Now that he saw it! Did not like it! I have a near acre of chartreuse cloth. What shall I do with it?"

"A tent, perhaps?"

Further comments indicated that Howe had not been at the shop since midwinter. Van Clynne sank into his chair and began thinking how he might shave a half-guilder off his debt and sample some of Quinton's fine beer besides when he happened to glance out the window. A white-painted carriage with elaborate molding and inlay was just pulling up in front, heading a procession of mounted redcoat dragoons and a second carriage.

The squire staggered to his feet, his face white and his strength suddenly sapped.

"What's wrong, Claus?"

"I, er, seem to have something caught in my throat," said the squire. "Would you have any water?"

"Not in the shop."

"Well then, let me use your back door."

"My back door?"

"And I'll take my coat. The repairs look quite excellent."

"But what about the rip at the sleeve?"

"What is a small tear among friends?"

Van Clynne's sudden interest in leaving was due entirely to the similarity of the carriage outside with one owned by Major Dr. Harland Keen, a man known to van Clynne as a rather dubious doctor and member of the British secret department. At one memorable juncture, Keen had subjected him to a full-body bloodletting, covering nearly every inch of his skin with leeches. The Dutchman liked a sanguinary experience as much as the next man, but this had been a bit extreme.

Van Clynne had taken Jake's word that Keen had drowned when he went over the falls. But who then was the man descending from the coach, his white hair pressed back, his coattails flaring with typical British audacity?

"I have a great need of your back door," said van Clynne, coughing as loudly as he could. "Quickly!"

"Don't choke to death. Come."

Van Clynne just managed to whisk through the door into the back room as the bell attached to the front door clanged as it opened. The tailor hesitated, but van Clynne pushed forward, confident that he would find the way on his own.

He had only just crossed from the back into the side alley when he realized he had left his gray-toned black beaver hat behind.

As a general rule, Claus van Clynne was not overly sentimental. He was, however, especially fond of his hat, which had accompanied him through considerable travail and was fairly unique in its appearance and construction.

Which meant it must surely be recognized by the all-too-perceptive Keen.

Easing up the side alley, just out of view of the mounted escort that remained in the street, van Clynne heard his recent host fill the room with honey-coated praise of his Loyalist and British guests.

"My good Earl Buckmaster," he heard Quinton say, "your suit, sir, is ready as promised. You see that I have taken less than a full day. It was an honor to prepare it for you. I think no tailor in this city so honored. And you will note the handsome stitching."

To relate more would surely sicken the reader nearly as much as it did van Clynne. It developed that the tailor was familiar with Keen, whom he presented with a shirt ordered several fortnights before, "and preserved, sir, against your return to our shop."

"Yes, well, hurry with it. We have several more stops, and my sister must see to a dress," said Bauer. He turned and addressed his brother-in-law and Keen. "Even with my man holding our seats, we must arrive at the theater before General Clinton. He creates such a god-awful scene. With luck, the little fop Alain will have finished eating before we get to the engineering office. His table manners are enough to turn the stomach upside down."

Van Clynne was starting to think the hat might escape notice—and be recovered—when he heard the doctor's distinct voice through the window. It was close enough to make his heart thump like the broken arm of a windmill smacking against the ground.

"This hat. Whose is it?"

A simple question, surely. But those are always the most dangerous.

"The h-hat," stuttered Quinton. "Well, some customer must have left it. Honestly, I am not sure. Would you like it? I can let you have it for a low price—no, let me give it to you. Yes, take it as a present."

Silence followed. Van Clynne imagined Keen taking up the beaver and examining it.

"I recently was acquainted with a fellow who had a hat very similar," said the doctor, the restraint in his voice obvious even outside. "Had I not seen him burn in a building, I would swear this was his."

"There are many hats like this," said the tailor nervously. "It is a common style."

"The owner was a Dutchman," said Keen. He was no longer bothering to control his venom; van Clynne felt his own body fairly warmed by it. "And do not lie to me or your tongue will be tread on by half the British soldiers quartered at King's College."

"Now that you mention it," answered the tailor, his voice trembling. "It does seem familiar."

The squire did not tarry to hear himself betrayed. He swept from the alley, bowed quickly at the mounted guard, and walked with as much balance as he could muster southward. He was nearly a block away when Keen's temper rose in a mighty fit; van Clynne could hear the sound of crashing tables and glass as he turned the corner and began running with all his might.

Van Clynne arrived at the infirmary just as Alison was trying to persuade Culper that she could serve the Cause as one of his agents in town instead of "visiting" a relative of his in Westchester, as he suggested. The girl had taken a flintlock pistol from the armory in the medicine closet. Seated at the large pine table that held the middle of the second floor wardroom, she was demonstrating her knowledge of its working parts by stripping it with the aid of a very large and pointed knife.

"Blindfold me, if you wish," she told the spymaster, waving the knife as if it were a harmless twig. "I will do it again. I can do it behind my back."

"It's a very useful skill," allowed the patriot leader. "I'm sure we will find great use for it. But first, we will have to make some arrangements for you."

"I don't want to be sent behind the lines."

"Quickly, there is no time to waste," blustered van Clynne, bursting up the unguarded stairwell so fast he nearly broke three spokes on the oaken baluster. "Where is Jake?"

"He's gone to the engineer's office," said Culper. "What business is it of yours?"

"A great enemy of ours is loose in the city," said van Clynne. "Quickly, he must be warned."

"Who is this enemy? What are you talking about?"

"Keen, Doctor Quack Keen, a man given to the most obnoxious poisons and a disgrace to his profession. He is heading for this Alain fellow, this engineering lordship. If Keen finds Jake there he will cover his body with leeches and set him on fire, and then prepare a proper torture."

"Jake told my men Keen was dead."

"Believe me, sir, he is very much alive. And I distinctly heard him mention Lord Alain."

"I've already sent the last men I can spare on other jobs."

"I'll go!" shouted Alison, starting for the stairs.

Culper grabbed her by the shoulder. "You're not going anywhere."

"You said I could serve the Cause. Here is my chance."

"I intend on warning Jake myself," said van Clynne. "I will enter the house under other pretense and sneak into the office to warn him away. I require only swift transportation, and a map of the place, if possible."

"There are two floors," said Culper hastily, necessity forcing him to put aside his doubts about the Dutchman. "Jake was to sneak upstairs into the offices while Alain was downstairs eating."

"I will warn him."

"How?" asked Alison. "You won't be able to climb up the side of the building."

"I will go in the front door, child, on some simple pretext," said van Clynne. There were no hatchets handy, and so he had to settle for the pistol Alison had just assembled. "There is no need for me to burglarize the place."

"Then you need an assistant to sneak upstairs," she said, volunteering. "I can easily slip away on some pretext."

The Dutchman threw her a doubtful look.

"Please," she said, taking up his hand. "Let me prove myself. I am very brave."

"I cannot dawdle."

"Let's go then," she said, running to the door.

"I will find Daltoons and have him organize reinforcements," said Culper as van Clynne followed her down the stairs with a series of oaths.

"A girl and a Dutchman," the spymaster added as they disappeared through the door. "What will Washington send me next?"

Twenty-three

Wherein, Jake does some impromptu carpentering.

*A*t roughly the same time that Claus van Clynne spied the crooked red bricks at the front of the tailor shop, a carpenter was walking in his oversized smock and apron down the city's east ward. He cut a tangled path toward the wharf used by the ferry from Brooklyn, smiling from beneath his broad-brimmed, if somewhat tattered, felt hat. Whistling a jaunty air—it might be "British Grenadiers," it might be "Yankee Doodle"—he headed back up the hill and, just as supper hour approached, found a large, dilapidated former creamery and set up shop on its rear porch.

It might be said that his chisel was strong but his saw not half as sharp as typical of the breed, for though he worked steadily for half an hour, he made so little progress that many a journeyman would have hailed him as an accomplished master.

The significance of this porch for our story is that it lay directly behind the painted brick building used by the British engineers to house some of their more important drawings and least important staff. The carpenter, who soon gave up his work to slip a long narrow bar and a pistol beneath his smock and apron, was none other than the well-disguised hero of our tale, Jake Gibbs.

Besides the costume and hat, Jake had added a wide bandage to his chin, wrapping it once around the bottom quarter of his face to obscure the rounded, often smiling jaw that was among his best features. Rubbing it, he made his way up the alley, crouching behind a barrel as the lone guard assigned to watch the building made his rounds in front.

A young maple tree, tall but too slender to provide more than token support, stood nearby. A window with a solid-looking brick ledge and frame would give Jake a good boost to the second story, where his metal shim ought to make short work of the hall opening.

The guard's pace wasn't exactly up to parade-field specifications. It was more a mopey shuffle, difficult to time exactly but ripe with the sort of lackadaisical effort that promised the alley would be unsupervised for long stretches. In addition, the guard had recently acquired a new set of boots, and so his approach was easy to avoid—the leather soles made a sharp sound as they scraped the pavement stones. As they became louder, Jake dropped to his knees and made sure his body was well behind the barrel.

Once the scrapes began heading in the other direction, Jake rose and peered in the window. As Culper's diagram had predicted, it looked in on the dining room. The table had been set, which meant that the secretary would soon be down for supper.

Jake was about midway up when the guard's soles began scraping again in his direction. He hurried upward, reaching the window that according to Culper opened into a small storage room.

Unfortunately, Culper's information was wrong. It opened into an upstairs hallway, in full view of the office where his lordship worked.

Or rather, the office where he was just now emerging.

Jake ducked away so quickly his grip loosened and his fingers slipped from the ledge. The distance to the ground was not enormous, but he still met the earth with a resounding smack, his legs groaning from the unexpected shock.

Jake groaned as well. He fell to his back, holding his breath as the scraping from the front of the house stopped.

Then resumed with much greater vigor.

The Segallas, cleaned and reloaded after the plunge in the river, was secreted at the top of his right sock. As he reached for it, the guard appeared over him and ordered him to stand upright.

"I am trying," said Jake. "But I have had a wicked bee sting here, and cannot even stand up." He rolled over, scratching at his leg as if injured—and hoping for a chance to remove the pistol.

"Never mind that," said the sentry. "Explain who you are."

"I am a poor carpenter," said Jake. "As you can see from my tools on the porch."

"What is a carpenter doing working on a brick building?"

"Begging your pardon, sir, but I am working on that porch there," gestured the spy. "A man named Baxter hired me to do some work. I was chased here by a nest of bees."

"Baxter? That building belongs to an old woman named Fife."

Jake grimaced. "Baxter was the name of the fellow who hired me." He rose. "Jesus, the damn thing is back," he said, swatting at the air.

The soldier was not fooled. But Jake was able to duck the butt of his gun as he swatted. He pulled his pry bar from his belt and smashed it across the man's face. A harder smash to his skull knocked him senseless.

Jake took off his apron and used its strings to truss the redcoat. Pulling him back to the porch, he fastened him below the steps, blindfolding and gagging him so he could not call out when he awoke. Jake judged it would be several hours, if not longer, before he managed to free himself.

By the time the patriot returned to the window, Alain was entering the dining room. Jake gripped the brickwork and hoisted himself quickly upwards on the side, his fingers clinging to the smooth clay like barnacles to a ship's bottom. He was at the upstairs hall window in a trice, pushing his slender metal bar between the sill and the sash and gently nudging it upwards. In the next second, he had slipped inside, confident that he would soon be on his way back to Washington with the whole story of Howe's pending invasion.

Twenty-four

Wherein, Jake examines diverse maps, drawings, and a maid's fine lips.

The chestnut floor planks were covered with a thin, fairly worn carpet, which provided little cushion for Jake's footsteps. With the first creak, he realized he had best proceed barefoot, and leaned against the wall to gingerly unbuckle and remove his shoes.

His destination was only a few feet away, not far from the top of the stairs. The house's owner, a hearty patriot, had taken the precaution of removing not only his furniture but many of his finely trimmed doors and shutters before fleeing. Thus anyone coming up the stairs would have an unobstructed view of the office, with Jake inside.

There was nothing to do but pray that wouldn't happen. Jake tiptoed across the hallway, shoes in one hand and cocked pistol in the other. Tucking the shoes by the door, he posted his gun on a chair within easy grasp and sized up the office.

Culper's intelligence had pegged the room as the most likely place plans for an invasion or other helpful records might be kept. In truth, this was but a guess based on its use by the senior staff, and Jake realized at a glance that only a thorough search would confirm or deny it. The place was hardly a model of bureaucratic efficiency. There were three small desks, each covered with a variety of books, loose papers and sketch upon sketch of maps. The center of the room was filled by a large table, whose smooth wood surface was neatly overhung by several layers of charts. Important papers and maps were stored without obvious order throughout the room, and indeed, throughout the entire house. The rumors of English efficiency were, in this department at least, greatly exaggerated.

Jake moved first to the central table; the pile proved a collection of various fanciful plans of world cosmology, replete with mermaids, phoenixes, and centaurs— obviously the sort of project a young subordinate filled idle hours with while his boss was far away. Much pain had been taken with several of these; on one edge of the table were tacked a series of studies for heads and faces. Jake had gained an appreciation for art while in Oxford for his schooling, and realized immediately that these drafts displayed considerable dexterity.

They were of little importance now, however. He turned his attention to the documents and books on the desks, going through them as rapidly as possible without creating too much noise. For the most part, the papers were plans for bridges and bivouacs that could be put into use anywhere on the continent; not one showed any geography or features that might hint where Howe was heading.

Jake's inspection was suspended by a knock so loud on the door below that it felt as if it were made at his shoulder. This was followed by a familiar *harrumph*, a not altogether pleasant clearing of the throat, and a general "hello there." The heavy steps of a butler sounded up the stairwell as van Clynne's voice boomed out, inquiring after his "good friend, the distinguished Lord of Marquedom, Count Alain, peer to the realm."

Had any other patriot knocked on Alain's door, Jake would have immediately guessed that trouble was afoot. But his long experience with van Clynne led him to believe that the Dutchman, as usual, was merely showing his face where it did not belong. Jake cursed silently, then told himself that at least van Clynne's loud voice would distract the servants and his lordship

from any noise he might make upstairs. Jake returned
to the desks and began pulling open the drawers to
examine their contents.

He was into the second desk when he heard a light
foot treading on the stairs. There was no chance to
escape; his only option was to hide next to the door
and hope whoever was coming up the stairs passed by.

Vain hope. Jake crushed himself against the wall as
the room filled with the light scent of pot marjoram. A
woman in her early twenties followed. She looked
down and asked aloud where the shoes had come from.

"They're mine, I'm afraid," said Jake, putting his
hand quickly over her mouth. As she began to struggle,
he found it necessary to use both arms to keep her still;
as it was necessary to cover her mouth, he used the
only device handy—his mouth.

Her lips were quite soft and surprisingly compliant,
and in a moment he felt her body slacken into surrender.

Claus van Clynne, meanwhile, made his way through
the house with characteristic bluster. The butler who
answered his knock gave the bearded, russet-clad visitor a quizzical look, as if he had opened a door and
come face-to-face with a ghost of the island's past.

The Dutchman saw the man's apprehension as an
invitation to proceed.

"Good evening, sir. Claus van Clynne at your service, here to express my severe condolences to his fine
young lordship. His marquess-ship is at home, I assume."

"I—"

"Allow me to introduce my young assistant, Al
Stone." Here van Clynne swept toward Alison, still on
the doorstep. "Despite his tender age, my friend is
quite a lion with arithmetic. He can multiply the nines
and even the odd eight as if they were tens, which is a
considerable talent in business. Hmmm, do I detect the
scent of roast capon?"

"It is quail, sir."

"Quail!" thundered van Clynne. "Properly prepared quail will triple the life span!"

Van Clynne led Alison and the attendant to the dining room, where the young lord was seated at the table with the air of a North Sea walrus awaiting his mollusk. Ever mindful of his manners, the Dutchman put his hand to his head, then belatedly realized he no longer had a hat. No matter—he swept an imaginary one off his head with the smooth gesture of a dancer opening a show for His Majesty himself.

"Lord Peter Alain! Greetings and cheery health, your most lordly lordship!"

The British ships advancing against the Spanish armada showed more reserve than van Clynne demonstrated as he swooped in on the young lord. Alain's only protection was an elaborate candelabra and a half-finished bowl of onion soup, his first course, resting on a pure silver plate.

"Claus van Clynne," said the Dutchman. "I am sure you are much too young to remember me. Your father appointed me to oversee his interests in the colonies. An excellent decision on his part, if I do say so myself. What is that you're eating?"

"That is odd," said the young man. "My father had no interest in the colonies."

"Of course not," said van Clynne with a dismissive wave of his hand. "Once I gave him my advice, he saw it would be foolish to even entertain the idea. Managing property and trade over an ocean—bad business, son, bad business. Your lordship, that is. Al, take your hat off as a sign of respect for his honor. Bend low—that's a good boy."

Alison did as she was told, which helped her suppress a certain look of displeasure at van Clynne's tactics. In truth, she rather shared Culper's opinion of van Clynne. The portly Dutchman was of a type her innkeeping father used to complain of as being late on bills and doubly long on gab. But the girl would have obeyed Satan himself to help rescue Jake.

Alain's attitude was one of unmitigated confusion. Unlike his older, now deceased brother, he had never been allowed much access to his father's affairs. Though he deemed it unlikely, he hadn't the slightest idea whether the Dutchman before him actually had anything to do with them. But he did like the slight blush on the youth's cheeks, and saw in Al's face the inviting naivete of a young schoolboy, barely his junior. So he made a gesture that the servant behind him understood to mean two more places should be set at the table.

"I would shake your hands, sirs," he told them politely, "but there are many diseases about and we must take precautions. My man will bring you a bowl to cleanse yourselves."

"No need," declared van Clynne as he pulled out his seat. "We were well advised of Your Lordship's precautions and washed before coming. We even took baths."

Lord Peter raised an eyebrow, but nonetheless ordered the butler into action. The servant did not exactly fly about his business. Nor would "glide" be the appropriate word. He moved with the deliberate speed of a blade of grass growing on a warm spring day as he faded into the bowels of the house.

"I see, my lord, that you are quenching your thirst with Madeira," said van Clynne after a short pause. "An excellent choice, as the water in this city is notoriously putrid. But if I might point out, as holder of, er, a lordly estate—"

"I am marquess of Bulham," said the young lord haughtily, before adding in a sweeter voice to Al, "You may call me Lord Peter."

Alison, unsure what the soapy tone was meant to signify, nodded.

"Your rank, my lord, gives you even more reason to forgo the Portuguese rot and drink the ancestral drink," continued the Dutchman. "It is only appropriate."

"Which ancestral drink would that be?"

"Ale, my lord. Fine ale. A British drink. Surely your father told you of the great contributions beer has made to your position?"

"My father was a teetotaler. I'm surprised you didn't know that."

Van Clynne ignored that bit of inconvenient intelligence, waving dismissively at the wine. "It never ceases to amaze me how a race can go to all the trouble of defeating an enemy and then sip their liquid. Imagine the great laughter as they trod on the grapes."

"To my knowledge we have not been at war with the Portuguese for some time."

"Would you call Spain a friend, my lord?"

"Of course not."

"And are the Portuguese not close to the Spanish? Twins of the same isthmus? Would you step on Romulus's foot and expect Remus to remain unaffected?"

"Your friend makes a good argument, though not much sense," Alain told Alison in a confidential tone. "He seems to have learned his logic in Circe's cave, rather than Plato's. Are you familiar with the ways of the Greek philosophers?"

Alison shook her head. Lord Peter smiled broadly.

"You would like the ways of the Academy, I believe. I will be departing for the theater with some friends following our refreshments. Would you wish to join us?"

"Well, my lord, besides extending my respects, I am here with a business proposition," said van Clynne, reminded by the reference to the play that Keen was on his way. "You have heard, no doubt, that the Seneca control a large store of salt in the upper province."

"I had not heard of that," said the young lord.

"Oh yes, the finest store of salt in the entire New World. Now, with the proper financial backing, we would be able to exploit—what was that?"

"What was what?"

"The noise upstairs. Al—quickly, go and investigate."

"I heard nothing."

"Tut, tut, my lord, there are spies everywhere. One has only to mention the word salt and they come rushing from the woodwork, like worms from a rotten ship's hull. A quick profit is a ready goad, as your father used to say."

"My father said that?"

"Al, quickly—up the stairs and investigate. I will talk no further of business until we are sure this house is secure."

"It was probably just the maid."

"Just the maid! If I had threepence for every business deal scuttled by a maid, I should have retired long ago. Up with you, Al."

"Perhaps I should go along," said Lord Peter. "I will fetch a few of my cigars while I am upstairs."

"My lord," said van Clynne, putting his hand on the young man's arm and easing him back to his seat. "There is a certain order to things. Even at your tender age, I am sure you understand that we must attend to our business before smoking. The Indians sometimes skip the order, and it leads them into all sorts of mischief."

While Alain tried to puzzle out van Clynne's meaning, Alison walked briskly to the stairs. She knew she must not run, yet felt her heart pounding fiercely. It was all she could do to control herself. Until a few days ago, bravery had been a child's game, played out in her mind as she drifted off to sleep, her eyes shut to the consequences of failure. But her father's last gasp came to her now, and Fear in the Gorgon's guise walked at her shoulder. With every step she took, the serious danger she faced stroked its icy fingers of dread across her neck.

*　*　*

As the servant surrendered into his arms, Jake deepened his kiss, pressing the young woman's ample bosom to his chest with a degree of pressure that might crush a bear, yet mingled with a softness that would tame a screaming baby. He slipped his fingers around the soft back of her neck, then with a flick closed his forefinger and thumb so sharply the woman fainted.

If asked, Jake would say that he had learned the complicated technique from an old Iroquois warrior. That was far from the truth; the confederation, after all, rarely sanctions the kissing of its enemies. The fainting grip was practiced as a parlor trick among certain London swains—but there is no time now to dredge up details of our hero's past.

The spy pulled the unconscious servant with him to the side of the doorway as footsteps approached from the stair. Holding her with one arm, he reached to his belt and drew his pistol, intending to wield it as a hammer on the newcomer's head—not as fancy a technique as the one he had just practiced, to be sure, but just as effective. Jake's hand was already proceeding downward when he realized the dark body in front of him had a familiar shape.

Alison ducked the blow by throwing herself to the floor.

"What are you doing here?" Jake said. He let the servant slip to the floor as he helped Alison up.

"Looking for you," said Alison. "If I knew you were having your way with a tart, I would not have come to rescue you."

"Watch your mouth, girl."

"Boy, if you please. I am in disguise. Your Dutch friend has a very peculiar way for a spy. He does not act like one at all."

"I'm glad to see you're such an expert on the subject. What the hell are you doing here?"

"We are here to warn you. Dr. Keen is coming."

"Keen? He drowned in the river above Albany. I watched him die myself."

"Not according to the Dutchman. He says he's seen him, and he's on his way here right now. You're to get out immediately." Alison shook her head. "That lord fellow is a queer duck."

"Quickly—go to the window and stand lookout while I finish going through these papers."

"But—"

"Do it."

Jake found a bundle of sketch maps with fresh ink piled at one end of the floor. The large pile was inviting, but he postponed his search through them, instead pulling open the books on the desk. He had just realized one was a thin ledger book showing payments to different informants when Alison tapped him on the arm.

"A carriage has drawn up."

"Downstairs," he hissed as he rushed to the front window to see. "Tell Claus—no, wait. Too late. It is Keen, damn him, back from the dead. He's already at the steps." Jake pulled Alison to the door. "Ordinarily I never kill a man twice, but in his case I will have to make an exception."

Twenty-five

Wherein, Jake takes further liberties in Liberty's name.

"Y̲ou'll have to go out the hall window," Jake told Alison, grabbing the ledger book. He reached into his sock and pulled out the Segallas. "Take this pocket pistol. Do you know how it works?"

Alison nodded. "I twist the barrels around for two more shots?"

"If anyone tries to stop you, pull both triggers and then run as fast as you can. I'm going to drop down this book to you; it's very important. The alley here," he said, leading her to the window, "connects with an old building. Run through it, then meet me at the infirmary. Hurry."

"But your friend is still downstairs."

"I will see to him," said Jake. "Come on."

Even hanging from the window ledge, it would be a long jump for the girl. She looked down and hesitated.

"But, Jake, if he really is in danger—"

"I'm glad to see that you have changed your opinion about him," Jake told her. "I will hold you out and drop you. Roll on your feet like a cat when you hit the ground."

"I know how to jump," she said indignantly.

"Out, then. And don't wait for me."

"But—"

"General Washington is waiting." Jake took her and dangled her out, then watched with some satisfaction as she fell with an "ooooff!" and immediately righted herself. He tossed the book down, then yelled "Go!" as she started to run toward the old creamery.

Jake's shout did not go unnoticed downstairs, though by now it was only one of a panoply of noises whose origin and meaning were a great puzzle to Alain. Van Clynne, of course, realized that his friend must have taken the warning to heart and was even now making good his escape.

Which meant that, despite the perfect moistness of the meat and the excellent—nay, superior—stout the butler had produced, it was time for him to exit as well.

"Well, my lord, I see by the clock that I must go," he said, rising with some reluctance.

"What clock? Herman, what the hell is going on up there? Where is Jennifer? Van Claus, what is your assistant doing, rogering the maid? Herman, go and see what the blasted hell is going on."

"Undoubtedly, my lord, I have overstayed my welcome." Van Clynne reached back to his plate and pocketed a healthy piece of the quail.

"You are not going anywhere," said Alain, whose voice had taken on a screeching tone. "Herman! Jennifer!"

"There is a knock on the door, sir," said the butler, shuffling forward. "Should I see to it?"

"Yes, see to it. What the hell was that thud? Was that a bird by the window?"

"I wonder," asked van Clynne, the color suddenly run from his face, "is there a back exit?"

"What?"

"Obviously, the Sons of Liberty are launching an attack," said the Dutchman hurriedly. "You secure the upstairs, and I will see to the back."

"But—"

"Quickly, sir. Young Al—"

"Yes, he is unprotected upstairs," said Alain, suddenly snapping up and dashing from the room.

* * *

Jake ran back to the office to grab the maps. He removed the silk ribbon from his ponytail, only to find the black cloth was not nearly long enough to hold all the papers. He tied together what he could and ran back to the window.

He had just reached it when his lordship began mounting the steps. The patriot spy went out in a head-first tumble, barely managing to tuck his legs below himself as he hit the ground.

It was a moment before he could recover sufficiently to pick up the bundle of maps and take the pistol from his belt. Alain had either missed his jump or gone to attend to the maid; Jake took advantage of this reprieve to sneak to the dining-room window. He reached over with his hand and flung it open, and in the next second jumped up, gun ready—

And came face to beard with van Clynne, wearing one of his more quizzical looks.

"Thank you, sir," said the Dutchman. "But I already am armed."

"This way. Keen is on the steps outside, with Bauer and his brother-in-law."

"The butler will be several years letting them in," said the Dutchman. "Lord Peter has gone upstairs. I assume the young lady is with you?"

"She's halfway back to the infirmary by now."

"Excellent. All according to my plan. I will proceed to the rear exit, through the kitchen."

"Hurry," said Jake, realizing the window was too small to accommodate van Clynne's girth. "Go through the old creamery behind the building."

"I have already made quite a study of the layout, with your friend Culper's assistance," sniffed van Clynne. "See to your own escape, sir. Mine is as good as done."

"Give me that case there," Jake told van Clynne, pointing at a portfolio. He placed the maps and pistol inside so he would appear just one more messenger on the street. "Get back in one piece, Claus," said Jake as he snapped the window shut. He noted with some satisfaction that the Dutchman left the dining room with more than his usual alacrity, then crept to the front of the alley.

The doctor succeeded in pounding his way inside the door just as a fresh coach pulled up beyond Keen's to the very head of the alley. This carried Lady Patricia, who had been detained at the dress shop. Jake crossed to watch her alight as she stepped from the carriage prematurely into the street.

Directly into the path of an oncoming wagon.

Dropping his portfolio, the patriot caught Lady Patricia around the waist an instant before she plunged into the horses' path. He swept her around, ignoring the deep splatter of muck that splashed on his back. No gentleman of London or Paris bowed as neatly as he when depositing her safely on her feet at the side of the road.

"You—what are you doing here? And dressed as a carpenter?"

"I was about to ask you the same thing," said Jake. "Was that Dr. Harland Keen who just went into the house?"

"The doctor was just looking for you," said Lady Patricia.

"Indeed," said Jake. "But I think I will delay our appointment a while longer."

"Jake—"

There was a certain note in her voice, a mixture of affection and apprehension. Whether it came because she thought he meant to dally with her, or whether it was intended to imply she wanted him to, was impossible to tell. In any event, her brother and husband were now coming down from the doorstep, and Jake decided he needed some expedient to distract their attention.

At least that was his official reason for taking Lady Patricia back into his arms and kissing her.

Her reaction differed from the maid's only in that

her lips pressed back sharply. In fact, despite the surrounding circumstances, this was quite a pleasant and lasting kiss.

"What in hell are you doing with my sister!" thundered Clayton Bauer, outrage mixing with surprise as he realized the fellow before him was Bacon's agent and Keen's friend.

"Thanking her for her assistance this morning," said Jake. "And saving her life."

Clayton's reaction was absolutely on key, but Lady Patricia's husband had not yet registered a complaint. Perhaps he had missed the kiss.

So naturally, Jake repeated it. This time there was token resistance, though he could tell from the way her hand pressed at his side that it was for appearance's sake only.

The dragoons strained from their horses to catch the show. A few gripped the swords in their saddle sheaths, but the bulk wore grins that betrayed admiration for the bold young man who had so overt a manner—and such fine taste in lips.

"Aren't you going to stop him?" Clayton demanded of his brother-in-law.

The earl was one of those men so accustomed to hiring others to do their work for them that they cannot take a stand for themselves, even when confronted by the most vigorous insult. He mumbled some words of shock in a soft voice.

"Stop," said Lady Patricia. It was the mildest rebuke imaginable, but it was enough for her brother, who stepped up and grabbed Jake by the arm.

"You will leave off, sir," he said. "You will cease and desist!"

"And who are you to order me about?"

Jake squared his shoulders as he confronted the man. Clayton was several inches shorter, with a waist that betrayed many second and third helpings at the feasts the British had thrown this past winter. Still, he had the fiery aspect of a self-made man, and the righteousness of his cause propelled his words.

"Do not think that because you are under His Majesty's protection that you do not have to observe the proprieties," said Clayton. "Why is everyone in Bacon's employ so damned arrogant?"

"It may be that we are arrogant," returned Jake, "but I understand now why all of your men bear a common idiocy."

The Tory's face twisted with anger and he turned to his brother. "Here, William, here is my glove. Demand satisfaction for his insult to your wife."

"I do not think—"

"No, Clayton. It was nothing." Lady Patricia's trembling voice revealed her great distress. She seemed torn by many conflicting emotions: admiration for her brother, a quiet contempt for her husband, and a definite desire for Jake.

"Then I demand satisfaction," said Clayton, slapping Jake's cheek with the fingered end of his glove. "For the family name and my sister's honor."

Jake stood still in the street for a second, playing the moment for its full drama. The entire world grew silent around him. He saw from Clayton's expression that the Tory was just now realizing the full implications of his challenge.

"You will lend me your glove, as I do not have my own," said Jake with all the dignity of a Spanish don.

The ritual proceeded quite properly. Clayton gave the place and the time: two days hence, at dawn, on the shore just north of Perth, a no man's land where the technicalities of the law would not follow.

Jake had the option of weapons and conditions. He briefly considered swords—surely this would please the Tory mentality—but changed his mind as a sharp rejoinder occurred to him.

"I choose pistols," said Jake. "I should not like your poor sister to cry over your slashed face in the coffin."

"You will supply them."

"It is only a matter of choosing which set," said Jake.

He smiled wryly, imagining the Tory spending the whole next day practicing for a showdown which would never come. His smile broadened to the widest grin as he swept down in a bow and bid the company—and especially Lady Patricia—a fond adieu. Retrieving the case with the maps and pistol, he began walking back toward the infirmary with the air of a man who had just snuck from under Death's nose without so much as dusting his clothes.

Twenty-six

Wherein, Claus van Clynne is discovered to have dawdled longer than expected.

While Jake had seen Claus van Clynne heading anxiously for the exit, it could not be said with any veracity that the squire made a very quick departure. He did, indeed, head straight for the back door, proceeding through the kitchen into the rear hallway and back rooms with all the haste commonly associated with a windstorm. Alas, upon his arrival at the rear of the building he discovered the passage had been given over to storage—and his escape was blocked by a broad cubbyhole stuffed with all manner of maps.

Cursing, he picked through the papers to see if the way beyond them might be cleared. It could not, but as he loudly cursed his frustration, his eyes happened upon the drawing in his hand, and he immediately retracted his angst. He pulled a second map out and examined it with great interest, temporarily losing all concern for the world around him.

Only one thing could divert the Dutchman's attention from the danger Keen posed—the prospect of retrieving his purloined estate. For the maps in his hands were copies of ancient Dutch documents, and clearly showed his birthright. The name was misspelled, with an extra "e" at the end, but here finally was perfect and legal proof of his family's ownership.

There is no describing the joy that enveloped the Dutchman at that moment. He felt as if every one of his ancestors had gathered round and begun pounding his shoulders while preparing the most glorious brown ale for celebration.

The loud growl of Keen's voice in the foyer brought him back to his immediate predicament. He took the maps and returned to the kitchen, searching for a way out. Here he found the windows filled with provisions for the lord's supper and snacks. Only a small portion of the top quadrant remained of each, not enough to allow van Clynne's dream of escape to take flight.

He picked up a large butcher's knife from the table, then with a firm resolve, shouldered open the door and proceeded toward the front, determined to fight his way clear to his land and destiny.

Miraculously, the front hall was empty. Keen had rushed upstairs, looking for Alain. Though not overly religious, the Dutchman began saying a prayer beneath his breath even as he passed the stairway.

"Mind you, I would have boldly faced him," the squire added after a humble amen. "A man such as Claus van Clynne is not frightened by the Keens of this world."

It was at that moment that Keen spotted him from above.

"You!"

The single word, hurled at him from the top of the stairs, struck van Clynne just as he reached for the elaborate brass doorknob. Like a tangled, prickly vine, it grabbed at his head and shoulders, slapping itself to his body as Keen's South American leeches had once done.

"You!" repeated the doctor, as stupefied and stunned at seeing the large shadow flitting before him as if the archangel himself had appeared to bring him to heaven. "I disposed of you weeks ago! Yet both you and your companion Gibbs have survived! How?"

Van Clynne swirled in an elegant turn as he answered—not by voice but by the long-bladed knife, which flew from his fingers with a well-practiced flick.

Alas, the squire had not much experience throwing kitchen knives. The blade sailed forward through the dim space of the stairway, missing the doctor's head by a good foot, and lodging in a large and overdrawn portrait of King George II that stood on the wall.

The projectile did have a positive effect on van Clynne's situation, however: Keen lost his footing as he ducked back out of the way. He tumbled over in a cursing heap, thrashing his head against the railing as he fell down the steps.

"I will forestall a proper discussion of your ineffective potions until we meet under more leisurely circumstances," declared van Clynne as he pulled open the door. "Lord Peter, your ale was most satisfactory. You must introduce me to the brewer."

Clayton, Lady Patricia, and her husband had recovered from Jake's insults, and were just knocking at the front door. The Dutchman bowled them over as completely as the front pins in a skittle game. He reached the street as Keen emerged from the house, pistol in hand.

Van Clynne had unholstered his own gun, and waved it back toward Keen as he headed around the corner of the building. The guards who had accompanied Clayton Bauer and his relatives hesitated at first, unsure precisely what side they should take in the conflict. Finally, their commander brought his horse forward, arranging his men in a protective cordon around Bauer and the others. This had the effect of leaving van Clynne and Keen temporarily to themselves, an arrangement neither cared to change.

"You won't escape me this time," said Keen, advancing to the alley. "I had not thought to find you here, but it is most convenient."

Van Clynne just managed to duck behind the large barrel Jake had used earlier as Keen fired from the street. In truth, the wood of the barrel would not have provided much of a stop for the well-muscled bullet. Pig fat, on the other hand, did quite nicely: One of

New York's many fine pigs, running loose in the street and angry that its favorite resting place had been usurped, chose that moment to take a run at van Clynne—and thus met a premature end.

Now it was Keen who retreated as van Clynne rose and cocked his pistol. The doctor ran back toward his coach, intending to grab another weapon. The Dutchman called out, but failed to fire; the doctor feinted to one side then dove to the other. Once more the squire took aim, but paused. Keen took advantage of the interlude to dive behind the coach. Van Clynne once again missed his chance to fire.

Actually, his failure to shoot was due to a problem with the pistol. So often in tales such as these, weapons go off right on schedule. But pistols fail much more often in real life than in literature, and this one was no exception, responding to van Clynne's vigorous pulls and curses with the nonchalance of a deaf elephant.

Sensing the problem, Keen opened the door of his coach and hastily climbed inside. Retrieving a wide-barreled blunderbuss from its compartment beneath the seat, he crept close to the door, listening for a moment to the Dutchman's loud complaints.

"You are quite correct," said Keen, kicking the panel open. "They ceased making proper pistols years ago." Keen steadied his gun, not wanting to take any chance of missing again. Though of ample girth and now less than twenty feet away, the Dutchman had shown a remarkable propensity to dodge bullets and Death himself. "Fortunately, they have not forgotten how to make weapons such as these."

"Just so," said van Clynne. "Just so."

Keen mistook the squire's comment and confidential nod as being directed toward himself, a typical show of empty rebel braggadocio. In actual fact, it was meant for the figure who had secreted herself on the coachman's bench atop the vehicle, taking the horses' reins in hand. For we had not seen so much of Alison's bravery to think she would leave a fellow soldier in need, had we?

The carriage lurched forward as Keen pulled the trigger, and the jolt—together with the squire's expedient flop to the ground—resulted in all fifteen balls sailing far wide of the mark. The horses decided the loud report had been meant for them, and began thundering down the street.

The dragoon captain now decided to spend some of his resources, dispatching two men to chase down the vehicle while the others kept up their guard on Bauer and the house. In truth, the redcoats' most difficult job at the moment was keeping straight faces. Keen's earlier curses had not inclined them toward helping him, and the Dutchman's antics were more than a little comical. From the safety of their horses they thought the dispute purely personal and not worth their intervention.

Keen cursed to high heaven as he rolled in the interior of the carriage, dust and smoke clouding his eyes and the door flapping back and forth in a great succession of crashes against his face. Several times he struggled upwards, intending to climb out and control the horses, only to be smacked down harder than before.

When she noticed the redcoats starting to pursue, Alison jumped from the bench and tumbled into the dirt, where she was plucked by van Clynne as he beat a hasty retreat back to the Sons of Liberty's sanctuary.

"You have your father's sense of timing," said the Dutchman as he led her up an obscure but convenient alleyway. "Another two seconds and my chest would have been weighed down with lead. Really, why does your race dally so when time is of the essence?"

Twenty-seven

Wherein, Jake launches a new plan, and Claus van Clynne offers his own revised theories of divination.

*J*ake was met halfway to the infirmary hideout by a loose group of boys and young men sent by Culper as reinforcements. He was not surprised that they had not met van Clynne or Alison; both were independent sorts and undoubtedly were proceeding by their own lights and circuitous routes back. At the hospital, however, he did worry, and he had hunted up Daltoons in preparation of mounting a rescue mission when the landless Dutch squire and the disguised girl appeared at the door, arguing about who had saved whom.

"Where have you been?" demanded Jake.

"We have been salvaging your operation," declared van Clynne. "As usual. I tarried long enough to make the entire episode seem a simple robbery, appropriating some cutlery along the way. Your friend Dr. Keen tried to upend me. Which raises another matter: I thought you had disposed of him."

"He has more lives than a cat."

"Indeed. Perhaps we should recruit several dogs to attack him. Now, on to more important matters: is there any ale in the house?"

Jake shook his head and turned his attention to Alison, telling her with great severity that she had disobeyed his direct orders by not heading straight back to the infirmary. The ledger book was more important than all of their lives together, he told her, as its accounts might well tell General Washington where the British were heading. That, in turn, might save the entire Revolution.

"It gives no more clue to Howe's intentions than the wind," said van Clynne as he pulled it from his belt. "I took the liberty of examining it on the way. It will show you quite clearly that the British have spies spread throughout the continent and pay them equally. But beyond that, nothing. Now, where is the ale stored? Must I attend to every phase of the operation myself?"

The Dutchman disappeared down the steps. His opinions on other things might be severely prejudiced, but he was an unbiased expert when it came to account books. The places were clear, but Boston was as well-represented as Philadelphia, which appeared as many times as Newark, which sprung up as often as Jamestown, itself mentioned nearly as much as Albany. The agents were listed by number only, as might be expected; the Americans employed a similar system.

The maps Jake had stolen were of even less value, being copies not of places in America but the lost continent of Atlantis.

After a brief and uncharacteristic burst of temper, Jake admitted to himself his plan had failed miserably. And while Culper had already gone to the coffeehouse to work on the problem from there, there was scant hope of quick results. The British were sure to increase their security because of the prison break, and might even guess what the Americans were aiming at. Any information gleaned could easily be part of a plan to throw off the patriots.

Not only had Jake failed to discover the British design, but he had announced to Keen that he was still alive—a development that would complicate his progress and have dire consequences for all who helped him.

Never in all his operations could he remember failing so dismally. And the stakes were incredibly high; Washington himself was counting on him.

Use your imagination, the general ordered. Create a solution. Untie this knot.

Create, Jake. The spy heard the general's voice in his head, setting notions into order.

"Alison, I want you to go with Lieutenant Daltoons to the coffeehouse," said Jake abruptly. "Then go where Culper assigns you."

"He wishes to put me into retirement," protested Alison.

"He merely wants you to be safe," said Jake.

"I can do much more good in the city," said Alison. "You see what help I've already been. The fat Dutchman wouldn't have escaped without me."

"I hope you are not referring to me," harrumphed van Clynne as he climbed the stairs back to the loft. "As you are wrong on several counts. I am neither fat, nor was I in need of your assistance." The mug of porter he carried with him was not the highest quality, but acceptable under the circumstances. "I merely delayed my departure long enough to retrieve a map of the area where my land is situated, to assist the good general in recommending my claim to Congress."

"You must go," Jake told her. "For your own good. No arguing."

"If I may be so bold as to make a suggestion," offered van Clynne, "I know a fine housewife on Long Island who would undoubtedly be glad to have her help. She is not Dutch herself, but married into the race. Granted, it is nominally behind the enemy lines, but the farm is safe enough."

"I do not like the Dutch, even by marriage," said Alison. "They are cowards."

"Cowards! After all of my efforts on your behalf!"

The pope would stomach insults to the cross with less emotion than van Clynne showed now, his nose twitching with such fervor that Jake feared he would issue a catastrophic sneeze.

"I will concede that you may be brave," said Alison,

retreating half an inch, "though it was I who saved you."

"You have much to learn, young woman," said the squire. "Who plucked whom from the city slop at the side of the street?"

"Please, Claus, you're not helping the situation," said Jake.

"There was a time when proper respect was shown for one's elders," he groused, walking toward a large chair in the corner where he could recover his dignity without further interference. "But mark my words, sir, your plan for gathering information is all wrong."

"Which plan is that?" said Jake.

"Whatever plan you are concocting. Undoubtedly it will entail much slinking about and additional fisticuffs. Brute force is unreliable in these situations. Finesse, sir—that is the Dutch way, tried and true. All you need do is discover the proper person, approach in the light of day, and ask."

"Like your tailor."

"A temporary setback," admitted van Clynne, feeling expansive. "It was the right forest but the wrong pew, the proper church but the wrong tree. The plan remains sound." He settled into the well-cushioned seat and pulled a small stool up for his feet. In truth, properly comfortable chairs had gone out of style thirty years before. This one with its wide wings and broad but firm seat would have to do.

"You have a plan?" Daltoons asked Jake.

"Not yet."

"Culper will be able to solve it, if anyone can."

"I doubt in time. General Washington has a difficult schedule to meet. Perhaps I should row out and ask Howe himself."

"The man has no taste," said van Clynne. "He believes wine better than beer."

"If I were Howe," said Alison, "I would attack Philadelphia. It's full of pompous puffs who will gladly bow to the king."

"So now you are a politician as well as a soldier," said Daltoons. "Shall we call you General Alison, or Congressman?"

"I do not think that I will allow you to call me anything," said Alison. "And why do you wear that red cloth around your neck? Is it your sweetheart's sign?"

The lieutenant turned red. "My mother gave it to me before I joined the army," he said. "I do not have a sweetheart."

"I could have predicted that," said Alison.

While the pair were engaged in their light fencing, Jake made a mental list of the men who must know Howe's true plan. General Clinton surely would know where his commander was going, even if Culper's efforts to infiltrate his staff had so far revealed nothing.

Kidnap him? If easier than swimming out to Howe, still difficult in the extreme. Nor was Jake likely to find any knowledgeable member of his circle an easy target. Keen would probably have alerted the entire British force by now.

He began thinking of prominent Tories who might have been let in on the secret, and once more came to Bauer. Surely his network of Loyalists would have been of use to Howe in his planning. Bauer had also helped organize Tory cabals in the city of New York before the invasion, and it would be logical to have him help or at least advise in setting the stage in Boston.

Or Philadelphia. Or Georgia. Or the Carolinas.

He had a company of guards, but that obstacle might not prove insurmountable. If he were kidnapped, he might be rowed from his own dock without an inordinate amount of trouble.

But how to get him to say what he knew? And how to know it was true?

Bauer's fierce reputation was not unwarranted. Fight off his guards, kidnap the man, torture the answer from him—and then be victimized by a simple if well-told lie?

Worse, kidnapping might alert the British, and possibly cause them to change their plans.

Brute force would be unreliable, Jake realized. Claus—dare he concede it?—was right about that.

Bauer must be the solution; Fate had not thrown them together so often today without some purpose. Too bad he couldn't just kill him, then dissect his brain for the answer.

Jake's mind lit with an idea.

"Do you think Bauer will show up for the duel?" he asked Daltoons.

"Of course." The lieutenant had laughed at the story earlier with a touch of envy; he wished he might develop his older friend's flair, as well as find his luck.

"Even if he knows I'm an American?"

"How will he know?"

"Keen will tell him." Jake reconsidered. "Well, perhaps he has reason not to. Bauer still thought I was a spy for Bacon just now. Lady Patricia seemed to think Keen and I were friends, which is an idea that could only come from Keen. He must have some reason for keeping my identity secret."

"In any event, I would think Bauer's reputation guarantees his presence at the duel," said Daltoons. "But why would you attend?"

"To kill him and then raise him from the dead."

"What?"

Jake jumped from his chair. "We are going to kidnap him and steal the answer, without anyone else realizing it. We will need some contingency to distract his dragoon guard, in case they feel obliged to attend the duel. Can you arrange an order to take them away from his house?"

"I'm sure we can find a diversion," said Daltoons, unsure what Jake was up to. "But don't you think you should consult with Culper?"

It was as useless to try and stop Jake when he was launched on a plan as it was to argue with van Clynne about Dutch superiority. The patriot spy waved him off as he ran to grab his coat. "The first trick is to kill him, the second to cure him. That way we'll keep others' suspicions down and only worry about his. Have everything ready for me. I must see a friend. In the meantime, organize some sort of order or delay for the guard. I want to make sure Bauer arrives on the Jersey shore without it."

Alison sprung after him.

"You can't come with me," Jake said.

"The British are looking for you," Daltoons told Jake. "And Culper specifically said for you to stay in hiding."

"The beauty of being on a mission for General Washington," said the spy, "is that I take orders directly and only from him. A mission has but one chief."

"I knew we would hear the theory at some juncture," muttered van Clynne as he slipped toward sleep. "Though usually it is to give me some base assignment."

"Deliver Alison to Culper, and tell him to continue his efforts. With luck, my stage tricks won't be needed."

"I want to help you." Alison caught hold of Jake's arm as he started down the stairs.

Jake reached back and took her arms firmly, gripping not quite hard enough to hurt her, but surely pressing his will into her rebellious flesh. "If you truly care about our Revolution, you will go with Daltoons and not utter another word."

"But—"

"And hand me back my Segallas."

Even in the dim light, there was no obscuring the look in Jake's eyes. Alison nodded meekly.

"I shall pursue my own plan in the morning," vowed van Clynne between his snores.

"Do that," said Jake, tapping his shoe as he left.

Twenty-eight

Wherein, Jake takes a not-so-leisurely stroll through the enemy city.

*A*fter General Howe and his troops succeeded in turning the American line at Brooklyn Heights on Long Island in the fall of 1776, General Washington orchestrated a daring nighttime retreat. Having escaped the cauldron, the Continental troops hunkered down in the city opposite, preparing defenses for the inevitable assault. The ensuing disaster of Kipp's Bay, where Howe routed our boys with a heavy rain of cannon, is nearly too depressing to mention. Only by the most heroic of measures was the commander-in-chief able to regain control of his army and retreat north. It was not until the brave battle at White Plains that the tide was finally turned. That skirmish may well have preserved our Revolution, and shall undoubtedly be praised by generations to come, once we have won our Freedom.

In the days following Washington's withdrawal from New York, a massive fire broke out in the western precincts. From Broadway west to the fort, from the water north to Barclay Street, no building was untouched by the flames. Even the magnificent steeple of Trinity Church glowed with the red flickers. The destruction was several times greater than that caused by the cannons of war; it may truthfully be said that no conflagration of similar proportions had ever raged on the continent. The wounded precincts have since become host to a city within a city built of ruins and canvas, the poor huddling for whatever shelter they can find.

But as Claus van Clynne would cheerfully point out, ever since its establishment by the Dutch, New York has been a city of great resources and strength. The presence of the British in the fort at the island's southern tip—and even more importantly, on the fields to the north and the waters to the east and south—proved a magnet to all manner of Tory. American industry, ignorant of politics, constantly seeks to build and grow, no matter who sits in the governor's house or mans the battlements.

Indeed, the city Jake proceeded through after leaving the infirmary hideout was enjoying what van Clynne's favorite philosopher Adam Smith might call an economic boom. Despite the late hour, the streets were filled with people going about their business. Even the notorious city pigs, supplemented by an occasional loose dog, walked with purpose. The air was as filled with the smell of money being made and spent as it was with horse dung.

Jake thought of pulling up the collar of his jacket to obscure his face. But on second thought, he felt this might unnecessarily attract attention. How often is it said that the most obvious hiding place is the one least expected? He straightened his spine and walked with a solid gait, hastening up George's Street toward the commons and then eastward. At every step, it seemed he saw a soldier or an obvious British functionary; Jake smiled and always endeavored to make direct eye contact.

It was a bold approach. While Jake had the advantage of moving through the city at a time when all of Howe's command and a large portion of his men had been removed to stew aboard ship, still, at any moment Chance herself might throw someone across his path who would recognize him and sound the alarm.

Not that he was unarmed. Beneath his belt Jake carried his Segallas, fully loaded and ready for action. He also had two full-sized pistols borrowed from the Sons' armory beneath his jacket, and a knife tucked into his right boot.

The spy's destination was a small apothecary shop off an alley on Cherry Street. Just a block off the docks and shipyards, before the Revolution the neighborhood was rough and thoroughly mixed, frequented by sailors and assorted ruffians who knocked shoulders with wealthy merchants, legitimate and otherwise. Any sort of deal in the world could be hatched here, and if the Devil were looking for a place to do his business, he could not have chosen a better spot.

Nor had respectability threatened this vale now that war had come. Jake adopted a certain aggressive gait, hands swinging and chin jutting forward as he nudged his way past the taverns and warehouses. He walked quicker, beginning to anticipate the meeting he had planned; he had not seen the owner of the shop he was visiting for several months.

But a half-block from his destination, a sensation grew on him that he was being followed. He took a left turn away from the building, walking up in the general direction of the reservoir. Sure enough, his fleeting glance revealed a figure in the shadows behind him.

The buildings lining the street were butted against one another too closely to give him a hiding place. He continued walking, his step brisk and deliberate but not panicked, making it seem as if this were his direction all along.

A shed that had been converted to a sales office for barrels of pitch sat on the next block, just on the out-skirts of the tanning yards. A porch stood over the front of the building, guarded by two large, rough-hewn posts. The posts had an assortment of barrels and coils of rope hauled around them; whatever function these were meant to serve, they provided an excellent hiding place for the patriot spy as he ducked behind them and crouched down.

The man following him turned the corner onto the

empty street. Not seeing his quarry, he broke into a trot, his full-length cloak flapping as he ran to catch his prey.

Jake slipped the knife from his boot and ran his thumb along the sleek steel blade. Just as the fellow passed him, Jake leaped over the barrel, grabbing the villain by the throat.

"Why would anyone wear a heavy coat in the summer heat?" the patriot asked his prisoner.

"Father!"

"Damn you, Alison," said Jake, spinning her around but not releasing her. "You almost had your throat slit. Why aren't you with Daltoons?"

"I told him I was going to the privy. He's very brave, but easily fooled. His coat is handy, though. It comes equipped with many pockets for weapons and such."

Jake scowled. If his knife had frightened her for even an instant, there was no trace of it on her face. "What you need is a good caning."

"Are all patriots treated this way?"

"Ones who don't obey orders. Where's Claus?"

"Sleeping like a baby, and snoring like a hound in heat."

"That's something, at least." Jake thought of sending her back alone, but dismissed the idea on two counts: one that it was too dangerous, and two that she was unlikely to follow such an order. "Come along."

The moon had continued her climb through the clear sky during Jake's brief detour, and now Night was serenading the city with her bright starlight and gentle bird songs. The building he sought had a large, multipaned glass window that covered most of its front. Several of the panels were made of thick, brightly colored glass similar to that found in the most lavish churches. Other than this obvious sign of prosperity, there was no hint of the building's owner or his business. Jake stood before the closed doorway for a moment, waiting as two men walked into the tavern across the way.

"Stay right here," said Jake to Alison. "Do not move. And do not go into that tavern. It is owned by a friend, but the sailors will have you aboard their ship before he spots you."

"I am not afraid of them."

"But I am," warned Jake.

He reached inside his vest pocket and retrieved a narrow, wedge-shaped piece of metal which he wielded like a skeleton key. In a second, he pushed the door inwards and slipped inside.

"Bebeef, are you awake?" he asked, walking toward the back. "Professor Bebeef?"

The only answer was a soft thud from the back room. Jake stepped gingerly along the wide, painted pine planks; the floor was littered with glass jars, boxes, and canvas bags. Only half contained what one might call the customary wares of an apothecary.

Nominally a druggist, the proprietor had a severe weakness for oddities and machines of all kinds. If the truth be told, he was a soft touch for any inventor or salesman who wandered in. On the floor and shelves were such items as an authentic Egyptian spyglass, a steel spring said to cure consumption better than Bebeef's own potions, and a large, winged contraption with which, under the proper circumstances, a man could fly. That such circumstances had not yet been discovered did not prevent the gray-haired chemist, philosopher, and veritable wizard from cheerfully trying to sell the device to anyone who strayed into his store.

"Bebeef?"

Jake knocked at the door to the rear room, where the proprietor customarily slept.

"Professor?"

There was a sound inside, louder than before. Jake pushed the door open, then fell flat against the jam as a large white ball exploded toward him.

The cat, Mister Spooky.

"I am being assaulted by all sorts of animals today,"

Jake complained to himself. His self-deprecating laugh was interrupted by a gentle but nonetheless obvious poke at his ribs.

"Do not move or this sword will pierce your flesh," said an unfamiliar voice. "It is tipped with a poison that will kill you only after the most painful seizures imaginable."

Twenty-nine

Wherein, Professor Bebeef's situation is found to be desperate.

"*I* have no desire to be poisoned," said Jake softly. In the dim light of the shop, he couldn't tell who might be holding the sword on him. It certainly wasn't Bebeef.

"Walk slowly with me, to the door. Too quickly, and I will plunge the sword in your side. Remember, I need only prick the skin for the poison to take effect."

"I need to see Professor Bebeef," said Jake, who realized the voice and shadow belonged to a boy, not a man, and thus dismissed his original theory that he had been surprised by a British soldier guarding the confiscated stores. Still, he was in no position to relax. "I am a friend of his."

"Move this way or you will die."

The question was not so much whether the blade was truly covered with poison, but which poison it might be; the nearby shelves contained quite a variety.

"You're not the apprentice who was here six weeks ago," said Jake. "You would remember that I borrowed a noise bomb."

"The apprentice is now a guest of the English, much against his will, and my uncle's," replied the shadow. "Your own path is clear: you are to leave immediately."

"Ah," said Jake, "you must be Timothy. I am Jake Gibbs. Surely your uncle has told you about me."

Before the lad could answer, he was interrupted by a loud crash at the door.

"Step away from Jake, or you will be filled with more lead than the weight of the clock in the governor's palace."

"I thought I told you to wait outside," said Jake indignantly as Alison waved her gun in the shadows.

"An ungrateful attitude," she replied. "But then, I have come to expect it, having saved your life so many times before."

"You've spent too much time with van Clynne," said Jake. "You're starting to sound like him." He turned back toward Bebeef's nephew. "We are all on the same side here. Light a candle and I will show you a sign your uncle would recognize."

"Why should I trust you?" said the lad, still holding his sword at Jake's side. "Anyone could claim to be his friend, and Mr. Gibbs is well known in several circles. His father's firm supplies many of the items in this very shop."

"Your uncle has a scar over his left eye that he got while escaping a Turkish prince who held him for ransom in his youth," replied Jake. "If you have not heard that story ten thousand times, you are not related to the professor."

"Everyone living in the province of New York has heard that story ten thousand times," answered the nephew. Nonetheless, he lowered his sword and retreated to light a candle.

Jake reached under his clothes and undid the money belt at his waist. The back of the belt was stamped with a Masonic symbol that the nephew quickly recognized. The symbol was shared by all members of the Secret Service, but the esoteric marks above it were a mnemonic Bebeef himself used as the abbreviation for a remedy for the Portuguese ailment—a disease King George was reputed to suffer from. The formula connecting the king with the disease and the cure with the Revolution was among the old professor's favorite if somewhat obscure jokes.

"I am sorry," said the nephew, who recognized the

marks immediately. "I am Timothy Hulter, as you surmised. The Tories and British are envious of my uncle's potions, and there have been several attempts at break-ins."

"Where is he? I need his help urgently. There is a potion only he can concoct."

"With my mother in Brooklyn," said the lad. "He won't see anyone. He won't talk, not even to her. He seems to have fallen into a deep spell, sitting day and night in the back garden, staring at a madstone."

"A madstone?" Jake squinted, as if suddenly presented with the unlikely object. Many people—including, it must be admitted, a few scientists—believed the special rocks able to cure fever and madness. Despite this, Bebeef had long dismissed such stones as mere superstitions.

"It is, sir, a rock such as one has never seen before. Until now, I thought such things were superstition. But there is much in this shop that I would not believe except for my uncle's demonstrations."

Jake was just wondering whether he might alter his plan for dealing with Bauer when the young man suddenly took hold of his arm. "Please, sir, come with me to the farm. You must find a cure for the spell that has taken him."

"I don't know," said Jake. "I have pressing matters to attend to. And I know nothing of magic."

"Nor does my uncle. There must be science to it. There is no such thing as magic, only formulas yet to be discovered, as my uncle puts it. He has spoken of you before this illness; surely he would help you if the places were turned."

Jake owed Bebeef much. Not only had his concoctions rescued him from many difficult situations, but the professor had sheltered him in the dark days of the British invasion. If it were not for him, Jake might well have suffered the same fate as Nathan Hale.

But the journey to Long Island was fraught with danger. Nor would it directly assist his mission.

Unless, of course, he was able to cure the professor. In that case, it would be more like an investment toward the solution, and not a delay at all.

"Tell me more about this ailment," said Jake. "No, wait—tell it to me on the way to the ferry."

"I have a small boat that is much safer," said the lad, starting toward the door.

"Alison, you go back to Daltoons," Jake ordered, "and tell him I will return in time for the duel."

But before she could go—or open her mouth to argue—a pair of shadows passed by the front window. Jake grabbed both Alison and Timothy and threw them to the floor.

The figures who had cast the shadows were members of the Black Watch, too intent on the tavern across the street to bother glancing inside the shop. Nonetheless, Jake decided Alison was safer coming along with him. She might even provide him with some cover, or at least a way of getting a message back to Culper if he ran into difficulties. In any event, he could not let her wander the city alone.

"Alison is a strange name for a boy," said the nephew after Jake told them they could rise.

"It will seem stranger still when I flatten you," she promised.

Timothy's boat was far along the road to Corber's Point, in a discrete yard where no questions would be asked no matter who came or went, day or night. The trio trekked north all the way to Division Street, making sure their intentions were not known and they were not followed. In truth, these precautions were overzealous, but considering the circumstances, understandable. Two hours later they were rowing as quietly as possible across the East River. Jake and Timothy had each taken an oar to use as an Indian paddles a canoe. Alison lay in the bow, acting as lookout as the skiff worked across the bay in the manner of mist stealing into a valley.

By the time they reached the small, tree-lined cove on the Long Island shore, it was well past midnight. Jake helped Timothy pull the small boat into the bushes. He and Alison followed the lad up to a dusty road and across a large, uncultivated field.

Alison was beginning to show the signs of fatigue. She had given Jake the pistol she'd "borrowed" from Daltoons, and left the lieutenant's heavy cloak at the rowboat. But her pace dragged nonetheless, the fatigue of the past few days starting to take their toll. In truth, even Jake's famous constitution was beginning to show signs of wear as the trio hiked across a country road and found another shortcut through a pasture. The warm summer day had given way to a cool night, and the chilly air rubbed at Jake's shoulders like a carpenter works a fresh tabletop.

"Just four or five miles from here," said Timothy as they climbed over a stone wall and found another road.

"Can we rest?" asked Alison, setting her hands on the wall.

Before Jake could answer, she plopped over on the ground.

"Mouthy for a girl," said Timothy, leaning over her to make sure she was merely sleeping. "But pretty, even with the short hair."

"I'd be careful what I accused her of," answered Jake. "She insults very easily. And would most likely be more than your match in a fight."

"I should like to wrestle her sometime and find out."

For all his protests against her behavior, Jake was starting to feel just a bit protective—and even fatherly. He scowled toward young Timothy, then hoisted Alison over his shoulder. "Come on, lead the way."

The Hulter farm was a fertile holding of nearly twenty cleared acres given over to the cultivation of corn. Indeed, it had been used for that purpose for several generations, spanning back to its original native owners. The house itself was not more than ten years old, a

replacement for a structure that had caught fire one
winter night when the fireplace was carelessly over-
stoked. A story-and-a-half, with finely decorated eaves
and handsomely carved shutters, it was typical of the
humble farmhouses that dot the island, save in one regard. This was its elaborate garden, which ranged on
all four sides at some depth surrounding the building.
All manner of bushes and flowers crowded together in
an elaborate though specially ordered jumble. Each
had its own medicinal purpose; more than a few were
rare to these shores, nurtured by Timothy's mother's
careful hand.

Grace Hulter was Professor Bebeef's youngest sister.
The natural philosopher had always doted on her when
she was small; as she grew, she returned the favor sev-
eralfold. They were close despite the years between
them.

Grace's husband had left to join the Continental
Army the previous year; she had had no word from
him since. Grace refused to countenance the neighborhood whispers that he had met his fate below White
Plains. True or not, the rumors filled even her most
vitriolic Tory neighbors with pity for the famously kind
woman. Grace administered mild cures to all in the
surrounding country without regard to politics. Thus
her husband's sins were not held too strongly against
her, though she was suspected of being a quiet rebel
herself.

By the time Jake unloaded the sleeping Alison from
his shoulder onto a wooden chair propped near the
front door, the sun was sending an advance party of
rays to test the horizon. Timothy led Jake directly to
the back yard, where the old professor was sitting beneath a rare and beautiful rose bush. In his hand was a
brown-colored rock not more than three inches long
and another inch wide, rough-hewn around the edge,
as if it were a petrified piece of wood. It seemed to
glow faintly; the old man's eyes, wide open in what

seemed like perpetual astonishment, shone with the reflected light.

Despite the fact that he was now well past sixty,
Bebeef's hair was full and thick, the magnificent locks
falling around his ears and draping across the velvet of
his fine cloak. He wore the doctor's robes of the
monastery where he had studied during his youth, as
was his habit when engaged in one of his more esoteric
experiments.

Jake had never seen him in such a stupor. He advanced cautiously. Despite all his learning and experience, he could not dismiss outright the possibility that
the stone did indeed contain some form of black magic.

"Professor, it's Jake Gibbs. I need your help. Professor?"

Bebeef's stare did not alter, nor was there any other
sign that he had noticed Jake.

"He does not stir for days at a time," said Mrs.
Hulter, coming out from the house. Dressed in a plain
white country dress, she seemed to float across the
stone path, her willowy hair tied in a modest bun at the
back of her neck. "He will not move or acknowledge
anyone and eats only a small bit of food."

"It's good to see you, Grace," said Jake, hugging her.

"And you, too." There was a look of regret in her
eye at that moment, and perhaps a veiled acknowledgment that her husband had indeed met his fate. She
quickly stepped back when Jake released her.

"What is the rock?" he asked.

"From looking at it, I would say a simple Bezoar
stone. It arrived unannounced, with a note proclaiming
its magic as a madstone. My brother scoffed, then took
it with him to the garden here. That was nearly two
weeks ago. Nothing I have done has helped."

"Have you tried to remove it from his hands?"

"I cannot seem to shake it loose. It is as if it were
glued."

Jake knew of madstones, even if his scientific studies
had not included them. Stones of various descriptions

had been known for centuries, and they were generally said to cure ailments such as warts and sniffles. Jake's family had even attempted to buy one famous for its fever cures in Virginia. But the spell this stone seemed to have cast on Bebeef was right out of *Arabian Nights*.

Or perhaps a very esoteric cure book.

"Is your brother's library still stored in the barn?"

"Of course," answered Mrs. Hulter.

"There is a book based on notes by Avicenna, the grand vizier and body surgeon of Persia," said Jake. "I would like to consult it."

Mrs. Hulter had no idea which book he was talking about, but was only too happy to do anything that might cure her brother. Most of his store of ancient texts was packed in crates in the cellar below the barn's main floor, protected by a ponderous guard of heavy rocks. It took Jake more than two hours to move the stones away and find the work, a translation in Latin of a text dating from the tenth century. Madstones were fully described, and though Jake's command of the noble tongue was rusty, he was able to ascertain that no such effect was documented. He therefore turned to Bebeef's own encyclopaedic study—not of madstones, but of paralytic poisons.

It was nearly noon before he had read enough to attempt a cure. As Timothy had gone off to bed and Alison was still slumbering, Jake enlisted Mrs. Hulter as an assistant. He made her wrap her hands in thick gloves, and cover her body with several layers of clothes, until only her eyes showed through. These he covered with gauze so tightly that she could barely see.

"I hope you're not expecting me to speak in tongues," she declared.

"Hardly," said Jake. "There is no magic here, just a powerful poison. The cure is surprisingly simple—largely coca powder and menthol. But first we have to strike the rock from his hands. If my guess is correct, the underside is covered with a gummy substance obtained from a bush in the French Alps, which acts as a glue."

Jake filled a pot with water and let it boil over the fire. As he waited, he too covered his body with the thickest cloths he could find.

His hands were so well padded that he was able to take the hot iron handle of the black kettle in them.

"Are you going to burn him?" asked Mrs. Hulter, the concern in her voice clear despite the rags protecting her face.

"I am afraid it will," said Jake. "When I give the signal, grab his head and pull him away from the stone."

They walked back to the garden, where the philosopher had not stirred an inch in the hours since Jake had left him. The patriot spy took up the kettle and held it over Bebeef's hands, then told Mrs. Hulter to be ready.

"I'm sorry to hurt you, professor," Jake told Bebeef's unmoving body a second before tilting the burning liquid. "But I believe the cure better than the disease, and I have great need of your help."

Mrs. Hulter grabbed her brother beneath the arms and hauled backwards as Jake started to pour the water. Bebeef fell from the chair, but the shock of the scalding water barely registered on his face. His hands were still stuck fast to the stone.

Jake kicked at his wrists and poured the rest of the water. Finally, with a loud, piercing scream, Bebeef began to writhe beneath his sister's arms, and the poisoned stone fell from his hands to the ground.

Thirty

Wherein, Alison becomes a butterfly.

"*T*here's no fool as an old fool," said Bebeef a half hour later, restored to consciousness and some comfort by a formula taken from his own book of cures. He had refused bed rest and was even now setting his laboratory in the barn loft back to order. The immense room was filled with even more tubes, jars, and bottles than his store in Manhattan. A long table ran through the center of the room, and a large cabinet of fancy walnut trays sat beneath a triangular window at the far end of the room. A jar of healing salts sat open on the middle rung, having been used to take some of the sting from the burns.

"Naturally, I should have suspected something was amiss when the package arrived. But I have such a contempt for these blasted stones and their superstitions. People look everywhere for cures these days, instead of consulting with those who have studied the body and its humors scientifically."

"I am sorry about your hands," said Jake. "But according to your notes, there was no other way to destroy the gum."

"Couldn't be helped," said the old man almost cheerfully. Thick gauze saturated with several ointments covered his hands, but otherwise he was in good shape. "These will hamper me, but I have suffered handicaps before."

"Do you know who prepared the stone?"

"There are only a few people with the knowledge to concoct something like this, and none bear me grudges," said the professor. "With the exception of one man, who has betrayed all his oaths and duties to the sacred knowledge he has gathered. He conducted human experiments for many years in London, and some friends have tried to have him arrested. I joined their petitions some months ago, but I had not heard if they were successful."

"You're talking about Harland Keen," said Jake.

It was one of the few times in his life Jake actually surprised the professor. "You know him?"

"He is an assassin for the secret department. He has tried several times to kill me."

"The secret department?"

"It is a coterie of men sworn to the king and charged with assassination. Keen has been after me for some time. I thought I had killed him a few weeks ago, but apparently he found a way to escape."

Bebeef tried to grab hold of Jake's arm with his bandaged hand. "You must be extremely careful. The man has a great store of knowledge—truly he is the incarnation of Faust, if not the devil himself."

Bebeef's gaze fluttered momentarily. It was as if he could see through the window's chintz fly barrier, out over the countryside, past the Heights, the bay, into the city itself, searching for his enemy.

"He is not immortal," the professor said finally. "No man can cheat death. But Keen's mastery of medicines and the body are more than those of the entire college of Edinburgh taken together."

"Beyond yours as well?"

Bebeef laughed lightly. "I am but a poor country scholar. You see how easily I am fooled."

"Keen must have prepared the stone some time ago. He has been busy of late."

"Perhaps we can assume from his presence in America that our petitions were successful. So that is something. But come, Jake. I hope you did not travel here just to save me."

"I would have," said Jake. "I owe you my life several times over. But I also have great need of your help. I want to kill someone. And then revive him."

"The first part of the equation is easily solved, but the second has given philosophers fits for centuries."

"Why else would I have sought you out?"

The professor's eyebrows began percolating, as if their roots were rubbing the furls of his brain.

"There will be witnesses, so the death must seem absolutely genuine," said Jake. "That is its whole point: I need to kidnap the man for a few hours without anyone realizing it. I was thinking of some sort of paralyzing powder," he added. "Something, perhaps, derived from a sea ray?"

"Paralyzing a man is not the same as killing him. He will continue to breathe heavily with that family of medicines."

"Something else then. I need only a few minutes. But it must be convincing and relatively safe," added Jake, "as I will probably have to die as well."

As Bebeef contemplated the problem, Jake studied the lines in the old man's face. Each seemed to record an entire library being investigated.

"The solution is not so elaborate as you think," said Bebeef finally, his face glowing as he remembered a formula used by certain South American natives in their religious ceremonies. "We will begin with a mandrake root from the garden. Bring me the green-spined book from the storage downstairs. Really, the formula is so simple to prepare I am surprised that you did not think of it yourself."

"That is what you said about the shrinking potion you gave my father for the dog."

"Oh yes, but I am sure this one will work."

Alison slept soundly upstairs for many hours, until well past two. Mrs. Hulter, realizing by some innate sense

that her guest was about to wake, walked silently into
the room and stood by the bedside, so she was with her
when she opened her eyes.

"It's all right, dear, you're among friends," said Mrs.
Hulter as Alison bolted upright in confusion. She put
her hand gently on her shoulder, urging her back.
"Rest a while longer. Jake has told me all about your
troubles. I am sorry for your poor father."

A strange sensation took hold of Alison's chest, and
suddenly she felt as if her heart had burst. Without
warning, she began crying uncontrollably. Mrs. Hulter
bent down and held her in her arms as the poor girl
was overcome by the grief she had held so firmly in
check.

She cried for a solid hour before finally falling back
on the bed, exhausted and spent.

"It is a terrible ordeal to lose your father," said the
older woman gently. "I cried for days when mine
passed on. And I hardly knew my mother."

"Me neither," said Alison.

"My husband now, too, is missing," said Mrs. Hulter,
her lips quivering. "There are rumors he is dead."

"Jake can help find him," said Alison.

Mrs. Hulter smiled weakly as she took control of
herself. "He has tried. Come. Let us see about getting
you something to eat, and some clothes."

"What happened to the clothes I was wearing?"

Her hostess wrinkled her nose. "Those things? They
smelled of the river, and several farms' worth of animals."

"They were my disguise."

"Yes, they certainly disguised you," said Mrs. Hulter,
in a tone that made it clear she was taking a propri-
etary interest in her young charge. "But you seem to be
ready to burst the bounds of any such disguise. You
have even excited some interest from my son."

"Really?"

"He's too young for you, dear; he's barely thirteen.

But he had a look in his eyes when he told me about you."

"A look?"

"Men get an expression in their eyes, as if the sockets will collapse."

"Is that love?"

"Well, it is something like it."

"Can I trust you with a secret?"

"Of course."

"I love Jake."

The words rushed from her so suddenly they surprised her.

"Many women love him," said Mrs. Hulter gently. "But . . ."

"Do you think he loves me?"

Mrs. Hulter sighed deeply, trying to be diplomatic without lying to the girl. "He is too old for you, dear."

"He's not much older than I, only six or seven years."

"The war has aged him in ways it is difficult to explain." Mrs. Hulter tugged her arm gently. "Do you think he loves you?"

"He saved my life. And I saved his."

"That is one type of love," allowed the older woman. "Still, I think you are after something else, aren't you?"

"How can you tell if someone is in love with you?"

"A person's whole being changes. You will see, when the time comes."

"I will make him love me."

Mrs. Hulter laughed. "I would think that quite difficult. In any event, he is too much a gentleman to take you as a lover, being both older and having been trusted with your safety. But as your guardian or friend, he is a powerful ally to have."

Alison was not ready to settle for that, even if she might suspect it was the truth. Instead, she changed the subject. Slightly.

"I have seen that look you were talking about," said Alison. "If that is love. There is a lieutenant in New

York. He tries to be mean to me, but I know he doesn't mean it. He's only seventeen, and already he is a lieutenant."

"Perhaps you should turn your sights on him," said Mrs. Hulter, rising from the bed. "Come, let's find you something to wear."

Alison pushed away the coverlet and followed her hostess to the next room. She was completely without clothes, yet felt no more shame than Eve before the Fall.

"This chemise is practically new." Mrs. Hulter withdrew a light linen shift bordered with fancy lace from the oaken wardrobe that dominated the small room. Alison stroked the lace as if it were some precious metal she had never seen.

Mrs. Hulter next produced a jump that had belonged to a niece. This lightly boned corset, not nearly as restricting as the elaborate metal affairs preferred by city ladies, nonetheless would be sufficient to leave little doubt as to Alison's sex—or beauty. Mrs. Hulter then brought out a light blue dress so expertly woven from homespun flax that it seemed like fine silk.

"I don't want to wear a dress. I want to serve our cause," said Alison, handing the chemise back.

"And so you will, no matter what you wear. This is a patriotic dress. It was woven in defiance of the king's ban on weaving. Women declared their independence first in this land. Men may boast, but it is women who take the risks and act first, protecting our homes and our rights. You will learn that as you grow older."

"I have already seen it," said Alison. She studied the dress a moment. "Do you think it will look attractive?"

"I think you would look as pretty as a butterfly in it."

Whether it was Mrs. Hulter's appeal to patriotism or her soft, reassuring manner, Alison finally submitted, allowing herself to be made up in a way she had scarce imagined possible. The bold patriot who had risked her life to save Jake and clamored continuously to help General Washington had not been banished; on the contrary, defiance shone all the brighter in her eye. Yet it had been magnified by a physical beauty that previously had been severely disguised.

"Your hair is our final problem," said Mrs. Hulter, stepping back. "It has a natural beauty to it, but it will be months before it grows long enough to curl. A wig would be too fussy—ah, I know just the thing."

She disappeared out the door and down the hallway. There was a small mirror on the bureau. Alison picked it up furtively, glancing at the image as if she might see something painful. She had worn dresses before, of course—her father absolutely insisted on them for church—but she had never felt like this.

Mrs. Hulter returned with a gauze-and-silk turban and a colored plume. Within a few minutes, Alison's face was set off by a colorful crown. The overall transition was so remarkable that Mrs. Hulter's son Timothy was knocked speechless, retreating to the wall as the two women descended the staircase.

"Well now, you certainly look beautiful," said Jake, meeting them downstairs in the house. He swept down as if introducing himself for the first time. "Jake Gibbs, on special service to General Washington. Pleased to make your acquaintance, Miss."

Alison turned red and found it impossible to speak, as if her wit had been left with her old clothes. It was difficult even to look at his eyes—though she strongly hoped to find the shadow there Mrs. Hulter had spoken of.

For his part, Jake wondered whether he should try and talk Mrs. Hulter into adopting Alison. But he decided the poor woman would have her hands full nursing her brother back to health and keeping her farm running besides. She had done yeoman's service merely getting Alison to wear a dress.

"We have to leave soon for New York," said Jake. "It will take us more than an hour to get to the ferry from here."

Mrs. Hulter insisted that they eat before they leave.

It was now nearly four, and all she had given Jake for breakfast was a half-loaf of rye. They sat down to a large dinner of boiled salt pork with some freshly dug potatoes. The meal was not a rich one, though Jake judged it must be as expensive a luxury as the good woman could afford during these difficult times.

"Alison, you have become very quiet," said Jake.

"I'm just—thinking."

"I see. Well, you may think a while longer while I consult with Professor Bebeef once more," he said as he rose. "But then we will leave promptly."

As accomplished as he was in affairs of the heart, Jake in this instance had made a mistaken interpretation, believing that Alison was infatuated with young Timothy, not himself. He went across to Bebeef's rooms feeling rather smug.

"I have prepared the bullets," the professor told him, looking up from the jars and tubes that arrayed the long desk where he was working. "I have adapted some simple copper balls and soldered them whole. They are somewhat fragile; you must not handle them too much before they are loaded."

"They will stay in their case until the duel," said Jake. He picked up the small ball and shook it; it seemed solid, if light.

The matched pistols were very plain, with only the slightest piece of scrolling at the very end of their butts. Their heavy, straight lock mechanisms betrayed their French design. No self-important English gentleman would condescend to use either to dispatch his ailing horse with, let along uphold his honor.

"They're the best I have," Bebeef apologized. "I'm not much for dueling."

"They'll be good enough. My friend may sneer all he wants, but he is obliged to accept them."

"The poison will work so long as it can penetrate the flesh. I have had to weaken the gunpowder mixture in your small horn there, to guarantee the balls will not explode in the barrel when the charge ignites."

"So there won't be much power in the bullets?"

"I would not vouch for their flying more than twenty paces with any real velocity," said Bebeef. "It would be best if they had an unobstructed path to the flesh when they struck. Even a thick coat might save the victim."

The thought of facing a bare-chested Bauer was almost too much for Jake to stand.

"The bullets will pass through a light shirt and still do their duty," said Bebeef hopefully, noting Jake's frown. "The liquid is red, so it will look like a very handsome wound. Aim for the chest."

"I intend to."

"Here is all I have left," said Bebeef, holding up a small tube whose glass ends had been melted shut. "The material that bonds the ingredients is very gummy, and will adhere to metal. If you rub a sword blade with it, the effect will be the same."

"But it's red. Anyone will spot it in an instant."

"It's a good thing you didn't choose swords then," said Bebeef. "It must pass through the skin, so you have to wound the victim lightly."

Jake took the vial and placed it in his vest pocket.

"Touch the wound with pure water to counteract the poison. Do not use city water by any means."

"I wouldn't even wash a horse with city water."

"You only need a drop. The effects will wear off in an hour without the antidote," Bebeef said. "The breathing and heart do not completely stop, but slow so much at first that it is difficult to tell. Gradually, they improve. After a few minutes, even a country barber could tell the victim is alive. I would advise you to shoot first, no matter the code."

"But professor, I have to stand on my honor."

Bebeef could not tell whether Jake was kidding or not. "I have been wracking my brain for a truth serum," the professor added. "There are several formulas in my books, but they are along the lines of love potions and very undependable."

As Major Dr. Keen had tried some such potions on

van Clynne with poor results, Jake shrugged. He had already concocted a ruse to fool Bauer once he was revived.

With luck, Culper would have solved the problem by the time he returned to the city. Then Bauer's information would be superfluous. In any case, the Tory bastard would be a fitting trophy to present General Washington with.

"I have also prepared a small supply of sleeping powder," said Bebeef, walking to the collection of trays standing below the triangular window. "I know it is one of your favorite concoctions."

"It's very useful for putting out guards without noise."

"And stunning cats, according to your father."

"I have not launched an attack on a cat in many years," laughed Jake.

"Take care, my young friend," said Bebeef as Jake started to leave. He reached up with his bandaged hands. "Do not discount Keen."

"I have not. But he is a man like the rest of us."

The professor's reluctant nod revealed that he might not completely share that opinion.

Timothy's eyes were wide circles, glittering as if he had seen the goddess Diana on the hunt. Jake could barely suppress a broad smile.

"Come," he told Alison. "If we are going to brave the ferry, we'd best do it when there is a crowd."

"I have been waiting for you," she replied, turning with a sudden swirl. She started out the door so quickly Jake had to trot to catch her as she swished past the blooming money plant at the edge of the walk.

"I will need a new cover story," she told him curtly as he fell in alongside. "I will henceforth be your wife."

"My cousin will suffice."

"A kissing cousin?"

Jake's scowl had little effect on her. She walked merrily with a breezy pace, the change of clothes having somehow increased her speed. He shook his head, thinking that he recognized both the signs and cause of a peculiar case of love sickness.

"Young Timothy is a handsome lad," he suggested after they had gone a few more yards.

"He is a little runt."

"A runt?"

"He is a full inch shorter than me."

"He'll grow in time."

"I could whip him with one hand tied behind my back."

"I'm glad to see that wearing a dress has not softened your spirits," said Jake.

"Do you like it?" she asked, swirling.

"It's very nice. As is the scarf."

"Grace helped outfit me. She is a remarkable woman."

"Indeed," said Jake. "I would think anyone who ended with her as a mother-in-law would be very lucky."

Alison gave him an odd look, as if she did not quite catch his meaning.

"Young Timothy will inherit his father's land," hinted Jake. "As well as his uncle's business. I would think he will be wealthy one day."

"Once a pipkin, always a pipkin," said Alison, turning up her nose and increasing her pace after calling her would-be lover an insignificant pot.

Jake had heard girls make light of beaus before; they liked to pretend they were sure of themselves. In such cases, it was useless to argue with them, as they would only pretend more firmly.

"You're walking quite fast," he told her.

"I can stop and wait for you, if I'm too quick."

"No, no, this is fine. At least I won't have to carry you all the way back to New York."

"I don't think I would give you the pleasure," she said, turning her nose up and increasing her pace.

Thirty-one

Wherein, Claus van Clynne offers to let go of his wits.

While Jake embarked on his trip to see Bebeef, Claus van Clynne undertook his own mission, starting with a pursuit entirely characteristic of the Dutchman—a twelve-hour nap. The Dutchman's eyes did not open until long after the local birds had gone about their business of catching the early worms. Indeed, there were few worms of any variety, early or late, to be found when van Clynne stretched his arms with a cranky growl and began rubbing his eyes vigorously. He soon discovered himself alone in the hideout. Daltoons had launched a full search for Alison upon finding her missing.

"Just as well," said the Dutchman to himself. "I am most efficient when unhampered by assistants. Or children. A spot of breakfast and I shall be back in order. Assuming I find anything worthy of the name in this town. Really, the quality of food has gone considerably downhill since the demise of the governor."

He being Stuyvesant, of course.

Van Clynne's hunger could not be satisfied at the Sons' hideout, which offered a cruel version of porridge in the kitchen downstairs. The squire did not complain about this; he considered that the few legitimately sick inmates in the small corner ward were aligned with the British side, and ought therefore to be tortured. Instead, he wiped a bit of water around his beard, borrowed a pistol from the armory, and went off to find himself a true breakfast.

Specifically, he wanted sausage. Now, one would think that, in a city with pigs constantly running underfoot, sausage would be an easy commodity. Not so. For there is a specific art to making sausage—a Dutch art, as van Clynne would have gladly explained had anyone asked.

In the event, he explained anyway, speaking loudly as he walked through the streets to a certain inn on Pearl Street owned by Samuel Fraunces. Though not strictly Dutch, Fraunces was a man steeped in the arts of hospitality, and his studies had led him to a formula for sausage construction that fairly rivaled that espoused by van Clynne's own mother. The fact that Fraunces was even now a firm and known member of the Whig party tended also to enhance the flavor.

His tavern was allowed to operate despite its owner's politics for a number of reasons, beginning with the quality of its ale. This morning the place was fairly empty, and van Clynne found himself greeted by the owner as he came through the portal to the main room.

"The sentries at King's Bridge are obviously sleeping," declared Fraunces in his faint West Indies accent. "They are allowing everyone into the city."

"As it happens, Samuel, I did not come via King's Bridge," said van Clynne. "I arrived by boat, with a personal escort."

Two young men sat near the corner window playing a card game; except for them, the room was empty.

"Your politics have not changed?" van Clynne asked the keeper in a soft voice.

"My politics are my own business."

"In that case, you may note that my feelings are as they have always been," declared van Clynne, pulling out a chair.

"I am sure Congress is glad of that," answered the keeper sarcastically. "And the king."

"Are you in the habit of talking all day, or will you ask your guest what he wishes to be served?"

"I see no guest before me, only a Dutchman who owes me ten pounds."

"Bah, ten pounds—a trifle." Van Clynne slipped off his shoe. "A double helping of sausages, if you please. Some fresh eggs, and if you can find any decent coffee in that cramped cellar of a kitchen, I will take that as well."

"You will take nothing until you settle what you owe me. I will have my sailor friends here kick you out." Fraunces gestured at the two young card players, neither one of whom made any sign to have heard. They were engaged in the arcane rite of cribbage. The Americans could have reinvaded New York and they would not have cared a whit, nor a Nobs.

But as the keeper set his fists on his hips, a smelly but genuine two-pound note drawn against Murdock & Company in Glasgow appeared in the Dutchman's fist. Fraunces grabbed the paper as it fluttered to the table, then retreated back to the kitchen, humming a song to himself. Coffee was issued, bread was found; within fifteen minutes a girl appeared carrying two plates of fine sausage and a large covered dish of eggs.

Fraunces nearly fainted when she returned to the back with another two-pound note.

A third appeared when the proprietor came to clear the dishes. By now he realized something serious must be afoot.

"I cannot take this money from you, Claus. Cannot, indeed."

Van Clynne looked up in amazement. "The Scottish bank is good for it, I assure you. And you will notice the elaborate engraving, protecting against counterfeits."

"Either you are very ill, or expect some great favor in return."

"Do I look sick?"

"Exactly the case. Exactly." Fraunces started to back

away. Van Clynne took the bill he had proffered and folded it neatly in his fist, where by some sleight of hand he managed to make it produce a twin. This had the effect of arresting Fraunces's retreat.

When a third note materialized in his hand, the keeper found his feet moving forward involuntarily. He knew the inevitable outcome but was powerless to stop himself from snatching for the bills, which naturally disappeared as soon as his fingers were extended.

"I am looking for Miss Melanie Pinkerton," said van Clynne, pushing away his empty plates. "I believe you know the family."

Fraunces frowned heavily. "What would you want with her? She's too young for you."

"I merely wish to speak to her." The squire opened his hand, thumbing the bills as if counting them. "She is no longer seeing General Howe, I trust."

"Baff—the swine claims to have thrown her over. He came within an inch of ruining the girl. For that alone he should be hanged."

"Agreed," said van Clynne, fanning the bills. "I wonder where I might find her."

"What are you up to, Claus?"

While the sum in van Clynne's hand was significant, it would not have been enough under any circumstance for the keeper to betray a trust. Van Clynne recognized this, and so he dropped a hint concerning the wishes of General Washington being involved. This only made Fraunces more suspicious.

"What have you to do with His Excellency?"

"I am on a mission for him."

"He wishes to see the girl?"

"She is but an attending player in a much grander scheme," said the Dutchman. "I assure you, no harm will come to her."

Fraunces frowned and turned his eyes to the bills. "Considering that I know your politics well, I suppose it would do no harm. The family took her north of Delancy's farm, past the encampments, to make sure she did not fall victim to Howe's depredations again. You would think one mistress would be enough."

"You do not get to be a gentleman by limiting your assignations," noted van Clynne with some distraction.

It was not nearly enough distraction to prevent him from whisking away his fist—and the notes—as Fraunces grabbed for them.

"I would be very obliged if you could find me a horse, on temporary loan. Some hatchets, too."

"What will you ask for next, a hat as well?"

"Tut, tut, Samuel, you are becoming quite excited," said van Clynne. "I am prepared to pay the lease in advance."

"In that case, I would be willing to lend you my wife's handsome black pony, barely in its third year, along with a fine cart that will match your exalted social standing," said Fraunces without noticeable irony. "At ten shillings an hour, then, I believe we could reach an arrangement."

"I will not be robbed in broad daylight, no matter who controls the city."

The hemming and hawing that followed was lengthy and resulted in a considerable price reduction. As a faithful reproduction would fill near thirty pages, suffice to say that van Clynne was found within the hour heading north at the bench of a two-wheeled, oak-paneled phaeton pulled by a short though not unvigorous pony. His armament now included a pair of axes, and he sported a black beaver hat that had been thrown in on good faith to seal the deal. The hatchets were a bit dull and the hat a size too big even for the Dutchman's prodigious skull, but at least it provided the Dutchman with something to doff when he was confronted by an English officer mounted on a white horse just south of Delancy's farm.

"Good morrow, major," called van Clynne cheerfully. "And what can I do for you?"

"You can call me colonel, for one," said the man

icily. "You will state your business and reason for being here."

Van Clynne grumbled to himself. It was difficult to keep up with the British army's habit of continually promoting its officers despite their incompetence. In the Dutch forces, this man would never have advanced above the rank of captain, obviously being far too nosey for his own good.

"Sir Colonel, I meant no offense. As for my mission, it is routine in the extreme. I am after some vegetables."

"You do not look like a farmer to me."

"Of course not, sir. I am a man of business. In fact, General Howe himself has asked me to look after this vegetable factor. It appears the soldiers are in great need of vegetative energy for their coming campaign."

"If you are working for Sir William, honor me with a letter from him."

"I will not, sir," said the Dutchman haughtily.

His new hat slipped to one side, ruining the effect. Deciding to change tactics, he grabbed it from his head and held it in his hands, hoping to strike a contrite pose. Though he looked the model of a penitent, the officer did not acknowledge the likeness.

"Stand down and present yourself for arrest. You are very much like the description of one of the prisoners said to have escaped yesterday from the city jail."

The colonel pulled his sword from the scabbard with a great deal of pompous flash. It was a most ornate device, with hand-crafted silver embellishments about the handle and considerable scrolling up and down the blade.

"You did not let me finish," said the Dutchman quickly. "I am under strict orders not to communicate my mission with anyone."

"Piffle."

"Well, I suppose I must make an exception, given your rank," said van Clynne, reaching beneath his hat toward his coat, then letting his fingers take a detour to the floor, where they found his hatchet. In the next instant, the Briton flew backwards as blood burst like a geyser from his skull, the ax having found its mark.

Van Clynne started to rise from the bench to retrieve the hatchet, but was interrupted by a shout from nearby in the woods. A half-dozen British soldiers appeared from their bivouac as van Clynne grabbed for his reins. The little pony Fraunces had lent him strained for everything he was worth as the soldiers let their muskets get some exercise.

The bullets did a nice job engraving their marks in the rear of the wagon. The Dutchman was, nonetheless, unscathed, as was his hat, which remarkably remained on his head despite the pace. But as he began congratulating his fortune and thinking if some way might be found to make the hat shrink a size, van Clynne realized one of the soldiers had appropriated the colonel's horse and was chasing him up the road.

"Come now, little one," the Dutchman told the pony. "Let us see if we cannot reach yonder bend before this galloping horseman. We may effect an ambush if we do. I have often thought a small pony more worthwhile in a pinch than a dozen large stallions."

The pony's ears bloated with the flattery as it strained its legs and pushed its shoulders forward in a manner that would have done fabled Pegasus proud. Alas, the animal was not used to such exertion, and quickly began to tire. When they were still several dozen yards before the turn, van Clynne realized they would not beat the redcoat there.

The soldier had taken the colonel's sword as well as his horse. He began waving it above his head, momentum building as he leaned over his horse menacingly. Van Clynne reached below the seat and retrieved his pistol, endeavoring to pull back the lock into the firing position while all the while urging his little pony forward. The space between the horseman and the cart fell rapidly; van Clynne managed to point the gun and fire just as the swordsman took a swipe at his head.

The blade missed. Alas, the same was true of van Clynne's bullet. The pony, exhausted, gave up his attempt at a gallop and fell into a strained trot, his body heaving with exhaustion. The redcoat pulled back on his reins, trying to gain a good angle for attack. Van Clynne threw down his pistol and reached for his remaining hatchet.

He nearly lost it as the pony jerked to the side to avoid the soldier's swipe. Van Clynne just managed to thrust the handle up as the redcoat slashed violently toward his neck. Sword and ax crashed together with a clang so loud anyone in the neighborhood would have thought he was being called to church.

Three times the weapons came together, and each time the Dutchman shuddered with the blow. The redcoat was a strong man born in northern Scotland and raised on red oats; he had ridden much as a youngster and by every right should have been at least a corporal, if not sergeant, except for some troubles he'd had as a young recruit.

But van Clynne was in no position to inquire after his personal history. He pulled back the hatchet, only to see it fly from his grasp, propelled by a quicker-than-expected blow. The redcoat, sensing that victory was but a moment away, pulled back his sword and took a deep breath, savoring his moment of glory.

"Well now," said van Clynne, doffing his hat as if in salute, "I am glad to finally be on even terms with you."

"Even terms?" said the Scotsman with a tongue so thick his words sounded more like *E turn,* "And how do ye figure that 'un, son?"

"Allow me to introduce myself," said van Clynne, taking the opportunity to slip down from the carriage on the side opposite the soldier. "Claus van Clynne, Esquire. You have undoubtedly heard of me."

"Whether I heard of ye or not, it dan't matter. Ye slain the colonel, and I'll be making mince pie of ye in return."

The redcoat pushed his horse forward and took another slash, nipping the oversized beaver hat but not its
owner. Van Clynne threw himself on the ground and
rolled beneath the wheels of the cart, using it for protection. No matter which way the redcoat attacked, van
Clynne flew to the other side. Granted, he suffered a
few close nicks and scratches, and the ground was not
very soft or smooth, but the soldier could not get close
enough to strike a serious blow without dismounting.

"Come out, ye damn coward. Out, or I will kill your
wee pony."

"A true Scotsman would not harm a pony born on
the heath," claimed van Clynne.

The soldier knitted his brow. He had never heard of
a pony imported to America from the heath, nor was
he altogether certain what distinguishing marks, if any,
a Scots pony would bear. Nonetheless, he held all
equines in high esteem and felt it beneath him to attack this poor animal, just because its owner was a
treacherous, murdering rebel.

Besides, the pony would fetch a nice price back at
the city.

"All right then," said the redcoat, jumping from his
horse. "But you yourself will get no mercy."

Van Clynne just made it out from under the cart as
the redcoat charged. He slipped onto the other side as
the sword crashed so heavily against the wood that
three inches of it were splintered.

"Stand and fight like a man!" declared the Scotsman.

"Oh gladly, sir," answered van Clynne. "But the
odds are little lopsided, given that you have a sword
and I have only my wits to protect me."

"Ye dan't object when ye had the gun and axes."

"I am only saying that I will put aside my wit, if you
put aside your sword."

This rather generous offer was answered by a vigorous flail of the sword. But as van Clynne circled the
cart and the terms of the standoff became clear, the

redcoat took a new assessment of the situation. Clearly, he could defeat the rotund Dutchman if they fought hand to hand—even without the dirk he had secreted in his belt.

"All right, laddie," he said, holding the sword at his side. "I will fight you fair, like a man."

He dropped the sword in the dust.

"Oh, you want to play at fisticuffs," said van Clynne, edging to his right. "I should warn you, sir: I am Dutch."

"So?"

Van Clynne's answer was a feint toward the sword. The Scotsman grabbed his knife as he performed a spectacular front-roll to the ground in front of the saber. He landed on his feet in a fighting position, quite prepared to take on an entire regiment of rebels, if need be.

He needn't. For the Dutchman had taken the opportunity to bolt not for the sword, but the soldier's nearby horse.

"As you were not prepared to completely abandon your weapons, I did not forsake mine," shouted van Clynne as he leaped aboard and thundered away.

Thirty-two

Wherein, Major Dr. Keen is sent to Brooklyn, for Squire van Clynne's health.

The battering at the engineer's office left Major Dr. Keen in the foulest mood of his life. It was one thing to discover that Jake Gibbs had fooled him; Gibbs was surely the Americans' finest agent, a man trusted by Washington with only the most delicate missions. He had been schooled in England and came from a wealthy if not noble family. In some ways he reminded Keen of himself as a young man.

But to find van Clynne alive and running through the streets of New York as freely as a rat—the humiliation was nearly too much to bear.

By the time Keen's horses finally stopped their panicked flight they were nearly trampling the rough wood of the docks. His eyes fairly closed by bruises, the doctor saw no alternative but to slink into some lair and lick his wounds. He did not want to rejoin Clayton Bauer and his relatives under any circumstances, as he would then be obliged to offer some sort of explanation for the tumult. Even the most convincing lie would be a degrading embarrassment.

Rarely had the doctor found himself in such mental disarray. He could not repair to his apartments on the city's west side for fear that someone—perhaps an agent of Bacon's—would seek him out there. Nor could he rule out the possibility that Gibbs had been sent to assassinate him, in a reversal of their previous roles. And so Keen spent a miserable night shivering in a shack owned by an acquaintance midway between Rutger's land and Corlear's Hook. The wind and sea ravaged his ears with their unrelenting drone as he pitched in the narrow cradle of his bed, wrapped in a thin and threadbare cotton cloth. Not even his potions could allow him a fitless sleep.

Still, the doctor had passed hard nights before, and the morrow brought him some hope and new priorities. He decided that he would no longer worry about Bacon and the consequences of the premature message announcing the death of his two enemies. There was nothing to be done about it one way or the other; he would have to accept whatever Fate delivered.

That decision gave him a certain amount of peace, and allowed him to reach his next: he would find and eliminate van Clynne before attending to Gibbs.

Van Clynne embodied nearly everything that Keen loathed, and yet he had beaten Keen consistently, escaping every encounter. To kill him, to rip the man's immense liver from his body and hold it above his head, to strip his gallbladder with a serrated knife and feed it to the rutting pigs . . . Keen nearly frothed contemplating such joyful enterprises.

He knew that van Clynne had a great propensity for drink and trusted that he would not be difficult to trace. The doctor began the day by making the rounds of the taverns and inns in the vicinity, gradually widening his net. All manner of owners and keepers knew his prey; van Clynne seemed to owe each inhabitant of the island at least five shillings. But the Dutchman's comings and goings were not regular, and none of Keen's interviews produced definite news.

Until, in midafternoon, he stopped at Fraunces Tavern.

"Owes you too, eh?" said the proprietor after Keen had one of the servers fetch him.

"He has owed me a great deal in the past," Keen told the aristocratic-looking man before him. He was aware that the middle-aged Fraunces shaded to the Whig side but was nonetheless confident he could be fooled. "In all honesty, it is I who owe him at present. I have business in Europe, and want to settle up before leaving."

Though the story seemed plausible and even admirable in theory, Keen could not have hit on a tale that would have made Fraunces more suspicious. To his knowledge, van Clynne never, ever loaned money; it was a violation of the Dutchman's most sacred principles. But Fraunces had considerable experience tending bar, and nodded with a face that would have fooled Saint Thomas himself.

"You are unlucky to have missed him," said the proprietor. "He was here before midday, and was speaking of going to Brooklyn. I believe he was paying off a debt among tavern owners there."

Keen did not bother to finish his Madeira before leaving.

"Add a shilling to van Clynne's bill," Fraunces told his bookkeeper when he returned upstairs. "I have just saved his life."

"Overvalued by half," remarked the man.

Clayton Bauer pulled back the pistol lock's hammer and steadied his aim, endeavoring to ignore his sister.

"Clayton," she insisted, "it is nearly midafternoon. Your dinner has become cold."

The pistol shot rent the air, but the paper Bauer had placed on the tree as a target remained untouched.

"Damn."

"It's a fine ham," said Lady Patricia.

"Please, Patricia. Leave me alone. See to your husband, or take a carriage into town."

The dismissive tone angered her, and Lady Patricia felt the bile rise in her mouth. Still, she fought to control herself, and when she spoke, her voice was nearly as conciliatory as before.

"Clayton, you can't go through with this silliness. It is beneath your station."

"On the contrary, my dear. To ignore the insult is beneath my station. It would finish me."

He bent down and picked up his ivory powder horn, refilling his pistol. Nearly half of his shots had failed to find the target. He decided to retie the blue ribbon around his white shirt-sleeve; perhaps it would bring him luck, if not improve his aim.

"Clayton, he is a foolish young man. In England he would be a commoner, if not worse."

"In England, I would be a commoner," he shot back. "You do not understand, Patricia. You do not understand the country or our ways. You have no notion what this war is about."

"And I do not care to." She could not control her anger any longer. "It is ridiculous. Let the colonists set their own taxes and rule themselves. What is the difficulty? The result will be the same. We are bred from the same soil."

"The result will be chaos and poverty. The issue is far beyond taxes. You do not understand the leveling of the mob, my dear. I doubt even your husband does. Nor did young Thomas."

"Don't speak of my son in that tone."

A twinge of regret flushed through him—Bauer had liked the young man a great deal—and he finished loading the pistol in silence.

"Are you going to practice all day?"

His answer was a shot that struck the paper square in the middle. Nodding with approval, Bauer began walking toward it to exult in his success. The high grass before the house flayed back with his boots, barely brushing his soft, smooth breeches. A redcoat sentry was posted a few yards to the north, along the stone wall that marked the former border of the property. The war had allowed Bauer to expand his estate for an extremely advantageous price.

"Come and eat something. William is worried sick about you."

"Lord William worries about nothing, not even your honor," said Bauer. He turned toward his sister suddenly. "Tell me, Patricia: did you enjoy that kiss?"

"Don't be ridiculous."

"I know you did. Bacon chooses his agents because they attract women. That is how they gather most of their information, from weak women."

"You think all women are weak."

"Everyone is weak," said Bauer, starting back to his mark. "It is just a question of how they show it."

Thirty-three

Wherein, the villain Egans is briefly rejoined, and Squire van Clynne goes courting.

*T*he renegade Egans had spent much of the time since his arrival in New York being abused by the British establishment. Not only was he denied prompt payment for his prisoner, but the lieutenant on Bacon's staff assigned to debrief him treated him with undisguised contempt. The man, Bacon's only officer left in the city, steadfastly refused to grant Egans his bounty or even his rightful pay until the entire business was complete. Given the lieutenant's intricate style of questioning, that might not happen for several weeks.

Egans was a stoic, and could weather many difficult trials without complaint, but he had a hard time stomaching insults. Nor did he feel it the best use of his time to be kept hanging around the city answering questions about how many horses were sheltered in obscure stables north of the chain at Peekskill.

When, at the end of his third interview the lieutenant still declined to approve the reward, Egans stormed from his office and headed straight to the jail where he had deposited his prisoner. If he could not have his money from the British, he decided, he would have it from the Dutchman, whose broad hints had included the possibility of a ransom.

And after that, some piece of satisfaction might be retrieved from killing him.

"Your prisoner escaped yesterday," sneered the

clerk who met him at the desk. "Along with a group of other rebels. Undoubtedly he was the ringleader. Perhaps we shall hang you for bringing him."

Egans instinctively reached for his pistol. As quickly as lightning flashes between clouds, three grenadiers grabbed him and flung him to the ground. His struggle ended when a muzzle appeared an inch from his nose.

"Do not harm him," said the clerk. "As pleasant as it would be, there are too many forms to fill out."

Egans was grudgingly allowed to his feet.

"Return with the fat Dutchman or your master General Bacon will have a full report. In triplicate."

The renegade was too smart to say that he considered no one his master. He met the British clerk's stare blankly, holding his eyes in a defiant gaze. Neither man blinked.

"Do you want the whole man or just his scalp?" asked Egans finally.

"His scalp will do nicely. The rest of him takes up too much room."

Van Clynne hurried past the British huts at Delancy's without stopping, despite a growing desire for something to quench his thirst. There was, at best, only a token force left guarding the small wood cabins built against the gentle hills and on the flats, but having just escaped British hospitality the Dutchman's mouth would have to be literally on fire before he would condescend to dally with any more redcoats or their German brethren. The colonel's horse proved a decent beast, not partial to either side, and van Clynne soon found the farm near Harlem where the Pinkertons had retreated to.

This was a Dutch family hard on its luck, or so van Clynne theorized, for otherwise he could not supply a reason for their staying in the occupied city. The tailor's example notwithstanding, by van Clynne's lights every Dutchman hated the British. If the truth be told, his estimation of Dutch patriotism was somewhat off the mark, but his assessment of the Pinkerton's financial status was correct. The family's attitude toward the British had hardened considerably since their daughter's interlude with Howe, though having voiced pro-English sentiments in the past they could not now risk the reception they might find further north.

They still had their pride, however, as the family patriarch made clear after ushering his old friend van Clynne inside.

"Imagine, hinting that we might be bought off by supplying some small infantry unit with grain," complained Veder Pinkerton. "Grain!"

"Truly an insult," agreed van Clynne. This was the typical British blunder: the Pinkertons had been corn dealers for three generations at least, and they considered anything that did not grow on ears as belonging to an inferior class. "I wonder if I might talk to Melanie."

"What do you want to talk to her about?"

"Oh—just idle chatter."

Veder looked at him suspiciously. "You want to talk about Howe?"

"Of course not," said van Clynne. "Naturally not."

"I will kill anyone who mentions his name to her. I can tell that her heart is still turned in his direction, despite all our arguments."

"A dastardly villain," said the Dutchman, who despite the warning was not about to retreat. "I think that when a man is at a certain age," he suggested quietly after a temporary pause, "there are certain contingencies in life one should prepare for."

Veder jolted upright in his chair. In the arcane etiquette of Dutch matrimonials, the squire's sentence amounted to a formal declaration of intent to informally decide on provisionally electing to eventually commence courtship—the all-important first step toward wedded bliss.

Whatever his faults, Claus van Clynne was not a man without means, and if his crusade to have his property returned were ever fruitful, he would easily rate among the richest men in the state. True, Veder realized, his clothes had long since gone out of fashion, and he had come to the house with a hat at least one size too large, but eccentricity can be overlooked in a rich son-in-law.

Veder ran from the room to fetch the girl. Van Clynne settled in the chair—a wingback whose high pillows kept his head well-cradled—and contemplated his next move. His present position was every bit as dangerous as the one he had just left on the road. More so, as he had already and quite honestly declared his intention to decide to intend to wed a comely lass in lower Westchester. Sweet Jane was busy preparing her wedding trousseau, which undoubtedly included several fierce weapons to enforce her claims.

Miss Pinkerton was not without her own charms. Standing a few inches below five feet, she had sharply curled red hair which flowed in grand tresses around her head, a veritable sculpture that set off her nicely rounded cheeks and helped impart a rosy glow to her face. Her yellow dress stood over a strongly curved corset, which plucked up the tops of her snowy white breasts like two large, European mountains.

During a previous mission to New York, van Clynne and Jake had foiled General Howe's proposed hunting expedition in that territory, and Melanie recognized the squire immediately. She greeted him with a warm and protracted kiss on the cheek just above his beard, her body pressing forward in a crush of silk and other things.

Momentarily flustered, van Clynne called for a cup of beer.

"We've no beer in this house," Veder reminded him. "But you are welcome to share my squeezings."

Made from corn, the liquid had an oily taste and was nearly one hundred percent pure alcohol. Van Clynne demurred.

"How is your friend Jake?" Melanie asked.

"Oh well, very well," he coughed. "And you? How is life on the farm?"

She shrugged noncommittally. "The corn grows."

Van Clynne, now back in control of himself, nodded as if this was the most interesting thing anyone had ever said to him. He shot a glance at Veder, hoping that he might hint at a strategic absence, which would allow him to get to the real reason he had come.

Unfortunately, custom strictly dictated a chaperone at this stage of the pre-pre-courtship ritual, and Veder was not about to blow his chances by committing an etiquette faux pas. Van Clynne frowned, then turned back to Melanie.

"So, do you hunt?" he asked the girl. The purposely awkward question had been prescribed by a codicil to the Hague Resolutions of 1643, directing the order of initial engagement conversations.

She shook her head.

"I suppose you spend your time mending," he suggested.

"Mending?"

"Socks and things."

"Why would I do that?"

"Melanie, dear, I'm sure you're getting tired," said Veder, pushing forward. The officially allotted time for a first meeting had nearly expired.

"I believe I will have those squeezings now," said van Clynne.

"Oh yes, the squeezings." Veder looked at van Clynne's face and concluded that he had completely fallen under his daughter's spell. He was obviously trying to move things along faster than anticipated, and the corn farmer was all for it. "Melanie, talk to Claus about the weather and I, I will just run into the next room."

"While you were with General Howe," van Clynne asked in a soft, hurried voice as soon as her father left, "who was his wig-maker?"

"His wig-maker?"

"Quickly, child, before your father returns. Did he mention a barber?"

"I believe it was George on Stone Street. Or was it Stone on George Street? One of those, definitely."

Van Clynne had no time to quiz her further, as her father announced his pending return with a merry song he hummed to himself. The tune sounded suspiciously like a wedding march.

"So, dear, you understand my intentions?" Van Clynne made his voice so faint she could not hear the last word, though her hopeful heart supplied it.

"Did you say, 'intentions'?"

Now his voice grew loud enough for even the corn outside to hear. "You will not have me?"

"But Claus—"

Van Clynne lifted himself from the chair as Veder, his tune banished from his mouth, ran forward.

"Claus, Melanie—"

"Claus, what did you mean? Intentions?"

"It is nothing, nothing. My poor heart cannot take the strain."

"Wait!" Veder appeared considerably more heart-broken than van Clynne. "Claus, you've rushed things. This is merely the first meeting. Your emotions have gotten the better of you. Slow down, my friend. All will work out, given time."

But the squire continued to the door. "Children cannot be expected to follow the Dutch order of things," he lamented, "if they are improperly raised."

"Are you insinuating that my Melanie was not raised properly!"

"Insinuating is not the word I would use, sir," said van Clynne, opening the door.

"Out and good riddance! Out!"

Van Clynne turned in the threshold, the very picture of brave but downtrodden dignity. "I am leaving, sir; there is no need to insult me further. My heart already has been quite riven. I despair. Who knows what I will do next? I may walk along the river. I may, perchance, enlist in the British army."

Veder, his emotions twisting in several directions at

once, settled to the floor and began sucking on the bottle of squeezings as soon as van Clynne departed, his brief dream of riches flown out the door with the squire's russet coat. Melanie remained in a state of severe confusion and finally salved her bruised intellect by pressing a few of her curls that had fallen out of place as a result of the interview.

Claus van Clynne possessed an encyclopedic knowledge of Dutch families in the province of New York— or New Amsterdam, as he occasionally referred to it. He was not equally informed about occupants whose genealogical roots had taken hold in other soils, however, and so he was not sure which, Stone or George, might be the proper wig-maker. As George Street lay closer, however, he decided to visit Mr. Stone first, via a road less convenient but completely removed from the one he had taken north. He also left his stolen horse behind, reasoning that it might be recognized from its fine equipment. These contingencies greatly increased the time it took him to carry out his mission, but van Clynne had always held that it was better to arrive at a place late and intact, rather than late in the most permanent sense.

The day had already progressed quite far without his having stopped for dinner; he felt obliged to hail a baker he knew in the northern precincts and see about some mince pie the man was always trying to sell. This transaction took considerable negotiation, not least of all because the baker warned that soldiers were proceeding through the city looking for the prisoners who had escaped from jail yesterday. He relayed their description of the ringleader: "a portly Dutch gentleman in old-style russet dress, with a scraggly beard, large Quaker-style beaver hat, talkative disposition, and a severe willingness to complain and argue at every turn."

"Fortunately, they've got the description all wrong," sniffed van Clynne. "The Quakers know nothing about proper hats."

Nonetheless, he took the hint and proceeded even more circumspectly. In sum, when the Dutchman finally arrived on George Street, it was late afternoon. There proved to be no wig shop there, or at least none he could find. Concerned about the hour, he walked quickly toward the southern tip of the island, aiming for Stone Street and Mr. George.

The fact that Stone Street lay exactly opposite one of the gates of the British fort, and was customarily filled with soldiers and British officers of every description, did give him some concern. Not fear—he was Dutch, after all—but further complications this close to achieving his goal would be bothersome. So he stopped at a small shop along the way and procured a large black cape that fit very nicely over his coat. In an alley nearby he confiscated a large and empty wooden box, complete with a snug-fitting cover. He hoisted it to his shoulder and held it close to the side of his face, pushing his hat far down on his head to help obscure his profile.

As well as his own vision.

And so when he felt his cloak rudely grabbed not a half block on, he jumped nearly two feet straight up in complete surprise.

Thirty-four

Wherein, the difference between fear and surprise is essayed, as are wig styles.

"*D*eclare yourself," said the redcoat tugging van Clynne's cloak. "What is your business here?"

"My business?"

Van Clynne turned uneasily and lifted the brim of his hat slightly, seeking his bearings. He saw that, in his haste, he had inadvertently walked down an alley exiting across from one of the fort's sentry posts. The guard had been increased for security's sake following the prison break, and van Clynne had nearly run down one of the redcoats, or more properly, the man's brightly polished bayonet.

"My business, sir, is business," van Clynne said boldly. He held the crate closer to his face as he gestured with his free hand.

"Are you delivering food for the fort?"

"Yes, that was exactly what I was doing," said van Clynne.

Thus we see the great difference between being taken by surprise and being overcome by fear: the former is quickly recovered, while the latter is only arrested by a vigorous run.

"I have a load of fresh vegetables for the fort here on my shoulder," continued van Clynne. "Fine vegetables. Here, let us examine them," he said, swinging the crate to the pavement. "You will want to search among the carrots, I presume. They are nasty things, always in need of a good examination. You never know when one will turn rebel."

"Enough, fool. Pick up your box and pass into the fort while the gate is open."

The soldier pointed his gun in the direction he wanted van Clynne to take, straight into the heart of the British camp.

"Well, I will not do so under those circumstances," he said, searching for a way to retreat.

"What is wrong here, private?"

"This arse wants me to search his carrots," the sentry told his superior, an officious but exceedingly young officer of His Majesty's Guard, who walked with such a stiff gait that van Clynne concluded a carpenter had forced a rusted hinge into his buttocks.

"What carrots?"

"What he's carrying in the box, sir. I already told him he could pass, but he insists on an inspection."

The officer frowned. Van Clynne, with some words about his honor and integrity being beyond question, reached to his crate—then showed great horror when he flipped off the lid to find it empty.

"I have been robbed," he shouted. "My wares have been stolen. Organize a search, call out the guard. Colonel, I demand an entire company of men to see to the thieves."

"Out of my sight, you fool," said the officer, hiding his flattery at the impromptu promotion with a sharp kick to van Clynne's rear.

The Dutchman complied, heading up Stone Street with considerable haste. Along the way, he spotted the wig-maker's shop. But he dared not duck inside while the sentry stood at the end of the block in full view. Indeed, he waited out of sight at the end of the block for nearly an hour until he spied the man being relieved. Thus it was nearly supper time before he was able to enter the shop.

"Here for a bloodletting?" asked the proprietor, who like many of his brethren was a barber.

"No, I was more interested in wigs," said the Dutchman. He settled into the large chair that sat at the center of the shop while he surveyed his surroundings and concocted a plan.

"Wigs?" The barber was a pudgy sort with a nose that, to van Clynne, betrayed a great interest in drink. Whether the conclusion was warranted or not, it suggested a course of action—provided he could overcome the man's initial suspicions.

"Wigs," agreed the squire.

"You don't look like a man who wears one. Though you could use a smaller hat."

"That is the reason for the room beneath my crown," declared the Dutchman. "I have come in search of the finest wig-maker in the city. You *are* Mr. George, I presume."

"Yes, indeed."

"Wig-maker to Sir William?"

The man patted his left palm with a barber's fleam retrieved from the center table. Ordinarily used for letting blood, the sharp instrument was an intimidating weapon under any circumstance.

"What business is that of yours?"

"No business," said van Clynne. "Merely that he recommended you to me, that is all. For a wig."

"As I said, you do not seem the type to wear a wig. The habit has largely gone out of style, except among the highest class of British officers. And even then—"

"Well that is where you are wrong, sir," said van Clynne. "Quite wrong. Indeed, I believe a club wig would look quite handsome on me."

"A club wig? On a Dutchman?" The barber laughed. He loosened his white apron and removed it, revealing a fashionably striped set of breeches and waistcoat. "No one has worn those in many years."

Van Clynne feigned confusion. "Sir William told me he had just ordered a dozen."

"He's pulling your leg. He's quite a prankster, Sir William. People don't realize he has a sense of humor.

I tell you, no one knows a man like his barber. Let a little blood, and a bond forms."

"Indeed. Are you thirsty?"

"Thirsty?"

"I came in for a wig, but now I find myself in a mood for a good bleed," lied van Clynne. "But in order to do so, I need a little, preparation shall we say?"

"A bit of Dutch courage, eh?" said the barber, reaching back to a drawer on the counter near his side window. "Rum'll knock you up in a second. Medicinal, of course."

"Actually, I was in mind of a strong beer or two. Perhaps you will accompany me. I will stand for it, naturally."

The barber looked at him doubtfully. "It is getting late in the day. I was thinking of going upstairs for supper before too long. The wife is waiting."

"She would begrudge you a beer with a customer?"

"If the truth be told—"

"What is happening in our city?" complained van Clynne, rising from the chair. "These rebels have put foolish notions into everyone's heads. Women no longer know their proper place. I tell you, sir, during Governor Stuyvesant's day, none of this would have happened."

"Now, now, relax, man. She is a good woman. Too given to church sermons, that is all. Trying to keep me on the righteous path."

"Well," said van Clynne haughtily, "from the way Sir William was bragging about you, I thought you would accept my invitation to a drink quite readily. But I shall have to tell him he was wrong."

"Just a minute now," said the barber, taking his arm. "Do you really require a letting?"

"I have been feeling most melancholy of late," said van Clynne. "Given to heavy moods. I also require a wig. I would naturally want the most expensive, in keeping with my station."

"That being?"

"Purveyor of purveyment. Contracting contracts. And the like."

"No horses' hair for you then, I daresay."

"Beneath contempt."

"Well, I cannot avoid my duty to my fellow man," said the barber, who also would not avoid the possibility of a handsome profit and free drinks. "After all, I have taken an oath."

The oath happened to be in relation to his wife's cooking—perhaps they could have a bite to eat as well.

"Which tavern did you have in mind?" he asked.

"You understand, sir, that the style was originally called an entire, as it contained hints of every brewing method known to man. Top fermenting—yes, that is the proper place for a porter to begin, at the height of the liquid, where the flavor noodles can take their proper perspective on the proceedings. You understand the theory of flavor noodles, do you not?"

The barber shook his head. He had been endeavoring to follow van Clynne's learned discussion on beer through several light ales, four lagers, and a very serious porter. The Dutchman had chosen this inn not merely because it lay in the opposite direction of the fort, but because it made a specialty of brewing several various styles of beer. It thus fulfilled his purposes remarkably well.

The poor barber had begun to show signs of inebriation with his third tankard, and now betrayed distinct symptoms of total drunkenness, finding not only that everything presented to him was pleasing, but endeavoring to be most pleasing in return. His new friend, in turn, was not only agreeable but generous: Van Clynne was willing not only to pay for the drinks, but had even agreed to twice the normal sum for the planned bloodletting. Plus, he had ordered dinner—a very fatted fowl, complete with fixings, still being prepared.

The Dutchman, judging that he had cooked his gander long enough, now pulled the fryer from the pan.

"And so, sir, onto the topic of wigs."

"Wigs?"

"You have fitted Sir William, have you not?"

"Oh yes. Sir William. Has me cut his nose hairs. They grow like a jungle."

"I suppose he has ordered a tye wig?"

"Tye wigs, no."

"Are they not popular in Boston?"

"Boston? I would not think so."

"Didn't Sir William enquire as to the popularity of wigs where he was going?"

"Isn't go'n Boston," said the barber, shaking his head. "He's going to Phil, Philkadelphia. And you know what they wear there?"

Van Clynne did not bother to listen to the reply, instead slapping two fresh notes on the counter. As he waved to the proprietor, the wig-maker abruptly fell over on the floor in a drunken stupor.

To say that the Dutchman was in as cheerful a mood as possible when he opened the door and stepped into the now darkened street would be to understate the obvious. To say that his spirits reversed with more speed than a bee on a spring morning would miss the mark by a similar distance—for the Dutchman suddenly found a large arm coiling around his neck.

It belonged to his former jailer, Christof Egans.

Thirty-five

Wherein, Egans's genealogical roots are briefly dug up, and concerns sprout regarding Jake's state.

"*J*ust the man I was looking for," declared van Clynne, barely managing to keep his balance as he was pulled from the doorway and pushed against the wall.

"You will shut your mouth for me, Dutchman," answered Egans. "I have spent considerable energy tracking you down, and waited here nearly a full hour."

"You should have come in," said van Clynne apologetically, noting the pistol in Egans's hand. "Surely I owe you a drink for delivering me to New York."

"Silence! You are worth as much to me dead as alive now." Egans loosened his grip and spat in disgust—a reaction, it must be admitted, to the somewhat sour odor the beer had imparted to van Clynne's breath. "I hate the damn Dutch."

"I do not see why," said van Clynne, smoothing his beard with as much dignity as the circumstances permitted. "Considering that you are Dutch yourself."

"You are a miserable liar!" screamed Egans, pushing the gun at van Clynne's face.

"Just so, sir, just so," tutted the Dutchman, casting an eye up and down the empty street before continuing. "But search your memory well after you shoot me. Remember your dear birth mother. When her face comes to mind, you will see it bore the strong, sturdy lines of an Amsterdam native. A fine beer-maker, I might add; no one could beat her hops."

"My stepfather was killed by a Dutchman, van Gergen."

"Your stepfather was a noble warrior and a great chief to his people," said van Clynne. "But he was killed by Von Gorgon. Von, not van. The vowel makes all the difference in the world. He was a German. They are a notoriously disagreeable people."

"I do not believe you."

"Naturally," said van Clynne. He reached into his pocket, smiling as Egans aimed his gun. "Allow me to show you a map."

He produced the small sheaf of documents he had taken from the engineering office and began leafing through them. In due course he came to the map of the quadrant in question and unfolded it for his captor. Von Gorgon's name was clearly marked.

As was Egans's, in a note indicating the German had usurped the property that had once belonged to "good Mr. Egans, his wife Gelda and child, miserably martyred by the native peoples."

Egans stepped back in confusion. Now it must be admitted that this last note was in a hand remarkably like van Clynne's, and that he had been examining this particular page in great detail upon his return to the Sons' headquarters the previous evening. Even so, it was not the map nor the argument that convinced the adopted Indian, but van Clynne's details of his mother's face, which conjured a dark but accurate memory in his breast.

"Come, sir, let us step off the street where we can talk," suggested van Clynne, gingerly extending his hand and lowering Egans's pistol. "I have not had supper. A good sturgeon steak, I believe, would revive me properly. And you appear in need of several strong ales."

Some time later, seated in a tavern located in the dock area and waiting for the well-buttered fish to be served, van Clynne unwound the tale of Egans's ancestors. John Egans had married Gelda Guldenwinckle of the Amsterdam Guldenwinckles, a housewife of the old school. Particularly adept at raising tulips, she was said by some gossipy neighbors to quite spoil her only child, young Christof.

At this point in the narrative, a tear formed in the ordinarily stoic Egans's eye, and the squire hastened to proceed. It took nearly three hours and four times as many cups of strong ale to relate the entire story of Egans's capture at the age of two by a small band of Mohawk, who in due course turned the child over to the Oneida. Van Clynne skipped over the womenfolk's role in the proceeding; this revealed his Western prejudice, as a native would have instead properly emphasized it. Nonetheless, his praise of Egans's stepfather was genuine and found a receptive ear.

Egans already knew much of the story well, but he had never heard it put so eloquently or fetchingly. For the first time in his life, he had something of an appreciation for his white parents as well as his red. It would not be truthful to say that the former had replaced the latter in his esteem, but the changeling now looked upon the world with completely changed, if somewhat beery, eyes.

Such was the power of van Clynne's tongue that, well before the end of dinner—marked by some creamy Gouda—Egans had not only given the Dutchman back his paper money and passes, but his political allegiance had shifted one hundred and eighty degrees. His hatred for the Dutch had been transformed into a complete loathing of the Germans—and thus by strong logic their allies, the British. The fact that the English had cheated him on countless occasions, and never shown him a quarter of the deference van Clynne made so obvious in his speech, clearly helped this conversion, though in the squire's opinion the shift was merely a result of Dutch blood winning out.

"I will murder every damn mercenary I see," declared Egans, slamming his fist on the table so hard that his tankard, thankfully empty, fell to the floor.

"Quiet now. We will find a more appropriate venue for your rage," said van Clynne, smiling nervously at their neighbors, including a pair of alarmed Hessians, before hurrying to pay the bill.

Lieutenant Daltoons paced through the large, empty room at the top of the infirmary. He had run out of fresh curses to use on himself for letting Alison slip away, and as the old ones were by now well-worn, he kept his vigil in silence. He assumed—he prayed—that she had found Jake. He further assumed—he further prayed—that Jake's failure to return as promised was due to some minor complication.

He had done more than merely pray. The undercover officer had spent much of the day searching the city, together with some of Culper's other men, but without result. Nor had Culper succeeded in discovering Howe's target, despite his best efforts.

. The spy ring itself remained in mortal danger. The British had reacted to yesterday's jail break with great indignation, to say nothing of increased patrols and a tripling of the normal guard at every facility. Nearly every soldier who remained in the city had been set to work harassing suspected patriot sympathizers, and there was word that the authorities were planning to conduct a house-to-house search for the escapees.

Culper had taken the precaution of sending men known to be wanted into hiding and emptying the places the Sons of Liberty had used with great regularity. This infirmary was one of them, but as it was the place Jake was to return to someone must wait here. And Daltoons had appointed himself that someone.

The Connecticut native had served Culper and the other members of the Sons of Liberty spy ring in a variety of capacities. He had never been more concerned than now, however. The lieutenant was not so much worried about Jake, whom he regarded as something of a mentor, but the spirited Miss Alison, whose beauty he had no trouble spotting beneath her rough disguise. She was a very remarkable girl, he thought to himself. More than remarkable. Were the circumstances different . . .

The reader may well fill in that last thought, as Daltoons had no time to do so himself. A loud wail rose at the far end of the block and sent the lieutenant to the window. He had not heard such a horrible sound since the landlord had packed five bags full of cats and kittens and tossed them into the harbor.

As his ears struggled from the strain, he realized the wail was actually a maudlin Dutch song of thanksgiving:

> *We gather together*
> *To ask the Lord's blessing.*
> *He chastens and hastens*
> *His will to make known.*
> *The wicked oppressing*
> *Now cease to be distressing.*
> *Sing praises to His name*
> *For He forgets not His own.*

Except that the words sounded more like:

> *We gather together*
> *To ask good Laura's blessing.*
> *She hastens to unbutton*
> *That her bosom be known.*
> *With lavish caressing*
> *We complete the undressing.*
> *Sing praises to her*
> *Whose lips are our own.*

"I assume this singing is some strategy of yours, meant to scare off the English," Daltoons said, meeting the two purveyors of this song at the back door with a sharp halberd as they concluded the verse. He had to retreat a step, so thick was the stench of beer from them.

"Just so, sir, just so," declared van Clynne, putting his finger to the point of the weapon. "We have pretended to be drunken revelers to put off the patrols. We are not, of course, though I daresay such accomplished tones have not been heard on these streets in many years."

"Thank God."

"Allow me to introduce my friend and fellow kinsman, Mr. Egans, a worthy Dutchman of the finest stock, and a fine tenor, all told."

Daltoons's head tilted forward incredulously as he examined the man before him. He did have white features, and they might perhaps be Dutch, but they were sheathed in garb that was so obviously Indian as to chase any other nationality far away.

The man greeted the young lieutenant's inspection of his tattoos and scalp lock with a prodigious and very beery burp.

"Inside, quickly, both of you," ordered Daltoons. "Drunken fools."

At this, van Clynne's dander stood up.

"We are neither drunk nor fools, sir," declared the squire, who was in fact a far distance from being inebriated, no matter how off-key his singing had been.

"Speak for yourself," said Egans. "I am drunker than a cat in an herb garden."

And with that, he fell forward into Daltoons's arms.

"Being Dutch, I naturally assumed he could hold his beer," said van Clynne after he and the lieutenant had delivered the man to a bed upstairs. "But perhaps the strain of the night has been too much on his humors."

"I don't know if we should trust him."

"You can trust him," said van Clynne. "And he will be a valuable agent to you. He is, after all, Dutch."

"You have admitted yourself he was raised by the Iroquois and served the British."

"The latter was due to a profound misunderstanding, which I have rectified," declared van Clynne. "As for the former, the federation is a powerful one, but varied in its nature. Many of its nations are indeed on our side. The Oneida are very much inclined toward us."

This was not so much a lie as a slight shading of the notion of neutrality.

"We'll see what Culper has to say about it," said Daltoons finally. "In the meantime, Jake is still missing."

"Tut, tut, he will arrive as appointed," said the Dutchman, walking toward the chair where he had spent the previous night. Having done a full day of work, he decided he would reward himself with a good nap. "And undoubtedly he will insist on carrying on with his plan, though I have already solved the problem. Be sure to wake me on the morrow."

"Wake yourself," said Daltoons. "I have details to see to. There are barely three hours till dawn. We will have to kidnap Bauer ourselves if Jake does not show up. I half hope he will not come easily."

"Always with the fisticuffs," complained van Clynne, drifting off. "You youngsters must learn the great Dutch art of finesse."

Thirty-six

Wherein, Jake and Alison reach the ferry—nearly.

For a man who knew he was likely to die in twelve short hours, Jake walked toward the Brooklyn shoreline with an easy step indeed. Granted, the knowledge that he would rise soon after being hit by the bullet added to his confidence, but he might nonetheless be taken as proof of the old proverb construing peace on those who face their demise mightily. The smile on his face was due to the thoughts of how he would fool Bauer when he was revived; there is little so amusing as making a complete ass of your enemy with the aid of a child's pretend game.

"It's colder than last night," said Alison, turning around just as they reached the road that led down to the ferry. "Why are the nights so cold when the days are hot?"

"Ssshh," said Jake, whose mood suddenly turned as heavy as the bag he was carrying. "Those are Loyalist rangers."

"How do you know? They have no uniforms."

"It's not much of a guess. Who else would be armed here? Pretend you are helping tie this bag."

Alison did as she was told. The road they were on led down into the cluster of buildings near the ferry landing, which was still a few turns away. If there were rangers here, it was a good bet there would be many more guards at the ferry itself.

Why? Yesterday's escapees would be leaving New York, not trying to sneak back into it. Was something else going on, or was the patrol merely the result of an overanxious subaltern, bored with his normal assignment?

"We need to do a little reconnaissance," Jake told Alison as he pulled her to one side to allow a man leading two sheep to pass by. "Do you think you could walk around the quay?"

"If you mean spying, I have been waiting all day for some chance at adventure."

He took hold of her arm. "This is deadly serious, Alison. They'll kill us if they find out who we are."

"I'm not a child."

The strong glance from her eyes shone with something he had not detected there before, a look that did not retreat. It was more than bravery. Jake wondered if, in changing her dress, Alison had made the transformation from girl to woman.

"We will stop, as if for supper," he told her. "While I talk up the customers in these taverns, you go down to the ferry and assess the guard. Try to discover why there are so many, but do not make yourself conspicuous."

"Do you think they are after us?"

"Probably not," said Jake. "They would have no reason to look here. Still, it's best not to take chances—even if they would be looking for a young ruffian, not a pretty young woman."

Her answer was a slight but definite blush on her cheek.

"The danger is not that they will recognize you," Jake warned, "but that they will try to take advantage of you. Stay as far from the guards as practical; ask the women and children what is going on."

"It's you who should be careful," said Alison.

"Well, now I know you've grown up, if you're starting to worry about me. Meet me in the Peacock there."

Jake pointed at the tavern down a small side street. "If anything happens to me—"

"I'll go straight to Lieutenant Daltoons."

Jake had intended on telling her to go back to the farm, but her reply was so confident—and exactly what an agent should do, in her position—that he let it pass. "Take no more than a half hour."

"I will be back before you can sneeze," she promised.

By now, the reader must be tiring of the description of every tavern and ordinary we stop at along the way. Truly, these are all of a common class, the same as any of us meet upon our daily travels. But it can only be emphasized that each has its peculiarities. The Peacock, for example, is a most curious mix of the modern and the ancient. The floor is packed dirt; one has the impression upon entering that cows recently trod there. The front room, however, is large and mounted by a balcony dressed in polished oak. At the center of the ceiling—so far overhead it must rival several European opera houses for its height—is a grand chandelier, with glass baubles pyramiding down in a style reminiscent of the finest French palace. Yet the tables below are rough-hewn from common pine, hardly squared and as level as the average mountain path. The wicker announcing the bar is wrought from common black iron—and not wrought very well, if the truth be told. On the other hand, the keeper pours his ale in magnificently tooled pewter tankards that would divert even van Clynne in a moment of thirst.

If there was an explanation for the contrasts, Jake did not seek it. When he entered the Peacock following a fruitless tour of several smaller and plainer establishments, he asked for a beer and sifted into the small crowd milling at the end of the room, ears open. Amid the usual talk of weather and crops, there were a few comments about the removal of the main elements of the British army from Staten Island, which these firm

Tories interpreted as a positive development: the damn rebels were finally going to get theirs.

"There still seem many troops around these parts," Jake suggested to his neighbors as he sipped at his ale. "It looks like a half-hearted offensive, if you ask me."

"Half-arsed, you mean," said the man next to him, whose belly pushed the buttons of his brown waistcoat nearly perpendicular. "Howe is as competent a general as I am a farmer."

"You're a better blacksmith than he is, too," laughed a neighbor. "Though not by much."

"I heard there was a prison break in New York, and they've doubled the guard," suggested Jake.

The others scoffed.

"They're always looking for someone," said a customer.

"They are trying to organize the Loyalist militia, so the civilian authorities look for a pretext to panic," explained the blacksmith. He had a ruddy face and short, naturally curled hair; there was ever so slight a hint of Sweden in his voice, as if he had come over as a child. "A man enters looking to settle a debt, and the guard is doubled and the shutters thrown. Haven't you enlisted?"

This was apparently meant as a joke, for the others all laughed.

"What do you do, stranger?" another man asked Jake. "You are not from here, I warrant."

"I have lately located to New York from above," said Jake, supplying a common story. "I am an apothecary by trade, and have been on Long Island to seek herbs."

"Manhattan weeds are not good enough for you?" asked a thin man clad entirely in white. This initiated a round of jokes about druggists' poor cures, all of which Jake had heard many times before. There was the cold cure that grew hair on a hen's chin; the bear who died with a toothache that reappeared in a patient. He laughed along and contributed his own story of a medicine intended for gout that transferred the stiffness to another member.

The sum of all this mirth was that Jake was stood to another beer by the company as being a good sort. Neither the beer nor the conversation brought anything tangible relating to the guards and the patrols, and Jake soon made his way to a table to await Alison.

The girl conducted her investigation with the aplomb of a seasoned veteran. Walking toward the ferry, she fell in with a group of women who were seeing a minister off after his visit to their homes. The women did not think the size of the guard unusual, and Alison soon drifted toward a young farm boy who was seeing after some pigs.

"Hello, sir, are you selling these animals?"

"Are you buying?" he answered, turning to see who had hailed him. When he caught sight of her, his wits seemed to flee. "I, a, excuse me, miss."

"No, I am not buying anything," Alison sensed her advantage and pressed it. "I am meeting a friend nearby, but I am wondering—are the soldiers out for any particular reason, or are they just bullying people?"

"Neither, I would imagine, or both," said the lad. "That is the prettiest dress I have ever seen. As is your kerchief."

She smiled and swept away. A few other encounters failed to yield any useful information, and Alison soon found herself passing directly before the guards at the ferryhouse. There were a few low suggestions. These were true redcoats, and as rude as any on the continent.

"I see that you men do not carry bayonets," she said presumptively. "It is just as well. Here you are obviously cutting yourselves with your sharp wits, and with knives you would truly do each other great harm."

"M'lady condescends to speak to the rabble," said

one of the redcoats, sweeping down in mock courtesy. "We are thrilled."

"It is clearly the most thrill you have ever seen in your lives," said Alison.

"I can suggest a much better thrill," said the redcoat, pointing the butt of his gun so that it just barely touched her dress.

"And undoubtedly you would suggest a price as well, as you are the type that can only find diversion by paying for it," she answered, pulling her skirts back.

The soldier's fellows nearly fell over themselves laughing. He could not let himself be humiliated so easily. Feeling himself growing hot, he reached quickly into a pocket and threw a shilling into the dust as Alison began walking away.

"Come," she answered, "your mother was paid twice that to conceive you."

The private was not the type to accept defeat gracefully. But Alison had learned a few things and gained considerable poise in the two days since she had faced a similar, if more inebriated, foe with Daltoons. As the soldier puffed out his chest and advanced, she slipped to the side and kissed him on the cheek. He stepped back in amazement—and tripped over her outstretched leg.

"Do not be so fresh from now on," she said. "And shave, or else no woman will ever kiss you."

The entire company of soldiers began laughing so hard tears streamed from their faces. Her victim bore as dazed and angry a countenance as King George betrayed when first presented with the Declaration of Independence.

His fellows caught him as he rose. A gray-haired woman stepped up and began scolding the men in a severe tone to be about their business. Her voice brought the men's sergeant, who barked that they had better get their dirty hides the hell back at their posts or face a prompt whipping.

"You must be more careful," the old woman warned

Alison when the danger had passed. "They interpret any remark as an invitation."

"I can take care of myself."

"I am sure you can, dear." The woman patted her scarf carefully. "Are you traveling alone?"

"My father—my cousin, that is, and I are going back to the city. I am to meet him nearby, at the Peacock."

"Be careful. There are many soldiers about. To say nothing of the lower types."

"Are the soldiers looking for someone?"

"A fat Dutchman who is a horrible rebel," said the woman. "He instigated a riot to escape prison in the city yesterday. It's the talk of the place, they say. A man has been going through the docks, looking for him and offering a reward. He is said to owe him a considerable sum."

"A Dutchman launched the riot?" Alison was truly incredulous, as she knew the real story and wondered how it had been twisted. "How?"

"He broke out from jail with a regiment of men, and then tried to rob a young lord of his valuables," said the woman. She nodded deeply, as if she had just confirmed the standing of ône of the Eight Wonders of the World. "He is the commander of a large army of rebels. He heads the Sons of Liberty. Be on your guard."

Thirty-seven

Wherein, Jake and Alison discover there is no pirate like an old pirate.

Jake was amused though not overly surprised to find that van Clynne had been promoted.

"He is becoming quite famous," he told Alison when she found him in the tavern a few minutes after her encounter with the old woman. "I have no doubt that he will eventually supplant General Washington as leader of the Revolution."

"There is a man going around looking for him but he has confused the description," Alison told him. "They think he is smart!"

"He is very clever in his way."

"Not as clever as you."

"Still, I think we had best wait for dark and find a more private way across the river. If they are looking for Claus, they may know of me as well."

Jake and Alison made their way through a good roast chicken with full trimmings as the spy considered his best course. There would be many boats available for the taking once dusk fell, though the heavy presence of guards did tend to complicate matters.

By now Culper and Daltoons would be worried about him. Perhaps they had solved the puzzle without his assistance. So much the better then. He would go ahead with his plan to kidnap Bauer in broad daylight and carry him to General Washington trussed like a prize pig.

Jake's contemplation of this happy sight was cut short by the arrival of a poorly shaven man with a rough jacket and open collar. He was not very tall, and as he stood over the table with a half-stoop his mouth was a few inches below Jake's ear. His whisper released an odor of gin so strong that Alison curled her nose and pushed her seat back.

"I could not help noticing, my friend, that you seem to be dallying here," suggested the man, whose appearance and manner showed great familiarity with the sea. His grin revealed he was several teeth short of a full set, and his left pinky, plopped with the rest of his hand casually against the chair back, ended at the knuckle. His black trousers dragged to his heels and his white shirt puffed out from a chest any rooster would be proud of.

"And what would it be to you if we were?"

"Oh, nothing, friend, nothing." The man pulled back the empty chair gently and sat. "Evening, miss. A very pretty blanket on your hair. Very becoming."

"It is an Arabian scarf," declared Alison.

"Yes, yes, I thought so myself." The man nodded, then turned his full attention back to Jake. "I believe you may be in need of discreet transportation."

"Why would you think that?"

The man laughed lightly and patted Jake's arm. "No pirate like an old pirate."

"What's that mean?"

"Nothing, sir, nothing. Two pounds, that's all."

"For?"

"Delivering you where you are going. The Jerseys, I assume?"

The uninitiated might miss the suggestive intonation of the destination. The Jerseys were a favorite destination for smugglers.

Jake shook his head. "I am neither a pirate nor a smuggler."

"Oh," said the man, starting to get up. "'Scuse me, then. Beg pardon, miss."

Jake caught the man's arm; there was just enough true surprise beneath the confident grin to trust the man.

"Tell me where to meet you. I will give you the destination after I arrive."

"That isn't the way it works, sir. Some destinations are more costly. The rowin', an' all."

"I will make it worth your while. Assuming, of course, you are a confidential man."

As he said these last words, Jake glanced down toward his lap. The old pirate did likewise, and saw that he was within aim of Jake's Segallas.

Again, surprise melted to a grin.

"Quite confidential, sir. A very confidential man, am I. I like your ways. They remind me of a captain or two I knew in the days of yore."

"Have a gin on me," said Jake, producing a coin.

"Obliged, sir, obliged." He tipped the cap he was wearing. "I will find you on the road," he said in a soft voice. "Wait an hour."

Before they left the inn, Jake sought out the tavern owner's wife and told her his cousin felt chilly with the night air. He persuaded her to sell him a shawl, then wrapped it around Alison loosely enough to give the small Segallas a nest at her sleeve.

Jake put his knife in his boot but kept the officer's pistol just visible beneath his jacket, where it would have some deterrence value. He tucked the vial of sleeping powder and the smaller bottle with the death potion into his waistcoat pocket; they could be quickly retrieved yet would be secure in their containers. The dueling pistols, loaded with their trick potion, were safe within their waterproof case in Jake's bag, hung across his chest by a rope.

Thus prepared, Jake and Alison left the inn and began walking warily up the street in the opposite direction of the ferry, parallel to the water. If anything, the number of guards on the street had increased, and there was nearly a full company of redcoats at the ferry.

On the other hand, the clear sky that had cooled the night had changed its mind, and was now unfurling a blanket of mist over the water to provide a little warmth. It was just the thing to steal quietly across the river in.

"I've never been a pirate before," said Alison, tugging her cape around her shoulders.

"And you are not now. Say nothing." Jake saw a shadow near a building a few yards ahead, but when they approached, realized it was nothing but the odd reflection of a drainpipe.

The buildings around them gave way to an open shoreline as they walked. Jake felt apprehension growing in his stomach, and began to think it might be safer just to steal a boat.

A hiss greeted them from a clump of bushes ahead.

"Aye, ya took yer time, but it's a pirate's right to go when and where he pleases," said the man they had met inside the Peacock. He stood and unsheathed a lantern. "This way then."

He skipped ahead on the road, taking them down a stony path to his boat. Even in the darkness, it was obvious the vessel had been recently painted. Jake took this as a good sign, for not only did it indicate the craft probably wouldn't leak, but that the man knew his business well enough to profit handsomely. Paint was a capital expense afforded by only the most successful smuggler.

"Up, with ya, lass. Before boarding, sir, your destination."

"Manhattan. Along the docks, but not at the ferry."

"Manhattan?"

"You know the place?" said Jake sarcastically.

"My business is strictly cash and carry," said the man. His disappointment was understandable; the close destination would bring a paltry fare, hardly worth his effort.

"Here is a crown for you."

"A full crown?"

"And five more shillings when we get across. Do not forget that we are well armed."

"Honor among thieves, sir. Best honor among pirates."

His spirits soaring thanks to the well-inflated fee, the little man helped Alison into the bow of the rowboat, then clambered in behind. They pushed off through the fog nipping at the shoreline, the oarsman stroking with an energy that belied his seemingly frail body.

By the time they were a quarter of the way across, the man had begun humming a light air vaguely reminiscent of "The Golden Vanity," the satirical ballad originally written of Sir Walter Raleigh. Alison soon joined in, and the two broke into a loud if slightly off-key chorus:

> *Sinking in the low land, low land, low,*
> *Sinking in the low land sea.*

"You've got a voice there, lass, a voice," said the boatman. His lilt now hinted of the West Indies and his eyes betrayed a tear from the song, which told of a cabin boy rewarded for sinking an enemy vessel by being cheated of his life. "A shame, really. A shame, a shame."

Jake suddenly sensed the man was not speaking of the song. Even as he pulled the pistol from his belt, he saw a long, low shadow looming in the mist ahead.

"Into the water," he told Alison. He grabbed her arm and flung her overboard.

Her scream was drowned out by a shot from the vessel that lay in ambush. Jake fired his pistol at the spark, and was rewarded by a satisfying splash, the gunman toppling into his grave. Behind him, the old pirate dove into the water, stroking for the shore behind Alison.

"You will be repaid," Jake vowed, "if harm comes to

her. I will pull your heart from your body through your nostrils."

"A fine curse, Colonel Gibbs," boomed an all-too-familiar voice from the nearby boat. "But I am afraid you won't live long enough to carry it out."

"I have been waiting for you to catch up to me for some time now, Keen. I am sorry to inform you that your operation proved unsuccessful."

"I suppose it depends on your perspective," answered Keen, his voice as cheerful as Jake's. The two men might have been old college chums discussing the day's laboratory procedures, each lying merrily to the other of his successes. "In science, there is no such thing as a failed experiment, merely negative results."

"Always the optimist. Tell me, what did Black Clay think of your failure? Or did you let him think you were dead?"

"I am glad my little ruse fooled you," said Keen.

"I never thought you were killed in the water."

"Come now, I'm sure you did. But then, I will admit you surprised me tonight. I was looking for your friend Mister Clynne, and here you show up instead."

"If you're referring to the Dutchman, I think you will find a 'van' appended to his name. He is rather touchy if you leave it off."

"Indeed. But then he is cantankerous to a fault, is he not?"

"I count it as his most endearing quality," said Jake. Alison's strokes were now far in the distance; if nothing else, Jake's banter had succeeded in purchasing her escape.

"It's you I have in front of me, colonel. I fear I will have to deal with you straight away. Your cleverness grows by the hour, it seems."

"I try to learn something new every day."

"Then this will be your most elucidating lesson," declared Keen.

"Much obliged, I'm sure. What lesson are we taking?"

"Ballistics, sir. Ballistics."

As the two men had been exchanging pleasantries, the hired minions in Keen's longboat had continued to row toward Jake. Their craft moved slowly, and not merely because of the current. The doctor had removed his swivel gun from the bow of his carriage and placed it at the bow of his boat; it was well-suited there, being of a naval design, though it tended to weigh against the craft's progress.

Jake slipped his knife into his hand, aiming to wait until the space between the boats was close enough to leap across.

But the British assassin had fought him before, and if he had underestimated him severely at the start of their mutual encounters, he now knew the American's capabilities all too well. He ordered his men to halt while the two boats were still a good way apart.

"This is quite close enough to eliminate my friend," Keen declared. "Make ready to fire."

Jake had sensed from the start that Keen was hesitating to shoot, but could not understand why until he realized that while the light of Manhattan was silhouetting his enemy's boat through the mist, his must be nearly invisible with the much dimmer Brooklyn shore behind him.

In that case, thought Jake, I won't help you find me any more.

As quietly as possible, he sank to his knees, crouching and willing the fog to fall in thick around him. Then he had a second idea, and took the bottle with the death poison from his pocket. The red liquid it contained was as thick as syrup, and coated the knife blade as strongly as any glue.

Perhaps if he hit Keen, the doctor's men might think him dead. Considering his usual treatment of subordinates, they would undoubtedly greet his demise with some joy, and might even leave off chasing Jake.

And so we see how Hope springs up unrealistically

in desperate times. Truly, Jake did not even know which dim shadow across from him was his nemesis.

He would have to get Keen to speak again. But doing that would reveal himself as well.

"I wonder, doctor—you never told me if you attended Edinburgh," said Jake.

"There he is," answered Keen. "Fire the damn gun."

In the split second it took for Keen's order to be carried out, Jake's knife flew toward the shadow standing midway back in the boat. He dove into the water just ahead of the cannon's crackle.

The patriot spy was not quite fast enough, nor lucky enough, to escape all its bullets.

Thirty-eight

Wherein, ghosts intervene, and a few redcoats fall asleep.

"Keen's dead."

"My God, the bastard's just pricked. The knife only caught his shoulder. How can he be dead?"

"Shitten hell, see for yourself."

"Christalmightygod. We must be fighting the devil himself."

"The rebel bastard's gone to the bottom, that's for sure. Boat blew right out of the water."

"What we do with Keen?"

"Take him back, I think."

"To hell with that. Wrap the anchor around him and drop the bastard overboard."

"Aye. See how far his threats get him."

"Deserves a decent burial for all that. He was a Christian."

"Seen no proof. Didn't he try to cheat us out of our price for the boat?"

"Promised a good reward, though."

"Got no sight of it. An' he hasn't a cent in his pockets."

"Throw him overboard then."

"Maybe the money is lined in his coat. Strip it."

The voices faded across the water. Jake gripped the piece of smashed keel and gave a silent kick beneath the waves, working his way in the opposite direction.

He had been hit in his leg and his left shoulder, though how badly he could not tell. The pistols in their case hung like a heavy weight from the strap around his neck. The only reason he did not let them drop was that he could not spare the energy to undo the rope.

The patriot spy guessed that the low shadows looming over his right arm must mark the Brooklyn shoreline; barely suppressing his moans, he pushed toward it. The natural action of the tide was sending him up the mouth of the bay. A salty spray of water lapped at his nose and eyes. He felt his body grow heavier and heavier, every inch pressed down by fatigue.

Alison must be somewhere ahead, he thought. It was unlikely she'd made shore yet. She was a strong girl, but Jake remembered the night on the Hudson. She had not been able to make the beach by herself, for all her energy.

He told himself he must push on and rescue her, must find the poor child—the poor woman—before she drowned. He owed it to her father.

He owed it to her.

He pushed on, until suddenly it felt as if Poseidon himself had taken hold of him.

Not Poseidon; this was a smaller and mortal hand grabbing him by the neck.

"Come along, now, sir; don't fight me or we will both drown. The girl is waiting on shore."

It took Jake a moment to recognize that the voice belonged to the old pirate, and it was another second before instinct told him he must trust the little man and his powerful strokes.

"I knew all the great pirate captains in my youth," the boatman told Alison, pointing out at the river as if the ships floated there still. "Aye, gentlemen every one. It is just bad politics that ruined their names. Politics and prejudice; steer clear of them, girl."

"Jake is waking up."

"Hush now, don't make no noise or we'll have the British marines down on us."

Jake lifted his head to consciousness, the voices taking shape before him. Alison and the old pirate were huddled cross-legged in the heavy mud of the shore a half-foot away.

"Jake, Jake, are you all right?" Alison asked.

"I don't know," he told her. "I seem to have all my arms and legs, at least."

"I repent, sir, of my perfidy," declared the old pirate. "I was tempted by gold and an evil man."

"The pirate saved us both, Jake," said Alison.

Even if Jake had been inclined at the moment to hold a grudge, his body ached too badly for him to do more than sit up. He examined his leg. A ball had ripped clear through the side of his thigh, taking a piece of the skin and bruising the muscle, but missing anything of importance. He took off his shirt and ripped part of the sleeve to fashion a bandage.

Alison, seeing that he winced when moving his arm, got up and examined his back and shoulder.

"You have a wound," she said. "God, I can see the ball right in your skin. It looks like a rock."

Jake took a hard breath, then flexed his muscle. It felt as if a giant were pressing his thumb to it. The fact that the wound was not deep was fortunate, but the bullet must be removed and the wound sealed.

"Do you still have your knife?" he asked her when he finished tying the bandage on his leg.

"Yes." Her answer was clipped by the shivers of her teeth; despite the mist, the night still had a hard chill.

Jake got slowly to his feet, testing his balance by hobbling through the heavy mud to the waterline where the old pirate had gone to keep watch. "I need you to start a small fire," he told him.

"Daren't do that, captain," said the man. "The sentries on the prison ships will see it right away, and send a patrol. They've already heard us talking."

"Where are we?"

"Wallabout Bay, in the mud flats."

"The burial grounds."

"Aye. Under the protection of the ghosts, I daresay."

No account of the perfidy of the British during this war can miss the horrors persecuted on those imprisoned aboard the *Jersey*, whose hulking hull loomed nearby. The soft murmur of horror that drifted across the water was not the lament of ghosts but the groan of suffering.

Jake told the old pirate to gather some driftwood quickly; they must start a fire no matter the consequences. Indeed, he hoped the British might send someone to investigate, for therein lay their salvation; it would be difficult to get off the mud flats except by water, and they dare not wait until morning when they would surely be discovered.

After the pirate had piled enough driftwood for a modest fire, Jake undid the calked compartment in his money belt where his flint lay and gave it to the old man.

"Old flint won't spark," complained the pirate after a few tries.

"You almost have it," urged Jake.

"Here now, the ghosts helped us," said the man as the fire sparked up.

"Get more wood, I want them to see the blaze," said Jake.

Already there were shouts and activity on the prison ships. The old pirate, not quite sure what Jake was up to, nonetheless began to hustle across the thick mud, seeking out more pieces of wood.

"Take the knife, Alison, and hold the blade in the fire." Jake dropped to his knees, keeping his eye on the water. He saw the outline of a longboat setting out from one of the moored ships. "When it burns red, use the tip to pry out the bullet, then sear the sides of the wound."

"But it will hurt you."

"It will hurt a hell of a lot more if you don't. Hurry, before that patrol reaches us. Be brave, girl."

Alison held the knife into the flames as the pirate continued to carry and pile on the driest driftwood he could find. She steadied the blade until it was so hot it was difficult to hold, even with her shawl as a makeshift glove.

Alison bit her lip as she worked the tip against Jake's flesh. He fastened his teeth on a part of his coat, trying desperately not to cry out with the intense pain.

The offending bullet popped out with a hiss; she closed her eyes and ran the flat of the knife around the wound.

Jake collapsed forward on the ground, but slowly willed himself back to his feet. Alison helped him up, tears in her eyes.

"Are you all right?"

"It hurts like the devil's own poker," he admitted. "But that's a good sign. It's the infection dying. Come on now, I have to meet this shadow. You stay back there on the firmer ground and say nothing, no matter what happens. Do you still have the Segallas?"

"It's soaked."

"Hold on to it anyway. Perhaps you can bluff someone, if it comes to that." Jake turned to the old pirate; before he could say anything, the man was helping her back up the beach.

While the others retreated, Jake warmed himself in front of the flames. He took the dueling pistols from their protected bag and case, cocking them carefully and leaving them within his reach. He would use them as a last resort.

The pain from the cauterized wound was starting to retreat. His heart was beating regularly now—or as close to regularly as could be expected, given the danger. Jake took the vial of sleeping powder from his pocket and loosened the cap, readying himself as the British boat nosed into the mud flat at the water's edge.

Four men had been sent to investigate the fire. A pair stayed with the boat; the other two fixed their bayonets and then splashed across the water into the thick mud, cursing at the muck.

Jake stood behind the fire, visible only as a dim shadow in the darkness and fog. "About time you got here," he shouted. "I have been waiting all night."

"Who are you?" asked the lead soldier, about twenty yards away. "Declare yourself."

"Don't you recognize me?" said Jake. "You buried me here just yesterday."

"Buried—who are you, rebel?"

Jake held his arms out, as if welcoming them forward. He walked through the fire. There was no danger of his soaked clothes catching as he passed through quickly, but the effect was impressive.

"Jesus, Fred, he's a ghost."

"Indeed—and I am the Queen's mother."

The unsuperstitious Fred advanced toward Jake, who held out his hands in supplication and continued forward. The man reared back to slap down the rebel figure with the butt of his gun—and then tottered over to the ground, felled by a fistful of tossed sleeping powder.

"Run for your lives!" said the second man, turning and running back toward the boat. "It's a goddamn ghost."

He might have asked his companions how many ghosts would have stopped to scoop up a musket. Jake pushed his bruised leg forward, trying to hurry after the Britons before they could escape into the water. For a moment he worried that his plan had worked a little too well. The scared redcoats might row away before he could douse them all with the rest of his powder.

Fortunately, the two men who'd remained with the boat were no more superstitious than the archbishop's wife. Unfortunately, that meant they dealt with the supposed specter in a very earthly manner. They raised their guns and fired.

Because of the mist, Jake did not realize he was being shot at until the bullets whizzed by a few feet from his head. It was only sheer luck—and the notorious inefficiency of the muskets and their operators—that saved him.

Of course, the Britons had no way of knowing that. They saw a shadowy figure hobbling forward in the mud flats toward them, apparently impervious to their weapons. They had buried numerous men in this same area over the past few months; it did not take much imagination to draw frightful conclusions and change their minds about the existence of ghosts.

The first redcoat dove straight into the water, gun and all. One of the men in the boat followed suit, leaving only a single marine to confront the apparition.

"I don't know who you are, rebel," said the man as Jake closed the distance between them to ten feet. "But I'll kill you where you stand, I promise."

"Attempt it," suggested Jake, bringing the gun up in his right hand as he continued forward. "You have already done so once."

Just as Jake decided he was close enough to fire, a new ghost began flying downward from the beach. This ghost was straight from hell, its horns pointed and tail flying behind it. The soldier dove straight backwards into the water and began flailing towards his companions.

Jake fell to his knees laughing as Alison ran up behind him, her dress and scarf fluttering in the wind. He was so grateful at this easy victory—and so used to her behavior by now—that he did not even bother to scold her for disobeying his orders.

A few minutes later, the patriots and their pirate guide had pushed the large boat into the water and begun heading away from the prison ships. Their progress was slow and the hour was now far advanced. Jake realized they must head straight to the dueling site, and even then might not make it in time.

"Their guilt was in our favor," Jake said, standing guard in the bow with the gun. The old pirate strained against the oars. "You cannot go day by day and see the horrors on the *Jersey* without it affecting you in some way."

"They were cowards," said Alison firmly. "All the British are."

"Not all of them," said Jake. "The war would have been over before it began if that were true."

"I would not say, sir, but that a real ghost may have played a role in their banishment," put in the old pirate. "The girl and I noticed several shadows behind you when the soldiers drew near. And none of their bullets managed to find you. That is a miracle not easily explained."

"You have never faced a British line," said Jake, who did not believe in ghosts, benevolent or otherwise. "A full squad can fire at a barn three paces away, and not a ball will strike it. Besides, it was very dark and they were scared."

"There are more things in heaven and earth than you dream in the imagination, sir," said the old pirate.

"Shakespeare's *Hamlet,* though you misquote it."

"I don't know what the ghost's name was," continued the pirate respectfully, "but I can tell you a tale of a haunted ship that routed half the Spanish fleet. And another that still sails the ocean, looking for its true captain, lost overboard in a fearsome gale."

"I have no doubt," said Jake. They were entering the mouth of the bay. Despite his age and seemingly small body, their companion was a strong rower; Jake began to feel confident they would make the duel on time after all.

"Were you honestly a pirate?" asked Alison.

"Still am," declared the man boldly. "With a privateer's license. Aye, one from England, one from Spain and one from France. I can plunder whom I please, when I please. Why, I know of many a pile of gold buried on this Long Island alone, and several dozen in the Jerseys where we are headed. Better hunting in the south, but I could tell you a story would make your short hair stand on end."

Jake slipped against the sideboards of the bow as the man filled Alison with tales of adventure on the high seas. How much might be true or not, only he could say, but it was a fact that privateers did frequent these waters. Indeed, a sailing man working for the patriots could make a fine fortune fitting out against the British.

And vice versa.

Whether he would choose this stretch of Jersey coast to stash his treasure was another story. The sun was just rising as they neared the shore; Jake saw a beached boat and a canoe. A red cloth lay casually over the canoe's gunwale.

Daltoons.

"Alison, you hide near that boat," Jake said quickly, pointing to the canoe. "You see the red cloth? That is Lieutenant Daltoons's sign. Show yourself to no one but him, do you understand?"

"Yes."

"I'm going above. Run up when you hear the pistols fire. If I am shot, tell them pure water is the antidote, and it must be poured directly into the wound. He is not to apply it to Bauer. Be positive about that."

Alison nodded.

"Tell him to make some excuse that he will bury Bauer himself. I expect he has already come up with a plan, but impress on him that it is important whoever is with Bauer think nothing is amiss. We must have secrecy."

"I could have told you that," said Alison. "But what are you going to do with Bauer?"

"Never mind. Just follow my directions for once. Do you swear?"

"Aye-aye."

"Swear it."

Alison pressed her lips together, then reluctantly held up her right hand. "I swear it."

Jake turned to the old pirate, whose toothless grin lit the grim morning.

"You, sir, thank you for your help. I will recommend you to the Continentals, if ever you should need assistance."

"And I will recommend you. You're a brave young lad. And you, young lady, you are as courageous as you are pretty."

Jake helped her out of the boat, and she dashed through the water, holding up the folds of her damp dress as she ran for the canoe.

"I don't even know your name," Jake said to the boatman as he put one foot in the water.

"Just an old pirate, sir. Nothing more, nothing less. Good luck with your revolution."

Jake hurried ashore, going as fast as he could manage with his wounded leg. As he started up the winding path toward the summit where the duel was to be fought, he turned and saw the boat and the old pirate were gone, as if into thin air.

Thirty-nine

Wherein, the lamentable death of Jake Gibbs is fully recorded and properly mourned.

"**I** might have expected the man was a coward. The city is filled with them these days." Clayton Bauer folded his arms and walked back toward the thick, gray stone wall where his brother-in-law stood. He had drunk two cups of strong whiskey before putting himself into the boat to come here, and another upon reaching the shore. His courage thus ran ahead of him, strutting heavily in the thinning mist of the morning.

"The sun is not quite on the horizon," said Daltoons, who had chosen the uniform of a British captain as his disguise. "The meeting was set for dawn. His honor entitles—"

"Honor." Bauer spat in derision and paced back toward his brother-in-law and the servant who had rowed them here. The hilltop seemed isolated and empty, save for the three Tories and Daltoons; the four men could easily be alone in the world. Not even the birds were out, the earth blanketed in gray desolation. A painter could not have created a better morning for a duel.

"A man who insults a lady has no honor," Bauer told Daltoons.

The disguised patriot thought for a moment how pleasant it would be if Jake did not show up: he would thrash the Tory bastard around the mouth several times before carrying him off for questioning. Culper's elaborate web had failed to turn up any new information of the invasion, and torturing Bauer for Howe's destination seemed their only option.

Daltoons had several men stationed in the nearby woods, dressed as redcoats and ready for any contingency. Each was armed with a pair of double-loaded muskets. Nor was Bauer's guard nearby. Reports that escaped rebel patriots in the area near his mansion had given them something better to do than traipse to Jersey.

In any event, Bauer was not so cowardly nor so confident of the outcome to invite them along. He stalked back toward Daltoons, wearing the face of an outraged suitor, though secretly glad at this easy victory.

"The sun is here, or would be, if this fog were not so heavy. Your friend has failed to attend. The insult against the lady is expunged by his lack of character, unless you yourself wish to uphold his honor."

"Who said I insulted her?"

The men turned in surprise as Jake walked happily across the hilltop, the limp in his leg barely noticeable. He had a large grin on his face and the sack with the pistols on his back.

"Here are my pistols," said Jake, presenting the bag to Daltoons. "You will have my opponent's second examine them, and then load them."

"Where is Doctor Clynne?" asked Daltoons, removing the gun case from the sack. He looked for some sign from Jake as to which gun to favor—or for anything that might indicate his plan.

"Doctor Clynne?"

"Our surgeon," prompted Daltoons. "I believe he went to fetch you this morning. He claimed to know all your haunts."

"I'm sure he'll turn up," said Jake, adding in a whispered aside that the bullets must be handled gingerly. He turned to Bauer. "A nice morning to die, isn't it? Gray and overcast?"

The Tory gave him a grimace. To his credit, there was

no show of fear in his face. "Etiquette requires that you be given a chance to renounce your insult."

"Hardly," said Jake. "A kiss is a kiss and can never be denied."

Lord William's hands began to shake as he took up the copper bullet to load his brother-in-law's gun. Daltoons reached over and caught the ball as it slipped toward the ground.

"What sort of bullets are these?" Bauer asked.

"I would not shoot you with common lead. A man of your circumstances deserves finer metal. If you object to copper—"

"The right of weapons is yours," said Bauer. He reached angrily for the gun Daltoons had originally loaded for Jake.

His brother-in-law put out his hand to stop him. "Perhaps it was not meant as an insult," said Lord William. "This is a silly matter for two civilized men to fight over. No offense was taken."

"Stand out of the way, William." Bauer sneered at the pistol's lack of ornamentation, then sighted down the barrel. The gun was lighter than the one he had practiced with and promised an easier kick.

Jake remembered Bebeef's advice that his victim's coat be removed to insure the poorly propelled bullet would prick the skin. He took off his own jacket, hoping it would entice Bauer to do the same.

It did not.

He turned to Daltoons. "It will look as if we are dead. Make an excuse to take both of us with you, and send Lord William back by himself."

"Easily accomplished," said Daltoons. "But are you going to be shot as well?"

"Alison is by the boat," Jake whispered, turning around as he heard Lord William behind him.

"I beg you, sir, to renounce this foolishness."

"I renounce nothing," said Jake. "It is an excellent day to die!" He took his pistol and began walking toward Bauer. "Is that the suit you're to be buried in? Where would you like the bullet hole?"

"Braggadocio ill becomes you."

"Hold my gun," said Jake, holding the pistol out to him. "Go ahead, I trust you won't shoot me before the proper time."

Unsure what his opponent was up to, Bauer took the weapon cautiously. Jake promptly stripped off his vest coat, exposing his white shirt.

"I want you to have a bright target. You'll excuse the tear in the back; a rebel and I recently had a disagreement. You will note where the coward struck me, but he paid for his impudence."

Jake grabbed his gun back and began walking to his mark. This last bit of bluster finally achieved its purpose. Bauer, deciding he could not be outdone, took off his own outer clothes.

"Shall we draw lots for the first shot?" Jake asked.

"The first shot is mine, by right," said Bauer. "If we are to observe the London etiquette."

"In that case," said Jake, "I choose position. Start here, three paces, and fire."

Concern flickered across Bauer's face. "I believe the general prescription is for a wider distance."

"I will concede five," said Jake. "Unless you are afraid—"

Bauer turned abruptly, aiming his gun toward the ground. "Your second may count us off."

Jake nodded at Lord William. "Recommend me to your wife. I wish her Godspeed back to England."

Lord William hesitated. He had lost his son a few months before, and now confronted the possibility of losing his brother-in-law. While he had not liked Bauer over-much, the man had always been decent to him and was, after all, his wife's brother. It was his honor at stake, in a way, as it was his wife who had been insulted, yet the entire matter seemed foolish and blown considerably out of proportion. But it was beyond his power to stop any of this; he nodded weakly and slipped to the side.

"Start, Captain Daltoons, before the insult is compounded," demanded Bauer.

"Wait!"

The men turned and saw Alison running from the ridge, her dress flowing behind her. Daltoons guessed from the frown on Jake's face that this was not part of the plan. The lieutenant reached to his back and took hold of the small pistol hidden there.

"Cousin, I wish to give you a kiss," said Alison, running forward.

Hoping the dress and dim light would keep the Tories from recognizing her, Jake stepped forward and was rewarded with a quite accomplished kiss.

"I might have known," he whispered. "Will you never follow my orders?"

"Three boats approaching," she answered. "There are many redcoats in the second and third."

"There's no need for concern," Jake announced loudly, turning away. "We will be done here quickly."

"What is it?" asked Bauer.

"Nothing. Our soldiers are patrolling below. Begin."

"There is a prohibition against dueling, and we should obey the law," suggested Lord William, seizing on the pretext.

But this attempt was brushed away by Bauer, who started the count himself. "One."

"Redcoats," Alison hissed to Daltoons as the two men began to pace, counting off their steps together.

"Too late to worry about them now," growled Daltoons. "Where the hell have you been? I sent out all my men looking for you."

"With Jake, of course."

"Two."

There is little a duel can be compared to. Stripped of its haughty speeches and overbearing emotion, it is merely walking and counting, turning and shooting.

When Bauer reached four, Jake became aware of

every wound and bruise in his body. His muscles ached with the great fatigue of the night and indeed the entire war. He felt every abuse he had subjected himself to, every deprivation. His right arm and shoulder were especially grieved with their fresh wound; the muscles tensed and it took great effort to turn and present himself at five.

He had sheltered a vague hope that Bauer might accept rules allowing him to fire first, or at least simultaneously; even the bravest man must flinch a bit at the moment of death.

Less than ten yards separated them. Bauer took a breath and pulled the trigger, and Jake felt the air reverberate with the sound of his pistol.

He thought Bauer had missed. Then he felt his chest tightening, and darkness clawing at his eyes. As his tongue thickened in his mouth, he jerked his arm up and just managed to squeeze the trigger.

The ball struck the Tory in the meat of his right shoulder, away from the heart. The impact pushed Bauer's chest back and straightened his head; he smiled, took a labored breath, then collapsed slowly to the ground.

As had Jake, a few yards away.

Though she knew the plan well, Alison rent the air with a terrified scream, a wail that under other circumstances might have woken the dead. In this case, the two men remained crumpled on the hilltop, oblivious to the commotion that suddenly broke around them. Daltoons's men appeared in bright red uniforms, bayonets drawn, charging from the woods under the direction of a medium-sized man whose markings of sergeant were matched by the self-important strut so typical of the species. He ordered his companions about with a haughty snap and a variety of curses, just the thing to direct privates and confuse officers with.

"What the hell is this, subjects of the king shooting

each other?" said the sergeant, moving toward Daltoons. "Speak, sir."

"You are in the habit of addressing a captain in such a manner?"

"I will damn well address who I want as I want," answered the sergeant tartly. "Declare yourself."

"Captain Mark Daltoons, His Majesty's Sixth Grenadiers." The unit was, of course, an invention, but it came from the disguised Libertyman with so much pretense that a colorful and glorious history was fully implied. "I am in charge here."

"Like hell. I have a report of rebel activity, and am to secure the area."

"You are speaking damn saucy to an officer, sergeant," said Daltoons, thinking his subordinate extending the part they had sketched. Alison's sighting prompted Daltoons to push the episode quicker than rehearsed.

"This looks to me to be a duel, sir, explicitly prohibited. A punishable offense, I might say."

"Talk to me privately, sergeant," said Daltoons. "That is an order."

"I'm not sure you are in a position to order anyone about," answered the sergeant, who nonetheless retreated a few steps with Daltoons—and was almost cuffed.

"Take Lord William back if he won't go on his own."

"We're letting him go? I thought we were arresting them."

"Do as I say. The real British are coming. Get Buckmaster the hell out of here. Jake wants him to think his brother-in-law is dead. Go now, before we're all shot."

The sergeant looked back. "Jesus, they look dead to me."

"Just go, you turnip-eating fool!"

"I would not use such intemperate language, captain," answered the sergeant.

As the redcoat captain and sergeant were having their tête-à-tête, Lord William walked gravely to his fallen brother-in-law. Tears had formed in his eyes, and he shook his head as he bent down to examine the prostrate body. The red liquid of the ball had done the job Bebeef had promised, not merely poisoning its victim but splattering him with Death's sanguine signature.

"Damn you, Clayton," said Lord William. "Damn you. He was nothing to die for."

Alison, meanwhile, was hunkered over Jake, sobbing quite convincingly.

"My lord, quickly." Daltoons reached down and lifted the man up. He steered him a few feet away. "Go back to New York while I deal with this. Have your man row you back. I will have your brother-in-law's body returned to you as soon as possible. We will invent an accident, and I will find a doctor who will sign a statement covering the death."

"But . . ."

Daltoons gave the sergeant a glance, and the man advanced, putting his hand on Buckmaster's shoulder.

"I would not want a stain to come upon your family because of this," said Daltoons. "This bastard of a sergeant is not settling for a light price. Go quickly before he changes his mind. More soldiers are on their way, and they may bring an officer of higher rank than myself. The scandal will be unavoidable then."

Lord William hesitated. Truly he had lost so much in these past few months that a blot on his family's name for dueling—or rather, for having lost a duel—was nothing.

"Your wife, sir. Go to your wife."

The indecision melted. Lord William nodded, and let himself be directed to the rowboat by the sergeant and his servant.

They were passed on the way by the "surgeon" whom Daltoons had waited on earlier. Huffing and puffing as he appeared from the waterside, in considerable agitation and complaining not only of the weather but the fact that no one in the country knew how to duel properly any more, Claus van Clynne made his very belated appearance at the top of the hillside.

Whereupon he saw his fallen comrade.

The cry that followed could not be described in any manner that would portray it with the least degree of accuracy. One might cite the tremendous, pained explosion that falls from a moose's lips when its mate is felled by a hunter in the wild; it might perchance be compared to the fabled sad trumpet of an elephant reaching the holy burial ground of its breed. The famous wail of trumpets that brought down Jericho could be mentioned. Yet none of these sounds would catch the nuances, the depth, the range of the Dutchman's vast and sonorous lament.

Forty

Wherein, a miracle occurs, and a pageant unfolds.

"If you had only waited for me," sobbed van Clynne, pulling at his hair. "Surely I would have saved you. How many times have I plucked you from danger in the past? We were an inseparable pair. What will I do for an assistant now?"

The Dutchman beat his breast with deep and genuine fervor. "Who will recommend me to General Washington? How will I get my property back?"

"Crocodile tears," said Alison.

"Do not think because you have finally found your proper clothes that I will allow you to be impertinent," said van Clynne. "There was a time when even young misses showed the proper respect for their elders. This is what the British have wrought: cynicism among the young. I am almost glad that you are not alive to see this sorry state," the Dutchman added, addressing his fallen comrade. "It would be more than your tender constitution could bear."

"Tender constitution?"

"Do not profane the dead with your remarks, child. Remember there is an afterlife. You, sir," van Clynne rose and found Daltoons. "I hold you fully responsible for this poor man's demise. The Revolution has lost its finest soldier. More harm has been done today to our cause than at any three battles on the continent."

Daltoons ignored him, hurrying his men to deposit

the seemingly lifeless bodies in the cart hauled by other
assistants and just now appearing from the woods. He
took a rifle and ran to the edge of the bluff overlooking
the shore, in time to see Buckmaster and his servant
push off. Two genuine British boats were just making
shore.

"I would have stopped this duel," wailed van Clynne,
turning back to his fallen comrade. "Had I not been
delayed by the perfidious tides, slow horses, and the
contingencies of, the contingencies—"

"Of breakfast?" shot Alison, borrowing a canteen
from the sergeant who had given Daltoons so much lip.

"He will have a fine burial, as fine a funeral as ever
mounted in this land. Washington himself will be a
pallbearer, and I right behind him, assuming my grief
subsides."

While van Clynne wove plans for the funeral, Alison
poured water directly into the hole the poisoned bullet
had cut. Jake opened his eyes slowly, then pulled up
with the soft groan of one interrupted from a pleasant
dream.

"He should be taken to Philadelphia immediately,"
van Clynne continued, addressing the heavens with his
upturned eyes. "Given a procession through the city,
and then interred in a place where the Congress can
visit his grave every day for inspiration. Near a tavern,
of course."

"Sounds like a lot of trouble," said Jake.

"Oh no, sir, it is but a trifle. I would think Congress
would be happy for the diversion." Van Clynne suddenly realized he was talking to a dead man. Daltoons
caught him as he fell backwards in a faint.

"A drug from Professor Bebeef," Jake explained.
"The antidote is pure water, as Alison has so obligingly
demonstrated. Our friend Bauer will be like this for an
hour. Were the others convinced?"

"Quite," said Daltoons. "But we must leave immediately. The soldiers arriving below are not ours."

Van Clynne, having recovered from his shock, gave

Jake a hearty pat on the back. "Well now, I think the entire episode has progressed very nicely. My acting clinched the effect completely."

"Your acting?"

"Indeed, sir. I knew you were but momentarily indisposed, and endeavored to give the best show."

"Uh-huh."

The body of the prostrate Tory was hoisted into the cart. The horse began moving before the lieutenant could even produce the whip.

"Smith's lies a league or so from here," Daltoons told Jake as the company double-timed into the woods. "Will that do for your plans?"

"Very nicely. Alison and I had quite an adventure reaching you," added Jake, but just as he started to tell Daltoons why he had arrived so late, a man appeared ahead at a bend in the path. Jake bolted forward, flying at him. Before anyone realized what was happening, he had thrown Christof Egans to the ground and pinned him beneath his knees. He pulled the white Oneida's long strand of hair through his fingers, threatening him with his other fist.

"This bastard is employed by the British as a messenger," Jake told the others as they ran up. "He tried to take me prisoner and sell me in New York."

"He's on our side," said van Clynne, huffing forward to intercede. "He has converted. He came with me, and was standing lookout in the woods, as he and I arranged. Come now, sir, you'll ruin what little hair he has left."

Jake looked at Egans doubtfully as the Dutchman told the full story. Despite his faith in van Clynne, he let his prisoner free with some reluctance.

Egans had not uttered a word in his defense, and did not do so now. "Two boats landed further north," he said instead. "Splitting off from the two approaching the landing below."

"Quickly," said Daltoons. "This way through the woods."

"I know of a better path to Smith's," boasted van Clynne. "We have only to follow a small detour this way . . ." He pushed back a tree branch to reveal a narrow and barely noticeable deer path beyond a small if strongly running creek. ". . . and we will arrive inside an hour. My path has the benefit of being nearly undetectable from the road," he added as the company veered to follow.

"Remarkable," said Daltoons.

"Smith is a fine brewer of beer, no doubt," suggested Jake.

"Top-fermented ale, to be exact," said van Clynne, with his customary air of superiority.

The placing of the bandage covering Clayton Bauer's chest was done smartly, but in fact, it was not secured well enough to prevent the few drops of water that splashed up from the creek as the men crossed from finding their way into the wound. Thus, unknown to Jake and the others, the Tory leader gained consciousness as he was driven through the woods in the wagon. Disoriented and confused, he did not grasp at first what had happened to him; he knew that he had been shot, but surprisingly felt no pain. For some moments he thought truly that he had died. But the voices around him gave sufficient hint that he had not, and Bauer was wise enough not to cry out. Some sixth sense warned him that the red uniforms that surrounded his wagon were not worn by true friends of the crown, and when he heard Jake's voice giving directions, he realized a trick had been perpetrated.

For all the patriot rhetoric against him, Clayton Bauer was a brave man. He had sworn that he would continue to serve his king until the moment of his death, and it was an oath he meant to keep.

"I tell you, sir, that I will not play the role of devil in your pageant. Play acting, sir; it is beneath me."

Van Clynne protested even as Daltoons's sergeant

took his measurements and began cutting a piece of red cloth for his suit. "I don't know if we have enough to cover him with," complained the man, whose pre-war talents as a tailor were being put to considerable test.

"You told me not twenty minutes ago that it was your acting that convinced everyone I was dead."

"That is a different thing, sir; then I was playing myself. Now I am the devil."

"You're not pretending to be the devil, Claus, just a British doctor."

"In the service of the king. It is the same thing. No Dutchman in his proper mind would deign to take up such a role. Never, sir, never."

"If you can give me another way to find out where Howe is going, I will take it."

"I have already told you: he asked his wig-maker for wigs in the fashion of Philadelphia. What more do you need?"

"Remember which package is which. The salts are harmless; mix them in the water to make it seem as if it is a cure. The sleeping powder will only work if it is loose in the air. Be careful; it is very potent."

"I should prefer a good knock on the head to one of your powders," countered van Clynne. "Perhaps we can pretend he has been sent to Hell, and make him confess the plans to Lucifer himself."

"What if this doesn't work, Jake?" asked Daltoons.

"Then we'll pull his arms and legs apart until he talks."

"We should try that first," suggested Egans.

"People are too susceptible to suggestion under torture," said Jake. "We do it my way."

The back room of the Smith farmhouse had been transformed from a humble closet for potatoes and onions to a well-appointed bedroom. The curtains at the window would not bear close examination, but the fine furniture at bedside, the white dressing table and fine mirror, along with the books casually strewn about, had all come from an abandoned and half-burned mansion not far away. It would not be difficult to convince the groggy patient he had been transported back to New York. But van Clynne and Daltoons must do better— they must pretend that weeks, not hours, had passed since Bauer fell on the field of honor.

Van Clynne, chafing under the burden of his red uniform, set a satchel at the foot of the bed, dismissed the others, and signaled to the sentry at the door that he was ready to begin.

"English, indeed," he muttered beneath his breath, before applying the antidote.

But Jake had not chosen van Clynne to play the role of doctor merely because he was unknown to the Tory. In the seconds before Clayton Bauer revived, the Dutchman's body underwent a vast transition, rivaled only by the changes that came upon his voice. His accent, as his patient opened his eyes, perfectly mimicked that of a native Londoner. If the squire was not an actor by trade, he was an accomplished man of business—nearly the same thing.

"It is about time," he told the revived man. "I feared you would resist this cure as well. Six weeks I have been trying to revive you."

Bauer started to push himself up, but van Clynne restrained him easily.

"Gently, my good man. Your constitution is at a very delicate stage, though your wounds have healed."

"Who are you?"

"Doctor Henry van Castle," answered van Clynne.

"You are Dutch?"

"Flemish. Actually, I have lived in England since I was nine, until coming to this cursed land three months ago. It is a mistake I regret every day."

"Where am I?"

"You, sir, are in the home of a British officer who rescued you from certain death. No other man in the colonies could have ministered to you as I have, day after day, night after night, for twelve, er, six long

weeks. At great personal risk, I might add. To aid a
dueling victim is a crime that can be punished by hanging, you know."

Bauer made a face. "Since when? Where are my sister and her husband?"

"His lordship is with General Howe," said van
Clynne loudly, as this was a cue to Daltoons, waiting
outside the door. "Or so I am told. We are making
preparations to abandon New York, and I haven't a
clue as to where anyone is at the moment, not even my
wife. Frankly, I will be only too glad to leave this dis-
eased vale; the very air we breathe swarms with pes-
tilence."

There was a knock at the door. Van Clynne admitted
Daltoons, who had given himself a promotion to major
to enhance the illusion that time had passed during
Clayton's sleep.

"Thank God!" declared Daltoons as he saw Clayton
propped on his pillow, eyes wide open. "I had despaired of your reviving."

"Where am I?"

"In the city. We are safe for the moment," answered
Daltoons. "But we will have to move shortly. The
rebels have taken King's Bridge and are marching
south as we speak. An entire army of them has appeared. If we cannot hold them at the woods near Harlem, the city will be abandoned." He lowered his voice.
"In truth, the order to evacuate non-essentials has already been passed. But do not say so in front of the
doctor, or the others."

"What? The rebels on Manhattan?"

Daltoons nodded solemnly. He endeavored to play
his role as well as van Clynne.

"What has happened to that idiot Howe?"

Daltoons's only answer was a scoff of contempt.

The plan was that Bauer would supply the answer
himself, with a statement such as, "What happened
when he reached Boston?" or "Cannot he be ordered

from Philadelphia?" But the star of this stage play had not studied his lines in advance as the others had.

"Where are my sister and her husband?"

"They believe you dead," said Daltoons. "They have gone to General Howe, to seek his help recovering your body. Rumor has it you were buried in the Jerseys."

"Buried?"

"Circumstances did not permit our enlightening them. They left to seek Howe shortly after you were shot, before this business. You seemed dead, at first."

Van Clynne sniffed. "I should have been consulted immediately. I have had cases like this before. Such cures are child's play for a scientist such as myself."

"Bacon is after you for killing his man. He seems to sense that you are still alive. I hesitated approaching General Howe, as I feared Bacon would find out. I myself do not have much influence, though perhaps if you sent word yourself, that would be a different matter."

Bauer, still obviously disoriented, struggled to prop himself on his elbows. "My mansion . . ."

Daltoons shook his head. "General Bacon has it watched night and day."

"Why are you hiding me?"

"As a matter of honor, nothing more. I hope your second would have done the same for my friend." Daltoons straightened. "Some men still have a sense of honor."

Bauer did not respond. Daltoons, trying not to show his disappointment, pushed on with the script. "There are not many troops left in the city. I doubt we'll be able to defend it."

"What the hell has Howe done, the incompetent windbag?" complained Bauer. "What of Clinton?"

"Summoned by Howe the very day you were killed. Or shot, rather."

"Should we send a message to his brother-in-law?"

van Clynne asked Daltoons. "There is, after all, the question of my fee."

"I am sure you'll be paid," said Daltoons. "Do you want us to send to them?"

Before Bauer could reply, there was a sharp volley of gunfire outside.

"Damn," said Daltoons. "The rebel sympathizers have launched many raids from within our borders, emboldened by their nearby army. I assure you, I will protect you as I have these past six weeks. It is a matter of honor. Doctor, take care of him. I will have a squad of men to escort you to the boat when there is no hope of defense. Do not hesitate when they arrive."

Daltoons exited. Van Clynne rolled up his sleeves and mixed the salt in a glass of water, as if preparing a treatment.

"What is this?" Clayton demanded as the glass was offered to him.

"An emetic," said the pseudo-physician. "Your spleen must be vacated."

"Thank you, I think not."

The Dutchman shrugged. "As you wish." He placed the glass on the bureau. "Should I send a message to your brother-in-law his lordship?"

Clayton hesitated before answering.

"Yes."

"Well? How shall I find them?"

"Send after Howe."

"The general or the admiral?"

"The general, you idiot."

"Excuse me, sir, but I think that you would show a bit more respect for the man who saved your life."

Bauer scowled. "If the general has taken Boston as he planned, then I assume they are there. Though they may just as well be back in England."

"Here, let me make you comfortable."

And with that, the Dutchman flicked some sleeping powder into Bauer's nose, sending him back off to slumber.

Forty-one

Wherein, the coffee is putrid, and a new plan is hatched to verify the results of the old.

Jake drummed his fingers on the pine farm table. The others—van Clynne, Daltoons, Egans, Alison, and two other Libertymen—sat at various stations around the stone-walled kitchen, waiting for his decision. Daltoons thought Bauer must have told them the truth, which meant Boston was the target. Van Clynne was convinced of just the opposite, contending that the Tory had somehow seen through their charade.

Jake wasn't sure. Their little play had gone off fairly well; he'd sat with his ear to the wall and heard every bit of it. But the ill logic of attacking Boston continued to bother him. And something about Bauer's replies seemed as fake to his ears as the others' lines.

"I have to have some other verification," said Jake finally. "Bauer may have seen through our charade."

"What other proof can we get you?" asked Daltoons. "Not even Culper has broken through their silence."

Jake rose and went to the small fireplace on the side of the room. He had to reach General Washington tomorrow morning with the information or the march for Boston would begin. Already he envisioned the soldiers gathering their things, advance parties readying the road.

Jake pushed away a bunch of dried onions hanging from the kitchen rafters as he walked to the side of the room. He turned there and walked back, trying to fertilize his thoughts with exercise. Alison had taken it upon herself to make breakfast, though given the meager cupboard this was more an act of conjuring than cooking. Three eggs, small enough to embarrass a hen or perhaps embolden a sparrow, were fried with the help of some pork grease in the iron pan at the fire's fore; these were multiplied in a sense with the help of a few stale crusts that the mice had not deemed worthy of attacking. The only things plentiful were onions, and Alison had populated her omelet with two dozen of them, a fact the others noted grimly as they picked through the scrapings.

Except for Daltoons, who gobbled it down as anxiously as if it were honey. "Just like my mother's cooking," he told the girl, who smiled at first but then resumed the businesslike pose copied from Jake.

Alison poked open the kettle and judged that the coffee was not quite done. The men did not seem upset; indeed, as they had watched the ingredients being prepared, they were not in a mood to hurry the concoction along. About a dozen beans, retrieved from the bottom of a grinder, were supplemented with a chicory weed, some grass and a handful of dried blueberries.

Or at least, they seemed to be dried blueberries. It was difficult to tell, as they appeared to have been dried several lifetimes before.

"If I return to Washington with the wrong information, it will be worse than not arriving at all," said Jake finally. "I'm just not convinced."

"It is a shame that you had no truth potion," said Daltoons. "Stuff some of that up his nose and we'd have the answer in a lick."

"Doctor Keen tried such a medicine on me during one of our meetings," said the Dutchman. He had responded to the news that his nemesis had died a second time with a contemptuous grunt. He had little doubt Keen would rise again. "It rendered me dizzy, but was insufficient to loose my tongue. Of course, our friend inside is not Dutch, but I would think no drug foolproof."

"My people have an excellent method for extracting information," said Egans. "Set him over a fire and put the question to him."

"I agree," said Daltoons.

Jake frowned. "Too many people admit fantasies under torture. We could never trust what he said, especially now."

"Too bad we can't just release him and see what he does," suggested Daltoons, rising to see if the coffee might be ready. "He'd be bound to make a report to someone."

"Why can't we do that?" asked Jake. "That's a great idea, Mark."

"I think, sir, the effects of the bullet's drug are lingering in your brain," said van Clynne. "Or else the fumes of the concoction our little friend is preparing. Release him and let him report to Howe?"

Jake stepped toward Egans, staring into the white man's tattooed face. The paint he had been wearing during their first meeting had faded, but a hard mask still obscured his emotions. "Have you met Bauer before?"

"Never."

The man whose eyes were locked with his had tried to murder him a few days before. Jake searched behind those green disks for some sign that he could trust him. But there are rarely obvious flags of a man's deeper intentions. The white Indian could easily be part of a ruse by Howe to throw the Americans off his track, just as his letter might be. Perhaps Black Clay Bacon himself had done Jake one better, arranging the show like an Italian puppetmaster.

Even Keen's death might have been faked.

"You will be a messenger for Howe," Jake told Egans. "Sent from Burgoyne. Claus can arrange for the necessary papers."

"I have them in my pocket," said the Dutchman, patting his jacket.

"We will deliver Bauer to his doorstep and revive him," said Jake. "Egans will arrive at nearly the next moment, exhausted from his flight south. He will be in the house when Bauer talks to his brother."

"How does this help?" asked Egans. "Am I to ask where Howe is?"

"No. You say nothing at all, only listen. Clayton will see that New York is not under attack. He will tell his sister what happened; he'll have to explain that he is alive. He will either be angry that he gave away the secret, or he will gloat that he fooled us. You will be in the room nearby; all you have to do is listen."

"He may not say where the attack truly is," said Daltoons.

"He will. He's too full of himself to keep his mouth shut in victory," said Jake.

"My opinion is firmly set on Philadelphia," van Clynne protested after the others had gone to see to the plan's contingencies. "The wig-maker's intelligence is impeccable, and I have never known one to lie."

"If I didn't think you might be right," said Jake, "I wouldn't be going back to Manhattan." He poured some of the strong liquid Alison had made into a cup for the Dutchman, then turned to the shelf to find one for himself.

"You're going back yourself? But Egans and Daltoons have just left."

"They have to find Culper's men at the rendezvous first. I'll still beat them."

One thing the Dutchman was good at: adding two and two and jumping to the proper conclusion. "You don't trust Egans, do you?"

"Why should I?"

"I would trust him as I trust my mother."

"You told me once you would never trust your mother." Jake sat at the table and began sipping the coffee concoction. Its taste was roughly akin to the squeezings of a tortured boot, following an uphill trudge through a berry bramble. "We cannot afford to trust him."

"You must rely on blood, sir. When a Dutchman gives his word, it is as good as gold."

"I have seen gold hammered into many shapes," said Jake. "Including a flask that very fortuitously fell into our hands—exactly as it would if a charade were being played. Doesn't his running across us both on our way south bother you? Especially given Keen's appearance?"

"A coincidence, surely. I converted him to the truth."

"If he has come over to us, then both he and I will have the plan. In any event, the true destination will come pouring out, no matter how complicated Howe's ruse."

"You are walking into the lion's den," said van Clynne. "If I did not know better, I might think you interested in stealing another taste of the lady's lips."

"I'll be safe enough," answered Jake, who could not conceal a slight smile.

Van Clynne sipped the coffee for the first time. "This is worse than the vinegar they served me in prison."

"I don't know. I've had worse."

"I had forgotten the extent of your torture by the Mohawk," said van Clynne. "I intend to complain to Culper of this at my earliest convenience. There are standards to be kept if one is to undertake a secret mission. The least they could have done was have Smith leave some of his beer in the house."

"You better keep your voice down; you'll hurt Alison's feelings. She's the only one left in the house."

"Her feelings are incapable of being trampled, that much is clear," said the Dutchman. "She has the spirit of a herd of wild horses, and more energy than ten boys loosed from school for the summer."

"Speaking of Alison . . ."

Van Clynne immediately increased his guttural garrumphs, pulling at his beard as if to amplify the effect. "I do not think, sir, that I should be charged with minding her. It is a task without reward."

"Now how do you know what I'm thinking?"

"Your embarrassed smile quite gives you away when you are preparing to hand over an odious mission." Van Clynne sighed deeply. "The Dutch are as fond of children as any race, but I am afraid you will find me an exception to the general rule. Children and I do not mix; we are like the proverbial cruets of water and beer."

"She's clearly not a child any more, Claus. She seemed to grow five years in the past few days."

"Do not let the dress sway you, sir," warned van Clynne. "Many a man has been wiled into submission by the strategic swish of a skirt."

"Granted. But I know you won't be."

Van Clynne signalled his frustration by twirling his beard around his finger. "She is at a difficult age," he warned. "Fresh on the door of adulthood."

"I'm not asking you to raise her, just to take her to Culper. He's promised to find a place for her in Westchester."

"I must point out that it is quite impossible to govern the young where love is involved."

"How do you know she's in love?"

"I would think it obvious," said van Clynne, "from the way she moons about in your presence."

"My presence?"

"Absolutely."

"Nonsense. There was a boy on Long Island she fell in love with. He is a year or two younger than she, but I think it an excellent match. They will be very happy together."

Van Clynne snorted. "I tell you solemnly, sir, it's you she's interested in."

"Impossible," said Jake.

"No it's not!" Alison burst through the door from

the other room, where she had stood listening to the entire conversation. "I'm not too young for you. Many girls my age marry."

Never on the battlefield had Jake been taken by such surprise. He stood stunned a full minute before replying.

"That's certainly true," he admitted gently, "but in this case, I think, it's more complicated."

"I shall like to watch you wrestle yourself out of this one," declared van Clynne. "I only wish I had some of Smith's excellent ale to assist my appreciation."

"Don't you have something to do, Claus?" asked Jake.

"No. Not at all. I have already spent a full day's exertion . . . but perhaps I had best be getting some fresh air." It was not the look from Jake that changed the Dutchman's mind, but a glance from Alison twice as murderous.

The girl flew into Jake's arms as soon as the door shut.

"I loved you from the moment you swept me up in my father's inn," she declared. "Couldn't you tell?"

"You are beautiful and brave," said the spy, his honey-sweet tone hinting strongly at the "but" that would follow. Well-used to breaking hearts, Jake had given this species of speech many times. Yet rarely had he felt this much tenderness delivering it.

"My heart is pledged to someone else," he told her, lightly pushing her from his chest.

"Someone older?"

"Yes."

The widow Sarah Thomas would have been greatly pleased to hear this, though she would have treated the words as someone does a clipped coin, not quite at face value. Still, they were meant sincerely. Jake might have made an even more eloquent case, his words rivaling many a poet's, had he explained further that before any earthly love, his life was pledged several times over to the cause of Freedom. But even Milton's tongue would have had no more effect on Alison than the simple shake of Jake's head when she asked if she might not change his mind.

"You must go with Claus to the city," Jake ordered. He pulled up his coat and prepared for her rebuttal and was greatly surprised when none came.

"All right," she said meekly. "You win. Let me just go and gather my things."

Jake narrowed his eyes as she left the kitchen to go upstairs. Nonetheless, he trusted the Dutchman would be more than a match for her. He himself had a great deal to do if he was going to finish this little puzzle.

Forty-two

Wherein, a happy coincidence procures a truce.

"*J*ake promised I could stay with him!"

Van Clynne shook his head as violently as if he were warding off a bee. "At least use more art in your lies. He charged me with taking you to Culper not ten minutes ago." The Dutchman puffed out his cheeks and set his hands at his belt, standing in the middle of what passed for the small house's great room. As soon as Jake had left, Alison had run down the stairs, veering from the front hallway when she saw it filled by van Clynne. She had then installed herself in a wooden chair, obviously reluctant to accept the Dutchman as her guide.

"I saved his life," said Alison sharply, curling her arms against the wooden Windsor chair as if van Clynne would try to physically pull her up. "And this is how I am repaid?"

"I might make the same claim several times over," agreed the Dutchman. "Gratitude has become a lost art. Nonetheless, you and I must attend to our mission. The lieutenant colonel has charged us with our roles, and as he often says, an expedition has but one leader."

The phrase proved considerably more persuasive than van Clynne had hoped, as the girl stopped sulking and nodded her head—slowly, to be sure, but nonetheless in the direction which indicates agreement. She unfurled her arms and rose from the chair meekly, walking across the braided rug to join him.

"We must set out immediately," said van Clynne, suspicious but nonetheless anxious to get started. "I know of a man not far from here who will take us across the river at a quite reasonable price. Along the way, we may be able to find ourselves a better breakfast than what we have been provided."

"I approve," said the girl so quickly you would have thought she was offered a chance to buy Manhattan for a bushel full of trinkets. "I had only a few bites of onions."

"Consider yourself lucky," said van Clynne, turning toward the door.

"You didn't like my cooking?"

"There was not enough of it," he said hastily. "You see the deprivations a soldier is treated to. You will be much more comfortable with Culper at the coffeehouse; food will be plentiful, and you may get your spying done between helpings of meat and potatoes, as it were."

"You're right," said the girl. But as she reached the threshold to the hallway foyer, she put her hand to her stomach and groaned heavily. "Oh, I think the onions are acting up."

"Are you sick?"

"No, I just—is there a chamber pot handy? Quickly!"

"Of course, child. Right in the kitchen cupboard, I believe, empty and clean."

"I will be all right in a moment," she said. "If you will excuse me."

Van Clynne nodded but followed along back to the kitchen. He was not so unschooled as to believe the stomach ache would not disappear the moment he was out of sight.

"You're not coming in to watch, I hope," she groaned, nearly bending.

It was so powerful a performance that van Clynne

retreated, closing the door behind him. He returned in an instant, however, setting a jar at the edge of a foot-stool where it would be knocked over when the door was opened. He then hurried outside to guard the room's only window.

Nearly ten minutes passed with no sign of Alison. Worried that he had overlooked some contingency, the squire took a peek inside the window and found the room was empty. Unsure if she had made her exit or was merely hiding, he propped his hat at the bottom of the window to make it appear as if he were sitting be-low. Then he ran back inside to find his stool and jar precisely as he had placed them.

"How in God's name did you manage this, child?" he asked aloud as he surveyed the empty room. "You have not gone out the door, and the window is still closed fast."

Van Clynne spotted the pantry closet at the side of the fireplace. Smiling to himself, he tiptoed forward, undid the latch as quietly as possible, then pulled the door open with a sharp flick of his wrist.

"A-ha," he shouted to the cobwebs.

After considerable beard tugging, the Dutchman de-cided there must be some secret panel inside this cup-board, perhaps beneath the floorboards.

"This is what comes of teaching children letters at an early age," he complained as he bent to examine them. "I have no doubt her parents were indulgent, and al-lowed her to read poetry at will. I would not be sur-prised if she had been given Shakespeare in her crib."

No sooner had van Clynne uttered these words than he heard a distinct creaking sound behind him. He whirled and just managed to grab Alison as she tried to spring from the pie-safe out the nearby door.

"You're ripping my dress," complained Alison. "Let go."

"You and I must reach an agreement," said the Dutchman, "whereby we are no longer enemies. Otherwise, I shall lock you in chains and have you carried on a mule all the way to the coffeehouse."

"I won't go to the coffeehouse," she said. "They're going to pack me off to upper Westchester, where my only excitement will be counting robins in a nest. I shall never be of any use to the Cause." Alison placed her hands on her hips and spoke in as plaintive a voice as ever Athena used to calm her father Zeus's famous rages. "How am I to stand for our enslavement by the English? Should not everyone do his or her duty according to their ability? And if their efforts are not used, will the Cause not suffer? Are not women to be the equal of men in this new republic? Otherwise, why fight at all?"

"Well spoken; I begin to wonder if perhaps you have some Dutch blood in you." Van Clynne stroked his beard thoughtfully. "But serving as a soldier would not be a good use of your talents, even if you could pass as a young man," he added. "You are too free-spirited for all that drilling and standing in line."

"I can be a spy like yourself."

"An operative, my dear. We involve ourselves in considerably more than spying, Jake and I. We are at General Washington's call for missions of every stripe. We are the upper class of agents, as it were."

The knit of van Clynne's brow grew to such proportions that not even Alexander could have untied it as he did the rope at Gordius. Scarce ever were the times the Dutchman had given such thought to a problem without the helpful lubrication of several barrels of fine ale: How to persuade the girl with a place where she might simultaneously be safe and fight the British at the same time?

The wheels in his head turned slowly but inevitably. For he was Dutch, after all, and the idea eventually settled into place like a great eagle landing on a treetop.

In truth, it did not take half the effort, though he made a great show of it. For van Clynne had made this suggestion to Jake several times already. But he had long ago learned that an idea that seems to suffer a hard birth is more easily accepted than one that slides into the world with nary a grunt.

"A friend of mine on Long Island may have need for a girl to help on her farm," he declared. "The woman is a brave patriot and often assists the Sons of Liberty. Her farm is behind the lines, and danger is always flitting past the threshold in some form or another. She is said to be Dutch by marriage only, yet has taken to the ways of the race so strongly that it is clear her ancestors found it necessary to obscure her Netherlands ancestry until now."

"Long Island?"

"Mrs. Hulter has lived there many years. Her husband was a soldier, but the rumor has it that he died near White Plains. As yet, his death has not been officially confirmed."

"Professor Bebeef's sister?"

"You know the family?"

Alison quickly told van Clynne the story.

"And here we once more have proof of Dutch superiority," declared the squire, who saw the coincidence not as a product of luck but of a plan he had intuitively if unknowingly placed in motion some time before. "There is a proper Dutch solution to every problem, my dear, as I'm sure the good missus will instruct. You will fight the British as fiercely as any Continental regiment. She is a fine brewer besides; you will do well to stay with her."

"I will go there on one condition."

"Name it," said the Dutchman.

"We cannot abandon Jake," said the girl firmly. "We must help him this last time."

"He has Daltoons's entire troop at his call," said the Dutchman. "They are meeting with reinforcements from Culper and will take over the farm and stand guard. Half the British army could arrive and they would be safe. We are as superfluous as a comb on a rooster."

"Perhaps I am," suggested the girl, "but what of yourself? What would have happened at the engineer's if you were not there to rescue him?"

"True," admitted van Clynne. "I did, after all, save the day. Many a time, I have had to pluck him from the fire just as his coat was singed."

"He has already died once today without you. What if you are not nearby a second time?"

The Dutchman contemplated that possibility. Actually, he did not worry so much about Jake as Egans, whom he believed would have a difficult time lying. This was a fatal flaw shared by all Iroquois, or so van Clynne believed. And the problem could, in turn, lead Jake to difficulty.

Besides, if they were starting from two different points, it would be difficult to coordinate their rendezvous on the Jersey shore. And despite Jake's long-winded assurances, he would undoubtedly feel obliged to leave for Washington without him. Van Clynne was loath to lose his opportunity for an interview with the general a second time.

"Perhaps we should reconnoiter the area as a reserve squadron," he suggested. "But they have already met you once; I'm not sure what pretense we can invent for your arrival."

"They know me only as a boy. They won't recognize me as a girl."

"Bauer saw you at the hill."

"There is an old dress upstairs, and I will wear a hat. You, on the other hand, have already been seen in your disguise as a doctor; you will have to find a disguise or stay hidden."

"Claus van Clynne never hides. That is a coward's way."

* * *

"I am warning you, girl, one nick and I will retaliate with appropriate measures. A strong paddling would do your soul good, I daresay."

"I used to shave my father every day. Now hold your mouth still—if that is possible."

"Impertinence. Impertinence in the young. In my time, it was unheard of."

"I am not as young as you pretend, and you are not as old," said Alison, who now had the advantage of seeing van Clynne's face—or a quarter of it—without its customary beard. "I doubt you are beyond thirty, if that. Now be quiet or we shall never arrive in time."

"Owww! What was your father's face made of? Iron?" Van Clynne reached up and grabbed her hand.

"Don't be such a baby," said Alison, freeing her wrist with a snap. She dipped the long straight-edge razor in the soapy warm water and prepared for another swipe. "A little bloodletting is good for your vapors."

"My vapors are in perfect condition, thank you. And I would expect you to show proper deference, now that I have condescended to allow you to shave me."

"Condescended?"

"Shaving is a sacred rite in the Dutch way of things, my dear. It is not every young woman who is accorded the privilege."

"Honored, I'm sure," said Alison sarcastically, plucking tightly at the next hairs and ignoring the ensuing howl. "When was the last time you washed your beard? I believe I have found a bird's nest here."

Forty-three

Wherein, Jake again kisses danger in the face.

The last time he had been in this mansion, Jake had arrived in a dazed condition with an armed guard at his shoulder. Still, he had enough of an idea of the layout to narrow Clayton Bauer's office down to one of two rooms in the western corner of the house. With Bauer gone, it would be the best place to hide—and would also give him a chance to search through the spymaster's papers.

Both rooms had windows facing the Hudson. Jake chose the corner to try first because it was closest to him as he moved through the woods from the side.

Though his wounds had been re-dressed at the Smith house, he did not want to push his battered leg harder than necessary. He walked forward slowly, glancing through the trees down toward the beach where he had washed up some days before. The disguised Libertymen had already appeared on the river; he had only a few minutes to get inside if he was to beat Egans.

The company of redcoats assigned to Bauer had returned in foul moods from the earlier diversion sent to them by Culper's men. Roused from bed to attend a false report of rebels attacking the rocky shore upriver, all they had to show for their adventures were skinned knees and bruised shins. The sentry posted at Jake's corner of the house was having trouble keeping his eyes open as he leaned against the building.

Jake kept the man's shiny coat in view as he half-crawled, half-trotted past a shed housing mowing equipment. He just managed to roll against the side of the building when he heard voices approaching from the rear; the low shrubs were enough to hide him only because the two sentries were talking rather than paying attention to their duties.

The men were discussing whether their company's assignment would be changed now that Bauer had been killed. Neither seemed to like the "uppity colonist," but they realized the chore of guarding him had been comparatively easy. The unit headquartered up the road a quarter mile away had been put on notice to prepare for an "expedition at sea." They worried over the cryptic phrase and whether it would soon describe their fates as well.

The talk faded as the guards called to their mate by the house. He shouted a one-word response and they reversed course, patrolling in the opposite direction. Their assignment doubtlessly called for them to walk the vast yard's perimeter in parallel, not tandem. Jake, ever the military commander, could not help but shake his head as he bolted to his feet and did his best imitation of a sprint toward the building.

The sentry did not notice him until the patriot's knife was slitting a peephole at his throat.

Jake propped the dead man against the house, hoping the others would not return before they were replaced by Daltoons's squad. In any event, he would look from the distance as if he were sleeping.

The window nearby was open a crack. Jake went to it, listened a moment to make sure the room was empty, and decided he was unlikely to find a situation more inviting. He slipped inside with less care than a sparrow entering her nest.

This was not Bauer's office, unless he had suddenly gained a very feminine side. Even if the rich yellow-

and-pink coverlet on the bed hadn't made it clear that Lady Bauer was staying here, the room was thick with her lilac-scented perfume.

Jake was adjusting his eyes to the dim interior light when he heard footsteps approaching from the hallway. He ducked and started to slide beneath the thick mahogany bed before realizing he couldn't squeeze in; the only other place to hide was behind the large curtain at the window he had entered. He was halfway there when the door opened behind him.

"You?"

Lady Patricia's voice held him suspended in midstep on the velvet rug. Jake took a breath, then turned to see her standing in her unclasped dressing gown, hair down, hands open at her sides. The hard soap of pain had scrubbed the pores of her face; rarely had mourning worn such beauty.

"I am Christof Egans, a messenger from General Burgoyne. I was ordered by the general to extend greetings to his honor Mr. Bauer before proceeding to General Clinton's headquarters."

The redcoat guard, standing at the top of the path from the beach, endeavored to keep his eyes off the strange markings on the man's face and chest. Nonetheless, his contempt for the visitor was undisguised.

"You're a white man?"

"I am an Oneida warrior. My Indian name is *Gawasowaneh*; in your tongue, it means Big Snowsnake. Do you wish my entire history, or will you do your duty and take me to your master?"

"Mr. Bauer is not here."

"I will wait, then," said Egans.

"You'll be waiting till Judgment Day. He's dead. Killed in a duel. Brother came back this morning."

"Take me to the brother, then," said Egans.

The English sentry had heard rumors of changelings and race traitors but had never seen one, much less found one in the employ of his government. Still, all

manner of arrangements were made during wartime.
When he searched Egans he found him unarmed. His
papers were in order. And so the private turned him
over to his corporal, standing on the shallow step before the front door, and retreated to his post—only to
find another guard in his place. As he protested the
unexpected relief, he was knocked over the head from
behind.

Egans, meanwhile, repeated his previous interview
with the private for the corporal, with roughly the same
stoic expression. Contrary to van Clynne's concerns,
Egans had no difficulty pretending to be something he
was not. The white Oneida soon found himself padding
softly behind the corporal as he was shown inside to
the parlor.

"I will attempt to find Lord William for you," said
the corporal. Like the rest of his men, he came from
the English Highlands, but his accent had been sup-
pressed by years of contact with his betters. He had
also learned a great deal more manners than his privates. "I must say that he is deeply grieved today. Your
audience may be strained."

"I am only here on orders," replied Egans. "As soon
as they are fulfilled, I will be happy to leave."

"Aye, I reckoned that." The corporal gave him a
crooked half-smile and turned on his heel to find
Bauer's lone servant, George.

Egans stood as erect as a statue in the well-appointed room. No rag rugs covered these wide floorboards; Persian and Flemish craftsmen had slaved for
many years so Clayton Bauer's guests could walk from
one room to the next without getting splinters in their
feet. At Egans's side stood a massive clock, taller and
wider than he, and filled with a mechanism as finely
and precisely tuned as the Oneida's own heart. Its deep
click filled his ears.

The reader should not think that the past few days
hadn't taken their toll on the adopted Indian's facul-
ties. The physical difficulties, to one so inured to a hard

life of fighting, were of little concern. Egans had en-
dured hand-to-hand warfare with bitter rivals; that was
a considerably greater trial, in his opinion, than any
fight with whites, no matter how extended. But the rev-
elations of his parentage, and more importantly, the
identity of his adopted father's killer, had struck the
core of his being. His hate had been so strongly held
that it guided his most important decisions since coming of age. It was one thing to shift alliances—Egans
had been taught the ways of justice and honor, and
knew firmly what he must do—but it was another thing
to face the grave error his life had been victim to. It
was a shortcoming he was responsible for; he must
somehow find a way not simply to amend it but to expi-
ate its consequences. Many men had been wrongly sent
to their deaths because of his mistake.

Jake need not have worried about his new loyalty.
Rather greater was the possibility that Egans might
suddenly do something very rash because of it. His
calm, stoic exterior, hardened by his years with his Iroquois family, hid the raging emotions of a volatile
white child, not yet tamed by civilization's conventions.
Sooner or later, the painted skin would fail to contain
the tormented soul bubbling below.

"Who are you, sir, and why do you come to my
brother's house?" said Lord William Buckmaster as he
entered the room.

"I am called Egans, a messenger for General Burgoyne. The general bade me directly to pay my respects, before I attended General Clinton. I have come
to fulfill my duty."

He addressed Lord William in a flat voice, and
seemed to take no notice of the man's finery, the well-
arranged powdered wig and black silk suit. Lord William had daubed his cheeks with rouge, but the lines of
his grief were obvious enough as Egans held his eyes.

Buckmaster dismissed the corporal, telling him to go
and check on his men. When he was gone, Lord William addressed Egans with a level voice, endeavoring

to take no notice of his odd appearance. He assumed such things were commonplace in this strange and violent land.

"My brother-in-law is dead," said Buckmaster. "I am waiting now on the arrival of his body."

Egans nodded.

"Would you care for a drink?"

"No."

Egans waited silently as Lord William called for George to bring him a strong whiskey.

"Sir," said the servant, "I believe that some additional soldiers are arriving outside. And I have heard noises in the north wing—"

"Just get me the damn whiskey. Now!"

The outburst represented Lord William's surrender. He sank into the blue velvet chair behind him, lucky that it was there to break his fall.

Egans stood motionless, observing, feeling only contempt for the weakling before him.

The same spell that had arrested Jake stopped Lady Patricia as well. Jake broke it first, moving quietly and quickly behind her to shut the door. Then he touched her shoulder with his left hand—his right still held his knife—not knowing whether she would cry out in alarm or fall into his arms.

She did neither, turning instead. A thousand emotions mixed in her face.

"You killed my brother."

There was a moment that seemed a century then, as if Jake might be somehow able to commit her soul to his memory, as if in the silence some essential part of each might mix. For van Clynne had judged his friend well; Jake had become enamored of the woman whose lips he first kissed for convenience only. Whether for her nobility in suffering, her strong yet charitable way, or the inviting curve of her body—it was impossible to say.

As the first moment grew to the next, the spy banished any weakness the attraction would bring. Yet some emotion remained; some regret tempered his strength.

"Your brother is alive." Jake took her hand as she started back in shock. "I am not an agent for Bacon, but Washington."

"Washington?"

He let her slip back to the bed, sitting on the edge and catching her hands to her mouth. He saw her next move before she attempted it, grabbing her mouth quickly as she rose to set the alarm.

"Let me go, you bastard." The words choked out between his fingers, not loud enough for anyone outside the room to hear. "You killed my son. You and your treacherous friends, you lying bastard!"

Lord William rubbed his face, as if he could pull the shattered shards of his soul back together. He looked up and offered his guest a wan smile of apology.

"Excuse me," he said. "My son disappeared—we have to assume he died—in the war, and now my brother. His wounds were more of the self-inflicted nature. Pride, really."

There was a shout at the front hall, and Lord William jumped to his feet, running to the door—where he found his brother-in-law, groggy but quite obviously alive, hanging on the shoulder of a sailor.

"If you yell out, your husband inside will die," Jake warned her. He moved his hand down and gripped his arm around her neck, trying not to choke her though keeping her secure. He had the knife in his right hand, but there was as much chance of him using it against her as there was of the sun rising a second time that day. "Your brother will be killed as well, this time for real."

"I don't believe you," she said, yet she made no effort to call out or get away as Jake leaned down to slide the knife into his boot.

Her long dressing gown was half buttoned, an inch of pink-white skin exposed between her breasts. Jake, still holding her around the neck, reached to the nearby table and pulled off the cloth, fashioning it as a light clasp for her hands.

"I did not kill your son," he said as he tied her hands. "And I did not make the promise to help find him lightly."

"You are a liar and a devil."

"You accepted my kisses readily enough."

"Don't flatter yourself," she said.

"I notice you're not trying to escape."

"I'm not as foolish as you think. You would grab me in a second, wouldn't you? And slit my throat. Kill me now, then. Go ahead. Kill me as you have devastated the rest of my family."

A sudden energy flooded into her body. Jake caught it just in time, clamping his hand over her mouth.

"I'm not going to kill you," he said, a second before she bit his fingers.

Forty-four

Wherein, several weapons are produced, as are some slight complications.

*D*altoons checked the pocketwatch warily as he squatted by the stone pillar along the roadway. His men would have deposited Clayton Bauer at the front door and ought to have neutralized the guards by now.

No matter whether in the city or not, operations on Manhattan were always fraught with danger. Daltoons, by now an experienced veteran of irregular warfare, habitually felt his palms sweating at some point during a mission. They had turned to raging torrents now, and he wiped them on his freshly bleached white breeches, anxious for his men to arrive and tell him everything was going as planned.

His hope was in vain. Hasty footsteps down the path and labored breathing announced a messenger.

"One of the sons of bitches got away," said the man. "He ran from the back when we secured the horses at the barn. You said not to shoot."

"Shitten hell." Daltoons turned his eyes back to the road. There was a redcoat encampment less than a quarter mile away.

"Pull everybody from around the building. March up to the crossroads with me," said the young lieutenant, loosening the worse curses in his arsenal as he began trotting up the hill, guns ready. "Shitten damn hell in a British dandy's rogering hatbox."

* * *

"It was some manner of rebel plot," Clayton Bauer told his brother-in-law as he was helped to the couch. "They were trying to get information from me on Sir William's plans. At least I believe that is what they were doing. I told them he was going to Boston." He managed a wry smile as he sat down. "The idiot has probably changed his mind several times now, and reversed course from Philadelphia, so lord knows I may have told them the truth. Who the hell are you?"

Bauer jumped upwards, still struggling with the effects of the drugs. Bebeef's sleeping powder had a nasty habit of leaving the joints knotted with pain for several hours after the primary effect had worn off.

Egans did not react.

"He's a messenger from Burgoyne," said Lord William.

"Gentleman Johnny is using clowns?"

"My name is Egans," the white Oneida said. "I was told to extend the general's personal regards before reporting to General Clinton."

"What the hell would you be told that for?"

"I am not in the habit of questioning my orders," said Egans. "If you wish me to leave, I shall."

"No, I do not wish you to leave," said Clayton, who waved off his brother's attempts to pull him back to the couch. "I want you to explain who the hell you are, and what you are doing here. The last time I saw Burgoyne I promised to see him in hell for his slander. He would no more extend me greetings than he would address a horse in the street."

Jake nearly screamed with the pain as Lady Patricia clamped her teeth on his fingers. He caught her as she tried to squirm away and pulled her back, hesitating to punch her but finally seeing no choice.

Just as his fist found the side of her head, a dark brown figure rushed through the door and flew at his back, snarling and barking. The mastiff that had once guarded him on the beach now sent him flying forward on the bed; Jake reached for his Segallas in his belt but lost his balance and fell over as the animal slashed its teeth into his side.

For nearly a full minute he fought the dog with his bare hands, wrestling desperately to keep its mouth from his throat. Finally he managed to fall to the side and roll to his stomach, his back and coat offering some protection from the angry beast's slashes.

Jake found the handle of the knife and pulled it from his boot, but dropped the blade as the mastiff slashed at his arm. He rolled over the knife and had to fight to his knees, the dog pulling viciously at his clothes before the spy finally managed to grab the weapon again. A sharp plunge with the blade into the animal's stomach drained the fight from it; he finished the job quickly by slitting upwards, all the way to its throat.

He rose to find a servant at the door holding a pistol on him.

"I have told you who I am," Egans said coldly. "If there is ill blood between you and my superior, it is none of my concern. I will take my leave. I am already several days late."

"Stop, Indian, or whatever you are," Bauer reached for the side of the couch. He didn't do so to steady himself. Ripping away the cloth, he retrieved a loaded pistol and pointed it at Egans.

"George, what the hell is going on with that dog!" Bauer yelled before turning to the sailor who had helped bring him into the house. "Get the guards from outside and have him arrested," he ordered. "Move, man, before I have you thrown in chains as well."

The sailor quickly headed for the door.

"Drop the knife, I say."

"Come now," Jake told the servant. "You're not going to shoot me for a brief indiscretion."

"Drop it or you're as good as dead."

Jake complied as the man steadied his aim. He was holding the pistol with more confidence than David displayed toward his slingshot.

"What have you done to her ladyship?"

"Just put her to sleep." Jake took a stagey glance toward the bed, but George was too smart to allow him an opening. He circled around to the other side, out of reach for a lunge.

Jake's blow had sent her slumbering, but otherwise left her unharmed. The servant placed his hand briefly at Lady Patricia's mouth to make sure she was still breathing.

There was barely six feet separating them. Still, it would take more than Jake's normal dose of good luck to keep from getting a gut's worth of trouble if he dove for the pistol. Nor did a plunge through the door into the house seem like a good option.

The Segallas was still in his belt, tucked beneath his coat. He tried to ease his hands down where he might grab it, but the servant returned his attention to him.

"Keep your hands up and walk through the door."

"And what if I don't feel in the mood for a stroll?" asked Jake.

"Then I will kill you here and not bother cluttering the courts."

Egans's face betrayed no emotion. He knew the "sailor" would soon return with either some story or his weapon drawn, or both. He already had the information he had come for; all he need do now was wait.

That he could do for a long time, as difficult as it was to stomach the stench of the cowardly Englishmen. If duty had not required his returning with the information Jake Gibbs and his friend the Dutchman sought, Egans would surely have attempted killing them all with his bare hands. In such a way, he decided, his mistakes would begin to be corrected, blood for blood.

"You are not a native," said Bauer. "Why are you dressed that way?"

Egans did not answer.

"Speak, you race turncoat. Speak. That is an order." Bauer waved the gun in his face.

"I was born white and adopted. I am an Oneida and a member of the bear clan. No one can steal that identity from me, for it has been sealed with blood."

"White blood, I would bet," said Clayton. "Your soul has been poisoned by the pagans."

Egans had many rejoinders, but offered none.

"Really, Clayton," said Lord William. "I think you should let the soldiers handle this. You are weak from your ordeal."

"He is undoubtedly another spy."

"He showed papers."

"Easily forged. I should kill him now."

"I don't think that would be wise," said the sailor, returning from outside. A Southerner caught in the city when the British invaded, James Dewey had joined in several clandestine operations against the British during his sojourn. Baffled by his compatriots' disappearance from outside, he'd decided retreat was now in order, and had produced a gun from under his billowing shirt to effect it. "Put down your pistol."

Bauer shook his head. "I believe we have a standoff."

"Not in the least." Dewey had been told by Daltoons that Jake would be inside the house, and so endeavored to tip the balance by calling him out.

"I'm here," announced Jake, answering his call as he appeared beneath the arch leading to the hallway. "But not alone."

The servant stood behind him, pistol poking into his ribs.

Forty-five

Wherein, a lesson in ciphers is well-learned, but does not prevent dire consequences.

Dewey had always prided himself on his ability at arithmetic, and fully realized that the patriot forces were currently one weapon short. Still, by his reckoning there was no immediate need to comply with Clayton Bauer's demand that he put down his gun. He was confident that the men who were supposed to be posted outside would eventually reinforce him.

"I can kill you as soon as you fire. And I will," he told Bauer.

"Brave words, rebel," said Bauer. "Bring him over there, George. Where's my sister?"

"Oh my God," said Lord William. He took a tentative step for the door, but the sailor's voice caught him.

"Move, and your brother will die."

"She's all right, m'lord," said the servant. "I caught this one before he could harm her."

"Your wife is sleeping," Jake told Lord William. "I found it necessary to give her a blow to the head, but there should be no permanent damage. At least she will stay out of the line of fire."

"My guards will be on you in a minute," promised Clayton.

"We have replaced your guards," said Jake. "Our men are just now disposing of them. Your best course is to surrender; we will spare your lives."

"I hardly expect, much less would I even accept, mercy from a rebel."

Jake shrugged and continued to survey the room for some implement or distraction that would change the precarious equation.

Egans made the first move. He had his eyes trained on Jake's guard, and when the servant began moving toward the window to see where the shots were coming from, he crashed against Clayton Bauer with the force of an angry bear. Bauer's bullet flew into the ceiling—but only after it punched a wide hole in Egans's bare chest.

Jake dove to the ground as the servant and sailor shot at each other, the servant's bullet crashing straight through the sailor's heart, killing him instantly. Dewey's aim was just as true, for in that same moment his bullet flew into his enemy's mouth, exploding with gore through the back of his head.

Jake jumped to his feet, Segallas in hand. He grabbed Lord William and fired a single shot directly into his temple. The bullet was too small to kill him instantly, and so the nobleman slumped to the floor, leaving his life to ebb slowly from him.

The patriot spy turned and found Bauer descending on him, wielding his pistol like a hatchet. Jake took a blow at the side of the neck as he shot the Segallas point blank into the Tory's shoulder.

The blow stung Bauer back to the couch.

"Where is Howe going?" Jake demanded, flipping the barrel mechanism around so two fresh bullets were ready to fire.

"Never," promised Bauer. He threw his gun at Jake, who ducked instinctively, choosing not to fire. If he did not succeed in getting Howe's destination, all of these deaths, and his entire mission, would be in vain.

The Tory took this chance to grab another pistol from its panel at the back of the chair where he was sitting.

Jake dove at him before he could aim. As the two

men crashed back and forth, the muscles in Jake's body cried out in despair, every injury inflicted over the past few days renewing itself. Half his body was covered in sticky blood.

Bauer surprised Jake by sinking his teeth deep into his arm—apparently the tactic ran in the family. The pain was so desperate the spy felt the hard shock in his backbone. Jake retaliated by punching the Tory with his head, moving him back but not loosening his grip on the pistol. Both men had their fingers on the trigger; both had their other hand on the barrel, flailing in a desperate struggle to aim or divert its fatal ball.

Suddenly, one of the fingers succeeded in slipping against the trigger, igniting the lock.

Whose finger it was, neither could tell. In the pure moment of silence that followed, it did not matter. Both men felt as if they had been transported, plucked from the tormenting fires of hell and deposited in the sweet clover hills of Oblivion.

And then Clayton Bauer's body fell limp, and Jake Gibbs fell back, the smoking pistol dangling from his bloody hand.

Daltoons's men had succeeded in surprising and dismounting the English soldiers, but he could see his troop was outnumbered and greatly outgunned. They had only enough shot and powder to keep on for a few minutes more; already he had lost two of his dozen men. Redcoat reinforcements kept appearing up the road. While the patriots had good firing positions, in command of the highway and the well-tended field before it, a concerted charge by the British would easily overwhelm them.

"Ames, you go back to the house and get them the hell out of there," said Daltoons. "We'll hold out as best we can."

Ames, realizing this might be the last time he saw his commander, nodded gravely, but hesitated a moment before putting down his rifle.

"Go, man," ordered Daltoons, and the young man was off, running down the hill.

It could well be that the moment of regret at leaving his friends cost him his life. For as he neared the house, a British sniper who had managed to infiltrate the woods spotted him, and with a single bullet sent his poor soul scurrying to Saint Peter's well-trod gate.

Jake rose and surveyed the battered room, littered with bodies. Once again he had failed, his finely crafted trick as useless as a child's game. But just as he was about to curse himself and all his damnable cleverness, he realized Egans was still alive. He bent over him and saw the wound was fatal; the red man born white would die in a matter of minutes, if not seconds.

"You must not try to speak," Jake said gently. He pulled the front of Egans's coat together, covering the bullet hole. "The ball has taken you through the lungs. You are a brave man and true to your word; I am sorry that I did not trust you before now."

"I had not earned it," said Egans, lifting his head. "I do not fear death. The sky has already closed around me. Howe is on his way to Philadelphia." He began to cough blood. "He told his brother."

"Philadelphia," Jake repeated.

"Yes," said Egans. "He said so freely. Father!"

The last word was uttered in the nature of a hoarse shout, emerging from his lips at the very moment his soul passed on. Jake followed the corpse's gaze across the room—right to Lady Patricia, who stood at the doorway with a rifle in her hands.

Forty-six

Wherein, the old adage, "Better late than never," is proven true.

Claus van Clynne's journey across the Hudson had been delayed by the contingencies of negotiation and logic, to wit: the squire could not understand why the ferryman deemed it necessary to increase the standard fee an extra two shillings, due to the fact that the British were now in control of the Manhattan coast.

"If you do not understand that, then I shall charge you three extra shillings, to cover the cost of my lesson," retorted the ferryman.

The negotiations proceeded at length until Alison dug into her own purse and tossed the man his extra two shillings. Van Clynne did not like this, but he nonetheless saw no reason not to get into the vessel while he complained.

While the Dutchman had spent considerable time on the water of late, his characteristic fear of the waves had not abated. Thus his eyes were closed firmly, and covered with his hands besides, when the vessel touched the rocks a hundred yards or so north of the point where Jake and the others had come in.

"They're shooting!" said Alison as the boat scraped onto the shore. "Look! Redcoats are coming over the hill. We must warn Jake!"

She was out and running before van Clynne could even open his eyes. The Dutchman's admonition that she halt might just as well have been uttered at the sky.

Cursing, he turned to the ferryman and told him he must wait for his return.

"Why would I do that?"

"Because I told you to," said van Clynne, reaching beneath his shirt for a purse. "And because I will give you a fresh ten-pound note if you are here when I get back."

"For that amount of money, I would wait for Satan himself."

"Satan would not pay you nearly as well," grunted van Clynne as he got out of the boat. He rushed up the shore to the two guards who were posted near the Sons of Liberty's boats.

"Come with me quickly," he ordered.

"The hell we will," said one of the men. "Throw up your hands you British dog, or I'll kill you where you stand."

"I'm van Clynne, you idiot. Don't you hear the gunfire? Why did you let the girl go on without a weapon?"

"Jesus, Jack, it's the fat Dutchman who is always complaining. Someone's snatched his beard away."

Under ordinary circumstances, van Clynne would have demanded to know by whose definition he was being declared fat. But there was no time to waste; he pushed down the man's gun and bade him follow up to the house.

"Our orders were to stay and guard the boats."

"Were your orders to let the rest of the party die in the meantime? Come on then, and follow me. Honestly, there was a time when enlisted men showed initiative. I hope your muskets are loaded with double shot, at least."

Spent gunpowder and smoke filled the room with a hazy gray air. Jake and Lady Patricia stood alone above a sea of blood and dead bodies. Her dressing gown was still unclasped; were it not for the rifle, she might appear an angel or one of the Fates, come to account for the dead.

Jake held his arms out calmly. "Lady Patricia, I had hoped you would not come to harm."

"Those are empty words," said the woman. "You have killed my entire family."

"I did not kill your son. Your brother-in-law and husband chose their own paths."

"It is the same. You rebels have no care for honor or the rule of law. I did not understand my brother until now."

"But we do. That is why we are fighting, as anyone who stays in this country more than a few weeks will learn. I do not mean to offer false hope, but if your son was not accounted for, it may be because he escaped alive. Perhaps he has deserted."

"I hardly think the son of a peer would run away from battle."

"He wouldn't be the first. He was a young man, and Justice is a strong mistress."

Tears were beginning to well in her eyes, but Lady Patricia was resolute. She lifted up the gun and with her thumb, reached to pull back the trigger.

"Jake!"

He dove to the side. Lady Bauer was pushed to the floor by a body leaping across the threshold onto her back.

Jake rolled to his feet and plucked the still-loaded rifle from the floor. He had to grab Alison as she aimed a blow at the noblewoman's head.

"She was going to kill you," cried the girl.

"It's all right, Alison." He gave her the rifle, then reached down and gently touched the poor woman's heaving body.

"Kill me, kill me," she sobbed. "I want to die."

Outside, the gunfire was getting closer—and thicker.

"I was not lying about your son," said Jake, still crouched over her. "And I promise to ask General Washington about him."

She made no acknowledgment that she had heard him. Jake stood over the prostrate, grief-ridden body. He knew many patriot women who had been made widows from this war; he felt no less for her than them.

Alison, standing at his side, saw the gentle way he knelt back and patted the Tory woman's shoulder. She remembered what Mrs. Hulter had told her of love— and in that instant despaired. The girl threw down the gun on the couch and walked out of the house in a cloud.

She was nearly run over by van Clynne in the hall-way.

"There you are, as usual, dallying with the distaff while there is considerable work to be done," announced the Dutchman in a huff as he entered the room. "We are under attack. Our forces are retreating to the perimeter of the house."

"I'm leaving," said Jake, rising. He stopped short as he turned. "Where is your beard?"

"I doffed it as a disguise," said the Dutchman.

"You look like a new man," said Jake, scooping up his Segallas and grabbing the rifle. "Come. We have what we came for, thanks to your friend Egans."

The battle outside was proceeding with great fury, as Daltoons attempted to beat the slowest retreat possible. His men were doughty volunteers, fully imbibed with the spirit of Freedom, brave souls all. But no manner of rhetorical flourish can overcome the fact that they were over-matched.

The British, sensing their superiority, advanced with an aggressive haste that gave Daltoons an idea. Loading his musket and pistol with double shot, he directed his men to continue their withdrawal past the house. He then hid himself in a thick bush as the British continued their advance.

The thick woods and rough terrain made it impossible to proceed as a line, despite the English officers' efforts. Bayonets drawn, but still occasionally stopping to fire, the redcoats continued down the hill.

The young lieutenant let the British vanguard, perhaps six men in all, pass him before he opened fire. He chose his first victim well, smashing the skull of a British lieutenant with both bullets from his double-packed musket. The shot from his pistol was borne of desperation, but no less accurate. He caught the company sergeant in the chest as the man aimed a shot in revenge. With great war whoops and hosannas, Daltoons gave the general impression that a full squad of men were launching a surprise counterattack.

The redcoats who had advanced down the hillside now had to retreat and deal with this new problem in their flank, or risk being cut off. The main company, meanwhile, immediately sought cover, having seen two of their leaders cut down by the troop of sharpshooters in the wood.

The feint relieved the pressure on his men and would give Jake and the others in the house a chance to escape. But Daltoons had suddenly made himself the acute object of redcoat desire. He dove over the large rock wall that marked the former edge of Bauer's property just as a fresh volley of musket balls punctuated the woods around him.

The lieutenant still had two small pistols in his belt, both loaded, assuming the charges had not been dislodged by his rough travel. Without bothering to check, he took one in his hand and began making his way along the wall toward the river as quickly as possible, half-crouching, half-running.

The woods and brambles, to say nothing of the smoke from their weapons, obscured the redcoats' vision and allowed Daltoons to gain a good lead before they realized where he was. Gradually, the Englishmen figured out that the attack at their side was merely a distraction, and endeavored to overcome its effects, redoubling their assault though handicapped by the loss of their lieutenant and sergeant.

As Daltoons reached the back garden of the mansion, they were testing the defenses at the perimeter on the other side of the house. Not hearing any gunfire, he leapt over the wall and began racing for the lawn overlooking the river. In truth, he thought the American side of the operation had by now concluded, and feared he would reach the river too late to join the boats. He had ceased worrying about being shot; indeed, he had ceased worrying about anything, focusing entirely on the river.

As he reached the path that led down to the waterside, the lieutenant became aware of two distinctly different objects in his periphery: the figure of a redcoat sharpshooter taking aim at the woodside ten yards from the mansion's front door, and a considerably more demure, willowy figure, walking as if in a daze from behind the brick wall out onto the lawn.

Alison, full in the aim of the redcoated demon and his gun.

Forty-seven

Wherein, bravery proves stronger than love, and vice versa.

*T*en yards might just as well have been ten miles, as far as the accuracy of the small pistol in Daltoons's hand was concerned. But the young lieutenant had no time to worry about that; indeed, he had no time to worry at all.

"Death to all redcoats!" he screamed, charging the sharpshooter. In the same motion he fired his pistol.

The bullet sailed well wide of its mark, but its effect was precisely what Daltoons wished. The Briton turned and fired not at Alison but at the blur attacking him.

"Mark!" shouted Alison as Daltoons fell to the earth, the side of his chest punctured by the wound. The spell that had taken hold of her vanished as she ran to the man who had just saved her life.

"I'm all right," he gasped. "The gun, the gun in my belt."

Alison looked up and saw the redcoat who had cut down Daltoons advancing with his bayonet. She grabbed the pistol and with a steady hand pulled back the lock at its side to fire.

Nothing happened. Whether the charge was knocked out by Daltoons's efforts or fouled by his blood, the effect was the same. Alison and the lieutenant were defenseless.

It took the redcoat a moment to recover his breath from the sudden fright of being faced down by a pistol.

"So, rebel, you thought you would kill me," he said, gripping his rifle so he could take a good plunge with the bayonet.

Retreat was cut off by the wall behind her, but in any event, Alison would not have left Daltoons. She threw down the gun and put her hands defiantly to her hips as she rose. "You're awful damn talky for a private," she said.

"I will show you the difference between talk and action, you damn rebel," said the Briton, preparing to lunge. "You will repent your tart tongue."

A shot rang out as the man started forward. The bullet took his head and snapped it sideways in a grotesque spiral toward death.

"Her tongue is her best feature by far, I think," said Jake Gibbs, vaulting over the wall. The rifle in his hand was still smoking.

Jake and company managed to make their boats well ahead of the British patrol, which was delayed by its need to search and secure the mansion. The ferryman hired by van Clynne now proved his patriotism, getting not only his vessel but the others started into the water as the Americans dove into the river. The man was soon humming a healthy tune, leading the tiny armada around a crag which cut off their pursuers' aim.

Halfway to Jersey, the patriots paused to take stock. Daltoons had lost several of his men, and the young lieutenant lamented not merely their passing but the fact that their bodies had been left unburied.

"You're lucky you're not dead yourself," said Jake. "Let me see your chest there."

"It's not even a scratch," protested the lieutenant.

"It needs to be examined," said Alison, pulling aside his coat to do so.

There was not a large amount of blood. A bullet had wedged itself at the side of Daltoons's ribs; though doubtlessly painful, it did not threaten his life.

"It can be plucked out with a knife," said Alison. "I

have performed the operation before. All we require is a bit of fire."

"And a good strong dose of whiskey," advised Jake. "You will be back in good health after a little rest. And perhaps some nursing. I sense you have a volunteer." He was not surprised to notice that both the lieutenant and Alison blushed. "Though I believe she is supposed to be elsewhere on Manhattan at the moment."

"The girl and I have reached an agreement concerning her disposition," announced van Clynne. "There is a certain woman named Hulter on Long Island, who has need of assistance on her farm. Apparently you have already made her acquaintance."

"I have indeed. But when did she volunteer to take on a girl?"

"Tut, tut, my good man, she is not taking on a girl, but rather a daughter. And perhaps a son-in-law as well. These things are well valued by the Dutch."

Jake rolled his eyes at the Dutchman's typically belabored speech. He knew better than to ask van Clynne for an explanation of how he knew Mrs. Hulter. But he sensed that the good woman would indeed accept Alison.

"Long Island would be a good place for a wounded soldier to recover," said Alison hopefully.

"It would indeed," answered Daltoons.

"I think Culper would approve," said Jake. "It seems a satisfactory arrangement for all parties."

"It is one I championed from the beginning," said van Clynne.

Forty-eight

Wherein, the past is fondly if questionably recalled as our tale ventures toward its end.

*S*everal hours later and some miles north on the Jersey shore, two tired but well-cheered travelers paused to let their horses drink from a stream.

"And so, it would appear that I have quite saved the day once more."

"You saved the day?" Jake's face twisted as he got down from his borrowed mare. Van Clynne had been uncharacteristically silent for nearly three minutes now, so he might have expected some such outburst as they paused. Still, it did not pay to allow any claim by the Dutchman to go unchallenged. "How, pray tell, did you manage that?"

"Through my usual pluck," said the squire. "Really, I would have thought by now you would be fully conversant with my methods."

"I will grant that you played a role in our escape," said Jake, "but frankly, I think you take far too much credit. As usual."

"Tut, tut, my good man, there is enough glory to go around. Though I would note that my intelligence proved correct; Philadelphia is Howe's target."

"Assuming he doesn't change his mind."

"Come now, the wig-maker would be the first to know. Nonetheless, your methods arrived at the proper solution eventually. I daresay that you ought not be over-criticized."

"Thanks for the compliment."

Jake stretched his legs, trying to fool his various pains into thinking they were temporary. In truth, he knew he had almost been too clever on this mission; all his plans had nearly come to naught. Nonetheless, he could not think of another way he might have tricked out the information. Howe's damnable golden flask had proven to contain a most difficult riddle.

"I shall make sure to mention your efforts to His Most Excellent Excellency General Washington when we meet," said van Clynne. "I shall reinforce your official report; a natural enhancement is needed for the dry tidings you render. Really, did your studies not include a proper recognition of the rhetorical arts?"

"When *you* meet General Washington?"

"Surely you are taking me with you to General Washington. Granted, my face is nicked, but that was in the line of duty."

"I'm not sure I will introduce you at all."

"Come, sir, I realize you jest—yes, you play the fox, twirling my leg. Well, sir, I will indulge you. Nay, I will encourage you. You have earned a little laugh."

"I've earned a rest, I think."

"We have many miles to ride, and then you will rest," said van Clynne, adopting Jake's usual line of argument in these conversations. "Really, sometimes I wonder how you ever became a spy with such a shallow constitution. Let us board our horses and be off. We have but a few hours before darkness, and even if we ride all night, we will be hard-pressed to make the camp on time."

And so once again Lieutenant Colonel Jake Gibbs found himself in the familiar position of shaking his head as he traveled with van Clynne. There was, it will be admitted, a vague pleasure attached to the Dutchman's company, even as he complained that the trees were no longer as green as they once were.

"You know, Claus, you look quite young without your beard," ventured Jake as he boosted himself onto his horse's back. "I think you are not half as old as you pretend."

"Thank you, sir, for your kind words, but there is no need to win my affections with flattery. I already hold you in high esteem."

"I am surprised that you allowed your beard to be cut at all. Did you harbor some secret admiration for Alison?"

"Please, sir, let us not be so impertinent. Nor should you forget that I found you holding a British noblewoman in your arms. What would General Washington say to that, I wonder?"

"He might well ask if I kissed her," said Jake, spurring his mount. "And I will have to say I did."

Van Clynne prodded his horse to follow. The white-gray stallion was a sturdy beast, provided by a Jersey patriot. For once the Dutchman had the faster horse, and he quickly caught up to his companion.

"There was a time when a gentleman refused to tell whether he kissed or not. Now, if Governor Stuyvesant were here, I can assure you, things would be different. There was a gentleman, sir, despite his occasional show of temper. A gentleman was a gentleman under his direction; he inspired them."

"Indeed," answered Jake. "Indeed."

HISTORICAL NOTE

Howe's "B—" letter and his attempt to confuse Washington is well documented, though there has always been some question of how and when the American general realized Philadelphia was the true British target. The existence of the New York spy ring, with the code-named Culpers as the organizers, is also amply authenticated by historical sources, though my interpretation is that the original writer of the Gibbs stories argues for a far more active—and I would think jollier—underground than previously known. While the records are understandably less than complete, no record of the activities described here seems to exist, though it will be admitted there are also no firm contradictions.

Students of history will realize that Alexander Hamilton did indeed fall in love with Betsy Schuyler, reputed to be one of the most beautiful women in America, though the first meeting between them has always been thought to occur several months after this tale claims.

Many young women donned men's clothes to fight in the war, as pension petitions and other records show, so Alison's bravery did not seem unusual to me.

I believed that we had finally caught the original author out with his far-fetched tale of the madstone. Yet Cynthia Blair, a fellow writer, graciously shared some of her own research on the subject proving that the stones were not only common but held in some esteem at the time.

As usual, I have received considerable help deciphering the old manuscript and making it somewhat presentable for contemporary tastes. Local historians and librarians, reenactors, and even my young niece

Domiana have all helped a great deal. Todd Keithely, my editor at St. Martin's Press, has been invaluable for his insight and enthusiasm. My agents at Wieser and Wieser—George, Olga and especially Jake—have all done yeoman's service. And of course without the support of my wife Debra and other members of my family, I should not have been able to complete the work. I'd also like to thank the many readers who have spoken to me at book signings and conferences, as well as those who have written to me, for their ideas and suggestions.

Avid followers of the series' first two books, *The Silver Bullet* and *The Iron Chain*, may be surprised to find that there is apparently a month's gap between the present installment, *The Golden Flask*, and its predecessor.

This is not due to a flaw in the publisher's work schedule, but an apparent gap in the original manuscripts. Clearly, big events took place in Jake Gibbs's career in the weeks immediately after *The Iron Chain* ends. As this book opens some six weeks later, the hero-spy has just recovered from wounds that apparently brought him to within an inch of his Maker.

What happened? The present author is as much in the dark as the reader. There remains a literal mountain of old manuscripts to sort through, and perhaps the answer lies within them.

—J.D.

Across the colonies, good men took up arms against the tyranny of England and King George. But as the Americans fought for their freedom, they needed someone who could go behind enemy lines, someone with a flair for danger, pretty women, and getting out alive...

THE JAKE GIBBS, PATRIOT SPY SERIES

BY JIM DEFELICE

In a new nation, each man became a soldier. One man became a legend.

THE SILVER BULLET
_____ 95570-7 $4.99 U.S./$5.99 CAN.

THE IRON CHAIN
_____ 95635-5 $5.99 U.S./$6.99 CAN.

THE GOLDEN FLASK
_____ 95762-9 $5.99 U.S./$6.99 CAN.